THE DICTIONARY OF FAILED RELATIONSHIPS

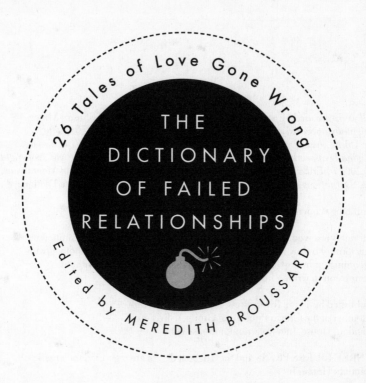

26 Tales of Love Gone Wrong

THE
DICTIONARY
OF FAILED
RELATIONSHIPS

Edited by MEREDITH BROUSSARD

THREE RIVERS PRESS
NEW YORK

Anthology copyright © 2003 by Meredith Broussard

Published by Three Rivers Press, New York, New York.
Member of the Crown Publishing Group, a division of
Random House, Inc. www.randomhouse.com

THREE RIVERS PRESS and the Tugboat design are registered trademarks of
Random House, Inc.

Printed in the United States of America

Library of Congress Cataloging-in-Publication Data
The dictionary of failed relationships: 26 tales of love gone wrong /
edited by Meredith Broussard.— 1st ed.
1. Love stories, American. 2. Short stories, American—Women authors.
3. Man-woman relationships—Fiction. 4. Dating (Social
customs)—Fiction. 5. Failure (Psychology)—Fiction.
I. Broussard, Meredith.
PS648.L6 D53 2003
813' .085089287—dc21   2002152193
ISBN 0-609-81009-X

10 9 8 7 6 5 4 3 2 1

First Edition

FOR MARY, EVELYN, AND LESLIE

CONTENTS

EDITOR'S NOTE

This epic and scholarly work began with a failed relationship: mine. I was dating a photographer in Philadelphia, the beautiful city where I make my home. One sunny afternoon, I told him, "I can't hang out tonight. Richard invited me to a cocktail party at the French consulate in honor of a visiting French designer." He heard, "I'm going out to have hot sex with a French lesbian." I have heard many stories about Mars and Venus, about miscommunication, about crossed signals, but this moment stands out in my mind as a truly exceptional manifestation of the great, unbridgeable gulf between human beings. And so this moronic photographer, who for narrative purposes we'll call Tony Columbo, heard what he wanted to hear—that his girlfriend was going out that evening to emasculate him.

Tony Columbo decided to strike back with the handiest weapon at his disposal (not counting the gun he kept in the trunk of his car, along with his golf clubs and camera equipment, the ammunition for said gun having fallen out of the glove compartment and bruised my knee on our second date). While I was at a mild-mannered cocktail party, drinking cheap Chardonnay and trying out my rusty, broken French half-remembered from college, Tony Columbo went and had sex with his ex-girlfriend.

It is important to note that the ex-girlfriend only became an ex-girlfriend because I had found out about her. Three weeks into my romance with Tony Columbo, I discovered that he was seeing another woman, who he'd been seeing for a year or so. I insisted that he choose between us, professing that it was his choice, that I didn't really care who he chose, but that I wasn't interested in a nonmonogamous relationship, and that it would be better to stop things before they really got started, rather than later when it might involve significant heartbreak. Secretly, of course, I hoped he'd choose me.

I didn't know at that point that the ex-girlfriend was the reason that Tony Columbo's wife had kicked him out a year earlier. I also didn't know that Tony Columbo had gotten her pregnant and paid for her abortion—the ex-girlfriend, not the wife—and I sure as hell didn't know that the ex-girlfriend lived two floors below me in my apartment building. These things were only revealed in the fullness of time, after I'd repeatedly had unprotected sex with Tony Columbo, invited him to Easter dinner with my family, and given him a set of keys to my apartment. Even when he told me that—surprise!—his divorce was not quite final, that technically he was still married to his ex-wife, I was too far gone to care.

I liked the long, lazy afternoons that Tony Columbo and I spent together. I liked the way his black curls drooped over his forehead; I liked the way his muscles looked in a wife-beater T-shirt. I liked having a boyfriend.

In my most paranoid moments, I wonder if I was brainwashed. When a person is routinely deprived of certain nutrients, she becomes highly suggestible. Cults use this technique to control the minds of their members—many "religious retreats" are actually opportunities to starve the minds of converts and plant the cult's beliefs. Celibacy isn't so far off from starvation. Take an otherwise intelligent woman who's been deprived of nooky for a few months, keep her in bed for a few hours every day, tell her she's beautiful and brilliant—and she'll believe almost anything. For three months, Tony Columbo and I were doing it three, four times a day, and I was so blissed-out, I didn't care that he was an obvious cad.

But then came the French Lesbian Episode. Tony acted strangely quiet for a few days after the cocktail party, occasionally asking me questions that came out of left field. Finally, after an interrogation worthy of Perry Mason, Tony admitted that he'd been with his ex-girlfriend. But only, he insisted, because he thought I'd been with the Hypothetical French Lesbian that night.

Not surprisingly, I freaked out. I'll spare you the gruesome details; suffice it to say that it was an episode of massive proportions, with copious amounts of tears, recriminations, accusations, and groveling. It wasn't pretty, and it lasted for days.

I wish the story ended there. I wish I could say I dumped his sorry ass when I found out that he cheated on me. I wish I could say I never looked back, that I went on to triumphantly write about my experience and that I became a heroic role model for all women whose boyfriends have ever cheated on them. *That* would make a great story.

The truth is, I took him back. Tony Columbo had sex with another woman *in my apartment building*, knowing full well that he was cheating on me and lying to the other woman, and I took him back. Someone should've hit me over the head with my copy of *Smart Women/Foolish Choices*.

Tony and I settled into our routine again, rapidly. We'd sleep late and hang around in bed, alternately giggling, bonking, and watching reruns of "A Dating Story" and "A Baby Story." Tony really wanted to get married again and have kids, he said, which made my recently discovered biological alarm clock start clamoring in my ears. Our days went like this: After breakfast, Tony would go off to the golf course while I wrote for a few hours. After his return, we'd go to bed briefly, go out to dinner, hang out with friends somewhere in the city, then crash, and start the whole thing over again in the morning. Occasionally, Tony dog-sat for his friend Carlo, and we'd set up shop at Carlo's place for a few days. It was a grown-up version of playing house—Carlo's town house was impeccably decorated, as long as you ignored the giant collection of anal porn in the bedroom closet. Tony was extraordinarily thoughtful toward the dog, a giant slobbering mastiff. The three of us would go to the dog run together, and I'd pretend it was our dog, our cute town house, and our happy-couple life together.

I loved the way I felt with Tony Columbo. He made me feel sexy, smart, capable, able to take on the world. His major problem was that he simply couldn't keep his dick in his pants.

Less than a month after the French Lesbian Episode, Tony told me he was going to Columbus, Ohio, for the weekend to photograph a wedding. It seemed perfectly plausible to me; I wished him luck and spent the weekend by myself in Philadelphia. Tony returned on Sunday night, called me Monday morning, and we met for coffee and took "our" dog out for a walk.

He'd brought me a refrigerator magnet from Columbus but was acting weird again. I let it go until Wednesday. That day, we walked to his place so he could pick up his car keys to drive me home. While I was in his bedroom, I noticed some letters lying on the bookshelf. I glanced at them and spotted "Dearest Tony" written in a female hand. Tony noticed me noticing the letters, and he guiltily shoved them inside a dusty book of Ansel Adams photos. We talked; we laughed; we made out. As soon as he went downstairs to the bathroom, I stuck the letters inside my purse.

I don't advocate stealing. I'm not even proud that I did it. Part of me promised that if I were wrong, if he weren't cheating on me again, I'd return the letters to exactly where I found them. But I was right. Tony dropped me off at my apartment building, and I dug his letters out of my purse while rushing through the lobby. In the elevator, I read "Dearest Tony," and I realized that the letter was dated only two weeks before. Most damning was the letter he must've received that morning, detailing how much fun the woman had with him in Ohio that past weekend, how he was everything she'd dreamed of and more. She had loved holding him in the bathtub, she said; she couldn't wait to see him again.

They'd met on the Internet. From what I gathered, she was an unemployed chiropractic assistant in Columbus, a single mom who'd had custody of her daughter taken away.

Tony Columbo's affair with Miss Columbus showed a truly egregious lack of good taste. Honestly, an unemployed chiropractic assistant? My ego couldn't take it. I dumped Tony Columbo that evening. I would've dumped him into the Fresh Kills Landfill, or at the bottom of a river, if I could.

In the subsequent weeks, I worked out my emotions by telling the story to anyone who'd listen—friends, family, strangers in restaurants, even the doorperson at my apartment building. I wrote so many e-mails about Tony Columbo's perfidy that I had to give up typing the story anew. I simply saved the text as a document on my computer and sent it, along with appropriate comments as to my state of mind at that moment, to anyone unwise enough to inquire how I was doing.

The first 547 times I told the story of the French Lesbian Episode, I cried. It felt good to be patted on the back and for various people to tell me that Tony Columbo was a jerk and that I was better off without him. By repetition 1,000 or so, I started to enjoy telling the story. Partly because it made great shtick, partly because people began telling me their own stories in return. At a Halloween party, a woman told me about the German photographer who'd taken her to a gallery opening in Chelsea—and asked if she was as turned on as he was by the photos of seminaked, preadolescent girls. An old guy at a bar told me about the heartbreak he had suffered at the hands of the She-Devil of the Harvard Club of New York City. And then there were the rehashings of past breakups that I discussed with my girlfriends—we'd go through our mental lists of past lovers, deciding whether the French Lesbian Episode was better or worse than other breakups. By the time I realized I was having a good time talking about relationship disasters, I was practically over Tony Columbo.

So, I began working on this anthology. I wanted to put together a directory, A to Z, of the myriad reasons that relationships fall apart. *The Dictionary of Failed Relationships* is the kind of book I'd enjoy reading after a breakup, before a breakup, or even in the middle of a great relationship. Think of it as the literary equivalent of Ben & Jerry's ice cream — delicious any time, but especially appropriate for times of PMS or heartbreak.

The story of this book ends where it began. As a side effect of focusing on failed relationships, I got over my heartbreak with Tony Columbo. Sort of. I met a really wonderful guy (a stockbroker, of all things) who reminded me that not all men are dogs. I learned that love, fidelity, and trust can do a lot to bridge the fundamental gap between human beings. I also learned that wanting to get married and have babies (me) plus fear of commitment (him) equals failed relationship. Oh, well.

That failed relationship story doesn't have a title yet; it's too raw. It doesn't even have a narrative. There's still a gaping, bloody, Grand Canyon–size hole in my chest where I think my heart used to be. It'll cost me at least ten thousand dollars in therapy to repair it, without a doubt.

But now, at least, here's a book to keep me company on the road back from heartbreak.

Word

*What it means;
usually not good*

EXPLANATORY CHART

By Meredith Broussard

author name here

gift: \ 'gift\ *noun* [Middle English; akin to Old English *giefan* to give] (12th century) need not be expensive, but should be abundant. Flowers work well. Even a piece of Bazooka Joe bubble gum tucked inside a lunch bag is a good gift. Gifts should appear promptly on birthdays, holidays, and anniversaries—wrapping paper is mandatory. Remembering to buy a gift for a friend from work who is getting married, then forgetting to buy a gift for your girlfriend's birthday two days later (even though you're spending the *entire weekend* with her and some friends at the beach) is unacceptable behavior.

Gender bias

The authors of the *Dictionary* entries are smart, funny, and quirky young women. Youth seemed especially important at the beginning of the project, because so many of today's most prominent women writers are postmenopausal. I wanted to collect the voices of women of my own generation, women with more style, intellect, and substance than Bridget Jones. At first, *younger* meant "under thirty." But since I'm going to be thirty (someday!), it seemed arbitrary to call thirty the upper limit of youth. Age ain't nothing but a number. These stories are by sassy women who are old enough to know better, and young enough not to care. Some of their stories are true, some are fictional, some are even stranger than fiction. It is an extraordinarily gifted and utterly delightful group of authors.

The story comes here.

THE DICTIONARY OF FAILED RELATIONSHIPS

AMBIVALENCE

By Heidi Julavits

am·biv·a·lence \am-'bi-və-lən(t)s\ *noun* [International Scientific Vocabulary] (1918) 1: simultaneous and contradictory attitudes or feelings (as attraction and repulsion) toward an object, person, or action. Such feelings may be constant in a relationship. 2a: continual fluctuation (as between one thing and its opposite). b: uncertainty as to which approach to follow, especially in the days preceding a breakup.

Let me put it plainly: It was summer. We drove down to Mexico.

This was not a vacation, because we were already on vacation. Vacation from a vacation from a vacation brings us full circle. "Business," Tim said to the customs official. It was July, and Texas wasn't hot enough for us, it wasn't screaming bloody cicada murder enough for us, so we had to drive down to Mexico in a white rental car and look for campsites with the word *superstition* in the name.

What's the word for *superstition* in Spanish? I asked. I sought Tim's advice when it came to certain languages. He was brought up by a grammarian mother, a feisty little Shreveport looker who raised her son to fear clichés more than venereal disease, who didn't give a hoot if he failed to make his bed for forty years, as long as he said *give it to Bob and me.*

Better you don't know, Tim said, fending off the little Mexican boys at the Nuevo Laredo crossing. They wanted money from the Americans in the white rental car. We were good-looking Americans, too, gleaming with a certain kind of ironic roadtrip sexy. Secondhand guayaberas factored in, and fake leather boots, and the paper-stink of truckstop potatoes extruding from our pores. Forget that I was a debutante, once, that I said crudité, once, at a party. Forget that Tim was pursuing a degree in comparative literature (he was a Lacanian with a concentration in Chilean protest poetry), forget that he grew a goatee to hide his thin upper lip, that he kept an antique prophylactic in the lizard wallet bequeathed to him by a dead man, his grandfather, that he was prone to saying things with a put-on Louisiana drawl like *you're so dang fetching when you're scared.* He believed there was no more novelty in the world, so the knowing cliché was the only antidote to banality.

This is the great thing about America. You can slum smartly in a fool instant.

But these little begging boys, they were not without a certain degree of original menace, in my opinion. They had a little mantra. Tim translated.

They claim we're having a party in our bank account, he said.

Did you tell them it's BYOB? I asked.

He didn't laugh. He blew past the little boys after giving them our Einstein air freshener. I saw one boy put it in his mouth as we cruised toward the Whatever Mountains, listening to Border Oldies.

This is bad, I said. The Border Oldies station played mostly seventies tunes that made me doomy.

What is bad? he asked. He liked to ask little things like they were big things, philosophical things, not like what is bad, but what *is* bad?

What is bad is the following, I said: That little boy will suck on the Einstein air freshener, because he thinks he'll ingest some glorious piece of America. His sister will find it clenched in his rictused hand tomorrow morning, and the authorities will trace the serial number back to your mother, who sent you the air freshener on your birthday as a joke-not-joke, because everyone knows your mother thinks you're a genius. Subsequent tests will determine that the air freshener—bought from your derelict brother's tchotchke headshop in Atlanta—was soaked in a tremendous amount of PCP. The Feds will prosecute your mother for drug dealing and for overestimating the very average intelligence of both her sons. Your SAT scores will be printed in all the national papers, corroborated by quotes from your elementary school teachers testifying to your mediocre preteen performance. You will be thrown out of your graduate program and forced to sell your grandfather's antique prophylactic on eBay to pay your student loans, which will come due immediately.

The wallet belonged to my grandfather, not the rubber. But that was a good one, he said.

Thanks.

Don't you ever worry you tell me too much about yourself?

Meaning . . .

Meaning, don't these morbid fantasies conceal an actual desire?

What *is* actual desire? I asked.

If you hate my mother, just say so.

I don't hate your mother. I am humored by your mother, which is a generous way to be exhausted by a person.

It just seems a little passive, he said. Thinking about doing things versus simply doing them.

He cranked up the Border Oldies until the bass line fuzzed. So, he said, changing the subject, what do all these songs have in common?

Death by vomit? I guessed.

They're all in minor keys. The seventies was a minor-key decade.

That's why we're such an anxious generation. We were children raised on popular menace.

So that's why, I said, licking the knuckles of his driving hand.

We never found the Superstition campsite. We settled for a roachy hotel in a big, noisy city. How come I've never heard of this city? I asked. It's so terribly big and noisy. We walked around the monolith and stared up at the Whatever Mountains. With confidence, he told me the word for "whatever" in Spanish was *zapata*.

I wanted to have sex all night to keep my mind off the roaches, but he wasn't up to it. It's all that Chilean protest poetry, I said, fingering his jellied crotch. The revolution is a flaccid cause. Viva la Deflation!

I drove twelve hours, he said, yawning.

But this is a road trip, I said. Carnality is part of the knowing cliché. We can have facile sex and I'll yell, *give it to Bob and me*.

He wanted to go to sleep.

But the floor is seething with roaches, I said. We'll wake up and they'll be in every orifice, laying eggs or just plain hanging out.

You're acting faux-scared and I'm fucking tired.

I was raised during the minor-key decade, I said. Blame it on Jethro Tull.

If you feel like I have a limited capacity for intimacy, just say so, he said.

Zapata, I said, over and over, into his sleepy ear. Worst-case scenarios were just another clichéd joke to him. There was no turning him on to the attendant promise of doom, there was no inspiring him, in short, to see the world the way I did: full of an inventively crippling kind of illumination.

The next morning we went to a museum. This was neither of our ideas, but we didn't know each other well enough to admit we hated museums. We were both scared of appearing artless.

There were photographs of motion in this museum. A man jumping over a wheelbarrow. A horse jumping over a dog.

I need a beer, Tim said.

We ordered beer and *churros* in the garden behind the brick museum. What do you think this place used to be? he asked, dipping his *churro* into his beer. A factory?

It was a motion factory, I said. This is where quickness was isolated. When quickness was first developed, no one thought it would catch on. The brains behind the operation, Señor Somebody, became a miserable pauper. His wife left him post-haste, using his own invention. His children changed their surnames to *Nafta*, which is Spanish slang for "inertia."

That's a sad story, Tim said, burping. Wanna fuck?

We fucked and then we went to the mountains. But Tim being Tim, he wasn't much of one for roads.

This isn't such a good idea, I said. We will be stranded and we'll hear nothing but wind. We'll be stalked by wolverines, or worse, I'll learn that you're a coward when it comes to confronting the more feral animals.

Tim didn't hear me. Besides, it's a rental, he said. The dirt roads had canyons in them. Our little white car was called a Malabar, but Tim renamed it the Malcontent because it had no-wheel drive and three pissy cylinders. The little tires dropped into the canyons. The axles made shivery, snapping noises. We were stuck.

I took the wheel while Tim rocked against the Malcontent's dusty white bottom, his aviator sunglasses slipping down over his goatee.

Tim dislodged us and the road improved. We were making good time now, two or three kilometers an hour. We crept through a tiny town. Chickens butt-waggled away from us, chagrined. A woman stood on her porch in a dress and apron, circa 1863. Her husband leaned on a hoe, dumbfounded. They're so Mexican Gothic, I said. Tim got mad. He got mad when people made references to things they'd only encountered through crappy third-hand culture. Like Proust's fucking madeleine, he'd gripe. People are always talking about Proust's madeleine, but how many of them have actually read Proust? A reference to a reference to a reference to a reference. So, he said, who painted American Gothic, do you even know?

It wasn't Samuel D. Clemens, I said. It wasn't Alice B. Toklas.

Samuel P. Clemens, he said. He flipped down his sunglasses and decided to forgive me, because the Mexican Goths were watching us fight and he didn't want to give good-looking Americans a bad name. Imagine waking up and seeing us, said Tim. Imagine seeing two blond people in a white car in the middle of the mountains. He honked and waved at the Goths. We're a dream, he said, patting my jeans. We're a first-world hallucination brought to you by Malcontent.

Soon it was time for lunch.

We had cheese, we had tomatoes, we had bread, we had meat. I insisted that it was very, very taboo to make a sandwich. We sat on the dusty hood with our parts spread out on plastic bags. It was acceptable, I said, to put two kinds of food in your mouth at once, but never three. Two foods was a combination, three was a sandwich.

Huh, said Tim, piling up his bread.

So what's the difference between a pederast and a pedophile? I asked. I was eating, at that moment, tomato and cheese.

I think I love you, he said.

You're just saying that because you don't know the answer. You'll say anything to keep appearing smart. Even in the wilderness.

He put a piece of bread and meat in his mouth. We're sitting on the hood of Malcontent in the Whatever Mountains and I said I think I love you, said Tim. And don't say *zapata* or I'll leave you here without a peso.

That would be very rude, I said. He kissed me and we were four foods now, we were in serious violation of something. This will come back to haunt us, I said. At the Superstition camp-ground, we will be haunted by this.

But back to your original question, Tim said, stroking his goatee for effect. One only thinks about doing, while the other does.

All in all, we spent four days in Mexico. We rode donkeys at one point, up and down gravel slides. Neither of us had health insur-ance. We slept in somebody's front yard and ate some very inspir-ing pork tacos. I'm making it sound like our business trip was all such fun, but really there was so much loneliness at work. There was so much anxiety at work, all those seventies songs in my sys-tem, driving me to ruinous thoughts. I told Tim: I am anxious in the mountains, I am anxious out of the sight of humanity. I longed for a monolith, a room seething with roaches. I didn't want to blame him, because we were in love apparently, so I blamed it on the mountains. I cursed them out, *Zapata, Zapata, Zapata*. Yet, somewhere in these mountains, I took the best pho-tograph of my adult life. It was a picture of Tim's arm. We found an abandoned house, all decrepit white plaster and gray porch boards. *Decrepit white* is an oxymoron, Tim said, a not-uninteresting one. He sat in front of the decrepit white wall and raised his arm over his face. I knew without ever needing to develop the film that this was the best photograph of my adult life, because if I am attuned to pretend ruin, I am also attuned to my modest moments of honest clairvoyance. This photo would prove that there was something desperately hopeful being expressed through my disaster narratives. It would prove that I was not an adult who could tour the world in a white Mal-content, with a man who raised his arm to protect himself from the imaginary menaces I might toss his way.

. . .

We drove back over the border.

I started to feel better, instantly, even though Nuevo Laredo and plain old Laredo proved to be big bright splashes of humanity that burned up quickly as we drove north. We were listening to Border Oldies, or maybe we were discussing the oxymoronic possibilities of *white malcontent*, but either way, we somehow forgot that we'd planned to get gas in plain old Laredo, and it was now almost midnight, and we were far away from humanity.

We passed a sign that said NEXT GAS — 15 DAYS, 47 NIGHTS.

This confused me. We do not measure distances in days and nights, not in America, I said. Those are miles, dumbass, Tim said testily, but somehow I couldn't see it. We were forty-seven nights away from gas.

This was not good. We did not have forty-seven nights' worth of gas. Tim's sunglasses were still pushed up into his hair, he still wore the same secondhand guayabera, and it didn't even smell, because he was superior in that way, a self-cleaning mammal. He was not bothered by the sign. For a man who'd barely had a break in life, he was unhealthily optimistic, especially when the odds were worse than terrible.

What's the plan? I asked. If I'd been a smoker, I would have shakily lit one up. Cliché, cliché, cliché. We cannot even be anxious in an original way.

A plan, why must you always have a plan? Tim looked at me, fake smoking like a little old lady. Think of the worst thing that can happen, and then you'll probably be pleasantly surprised by the outcome. That's the plan.

This was mean. This was just downright mean.

I'm coincidentally an expert on worst-case scenarios, I told him, puffing away.

Great, he said. Go for it.

Okay, I said. We've run out of gas.

Obviously.

We have to pitch our tent. I don't want to go into the woods because of the scorpion nests, so we pitch our tent on the shoulder. Fortunately, nobody's driving at this time of night. But then we see headlights. A semi. Bringing Einstein air fresheners over the border, tinged with PCP that will kill many adults in America and children in Mexico. We see the lights for miles before they reach us. We hold on to each other as it passes. It's like a tornado. Our car keys and eyeglasses and money are blown away. We are nobody now; we are without a vision for the immediate future.

Tim held up a finger. But why don't you jump out and flag the truck down? he asked.

Good question. Because my mother was raped by a trucker. There's no love lost between my family and truckers.

Your mother was not raped by a trucker. Your mother gives voice lessons in Pacific Palisades.

This is a worst-case scenario, I reminded him. The back story is fair game.

Tim grumbled. He disagreed about the back story, but let me continue.

So. We move our tent into the woods. We sleep fitfully until the scorpions start oozing through the seams like some kind of creepy jelly. You have to cut the roof of the tent with your knife to get us out. We escape farther into the woods. I am—it goes without saying—apoplectic with fear. My brother, I've never told you this, was killed in an Alabama backwoods fry-up by a band of white-trash cannibals. Soon we find a hunting cabin. The door's locked, but I convince you to break a window. There's a decent bed and even a few cans of warm beer. We drink the beer and sleep pretty decently until we hear the ominous strumming of . . .

Not banjos.

I paused. Do I detect a slight prejudice against banjos?

It would just be a little . . .

I held my "cigarette" high; I wanted to drive it into his sunburned forearm. Don't say clichéd, I said.

Well?

Basic human foreboding toward stringed instruments is not clichéd! It is basic!

Tim ignored me.

Is the human condition clichéd to you? I asked. Is plain old terror and despondency and strife just a stupid . . . hey, there's an exit.

Tim took the exit without comment. At first, the exit seemed deeply unpromising. Thickety, overgrown porches and black storefronts. I heard banjos — oh Christ I did. Then we saw a sign. I could not believe it. We were in a town called Zapata.

Zapata, I said, with a kind of fearful wonder.

There wasn't a single sign of humanity until we turned a corner. Then we saw all the humanity Zapata had to offer, or rather humanity's trucks, parked in the lot of the most shackity shack imaginable, with neon and beer signs and . . . banjo noises.

I did not say Ha! but I thought it. Ha! Ha! Take that, you swashbuckling crusader against cliché! Sometimes a cliché is a cliché because it is goddamned, goddamned true!

Tim parked the car. He didn't comment on the banjos. He said, Somebody in there's bound to have a gas tank. The door opened and shut behind him. Louder music, then quieter music. The sign over the door said JETHRO'S, and I did not think, huh, or wow, or anything. I thought, I am trapped here, I am trapped in this recursive shitty joke of a life.

I waited outside, leaning against the Malcontent. It stank of gas, like out-of-gas cars do. Tim emerged five minutes later behind a man. Honey, Tim said. He had a Texas drawl, all of a sudden. Honey, this here's Bobcat.

I shook Bobcat's hand. *Give it to Bobcat and me.* I said, We sure done do appreciate your doing this, Mr. Bobcat. Tim glared at me, but Bobcat didn't blink a whisker. He nabbed his gas can and handed it to Tim. Five gallons in there, he said, go ahead and take it all. If I wasn't mistaken, Mr. Bobcat spoke with something like a lockjaw. Rabies, maybe. Or just another stranger to true American wildness, slumming in the outback like us.

Bobcat went back inside (I love this song, he said), leaving us to fill our tank. Tim unscrewed the gas cap and sank the nozzle in deep. He looked up at the stars and wondered to me, How far to the next gas station?

Forty-seven nights, I said.

Probably more like thirty. We are in Zapata, after all.

I watched as he weighed the gas can carefully. He held it up to the light from the neon signs to see how much gas was left.

I figure half will do us, he said, replacing the can in Bobcat's truck.

Don't be an ass, I said. Take all five gallons. Bobcat said you could.

Naw, he said. I figure we can make it on two and a half. He actually said *figger*.

Tim, I said. Please. Just take all five gallons. I'll pay for it.

Tim put his sunglasses on. The light from the bar reflected off them. He looked like an insect to me, like some kind of shiny insect. What's the matter, honey, Tim said, don't you trust your daddy?

I . . . that's not the point, I said.

What is the point then, little flapjack? he asked. What is the plan? The plan? The point?

I stared at him. And stared. I would not take responsibility for this meanness. He'd poked it out of me.

The point is that you're no cowboy, I said. The point is that you're just an all-but-dissertation grad student who spent most of last Tuesday looking for a wad of cheesecloth for an herb sachet.

That hurts, he said. Get in the car.

But . . .

Get in the car, he said.

I stared at my hands. They were very white and parsnippy-looking in Jethro's floodlights, flexing and unflexing. *One only thinks about doing while the other does.*

Not until you put the rest of Bobcat's gas in our tank, I said.

What are you so worried about?

It's not about worry, I lied. It's about exhaustion.

Why are you so tired, Scheherazade?

I'm tired of being scared in order to be fetching, I said.

Tim smiled. This was all a big joke to him.

Lucky for you, there's only forty-seven nights' worth of talking you have to do, he said.

We faced off silently over the hood of the car as the banjos inside Jethro's achieved a conveniently tense peak. I wanted to impose on him my notions of pure affection, but this was not a language he could understand. He wasn't a bad man. He was just ungenerous in a very small, hardly noticeable way.

I got in the car. Soon we were far away from Zapata, we were on the highway again, and Tim whistled the banjo tune while eyeing the gas gauge like he'd put money on it. I sat shotgun and fake chain-smoked, taking periodic glimpses of his profile. It begged for disaster. Driving in the dark, I thought, our front left tire would hit a long metal pipe that had fallen off a semi driving north from Laredo. The pipe would kick up over the hood of the car, numchuck fast, straighten itself out, and harpoon through the windshield, aiming straight for Tim's left eye. I heard the screech of metal, the crack of glass. I could see the pipe's end, hovering right before Tim's face, twanging like a tuning fork. It hung there. It hung there. But I could not drive the pipe through his skull, the pipe noodled up, it dissipated into the air like a gray coil of smoke. I summoned the pipe again and again. I started to panic until something bleaker and more terrifying occurred to me, it was so terrifying that it cauterized every fear-firing synapse and made me deathly calm, as the gas needle fibrillated below empty and we still had more than twelve nights to go. The moment you cannot kill a person, what does that say about love?

Berniced

By Eliza Minot

Ber·niced \bər-'nēsd\ *adverb* [origin unknown]: When something gets trampled, it gets Berniced. <Bad date last night; I got totally *Berniced*. Am I some sort of magnet for freaks?> *See also:* RAILROADED, OVERWHELMED, UNDERTIPPED, FREAK MAGNET.

Sometimes, I just, like, look out the window? And watch the cars going by? It's so totally boring when it's slow at the restaurant, but it can also be a relief when you're just not in the mood. Some of the other waitresses? They do crossword puzzles and stuff? Or read the paper or magazines? The managers don't like that, though, because then it looks like we're just hanging around. So when customers come in, they're like, excuse me, are we, like, bothering you guys? When it's slow, I usually stand by the salad bar and just look out the big, long windows. I end up watching people pass on the sidewalk. I end up looking out at them and wondering things like, could I like that man? Could I like that woman? Am I like these people? What does he do? Where is she going? Mostly, everyone seems really busy and hurrying someplace. Me, after work I usually don't hurry anywhere. I go to the mall, to, like, Strawberries, and check out the clothes or buy some earrings, or maybe go to Coconuts and listen to CDs on the headphones.

Some brunches, though, are so busy. Like on Sundays. There's, like, no time to pee it's so so busy. It's not, like, families, really, because this part of the city's not, like, family? It's couples mostly, groups of friends, that kind of thing. I end up waiting on a lot of couples because usually my station's station number three? Which is mostly the two-tops? So it ends up being couples. I walk right up to their tables and say, you guys ready? Some of them are really nice! Some of them are really funny! Sometimes, while they have their eggs and stuff, they don't say anything to each other? But it's not like they're not talking because they don't have anything to say. They just look like, well, there's no hurry. Like they've got all day to talk, or maybe, for all I know, a whole life-time, if they're married.

Which brings me to Tad. Yeah, right, like we're married! But still it's, like, weird? I don't know what happened? I mean it's weird! He just—*poof!*—disappeared! Which is totally fine and everything because he was basically a big jerk. But still it's, like, so crazy, right? Okay? But. So. We were down in the park? We went down there? It was way too cold to be out there, but pretty sort of because the sky was this total blue and there was snow everywhere from the storm, so it was totally bright. It was too cold, though. I wasn't dressed warmly enough. My boots totally suck! But any-how, we were going to see if we could walk across the river to the other side? That's how cold it was? Like the river should be frozen? Like everything was frozen? People on the street were, like, running to where they had to go. They were all bundled up except for, like, the top of their nose and their eyes! My nostrils did that thing where they clog together. Where they squinch up and stick? Anyway, when we got down to the park, the river wasn't that frozen. It was actually not frozen at all out in the middle. It was, like . . . regular water. Like a big, flat, dark spot out there in the middle. The sides of it were all icy, though. With, like, slushy stuff around the water part?

We were sitting on a bench? We were sitting there for a while, and there was nobody anywhere. A big dog came around, though, and was jumping in the snow. Dogs, they, like, attack snow! They're so funny! They, like, pounce like big tigers or something and then snuffle up their noses in it and go nuts wagging their tails! Crazy dogs!

There's this dog at the restaurant? It belongs to this guy who's a regular? A pretty new regular, like I guess he just moved in around the corner or something. I don't know. But he's allowed to bring him in? The dog? Since he comes in so much, and plus the dog's kind of small? His name's Boob. The dog's. Can you believe that? He's this little dog. Not too little. He's kind of scruffy and dirty but cute still since he's just old and has those cute eyebrow things that poke out over some dogs' eyes. Like Muppet hair? Those hairs that float around wavy, like tiny feathers? They're so cute!

So Sarah? This sort of bitchy waitress? She said she thought he looked like that movie star dog Benji. And then Michael, this bus-boy who's always totally greedy for any kind of gossip, was all, "Who's Benji?" but he was trying to make it sound like it was just a simple question? Like he didn't really care? But really he proba-bly thought it was some cute guy who'd been in the restaurant? Or someone we all knew and so he should know, too?

So I told him, "Benji's a dog." It's so cool when I can say things, totally knowing what I'm saying. I mean, I know what I'm saying, but, like, when someone says, "He looks like so and so," or some-thing like that, and I know right away what they're talking about and can, like, get it right away. It's so cool.

Then Michael asked me, "Whose dog, Bernice?" He thought there, like, might be some gossip on the dog?

I told him, "You know, that dog in the movies? Benji?"

"Oh, that Benji," said Michael, all disappointed-like and bummed.

"You mean like Lassie?" asked Tammy. Tammy was over at the staff table, marrying the ketchups. She goes off talking to herself a lot, practically, Tammy. She does it a lot. "There was that Lassie movie," she was saying, going on, "with the guy who was looking for the Heart of the Ocean in *Titanic*. He played the dad. That is, I think he played the dad. Does anyone know what I'm talking about?" Tammy says that a lot—does anyone know what I'm talking about?—then rolls her eyes up at the ceiling, then laughs. "It's just *Titanic*, you know, you guys," Tammy said. "Not *The Titanic*." Tammy moved from Ohio with her husband? To try to be a dancer? She's, like, my age! And totally married! Her husband's really hot, too! Why would a guy that hot get married so young? It's weird, but I guess kind of cool!

So, Sarah came back from the guy with the little dog's table and told us all that the dog's name was Boob. We were all, like, "Excuse me? Boob?"

Denise, my manager, said that wasn't a very nice name, like it was a mean name? Denise was all busy erasing and fixing up the reservations book. All it is is, like, these pages in a binder with big black circles in different sizes that we write the parties' names on and then the different times. Denise was whispering so that the dog's owner couldn't hear her. She was whispering, what does he say to it? Sit, Boob? Fetch, Boob? Here, Boobie, Boobie!

Sarah told us that the guy—his name's Gene?—that when Gene got the dog? It was already named. But Denise said you could still change a dog's name. Right? As long as it rhymes? And Michael said, yeah, you could call him Tube! Or . . . Lube! Or Doob! And Denise was saying, like, sure, Michael, those are a lot better. I said, what about Scoob and was, like, so proud of my suggestion.

But anyway—ohmigod! I'm, like, talking about dogs! So me and Tad. We were just sitting there on the bench? Me, like, *freezing* my little butt off, and then Tad was, like, yo, wait a minute, what's going on? I looked, okay, and there was this guy down at

the edge of the river, like, getting ready to walk on it or something? He was, like, bent over? He was wearing one of those furry
Russian hats and a black coat that came down to his knees. He
looked, like, dark and creepy, sort of, against all the white snow
everywhere, like in some movie? I love movies! But he was right
on the edge of the river, on the ice. So he was, like, bent over
there, and we were all, "What is he doing?" We couldn't tell if he
was, like, hurt? Or thinking? He was sort of far away, so we
couldn't tell? Tad was all freaked about it, like the guy was about
to walk out onto the ice and the ice wasn't strong enough, and I
was telling him that the guy wouldn't do that, just walk out on it.
But Tad started calling to him, Hello! Hello! And then the guy—
I don't think he heard Tad yelling or anything, but it didn't matter, right? Because then? Then, the guy started walking out. He
did. He started walking out onto the totally thin ice. We were like,
"What?"

Then Tad, like, turned and looked at me with this look on his
face, like it was my fault or something that this guy was going out
there. Maybe he was just surprised? But always, these guys, these
jerks look at me like that? I mean, I was still getting used to not
having to look all over the place all the time for this guy Jed who I
thought seemed really nice at first—he was cute! He was this cute
little guy, but he ended up being a total freak and had a lot of
things wrong with him. I mean, he was really needy and said he
never liked a girl before? Ohmigod! Like, never? He ended up
following me around to my decorating classes and everything? He
always looked, like, so tired, and I felt really bad for him, you
know? So I helped him sort of, I guess? Just by being nice? And
then he, like, broke in through the fire escape and stole my CD
player! I had to change the locks, and it was, like, so stupid! Like,
a big waste of my time. I mean, me and Tad we had dramas, too,
but you know, I keep things relative. He never, like, stalked. At
least not yet anyway! Ha ha!

But, yeah, we had our, like, drama, me and Tad. It's gloomy I guess. Sometimes he'd scare me. Sometimes I'd feel like throwing up practically or sometimes I'd just be, I don't know . . . scared? I, like, wouldn't know what to say? He had a bad temper. Ohmigod, he could go, like, totally mental! Sarah at work says, "Bad temper? Read my lips: how about *asshole*," and she says *asshole* really long and loud. Even though Sarah's sort of a bitch? Still, she's pretty funny. She says all the guys that like me are total jerks. That I'm, like, a magnet for them? I don't get mad, because she's usually right! It's like they're losers and, I don't know, I feel sorry for them? Or just I'm a loser, too? I don't know what my problem is! What's my problem? But Sarah, like, named it after me! When she somehow has to deal with a real jerk? Like if she goes on a date and it turns out badly, she'll say, "I got completely Berniced." Or, "It turned into a total Bernice job." Even, like, when someone in the restaurant ends up with an asshole table somehow? Like a really jerky table or a table that barely leaves a tip? They'll say, "I'm completely being Berniced." Or, "That was a classic Bernice situation." I mean, I laugh, too. They all don't mean it, like, mean?

But right. The Tad drama. It was nothing that's, like, really bad. I mean, I know about the really bad stuff that goes on out in the world? I mean, I guess I do? I, like, read the paper. Believe it or not! The other day I read about this young guy? Like, practically a boy still? He was stripped by some group, and then they, like, cut off his ears and shot him in the knees. He had, like, cigarette burns all over him! Then just yesterday, I read about this woman who was, like, partly retarded? And this ex-con became her friend so he could collect her government money? They found her in a bathtub with jumper cables on her nipples! I could kill that guy! And, oh! This one's so totally sad! I read about this old man? Like, a minister? From the Caribbean? He came up to retire to, like, Boston or somewhere to be near his daughter? He came all the way from the Caribbean, right? Then the local police came busting into his apartment! They came just busting in on a drug raid or something? And scared him so badly he had a heart attack! But they had the wrong apartment! They, like, read the floor plans wrong!

I remember once looking at a book? It was, like, a big picture book that my brother had at his girlfriend's? Why am I thinking of this? But it was weird. There was a picture? Of these people on the beach? Somewhere like Italy or someplace? The photo showed this really hot guy. He was, like, lying in the little waves on the beach? Lying there, like, practically drowned? There were lifeguard people all around him, trying to help him, like, all over the place. Then, like, right in the middle? Right in the middle of the picture with all this stuff going on? There's this girl. She's, like, crouched over, too, like the lifeguards? She's the guy's girl-friend, probably, or wife, or fiancée or something. She's really pretty, but anyway, she's, like, right there in the middle of every-thing? Like, looking right at the camera? She's looking, like, *right* at the camera and, like, smiling! Her husband's, like, *dying* and she's smiling! And underneath the picture? The caption thingy? It said, *Why is this woman smiling? It is the effect of cameras and media on our culture today.* Or something like that. Weird, right? I read about weird, bad stuff all the time. But you, like, hear about stuff, and you can only sort of take in a certain amount, right? Like, where do you begin to, like, really figure out what's wrong? It's, like, so totally crazy, everything that goes on.

So, anyway, back to the river with Tad and the freezing cold. So Tad was basically just wondering what the guy in the long jacket was doing? He was only a little ways out? On the ice kind of? But it didn't look like he was stopping? So Tad said we should go down there, and then he ran down through the trees. When we got down there? The guy was off to our left? Walking away from us? Totally walking out! And the middle of the river was totally water! There was no ice! And he wasn't really that far from it! I turned around and looked up to where we came from? To see if there were any people up there watching? But the park was all empty. Then Tad, like, pulled at my arm saying, "We've got to get closer to him, he needs help," or something like that. It was really weird, because all of this was happening, right? And for me, it was like . . . like I didn't really care? I mean, this guy was walking out onto some ice that he'd totally crash through, and I, like, didn't care. It kind of felt like a drag? Instead of an emergency?

So Tad went running along the bank and I ran after him—I, like, killed my knee! It did this thing, it went, *pop!* So I kind of stumbled along. Tad was calling to the guy still? Trying to talk to him or at least get his attention? He wasn't answering or anything, so I called, like, "Hello?" As loud as I could but sort of sarcastic like? And Tad was really mad and sort of pinched me and he said, "This isn't funny, Bernice!" Or, "This is serious, Bernice!" Or something. Then he told me to run back up to the street to go get help, and I was like, "Excuse me? I don't want to go all the way back up there! Plus, my knee!" And then Tad was like, "What is wrong with you?" and I said, "What is wrong with you?" and he told me I was acting idiotic? That we really needed to try to help the guy? I told him not to call me an idiot, and then he started to get really upset, telling me I was missing the point, and he started running away to get help. Then, like, right as he ran away along the bank we heard this, like, dull crack, like, muffled. From the river? It was the ice? And we both yelled, No! Then before I really realized what was going on, Tad was running up the hill, yelling about getting help. So then I just stood there for a second? My knee kind of hurt? I looked out over the ice again. It was totally empty. The water out in the middle was sort of twinkly in the sun. It looked like no one was ever there.

When I finally got up to the street? I looked to my right and the promenade was completely empty? I looked to my left, and I could see Tad in the distance, talking to a cop. Tad was waving his arms all over the place. The cop had his hand raised up in the air? Like he was saying, settle down? When I got to where they were? Tad was telling the cop, "Like, you've got to call someone, you've got to get down there!"

The cop was going, "Easy, slow down," to Tad, then he turned and asked me if I saw anything. And I said something like, "Excuse me, sir?" And Tad was all mad saying, "What is with you, Bernice?" Talking really fast and saying, "We've got to go down there now," to the cop, saying, "You think I'm lying? Someone's drowning!" And then the cop, like, very slowly started to get out his radio, and he radioed someone else, going, "Yeah . . . yeah . . ." really slowly, like he had all the time in the world? And then Tad started saying, "What's wrong with you people?" Really loudly, and it really bugged me, because to me it was like he was showing off how worried he was or something. Like he was being melodramatic for attention? But still, I knew something serious had happened? But I, like, didn't feel it? It was like I was lifted away? Like I was gone or, like, not really there practically? I never used to feel that way. Like stare off with nothing to think about?

So the cop was radioing and Tad was all upset. Tad was looking at me, so I said to him, "What?" For something to say I guess. Then he looked really weird, so I said it again. "What?" And he said something like, there's nothing that, or, there's no, or, well, I can't remember what he said, but he said something, and then he just turned away. And started to walk away! Then he, like, sped up! So I called, "Wait!" Or, "Don't worry!" Or something. But his head just kept on going, like, bouncy down the path toward the underpass. And that was that!

I don't even know what happened to the guy who fell in. But I can guess? He probably killed himself? Right? And as for Tad, good riddance! I mean, it was good riddance from the start? That was obvious? I mean it was like I was waiting for him to somehow make it all end the whole time? But did I do something wrong? What am I doing wrong? I mean, not just with stupid guys or, like, helping drowning people, but, like, with everything? With, like, me? I mean, I know I was wrong to not care about the poor guy on the ice. Would it be better to fake it?

The thing is, I'm, like, tired every day. I know it's important to stay cheery. Yay! But it's, like, I feel like I don't do anything? Like

I don't do anything that's, like, good or special somehow? It's so bizarre, like, I forget what I'm supposed to do? What I do usually? Like, what have I been doing all along? I don't know how to, like, stay still? But it's also, like, I don't know how to, you know . . . move. It's like I know where I am, but it's crazy, because a lot of the time I feel like I totally don't? Like I'm here, but I'm not here? That sounds so stupid, right? So totally dumb? But it's like I think all the time lately that other people would do it so much better. Other people would know how to be me way better. They'd live my life really well.

Back at home? I can't sit still. My roommate, Julia, went to the Adirondacks. I walk from the kitchen past the front door? Then through the living room into the bedroom? Then I turn around and walk back through to the kitchen again. I try to stand still to look out the window. The guys in the parking lot on the corner never stop parking and reparking cars. In the apartment? I keep on, like, smelling gas? But every time I go to the stove to make sure it's not on? It's not? And then I'm, like, afraid to open the oven and stick my head in to check, because it's like it might turn out to be the actual second it explodes. I, like, walk around *clop-clop-clop*, waiting for something to happen. What am I doing? What am I waiting for? It's not like I want something to happen? It's not like I even know? I don't know! And all these jerky guys like Tad. What a jerk! He hit me! Hard! I don't care about them! I don't know really what I care about? I don't care about having a boyfriend or anything? It's not marriage I care about? Or being alone? It's love, I guess? Just, like, feeling it? Like not just for some guy, but for anything. Sometimes I feel like I can pretend I know how it feels? But it's like I'm not sure, like I haven't felt it, like, since I was little? Or, like, I don't remember?

Ohmigod! What am I saying? This is like, what? I'm such a freak! Am I? Why am I telling you this, like, blabbing my head off? Right? Ohmigod! But I think about it! I try to think about stuff! I try to think about me as a person, like, making my little tiptoey way through the world? And how I'm doing? And I end up thinking about love and what it would be like. To have it. And what I'm doing wrong to not feel it? I think about the feeling of it? I think about having love in a little bubble, like a glass one. Like hope, if it was a thing? Like air?

CALL-HELL

By Amy Sohn

call·hell \'kȯl-hel\ *noun* [insp. by Dorothy Parker]: the state of severe anxiety following a date or sexual interlude, when the woman wonders desperately if the man will call, and the man does nothing to eliminate this severe anxiety. Symptoms of call-hell include: obsessive checking of telephone messages; calling oneself to make sure that voice mail/machine/phone service is functional; refusal to take out trash or do laundry lest one miss the all-important phone call; telling friends that the line can't be tied up; disappointment/frustration at perfectly ordinary phone calls, simply because the ordinary people are not The Man. *See also:* DELAYED GRATIFICATION, AWKWARD PARTINGS, AFTERMATH OF A DATE. *Also:* consult Appendix A, Eternal Questions. *Specifically:* Question 547: "Does he like me?" and Question 548: "Does he like me, or does he *like* like me?"

Every Valentine's Day, Rose Brody went to a party at a bar in the East Village, and every year she left more despondent than when she had entered. The party was held at a huge hot spot with high ceilings and was hosted by three entrepreneurial promoters who gave each guest one hundred dollars' worth of funny money upon entry. Over the course of the evening, as the revelers drank more and more Stoli tonics and found negligibly attractive strangers more and more appealing, they would begin to take out the fake cash and dare each other to do illicit things: "I'll give you five bucks to French-kiss me for five Mississippi seconds," or "I'll give you a hundred to leave with me now."

If the daree were interested, she would accept the dare and the money; if not, she would give the darer the same amount of money instead—and he would walk away with his tail between his legs. If a darer felt timid, she could have a friend make the entreaty for her, and then act as though she herself had no idea why she was being asked to lick the chest of a Greek god–like stranger. Whoever had the most money at the end of the night won dinner for two at an expensive restaurant, which Rose thought was a silly prize, given that anyone attending a Valentine's party to begin with probably felt uneasy at the notion of dinner for two.

At last year's party, Rose had met an attractive, muscular Jewish painter named Sam, and, convinced there was mutual chemistry, she'd dared him to kiss her. He obliged, seemingly delighted, and the embrace was so intimate, long, and lovely that Rose felt certain he was smitten. As she was contemplating which font to use on the save-the-date card, he said, "Will you excuse me? I have to go to the men's room."

"Of course," Rose said, understanding that nature's call sometimes competed with love's. She looked at him dotingly. He looked at her less dotingly, hesitated for a moment, and then picked up his beer bottle and took it with him.

Given her track record, Rose was nervous about attending the party this year, but at the last minute she changed her mind. She had no other plans and decided the upside was that she would be unlikely to have a worse experience than she had the year before. She wore confident clothes, hoping they might bring good luck: a new pair of jeans called Sevens that made her derriere look round but not too big, a black rock-and-roll tank top with a print of a unicorn on it, and a belt with a buckle that said INDIAN.

When Rose walked into the party, one of the promoters gave her a hundred dollars and said, "Have fun." She slipped the money into her pocket and spotted Tom, the ex-roommate of her ex-best friend. He was talking to a skinny boy who had mussed black hair and a strange elfin look, as though he had been the runner-up for lead hobbit in *The Lord of the Rings*.

"Hey, Rose," said Tom. "This is my friend Matt. Matt, this is Rose Brody."

"Do you bike, Rose?" Matt asked.

"What?" she said, thrown.

"Indian motorcycles," he said.

"Oh," she said. "I didn't even know what *Indian* meant. I bought this at a high-end women's clothing store because the saleswoman pushed it on me."

"It's good she pushed," Matt said. "You got a lot going on there! I wouldn't mind clinging to your waist." He put his thumbs in his belt loops, jutted his chin out, and nodded slowly. His delivery was so over-the-top that Rose decided he wasn't so much sleazy as sending up the notion of sleaziness. The half-kidding style made her so uneasy that she mumbled, "Nice meeting you," and moved along.

For the next few hours, Rose circulated and made small talk with others in the crowd, which was comprised mainly of actors and screenwriters. Rose was a freelance copy editor and was half-afraid of, half-entranced by the beautiful people.

Around midnight, the music got loud and the group danced and sang along to the only black songs that white people know the lyrics to: "ABC" and "Dance to the Music." Rose could see all the young folk beginning to dip into their funny money and dare each other to do strange things: A slender performance artist climbed up on a table and was mooning the crowd; a buttoned-up blond was giving a lascivious lap dance to a guy on a couch.

As Rose was gaping at the lap dance, an overconfident, wan guy came up to her and said, "Would you kiss me on the lips for ten seconds?" She looked around to see who he had made the suggestion to, but everyone around her was shimmying to Sly.

"All right," she said.

He used too much tongue, though, and rubbed his hands too vigorously against her back. He must not have been too big a fan of her kissing, either, because when he pulled away, he handed her the money, said, "Thank you," and quickly left.

Rose found herself thinking about the ironically sleazy hobbit boy and took a promenade around the room. She ran into Tom, who was getting his coat at the coat check. Since she had tossed back a few Stoli tonics by this point, she said a little tipsily, "You're such a funny guy, Tom. I need to find someone funny." She had realized this a few weeks ago, when a girlfriend of hers had told her, "Sometimes my boyfriend makes me laugh so hard that I'm crying and can't even move." Many of Rose's ex-boyfriends had left her crying and unable to move, but it was never because they'd said something funny.

"You don't date funny men?" said Tom.

"No, the nicest ones are bland and the interesting ones are mean, but none of them are funny."

"Matt's funny," he said. "You should talk to him."

Before she knew what she was doing, she had pulled a ten out of her pocket. "Give him this and tell him to come over here and make out with me."

Tom grinned, took the money, and disappeared. Rose sat in a banquette to wait. Fifteen minutes later, she spotted Matt across the room. He looked at her sideways but didn't approach. She beckoned him in an exaggerated, cartoonish style, and soon he was sitting next to her.

"What took you so long?" she said. "Didn't you get my offer?"

"Yeah," he said, "but I thought ten was a little low."

Matt's drink was sitting on a cocktail napkin in front of them, and there was a red cherry in it. She plucked it out, ate the cherry, and asked, "Want to see me tie the stem in a knot with my tongue?"

"You can't do that," he said. She stuck the stem in her mouth and pulled it out in a perfect knot a few seconds later.

"How'd you learn to do it?"

"My cousin taught me at a wedding, when I was five," she said, "and I've been screwed up about men ever since."

He raised his hand to her face and ran the back of his fingers up and down her cheek. "Your cheek is so smooth," he said. She decided he wasn't so strange looking.

"Let's make out," she said, curling her arm around his as if they were walking, even though they were sitting.

"Have you kissed anyone else tonight?"

"Just one guy. He was bad."

"Then I can't kiss you."

"Why not?"

"I'm germ-phobic. I've been afraid of germs ever since I went to India."

"When was that?"

"Twelve years ago." She looked at him uneasily. He paused a second, then said, "Just kidding." He leaned in and smooched her, soft and just a little wet.

"Let's go somewhere," she said.

"I really shouldn't," he said. "I wanted to get some sleep tonight."

"Then let's get in a cab, drive around, and make out. We can drop me off first and then you."

"Where do you live?"

"Brooklyn."

"That's too far," he said.

"Are you kidding?" she asked.

"No," he said. She sighed, weary from the effort, and it must have had an impact on him, because immediately he said, "OK. Let's go back to my place for a drink, but only one."

"One is fine," she said.

. . .

His apartment was a tiny one-bedroom without a separate kitchen. Rose beelined to the bathroom. In front of the toilet, where everyone posts their most prized achievements, was a framed poster for a film called *Party Line*, about a telephone operator who eavesdrops on people's calls. Rose hadn't seen it, but she had seen the trailer. Someone named Matt Bell had written it, and Rose assumed it was this Matt.

She flushed and came out of the bathroom. "Did you write *Party Line?*" she said.

"Yeah," he said, from the kitchen, where he was mixing a drink. "Did you see it?"

"No, but that was a big-deal movie. I'm very impressed."

"Thanks," he said.

"How come you have such a small apartment if you wrote a big-budget movie?"

"Don't ask me that," he moaned. She realized she had done the one thing a woman should never do to a guy on the first date: criticize his size.

His desk was by the bathroom door, and Rose sat down at it, picked up the fax phone, and said, "Hello, Matt Bell's office. No, this is his secretary. Who's calling? Mr. Lingus? All right, Mr. Lingus, I'll give him the message." She wrote *Mr. Lingus* on his blotter, on February 14. Matt came over and handed her a drink.

"What is this?" she said.

"Gatorade and vodka," he said. "It's all I have."

He disappeared into the bedroom. A few seconds later, Rose heard "The Girl from Ipanema," playing with just music and no lyrics. She had never had a guy play "The Girl from Ipanema" as a precoital warm-up before. She felt romantic and light-headed, as if she were living in an old-time movie.

She went into the bedroom, where Matt was adjusting the volume of the music, and he turned to her with his arms extended and a decidedly unfunny look on his face. They danced well together, and because he was short, they fit. She became so taken with his small, strong body that pretty soon she toppled him down onto the bed.

"I'd like to be naked with you," he said after a while.

"That sounds like a good idea," she said. "We could do it like in *The Heartbreak Kid*." He was a screenwriter; she felt sure he'd get the reference.

"I don't know that movie," he said.

"How can you not?" she said. "Cybill Shepherd and Charles Grodin stand in front of a fire and take off all their clothes, item by item. After each piece is removed, they take one step closer to each other, but she says they can't touch."

"What a good plan," he said.

They lay side by side. She took off a sock. He took off his shirt. She took off another sock. He took off his pants. When she got down to her bra and underwear, she was embarrassed because she was wearing a cheap green-and-black leopard print thong. She decided to take it off first.

"Uh-oh, I'm getting nervous," he said. She slithered out of the thong, and he said, "That's a very interesting shape you've got there."

"It's an overgrown Brazilian," she said. "So I'm two-toned. So sue me."

He took off his boxers. She took off her bra. They touched.

The sex itself wasn't so much bad as hesitant, on both of their parts. They were torn between wanting to go all the way, to make it a bona fide one-night stand, and not wanting to go all the way because neither of them was really comfortable with that sort of thing, generally speaking. He was the first to suggest they do it. Thinking he meant it and really wanted to, she agreed, and then he ran into the bathroom to get a condom and had trouble getting it on, and she said, "Maybe we shouldn't," and he said, "You're right, let's not." They rolled around a little more, and he went upside down on her, and after he made her very, very happy, she said, "I think we should," because she felt generous, and he said, "That's a good idea," and they did for a while, but the condom was thick and dry and after fifteen minutes she suggested that they stop, and he seemed more relieved than dissatisfied.

In the morning, as Rose dressed next to Matt, she found her unspent funny money in her pocket. She put it down on the nightstand and said, "Thanks for last night."

"Good one," he said.

They went into the main room to leave, and he asked her for her phone number before she had even offered it. That, combined with her one-liner, made her feel elated and secure. She went to the desk and scribbled her number underneath the name Mr. Lingus.

"You'd better not throw out February," she said. "I'm unpublished."

"How come?"

"I don't want the wrong people bothering me."

"I know what you mean," he said. Then he walked her to the subway station and kissed her for a long time before she went down the stairs.

That afternoon, as Rose was sitting at her desk, editing a revised, expanded, annotated edition of *The Yellow Wallpaper*, the phone rang.

"Last night was really amazing," Matt said. "You are really something else, Rose."

"Thanks, Matt."

"Do you not like it when I call you by your name?"

"I don't mind it, but I can't tell if you're being funny."

"I call people by their names. It's a habit I have. I'm bad with names, and it helps me remember."

"So you were about to forget mine?"

"Not at all! I won't say your name anymore. I won't say it."

"You can say it."

"All right, Rose."

They talked a little about their families, and Rose told him a joke she had heard recently about an old man who complains of pain to his doctor. The doctor asks for a stool sample, a urine sample, a mucus sample, and a semen sample, and the man says, "Why don't I just give you my underwear?"

Matt laughed appreciatively, and Rose felt relieved that he wasn't grossed out. "So, Matt," she said, "why don't you tell me something about you that I don't know?"

"Like what?"

"It could be about anything, not necessarily dramatic. About your favorite food, even."

"Food is OK?" he said. "All right. More than any other food, I eat boiled chicken. I like to boil it in a pot, take a shower while it's boiling, and then dry myself off and eat it." Rose didn't know why she was charmed by this image, but she was.

They talked awhile longer, and Matt seemed solicitous and very interested. He asked her a bunch of questions about copyediting and kept calling her "lofty" and "smart." At three different times, he said what a great night it had been, which Rose thought was odd given his lack of fruition. Maybe the world was becoming more egalitarian. Then he said, "I'm going to visit my uncle in Connecticut this weekend, but I'll be back Sunday. We can go out early next week if you want."

"I'd like that," she said.

"Actually," he said, "I have birthday parties on Monday and Tuesday. But let's talk in the beginning of the week and do something late in the week." Rose didn't understand why he didn't invite her to the birthday parties along with him. "I'd invite you with me," he said, "but my friends are really weird, and if you met them, you'd think I was weird, too. Besides, if you were there, I'd want to focus all my attention on you." Rose liked the idea of his focusing all his attention on her but still thought it was strange that he wouldn't invite her.

"Well," she said. "Cawl me latuh." Rose said this to emphasize the point that *he* should call *her*, but she said it with an accent so it would seem joking and off-the-cuff instead of insistent and controlling.

"I will," he said.

Rose lived in a tiny studio apartment, so her desk was only ten feet from her bed, but her phone was on the nightstand. It was a white, cordless Radio Shack model, and although she had to replace the battery more often than she liked, she was pleased with the unit and the ring, which was friendly without being too loud. Her answering machine was a Panasonic digital messaging system that had twenty minutes of recording time. Rose's friends all thought she was crazy for not having caller ID, but she was old-fashioned and felt the world was getting stale from lack of surprise.

On Monday morning, she moved the phone to her desk, right next to where she was working on the manuscript. It was eerily quiet all morning, so quiet that she became convinced the phone was broken. On three different occasions, she pressed "Talk" on the receiver to make sure nothing had happened, and each time she was greeted by a kind, infuriatingly efficient dial tone.

The only time the phone rang was at twelve-thirty. Rose felt her heart race and said, "Hello?" There was a long pause—Rose felt sure it was Matt, mustering up the courage to speak—then a woman's voice came on, telling Rose that she wanted to offer her an unlimited calling plan from Verizon.

On Tuesday morning, she decided to leave the phone in its cradle so she wouldn't look at it or think about it. She was pretty sure that Matt would call, but she knew if she focused on it too much, he wouldn't, since that was what always happened. It rang at three-thirty. She jerked around nervously. She was certain it would be Matt, since this was the middle of the middle day of the beginning of the week, so she answered in a low, breathy voice like Jessica Rabbit's.

"Hell-o," sang her mother, who was calling to give Rose the date of the Passover seder, which was six weeks away.

"What's the big rush?" said Rose.

"I'm just trying to be considerate," said her mother.

Wednesday was the longest of the three days because when Rose woke up, her first thought was, "This is the day he'll call." She was sure that if Matt had any doubts about when to call or any logistical problems on Monday or Tuesday, he would surely be over them by now. The phone rang twice that morning. Once it was Rose's editor to check in on her progress, and the other time it was her gynecologist, reminding her of an upcoming appointment. Rose was rude to both and felt guilty that the cause was a boy.

At noon, she went for a walk to clear her head, but she took her cell phone with her and called her home machine three times within twenty minutes. By three o'clock, she was wondering if maybe Matt were dead. She thought he might have gotten into a car wreck on his way back from Connecticut, and this thought made her happy. She knew it was bad to be happy he might be dead, but it soothed her. She imagined herself in black at his funeral, his whole family knowing she could have been the one he married if only he hadn't been killed.

But if Matt were not dead, it meant that he had consciously decided not to call her again for some other reason, so she began replaying every line and inflection of their conversation to determine what she had said that might have been misconstrued. She decided her dirty joke was too dirty. She decided she had seemed, in general, too eager and fond.

At four-twenty-two, the phone rang. Rose let it ring three times before she picked up. Her heart was beating very fast, but she tried to sound calm. "Hello?"

"Rose, it's Steve. We're all going to dinner tomorrow night, and I wanted you to come." Steve was a married guy in his fifties whom she had met at a magazine party several months before. He and his friend Richard, another fifty-something married guy, liked to double-date with Rose and her friend Jane, a single girl in her twenties. They would gather at a SoHo restaurant to eat, drink bottles of red wine, and flirt. At the end of the night, the men would drive home to Westchester, and the girls would split a cab back to Brooklyn. It was a symbiotic relationship—the men got to leer without guilt, and the girls got free food and nonstop compliments.

"That sounds wonderful," Rose said. But she couldn't help thinking that if Matt had called her when he was supposed to, she would have had to tell Steve no, she couldn't go, that she had a date. She even worried that if Matt called later in the day to ask her out for Thursday, she would have to say no to him. But she felt that one day's notice would be way too inconsiderate, and in any event, the dinner could be an opportunity for her to live her life, stay busy, be her own person.

When Rose showed up at the restaurant the next night, her face was pale and her hair beginning to thin. She hadn't been eating well and her mouth was dry. She kissed everyone hello and collapsed into a chair.

"What's wrong?" asked Steve. She told them the story. "Maybe he meant you'd *talk* at the end of the week instead of make plans the end of the week," said Steve.

"He's not that dumb," she said.

"Hmm," said Steve. "I say give him till tomorrow, and then AMF."

"What's AMF?"

"Adios, motherfucker."

"How much do you like him anyway?" said Richard.

"To tell you the truth, I don't really know anymore."

"Do you have his e-mail?"

"No."

"Too bad," said Richard. "If you did, you could send him something snarky."

"Like what?"

"Like, 'Did ya fall off the face of the earth or something?'"

"That's not snarky!" said Steve. "That's obnoxious."

"That was just my first draft," said Richard. "Give me a second."

"Don't listen to either of these guys," said Jane. She was red-headed and gamine and always had at least five men in love with her. Because of this, she took great joy in playing den mother to other single women. "Don't call. He knew he was supposed to call and he didn't."

"But it's only Thursday," said Rose. "Should he get a buffer?"

"When they like you, they call," she said. "No buffer. Five years ago I might have advised you differently, but now that the Book has permeated our culture, it's a different story. It's done for women what Viagra's done for men: ruined everything. Every other girl's doing it, so if you don't, you come off as a desperate freak. But anyway, he's not worth your time. Palmolive!"

"What do you mean, *Palmolive*?" asked Rose. Jane mimed vigorously washing her hands.

The food arrived, and as Rose ate her salad, she had a thrilling thought—the kind so intoxicating that it is hard to keep it to yourself. Richard and Steve were engrossed in a conversation about basketball, so Rose tapped Jane on the shoulder.

"What if all I want is a sexual relationship with him?" Rose whispered.

"Oh," said Jane, who was chewing a piece of endive. "Then a completely different set of rules applies."

"Really?" said Rose. "What are they?"

"You can call whenever you want. Every decision is based on one single goal: the procurement of sex. There's no ego, and full humiliation is acceptable." Rose decided she would go to the bathroom and call him from inside.

"Though to tell you the truth," said Jane, "when people say they only want a sexual relationship, they're usually just saying it as a justification to do what they want to do. They can't see any way to do something so humiliating and wrongheaded if they actually like the person, so they convince themselves that all they really want is sex when in truth they want much more. How was he?"

"That's an awfully personal question!" exclaimed Rose.

"Just as I suspected," said Jane.

Rose started to feel a little dizzy. She had sought more clarification and was only getting less. She decided to go to the bathroom — not to call, but to throw some water on her face.

The bathroom was at the back of the restaurant, and there was a woman in her sixties waiting outside the door. She had spike-heeled black boots, red lips, and a wild, crazy look, as though she had once lived a little. Rose stood behind her in line. "What's the matter?" asked the woman. "You look like you've just been run over."

Rose deliberated for a moment, and then told the woman about Matt. She knew this was an extreme move, but felt that maybe a stranger would be able to offer better advice than people who knew her well. Maybe a stranger would tell her to call.

When Rose finished the story, the woman said, "Have you ever heard of Ferrara Bakery & Cafe?" Rose hadn't. "It's in Little Italy on Grand Street, and they sell the best cannoli in the city. It's so popular that every time you go, there's a line out the door. Each new customer has to pick a number, and the bakery girl, who is a very attractive young lady, calls out the numbers one by one. When a customer hears his number, he steps up to the counter and she takes his order. If the girl calls number fifty-one and no one answers, she calls it once, maybe twice, and then she calls fifty-two.

"You need to think of yourself as the counter girl at Ferrara

Bakery & Cafe. If you call a number and no one answers, you need to move on. You don't have time to waste. You got a line of people waiting to be helped. They would not take it well if you kept shouting, 'Fifty-one! Fifty-one!' until the end of time. As a matter of fact, they would go somewhere else to get their cannoli even though they all knew Ferrara Bakery & Cafe was the best in the city."

"Wow," said Rose. "That's the best advice anyone's given me in my entire life."

A thin, drawn woman in her thirties had taken her place next to Rose and was applying powder to her nose. "I couldn't help overhearing," she said. "Are you in call-hell?"

"I think I am," said Rose. "This lady here said something very wise, but it takes a lot longer than one conversation to internalize the concept of healthy self-worth."

"Tell me about it," said the second woman. "I'm better at getting through call-hell now than I once was, but it's only because I took up crochet."

"Crochet?" said the red-lipped woman.

"Every time I'm about to call a guy who's bad for me, I crochet a couple rows of a blanket instead. I keep doing it until the urge passes."

"How big is the blanket?" said Rose.

"Which one?" said the woman. "I've made twelve."

A muscular guy in a white fishnet cutoff top looked up from a nearby table. "I used to do stuff like that to control myself," he said, "but now I just call. I took this course on radical honesty and learned that anyone I scare away by being clear isn't worth my time anyway."

"I hate the 'not worth my time' argument!" said a petite, spiky-haired woman dining alone a few tables away. "If she could accept the fact that this guy wasn't worth her time, she wouldn't be thinking about him all the time anyway! No one believes in predestination when they're conflicted by matters of the heart.

People get into ruts like the one Rose is in because the American ethos is built on an assumption of free will."

"How'd you know my name?" said Rose.

"We were raised to think we could make our own fate, like Horatio Alger," the woman barreled on. "So when our actions don't lead to a desired result, we convince ourselves we must have taken a wrong turn."

"It's not about predestination or free will," said the leggy, platinum-blond bartender, roller-skating out from behind the bar. "She shouldn't have slept with him on the first date!"

The entire restaurant became hushed. Every face turned to stare at Rose accusingly.

"But he didn't come!" Rose shouted. "I did, but he didn't!"

The patrons began to murmur and talk among themselves. "It doesn't matter," said the bartender. "You ruined it. I'm Swedish, so you might think I'd have more liberal notions of sex, but in my experience, nothing long lasting ever comes of first-date sex. Even in Sweden."

Rose felt a huge gust of wind from up above. Julie Andrews floated down from a hole in the roof, carrying a black parasol. "My vocal cords are broken, but I had to weigh in," she said. "It all went downhill when you used that fake accent on 'Cawl me latuh.' He knew you were uncertain that he might not follow up, and though he wasn't conscious of it, he decided you were too needy. What man wants a needy girl?"

The room started to spin very slowly, like the restaurant at the top of the Marriott Marquis. Rose felt nauseous and dizzy. A sleek, fit lady whom Rose hadn't noticed before stood up from her table and put her finger in the air. "Narcissistic and uninterested in other people's personal dilemmas as I usually am," she said, "I can't help but opine. I'm a lesbian and the rules are very different, but what I've learned from the Forum, which is not the same as EST, is that it matters not what you do but how you feel about what you do."

"I don't understand," said Rose.

"If you imbue Matt with a power he's not worthy of, then it doesn't matter if you call or not. You've already lost, by defining yourself according to his view of you. Granted, this dilemma stems from a long history of patriarchal marginalization of women, but you have to rip those shackles off! Until you can stop elevating men so that they take over every aspect of your life, you'll continue the same sad cycle of projection, obsession, and depression."

The walls were spinning faster, and although Rose stayed still, the other patrons moved along with the walls, oblivious to the motion. "It all comes down to women and men!" shouted a small terrier in the lesbian Forum grad's shoulder bag. "You were too aggressive early on. He felt his role being usurped and had to flee. Male fear leads to male exit. It was doomed from the moment you paid him to come over."

"Everyone here is full of it," said a member of the Australian women's Olympic bobsledding team, who was drinking a Foster's at the bar. "If you're spending so much time thinkin' about him, you should just call him. Get it over with. That's what I'd do. If you got a question you want answered, get it answered. Call him! Call him! Call him!"

A couple dozen other patrons joined in with the Australian's chant. The anti-call lobby inserted quick "Don't"s in the spaces between the "Call him"s, in a deafening oom-CHA-CHA rhythm. The terrier was now yapping, high-pitched and angry. Julie Andrews was parasoling above Rose's head, lip-synching so she wouldn't further hurt her vocal cords. The walls began spinning faster, the faces blurred together, and the voices became an inaudible jumble. The floor shook violently, and a jagged portion of it dropped out beneath Rose's feet, causing her to be sucked down with an enormous *whoosh* into the blackness below.

Rose found herself traveling a thousand miles an hour through a twisty, narrow tunnel. She clawed the sides to stop her downward motion, but her fingers slid helplessly down the slick walls.

As she came around a bend, she felt an invisible though stable surface materialize beneath her feet. She abruptly landed on her rear and rubbed it in pain. There was a warm patch of light in front of her, so she stood up unsteadily and headed toward it. She came to a large wall of Plexiglas. Behind it, she saw Matt in his apartment, as if he were an exhibit at a museum. He looked healthy—by no means dead—and he was pacing around with great agitation.

He went to the desk, pulled out the garbage can below it, and began strewing refuse onto the floor. He sifted through the cards and scraps, and when he didn't find what he was looking for, he opened his wallet and emptied it onto the blotter. As he removed bits of paper, he would inspect them desperately, longingly, insistently, and then return them to his wallet. When he had gone through every paper he had removed and had still not found what he was looking for, he ran his fingers through his messy hair and lowered his head to his desk with a moan.

"The blotter!" Rose shouted.

Matt got down on his knees and searched under the desk. "MR. LINGUS!" she cried. "It's UNDER MR. LINGUS!" She knew she sounded ridiculous, like a spectator at a horror film telling a heroine to run the other way, but she didn't care. As Rose pounded against the Plexiglas, the prostrate Matt, his desk, and his entire small apartment began to disappear, becoming more and more faded and imperceptible, like a Polaroid in reverse—until finally they were no longer there.

The surface Rose was standing on lurched forward in the manner of a moving sidewalk. Rose half expected the theme song to *The Graduate* to start playing. She was conveyed forward to another sheet of Plexiglas, once again with Matt's apartment behind it. She was alarmed to see that Matt was not at all distraught. He was leaning against the refrigerator, kissing a blond girl who was the spitting image of a young Cybill Shepherd. Young Cybill lifted her leg up over Matt's ass, and Rose heard him say, "Oh, Melissa, I'm so glad we met the other night. You're the hottest girl I've ever seen."

"I know," said the girl. "And to think I almost didn't go to Johno's party."

"I've never felt so instantly intrigued by anyone before," said Matt. "I know this might sound hasty, given as how we hardly know each other, but how would you like to become my wife?"

"Oh, Matty!" she exclaimed. "You've made me the happiest woman alive!"

Matt lifted the girl up and carried her into the bedroom with great ease, despite his weak frame. Rose scooted to the left as they moved, so that she could see. He gently placed the blond on the bed as if she were a china doll, then he began dry-humping her and whispering terrible things into her ear—things like, "I love the color of your hair," and, "I've been commitment phobic my whole life, but now I feel I can stop running," and, "You're so different from all the other girls I've dated." As Matt whispered, the girl nodded with great certainty and joy. Matt kissed her repeatedly on her white neck, then removed her skirt, revealing her hairless thighs, which miraculously had the same width as her calves.

"How weird is this?" the blond cried. "We just met, and now we're going to take this beautiful leap?"

"I know!" he exclaimed. "I've had one-night stands before, but usually afterward I want to kill the girl. It wasn't like that when we slept together at all! With you, I feel like making a baby!"

"You took the words right out of my mouth!" she cried. "Let's get to it!" He tore off his shirt and dove down on top of her with great relish. She giggled loudly, and as he mauled her, they slowly disappeared.

Rose felt a huge lump in her throat. Even when she swallowed, it didn't go away. The moving sidewalk lurched forward again. She came to a third version of Matt's living room and sighed nervously.

This time, he was sitting at the desk, talking to a brown-haired man, who was leaning against the kitchen sink, his back to Rose. "I don't know," Matt was saying to the back, "I feel like I keep dating the same girls over and over again. They're all so aggressive. It really harshes my mellow."

"I know what you mean, dude," said the back.

"The last girl I did it with I was into at first, but then she came on so strong it freaked me out. She chased me down and forced me to kiss her. I should have known not to mess with her. Her underwear was Skank City and then she told a really nasty joke."

"But you laughed!" Rose cried.

"What party did you meet her at?" said the back.

"Some Valentine's thing in the East Village, where they give out fake money. She gave me ten bucks to make out with her and then yelled at me when I didn't come over right away. I was like, Whoa there, cowboy."

"I've been to that party," said the back, taking a step forward and heading toward the desk. Rose saw that it was Sam, the muscular Jewish painter. She let out a choked sob. "And I just got a bad case of the zacklies."

"What do you mean?"

"'Zackly same thing happened to me last year. Chick was all on my tip and I was like, Girl, you need to chill. I tell you, man, women in this town are des-per-*it*!" He slammed his fist down on the desk.

"I know," said Matt. "I need to find a girl who's relaxed, who does her own thing."

"You need to move, man," said Sam. "I hear they got chicks like that in Austin."

"Maybe I should move. Maybe I should."

"Did you call this girl after you did her?" asked Sam.

"Yeah," said Matt, "but only so she wouldn't think I was an asshole. When you don't call at all, they think you're an asshole. But that's it. I did the I'm-a-nice-guy call and now, as far as I'm concerned, she's dead to me. D-E-A-D dead. I'm *never* calling her again! NEVER!"

He threw his head back and laughed maniacally, and Sam did, too. They looked like evil swallows, their tongues flickering in the air, their Adam's apples bobbing with glee. As the image evaporated, Rose felt a terrible melancholy rise to her chest. It was as though she had just watched a ship with all the world's most valuable possessions capsize in a monsoon. She was helpless and angry, and the combination felt like being in mourning.

Suddenly, the invisible floor beneath her dropped out, and she was sucked down into the tunnel again. Rose was certain that when she stopped, she would be dead. But after just a few seconds, she landed with a huge *thunk* on something soft and very familiar.

She felt her warm comforter beneath her, opened her eyes, and saw the cracks in her ceiling. She was bone-tired, but calm. She spotted the poster of *Don't Look Back* across from her, Bob's eyes low-slung and cynical, and next to it the framed photograph of herself at her Bas Mitzvah, surrounded by her four brothers and her parents. Her breathing slowed and came from her diaphragm, even though despite three years of yoga she had never been able to master this style of breathing. She felt her vision begin to sharpen, her senses begin to return to normal. She rolled over onto her side. Her nightstand was still in place, her phone still sitting in its stand.

And then it began to ring.

The sound was high-pitched, birdlike, and sweet. To Rose, the ringing was different from all other times, as though it contained some bright good news. She was not afraid and not at all uncertain. She was filled with an overwhelming, all-encompassing sense of relief and calm, as though every cell in her body that had ever been unsettled, every neuron in her brain that had ever felt unsure or lonely, was about to be massaged into a sublime state of completion.

But as she reached to pick up the phone, her hand would not move. Though her brain could send the signal, the fingers would not rise or even twitch. She tried lifting her left hand. It was locked down tight by her side, as though the palm were glued to the bed. She tried to lift her cheek from the pillow, but her head was as heavy as a sleeping child's. She felt a panic rise from her stomach to her throat.

Her answering machine was right where it always was on the nightstand, but it wouldn't pick up. The signals persisted, a two-second ring followed by a two-second pause, two-second ring, two-second pause. After ten, she waited for the caller to give up and hang up; and after twenty, she waited again. But even then the phone would not hush. Rose stared at the receiver, blinking in rhythm to the rings.

Dagenham

By Anna Maxted

Da·gen·ham \'da-gən-ăm, 'dag-nəm\ [geographical name] 1: former municipal borough Southeast England in Essex, now part of Barking and Dagenham, a borough of East Greater London, England, population 139,900. 2: okay, so strictly speaking, the place name isn't important. Everybody has their own geographic location for it. What's important is it's where the story began, the story of *him* or of *the two of you,* and it's a name that causes either great sadness or joy.

There is, thought Tamara, simply no excuse to look a mess on the beach. All that seaside perfection requires is a little planning and no piggery. (Why do some people make such a *meal* out of dieting? Eat less cake. And do Pilates, not aerobics. Aerobics is undignified, and probably oppressive.)

Once you have the correct body, book your salon toffee-cream tan, commission a hard-liner fascist beautician—you want an effective bikini wax, not some twit picking daisies—and find the Jackie O. of shades. Your hair should be long enough to tie back unless, of course, you *wish* to resemble Don King in a gale, and your designer swimsuit should be a gorgeous, extortionate feat of engineering. The beachwear equivalent of a plasma TV.

This isn't exactly rocket science. More like junior high science.

And yet, thought Tamara, frowning behind her D&G sunglasses, almost every woman on the beach looked a mess. Bright white, or scorched red, most were heavy with sag and wobble. And blotchy. And frizz-haired. Not to mention the hair on their heads. And where had the poor dears been tricked into buying their costumes? Did Target sell beachwear? A host of floral atrocities, each one with a low-cut *pant*, the nasty sheeny material covering every bit of those generous bottoms. Was there anything more suburban than a thick-sewn gusset? And as for their accessories! Navy-and-white striped shoulder bags, with golden anchors embroidered in the middle as a final monstrous touch!

Nicholas, surveying the men, was equally appalled. One didn't fly first class to one of the most exclusive hotels on the planet (courtesy of Elegant Resorts) to share the private beach with *this* sort of person. The entire point of holidaying at the Datai — "an idyllic retreat on the beautiful Malaysian island of Langkawi, set on the edge of an ancient virgin rain forest" — was that this sort of person wouldn't be able to afford the Datai. Nicholas rolled over on his sun-lounger in disgust and groped for a Camel. "Tammy," he said, tapping gray ash onto the golden sand, "I don't want to alarm you, but take a look at that."

A fifth Pimm's had made his voice loud, harsher than usual. He jerked his chin toward a man with shaved hair, a pale, untoned stomach, and a smattering of freckles on his back. Some sort of hooligan, here to get laid and lagered and to read bloody John Grisham, no doubt. Only language those sort of people understand, John Grisham. (Nicholas himself read bloody John Grisham, but he read him ironically, which was an altogether different affair.) He squinted at the thug's book, a lip curl at the ready. *The Mind of God.* Eh?

Tamara's cool blue eyes followed his gaze. Nicholas, never one to let fact get in the way of a mediocre line, bawled, "Dagenham comes to the Datai!"

Tamara, for whom spite also took precedence over reality, added, "Do you think he's looking for the pictures?"

Together, they hooted with laughter.

Julie tried to concentrate on *The Portrait of a Lady*, but it was difficult. If you asked her (although this was unlikely, as when you come from Brentwood, people are not overly interested in your opinion on Henry James), she would have said that the book needed a good edit. From what Julie could gather from the leisurely introduction, the man had written the tome primarily to impress his literary mates. Apparently, James's brother had had the temerity to accuse a previous effort, *The Europeans*, of being "thin." *The Portrait of a Lady* was thick. Five hundred and seventy-eight pages thick. Julie preferred Jane Austen.

Not that she was a snob or anything. She wouldn't chuck Maeve Binchy out of bed. And an Elizabeth Berg was like a warm hug. But Jane Austen was her favorite. Such lovely manners they had in her books! (Julie had been raised on the premise that "manners cost nothing"—her mother had been a devout fan of anything that cost nothing. Consequently, her daughter was polite and clean, and every glass from which she drank had once contained Nutella. When a pensioner hobbled onto the train, and the pudgy young men and hard young women remained in their seats, Julie was as shocked the tenth time she saw such an occurrence as she was the first.)

"You know," she said to Darrell, "this isn't half as good as *Emma*. With *Emma*, everyone spoke in character, and the plot was spot-on. With this, everyone just says what the author wants to say himself. And the plot is *weak*. There's no motivation. And critics accuse Jane Austen of being narrow. As far as I can tell, James doesn't have any more, like, breadth; it's just that, occasionally, he sticks in a pompous paragraph about America or Europe. I'm halfway through and I still can't get a grip on the heroine. Maybe it's just me."

Darrell raised an eyebrow. He was not a reader of fiction, preferring fact. Whether it was history, philosophy, biography, or superstition, *How to Defend Yourself Against Alien Abduction* or *The Fall of Che Guevara*, Darrell sucked up knowledge like spaghetti. If he wasn't learning, he was bored. And where he came from, if you were bored, you got into trouble. Like throwing a trashcan through a shop window just to see what would happen. (Which, any way that you looked at it, was not good.) Happily, Darrell had a little more imagination than this as well as the sense to put his computer-literate mind to lucrative use. He waved his own book about in reply.

"This bloke. Paul Davies. He's wicked. He's top. He's a cosmologist, which, next to being an astronaut, is really cool. He's writing about the whole meaning of existence—pretty much that the universe is far too complex and peculiar to be the result of coincidence. That maybe there's something else that aided it— it's really hard to explain. It's just like that there might be a God, and the universe and our reality might be an expression of that."

"Wow," said Julie, who was more comfortable with escapism. (Julie had spent most of her life escaping. Via willowy romantic novels, hard work, Saturday jobs, and by pronouncing all her consonants—anything, basically, that would remove her from where she came from.)

"I'm boring you. Never mind. I'm going in the sea. Coming?"

"Later." Julie reclined on her lounger and watched her friend pad toward the water's edge. A bubble of happiness welled to the surface, and she smiled. To be here. In this place. It was amazing. She dug her Wal-Mart sun lotion out of her new bag—she was proud of that bag; like yacht-wear, it was appropriate—and blobbed cream on her pale sun-starved legs. She stretched, luxuriating in the toasty heat like a cat. The *colors* of the place.

Aquamarine. Bright blue. White. Green. She was Dorothy in Munchkinland after a lifetime of Kansas gray. As a teenager, Julie had vowed that when she was a grown-up she would have *foreign* holidays. She had made the vow on the day she heard her mother whispering about Cheryl Cooper's girl, from next door, dead of breast cancer at thirty, and never been abroad.

A raucous laugh rang above the *sh-sh-hush* of the sea. A short distance down the beach, a lanky man in loud shorts and a hard-faced woman in oddly large sunglasses (she looked like a blue-bottle, thought Julie) were haw-hawing with their pink mouths open. Julie tensed. Their noses were pointing at Darrell. She couldn't hear their conversation, but she didn't need to. They were laughing *at* him. She knew it. Julie—who'd been a fat kid at a rough school—could spot a sneer at ten paces. Such people wore a furtive look and a gleeful aura. Julie tried to hear what had already been said, spooling back the tape of her subconscious. It turfed up "Dagenham."

The arrogance of those who have enough money not to give a damn. Hurt, she looked at Darrell again and tried to see him through their eyes. He'd razored off all his hair the night before, as it was "easier." Berk. His soft stomach. Well, the man *had* survived on economy sausages all through college, and he refused to believe that a Snickers bar was fattening (because it was "tiny"). So. A bit of pudge and the wrong haircut. Shame fought pain.

And then, a rip of rage tore through her. You never could get away. Darrell himself said that. If not proud, he was *defiant* about his roots. But Julie had been running since the age of nine. After educating herself sick and training in accountancy (what could be more middle class?), she had presumed her new identity complete. But this rich couple saw through her Penguin Classic and her careful speech to her common core.

But that was the thing with *other* people. If you came from Essex, no one allowed you to be intelligent. Not your friends, not your teachers. You were conditioned to be thick. If it hadn't been for their parents' vicarious ambition and their own desperate claustrophobia, Julie and Darrell would be working in the local supermarket. At college, expectations of stupidity subsided (there, the Ilford accent was emulated by students from Hampshire to Hampstead), then, upon graduation, resurged. Julie recalled the football thugs running riot through Amsterdam a year back. One man, in particular, had the legend *Pussy Hunter* tattooed on his huge gut. Yet these people couldn't differentiate between Darrell (who, incidentally, loved cats) and Mr. Pussy Hunter!

When Darrell sauntered back from the sea, Julie smiled, but the gorgeous light had been leached from the day. "Let's go in," she said. "I'm sunburned."

Although Nicholas and Tamara always availed themselves of the finest that Elegant Resorts could offer, they might as well have stayed in London and paid their local builder to tip a skip of sand into their garden, for all the exploring they did. Nicholas despised any culture other than that of greed, and he wouldn't shift his (rather big) womanly bottom off its sun-lounger for the whole fortnight—except to use the Mediterranean Sea/Indian Ocean/Andaman Sea as a luxury open-air urinal. Yet, here they were, on a tour of the coastline. Tammy was determined to return to work browner than thou—and a day on a boat would accelerate her tan. Nicholas occasionally deferred to his girlfriend so that she would indulge his sexual peccadillos (nappy, nipple, nanny— don't ask).

"I thought this was private," exclaimed Tamara as she saw the other couple already sitting in the motorboat. "Yes," said the guide, grinning. "Only four people—private!" Someone should teach you how to floss, thought Tamara. Nicholas nudged her. "We should have stayed on the beach," he said, not bothering to lower his voice. "We'll pick up all sorts of common habits."

When she saw *them*, Julie's heart shrank inside her ribcage. She turned away as Tamara climbed into the boat. It wobbled and so did Tamara. "Careful," cried Darrell. He instinctively held out his hand, and instinctively, Tamara took it, then a moment later let it go.

Tamara arranged herself so that every socially acceptable body part was exposed to sunshine. She decided that Dagenham looked less, mmm, *trailer park* clothed: baggy shorts, a red crew-necked T-shirt, Adidas sneakers. (Nicholas wore his holiday uniform: navy baseball cap, Mambo shorts, Lacoste top, and deck shoes.) Tamara closed her eyes. Dagenham insisted on chatting to the guide, and his voice grated. It was so . . . naive. His frowsy girlfriend—a secretary, no doubt—remained silent. Tamara noted that the woman's lipstick was bigger than her lips. Really! Collagen was invented for people like you, she thought. Nicholas yawned without covering his mouth. Tamara could see strings of saliva, tacky and white. He'd overdone it in the sun yesterday and was broiled red—a good color for an angry person, but it didn't flatter him. She twitched. Occasionally, you wanted charm with your diamonds.

"So, where you from then?"

Tamara realized in shock that Dagenham was addressing her.

"Kensington," she replied (rewriting his question as "Where do you live?" as she didn't wish to answer "East Croydon").

"Rude of me," added Dagenham, extending a hand. "Darrell."

"Tamara." She didn't bother to introduce Nicholas. On her salary, she was above manners.

"Wotcha," said Darrell. Tamara tried not to smile and succeeded.

Julie stormed into the lobby, Darrell trotting behind her like a bewildered puppy. "What? *What?*"

"Nothing."

"Nah, go on. What?"

"Nothing."

"Please, Jules, what?"

"Nothing." That bitch. That cow. And her boyfriend with a jaw like Judge Dredd. They were both too haughty to acknowledge her and Darrell's presence. That witch, deigning to humor Darrell, like Queen Elizabeth meeting a homeless person. And Darrell, too artless to realize he was a clown to these people. Six feet tall, but in need of protection. Julie felt possessive. Not that she . . .

"Look," said Darrell, later by the pool, nudging her from quite possibly the longest paragraph in the world.

"Don't pretend we're speaking!" snapped Julie, hating herself. She hated herself for having pale English skin, for finding Henry James a bore, for liking the maraschino cherry in her daiquiri (you can take the girl out of Essex . . .), but most of all she hated herself for behaving like a *wife*. The whole point of being Darrell's oldest and dearest friend was that her status was higher than that of squeeze. The Michelles, the Nicoles, the Simones, they'd come and go, but her relationship with Darrell was a constant. And now, after one morning with that braying horse of a woman, Julie found herself reduced to a sulking cliché. She had felt threatened.

"Look, though." She looked. A small gray-brown monkey scampered along the poolside, whipped a banana slice from the side of a cocktail glass with his curiously human fingers, and crouched to dig through an open bag. (He had good taste for a monkey, as he'd ignored Julie's $12.99 thrift-store bargain and had gone straight for Tamara's pale pink Hermès number.) "Nicholas!" shrieked Tamara. Nicholas took three threatening steps toward the monkey and roared, "Sod off!" The monkey took three threatening steps toward Nicholas and roared something as rude in monkey language. Nicholas saw the large yellow pointed teeth, and he backed away.

"Bit of a berk, innee?" said Darrell. "Wonder what she's doing with him."

"What do you care?"

She was tempted to tell him about the Dagenham jibe. It wasn't that she wanted to hurt him. She wanted to share *her* hurt — as if telling him would dilute it. She couldn't bear that Darrell was intrigued by this woman, like Mellors lusting after Lady Chatterley.

"She's all right," said Darrell. He winked at Julie. "I might have a pop."

Julie forced a smile. Suddenly, despite the beauty and the sunshine and the sharp colors, her head was as gray and congested as a motorway. She couldn't hear herself think for all the dirt and noise, heat and fury inside her. She wished for regression — to be a speck in the womb, with a mind fresh and clean, a blank slate unblemished by the endless layers of grime that life heaps upon you. The irony was that she'd come here for peace.

Nicholas and Tamara were eating dinner on their fantastic balcony with its endless view of the sea and rain forest (and pool area), and Tamara was trying to get drunk. She had a better time with Nicholas when she was drunk. His jokes would become funnier and sex would be more bearable. Sex was a pastime they undertook more out of a sense of obligation than passion. Because Nicholas wasn't great with women. His world as a rainmaker was one of silver Porsche Carreras, and yes sirs. Of twenty-hour working days and dinners at Nobu (a cold restaurant for cold people). Of brands and bonuses and closing deals on slopes. Women were merely another commodity that became increasingly available in proportion to your wealth. (Tamara knew about the lap-dancing clubs and the fifty grand blown on coke and hookers.) But Nicholas was awkward with women. If Tamara were honest, their one shared interest was the denigration of the rest of the human race.

A shadow down by the pool caught her eye. Tamara stubbed out her cigarette in the remains of her lobster and stood up faster than she had intended. "I'm going for a walk," she announced and walked out, leaving Nicholas to his Cristal and Tom Clancy.

Darrell stared over the luscious trees to the glittering ocean and saw none of it. *Women*. What was it with them? Or rather, what was it with *her*? They required you to be telepathic, omniscient — a cross between God and David Blaine. That silent treatment was a killer. He couldn't stand the dishonesty of it. Obviously, he had committed a foul, heinous crime (in his sleep, perhaps?) and was being punished. It was totally out of character. The reasons he prized Julie as his great mate were that she was fun, funny, and, that rarest of female attributes, *reasonable*.

Unlike Simone — or was it Nicole? — who had forbidden him to drink water after nine P.M. because she couldn't stand being woken in the night by his trips to the toilet, Julie was rational. Sensible. Balanced. This was why he adored her. (Plus, she was well-stacked, he couldn't tell a lie.) So why this abrupt and terrifying bout of insanity?

"Oh, look, it's the heavy mob!"

Darrell jumped. The posh bird was standing beside him. She was wearing an alarming red item — the material was crinkled like a fan, and it rose from her back like a dragon's wing. He guessed it was designer and very expensive. He supposed that made up for it looking ridiculous. She waved her cigarette packet at him, and he saw that she was as drunk as a lord. Her well-preserved face had a pale-greenish tinge, and she didn't have full control of her neck muscles — her head alternately wobbled and went stiff.

Even so, it was a bit much: to bowl up to a bloke minding his own business and merrily accuse him of being a gangster!

"So, what car you driving at the minute, Darren?" She laughed, as if this was the wittiest line in the world. Darrell, with the ease of a man comfortable in his skin and with his choice of motor, replied, "An old Merc." And then — because although Darrell was placid, he wasn't a pushover — he nodded at Tamara's crinkly wing and said, "You paid for that, did you?"

But Tamara didn't hear. Her green-tinted contact lenses had almost popped out of her head. "We were certain you drove an Escort," she cried. "I bet Nicholas a grand! What a surprise! Do you have any other surprises for me, Darren?" Tamara's attempts at flirtation were clumsy. After years of working as a stockbroker, the small amount of empathy she once had had flaked away like dandruff, and her social skills were those of a young Jeffrey Dahmer.

"It's Darrell, actually. What do *you* drive?"

"Audi TT," purred Tamara, rearranging her Issey Miyake dress, lighting up and tossing her match into the murk of the five-hundred-thousand-year-old rain forest. "Back where it came from," she sang, to Darrell's look of dismay. She leered at him. He had beautiful eyes. She remembered the feeling of his hand in hers. Rough. Mmm. She fancied a bit of rough. Her gaze flicked downward. She wanted to touch him. And what Tamara wanted, she got.

"Where's your little girlfriend?" she murmured, hosing him in alcohol fumes.

"She's a friend."

"Oh? Then she won't mind me doing *this*." Tamara gripped the back of Darrell's head and pulled him toward her. Darrell's thoughts, in no particular order, were these: That was a come-on? Seafood. Suction pump. Liz Hurley gone to seed. Why not? Sod him. That idiot. Fling. Good. Blimey. Scary. Why not? Ouch. What, *here*? I suppose time is money. A use. Not bad. Bit of rough. Bit of posh. She's done this before. Not my type. Tongue like a salmon. Why not? Julie. *Julie*.

"Wait."

Darrell tried to wriggle from the embrace. It was like attempting to escape from a killer octopus.

"What the *fuck* is going on here!"

Reluctantly, Tamara let Darrell go.

Nicholas—red eyes, red skin, red hair—was now seeing red. The whore! How grubby!

Sneaking off to cuckold him with a . . . a . . . a—Nicholas had difficulty conceiving of a word foul enough to describe the creature in front of him—a *tradesman!* This person *might* earn in his lifetime what Nicholas earned in a month. Was the man a lottery winner? How else could he infiltrate the Datai? Why wasn't he in Tenerife? But hang on. If he earned less than Nicholas, and Tamara was kissing him, then he must have something else, something that he, Nicholas, didn't have. What? Nicholas galvanized the meager resources of his entire brain into answering this question, and failed. "I'll fight you!" he roared.

"That," said Tamara smoothly, "is not a good idea. Darrell has big muscles"—she giggled—"*everywhere.* And you don't. Don't make a fool of yourself."

As she said the words, she realized that she no longer planned to marry Nicholas and give up work and let him buy her ever-increasing circles of pearls, diamonds, rubies, and whatever else he could order from Tiffany's without actually setting foot in the shop. Nicholas continued to stare at Darrell, but he still couldn't see it. He was so devoid of generosity, with a soul as dried and shriveled as an old raisin, that he never would be able to see it. All he ever saw in anyone was profit or loss. He saw other people purely in terms of what he could gain from them, and how inferior they were to him. Goodness was invisible to him. Like a spoiled child with no imagination who would never see Tinkerbell, Nicholas was blind to a pure spirit as only the truly ignorant can be.

"Darrell," said a cool voice. "What exactly are you doing with these people?"

"Snogging my fiancée, that's what!" shouted Nicholas.

"Ex-fiancée," corrected Tamara, removing her two-carat diamond engagement ring and tossing it over the railing, where it joined the rest of her discarded nonbiodegradable detritus on the rain forest floor.

"You . . ." Various anatomical vulgarities suggested themselves to Julie, but eventually she chose the noun that she felt described Darrell best: "Fool." She stalked off.

"Julie, wait up!"

Julie ignored him (although to her annoyance, she couldn't stalk very far—it was a choice between the hotel lounge or the computer room). She refused to go back to their jungle villa, with its luxurious interior and prim twin beds. Twin beds because Darrell wouldn't dream of making a pass. Oh no, not in fifteen years, not even after his twenty-fifth birthday, when he drank thirteen pints of beer—not so much as a crude fumble! (He'd vomited meekly in her toilet, said, "It's OK, I feel much better now," and passed out on her sofa.) And yet, this hard-faced Pegasus look-alike, who despised everything about him without knowing anything about him, had seduced him in minutes!

"Julie, please!" Darrell had left Tamara and Nicholas to their rich, joyless lives, and finally caught up with her. Gently, he touched her upper arm.

"Off me!"

"I'm sorry," he said, releasing her. "I know you don't like them."

"They don't like *us.*"

He laughed. "I know that. The woman was just about coma-tose. She probably mistook me for a plumber she once fancied."

"You didn't have to kiss her back then, did you? What are you, a gigolo?"

Although he knew it was unwise, Darrell couldn't help gig-gling at the word *gigolo.*

Julie, who was desperate not to giggle with him, bit the inside of her lip hard enough to draw blood. This maneuver enabled her to glare convincingly, until she reminded herself what he had done and found that she was able to glare quite happily, without the aid of self-imposed torture. "Don't think just because I nearly laughed then that I've forgiven you. You've ruined my holiday!"

As she raged, Darrell watched her, and a faint squiggle of hope began to squirm inside him.

". . . It was meant to be a nice, relaxing holiday! A celebra-tion . . . to celebrate my qualifying and your being promoted *again*, a sophisticated holiday, not a . . . a . . . an orgy with people who don't even like you!"

"So tell me," blurted Darrell. "Have I no chance of ever succeeding?"

Julie blinked. "You what?"

Darrell blushed to his soul. Excruciating. Mortifying. The most embarrassing moment of his life, however long he lived. Why the hell did he say it! He hadn't meant to. The ludicrous phrase had been circling his consciousness like a shark. He'd only picked up *Emma* because Julie was forever going on about it and how romantic it was, and he wanted to see what all the fuss was about. What *she* considered romantic. And he'd found that what she considered to be romantic was several centuries and classes away from everything that he was. Secretly, he thought the hero, Mr. Knightley, was a pompous ass. But if that was what appealed to Julie, then Mr. Knightley was spot-on. He, Darrell, had sod-all chance of ever succeeding.

She was laughing at him. Julie was practically on her knees with laughter. He couldn't blame her. "I don't believe you," she gasped. "When? When did you read *Emma*?"

"Last weekend," he said through gritted teeth. He couldn't look at her. She grabbed his hand. "Nice," she told him. "But that line is not you." She paused. "Try again."

Darrell forced himself to meet her eyes. "Right." He breathed deeply. "Julie. I think you're a bit all right, and I, I love you. Er. That's it, more or less. I — "

She kissed him. And the next day, she gave up on *The Portrait of a Lady* (Darrell suggested she save herself the time and look in the mirror). And because she *was* a lady, she never did tell Darrell about the Dagenham jibe. And because Darrell was a gentleman, he never told her that he'd known all along.

ETIQUETTE

By Thisbe Nissen

et·i·quette \'e-ti-kət, -ˌket\ *noun* [French *étiquette*, literally, ticket] (1750) 1: the conduct or procedure required by good breeding or prescribed by authority to be observed in social or official life. 2: that which should be adhered to more closely by certain members of a certain gender, after meeting other members of a certain other gender, so as to avoid confusion and entry into call-hell.

1. Don't say you're going to do something unless you actually plan on doing it. *You and I were playing "I'll show you mine if you show me yours." We said 1-2-3, GO. I pulled down my pants, and you laughed and ran away.*

2. If it's going to be a one-night stand, let it be a one-night stand. *Say: "Hey, it was nice meeting you. Maybe we'll run into each other again someday at some other wedding." Don't say: "Let's talk soon." Don't call from O'Hare when your connecting flight home gets delayed. Don't send cute postcards, each time promising the next card will be "more scenic," each time promising a "next."*

3. Don't get angry when someone uses things you said against you. *Especially when those things were said under the influence of more than your share of Bloody Marys, and before some heated foreplay in the backseat of a taxi to the hotel, where the bride's parents were so graciously putting us all up in the charitable hope that their daughter's wedding might get a few of her friends laid as well, and a few hours of sex that made me think I might finally be able to understand how people decide to get married at all.*

4. Certain things are not to be said during sex if one would like to maintain that sex is just sex and nothing more. *Like, "God, I love you."*

5. When your mother told you not to say anything at all if you couldn't say something nice, she wasn't referring to relationships, *in which case it's much nicer to say something: "I'm not really interested," or "I don't do long-distance," or "I've met someone else," or "Relationships scare me," or "Did I forget to mention my wife and seven children?" or "Yo no hablo inglés."*

6. Misrepresentation can be grounds for a lawsuit. *Did you know that?*

7. Life is confusing enough as it is. *And would still be plenty difficult even if everyone actually did tell the truth insofar as they could discern what the hell that might be. I have little patience for guessing games and no patience at all for the rules of courtship—both those unspoken and those outlined in a best-seller I refuse to read—so I don't do coy, hard-to-get dances or spend my time dangling carrots.*

8. There's nothing more pathetic than a woman waiting around for some guy to call . . . *reading and rereading the words he left scrawled on a scrap of hotel stationery, trying to find within those simple lines—name, street, city, state, zip, area code, phone—some explanation as to why she now feels that to use*

any piece of that information would be to push and pry on the door of a life that's been suddenly and inexplicably slammed.

9. It's courteous to give a person a little warning. *Like, maybe you could have said something before you went and slammed the aforementioned door, since I happened to be standing in the goddamn doorway.*

10. *When it starts to feel like you're at a SoHo dinner party where everyone's skinny and wearing black and you're laughing gaily as you sip your cabernet, when suddenly you feel something fuzzy against your leg and it turns out to be the girl you just slept with, and she's under the table begging for scraps, then you know that something's seesawed way off-kilter in the power dynamic. I am not a basset hound.*

FAQ

By Elizabeth Benedict

FAQ \'fak\ *noun* [Internet terminology] (c. 1990s) 1: acronym for "Frequently Asked Questions," a popular way of presenting detailed or complex information on a Web site. 2: a list of questions and answers presented in a simple-to-follow format.

What were there before FAQs?
Philosophers. Questions with no answers.

Are FAQs available on every subject?
There is a shortage of them pertaining to "female troubles."

What are "female troubles"?
Men.

But haven't women always had trouble with men, even before FAQs?
The questions used to be different. And there were never any answers.

For example?
Between 1945 and 1963, the average women was tormented by these questions: "Should I call my mother-in-law Mom?" "Should I go to a doctor who doesn't make house calls?" "Is it permissible to disagree with my husband's views on Red China?" "How many times a week should I wax the kitchen floor?" "Is this all there is to life?" "How will I know if I've had an orgasm?" The average woman was often too ashamed to ask anyone, even her mother, these questions.

How have the questions changed?
Today's FAQs on female troubles concern matters involving the intersection of etiquette, law enforcement, mental illness, addiction, and technology.

Can you give us an example?
Can we ever! These are the most frequently asked questions on our site:

1. What are the benefits of dating a recovering crack addict?
    a. Drama. Will he pick up again? Will he pick up if I do something he doesn't like? Will he pick up when he realizes I've changed the password on my ATM card? If so, will it be as bad as it was the last time I changed the password? Can I believe him when he says he will never sell my dog again?
    b. You get to feel needed without ever being sure that you are, so there is always plenty to hope and strive for.
    c. Even though addiction counselors say you shouldn't, you can blame yourself if he does pick up again!

2. How many Internet porn sites do you need to discover on your boyfriend/husband/fiancé's computer (e.g., analsexwithpuppies.com, slutsandchildrenfirst.com, cumhardandfastwithdebbie.com) before you confront him?
    Three to five.

025

3. What is the best way to confront him in this situation?

   Despite the prevalence of this problem, we have no idea.

4. Should you ever date a man over forty-three who has never been married?

   No. In the words of one of our consultants, "Better he should have murdered his wife than never to have been married, because then at least you'd know he can make a commitment."

5. Should you ever date a man who is attempting to divorce a woman who has never had a job?

   No. No exceptions.

6. If a man tells you he wants you to have his child, does this mean he is seriously interested in you?

   No. There is no correlation between this statement and his feelings for you. In fact, there may be an inverse relationship: Having said something so bold and serious, he is likely to have scared himself half to death and need to retreat at the first opportunity.

7. Is it better to date a man with an ex-wife or a dead wife?

   Most women would instinctively answer "dead wife," but they would be wrong. The dead woman's physical absence is often a trick to make you think the man is available.

   One of our consultants filed this memorable and heart-rending case study:

   Jake and I met on the Internet and were having an awesome long-distance relationship. We spent a sexy weekend together in New York, halfway between his hometown and mine. We spent a weekend together in Chicago. Then Jake called and invited me to spend Memorial Day weekend at a bed-and-breakfast in Napa Valley, wine country, California! He had a favorite place he stayed at: a detached, two-story mini–town house with a Jacuzzi, a water bed, a private sommelier, a daily massage, room service, and Internet access. We would both fly to the San Francisco airport; together, we'd rent a car and drive to the wine country. I needed to decide within the hour because that's all the time the owner had given Jake, and this was a premium room. I rearranged my entire work schedule, swapping shifts with another woman; bought the only plane ticket I could afford (nonrefundable, changing planes in Chicago, Minneapolis, and Salt Lake City); and took three calls from Jake, reminding me that I only had an hour to decide. For two weeks, we talked every night about our upcoming trip. But he sounded funny when he called the week before we were to meet there. "I just spoke to my daughter," he said softly. His daughter was twenty-three. "She really misses her mom." The wife had died two years before, but Jake didn't talk about her much.

"Gee, that's too bad."

"Really misses her."

"I can imagine."

"It's got me in a funk. Of missing her myself."

"I'm sorry to hear that."

"You can't imagine what it's like. The agony."

"Agony, tough word, big word. Sorry."

"I'll never meet anyone like her. The place we're going will remind me even more. We had blissful times in that room. Just the two of us."

"You went there with her?"

"Of course. How else would I know so much about it?"

"You didn't mention that to me."

"I was trying to pretend I could forget. But I see now— how could I ever forget the times we had in that room? Jeepers, I hear my call-waiting beep. Can you hold?"

I said I would, but I didn't. I hung up. And he never called me back, the miserable, grieving SOB. But here's what I don't know: How could I have protected myself from this? Shouldn't

I have guessed he'd gone there with his wife? Was I total jerk not to realize this, even though he didn't tell me?

8. Is it always up to the woman to look out for the trouble spots, the danger zones, the bad moves, the foolish vacation destinations?

 Yes.

9. During the first week of a relationship, is it a good sign when the man sends you flowers, buys you a bauble from Tiffany's, and invites you to Paris for Christmas, which is eight months away?

 No! Beware! We approve of the flowers, but the Tiffany's tchotchke and the trip to Paris may indicate someone with Narcissistic Personality Disorder.

10. What's that?

 A common misconception about narcissists is that they love looking at themselves in the mirror. But those with Narcissistic Personality Disorder (NPD) are afflicted with problems far more serious and destructive. Narcissists cannot empathize with others, but they are excellent at pretending they can, using lavish gifts and grandiose promises to lure others into their orbit. Once the lover is hooked, however, the narcissist wants only to be worshiped and adored, and at the first sign of criticism or withdrawing from his affections, he suffers a "narcissistic injury," seems to "come apart," and turns on the lover suddenly and viciously.

 And, make no mistake, this *will* happen—long before you get to Paris. Sadly, you're likely to experience the first attack well before the flowers have lost their bloom.

11. How can you predict all that mental illness from a dozen roses, a piece of jewelry, and an invitation to Paris?

 That's why we're here, to save you the trouble.

12. Just because a guy comes on strong—you're labeling him a psycho?

    We are merely suggesting that it is unwise to draw conclusions after the first week of a romance, even when that week is blissful. At the start of things, we advise you to "just say maybe."

13. I'm sure I'll have more questions. What if I can't always reach you?

    The Internet is a thriving democracy. Information is available to all, 24/7, regardless of education or training. Just go to your favorite search engine and type in the problem. Fast, easy, free.

14. What are the other problems I can learn about?

    The dirty dozen: alcoholism, codependency, drug addiction, gambling addiction, sex addiction, passive-aggressive personality disorder, borderline personality disorder, histrionic personality disorder, manic-depression, depression, obsessive-compulsive disorder, and antisocial personality disorder. If there's an affliction, believe us, there will be Web sites.

15. Are you saying that reading these sites, making our own diagnoses, will make us happy? Help us have better relationships?

    Heavens, no. But understanding that your boyfriend has a personality disorder and is not just stubbornly unavailable may empower you to move on, instead of buying him *Men Are from Mars, Women Are from Venus* for Valentine's Day. I think we've got time for one more question.

16. Do you ever yearn for the days when all we had to worry about was whether to call our mothers-in-law "Mom"?

    No, never.

17. Don't go yet.

    It's getting late.

18. But time doesn't exist on the Internet. It's always open. And you're about to vanish. This is all so scary to contemplate on my own. Will I ever find a man who isn't riddled with disorders and addictions? Are there any out there?

   Of course there are.

19. How will I know if I've found one? Is there a secret handshake?

   Your question indicates that you are well on your way. An ability to laugh at life's leftovers is an essential ingredient in your search. Knowledge is power, and so is humor.

20. That's it? That's all you're willing to say?

   We think that is saying a great deal. Happy endings, my dear, are for fairy tales.

GREEN

By Susan Minot

¹green \'grēn\ *noun* [Middle English, from Old English *grene;* akin to Old English *grōwan* to grow] (13th century) 1: a color whose hue is somewhat less yellow than that of growing fresh grass or of the emerald or is that of the part of the spectrum lying between blue and yellow. 2: something of a green color. 3: money; *especially:* GREENBACKS.

²green *adjective* (before 12th century) 1: pleasantly alluring. 2: youthful, vigorous. 3: not ripened or matured: immature <tender *green* grasses>. 4: fresh, new. 5a: deficient in training, knowledge, or experience. b: deficient in sophistication and savoir faire: NAIVE. c: not fully qualified for or experienced in a particular function <*green* horse>. 6a: marked by a pale, sickly, or nauseated appearance. b: ENVIOUS— used especially upon meeting a partner's former lover(s) as in the phrase <*green* with envy>.

"Will you-know-who be at the wedding?" Fran said.

"Yes," Tom said, reading the paper. "She will."

"You know?" Fran stood in the doorway that led to the narrow kitchen slot.

"Yes, she called me. The other day."

"She called you again?" Fran came out into the room. The apartment had one other small room, just big enough for the bed. "She was the one who left you," Fran said. "Why doesn't she act like it?" Fran turned back to the kitchen. "She should act like it."

"She did not leave me," Tom said. "It was a mutual decision. Things had been over long before she left."

"Did you leave?" Fran said.

Tom shrugged. "She just happened to mention it first."

"I don't see why she calls you all the time," Fran said.

"She does not call me all the time." Tom put down the paper.

"Enough, she does."

"She's a friend. We've known each other a long time."

"A friend?" Fran said.

"Yes, a friend. That's what it was like. That's why it didn't last."

"Six years is a pretty long time for it not to last," Fran said.

"We weren't together the whole time," Tom said. "We broke up, a lot."

"And got back together every time," Fran said.

"I felt guilty," Tom said.

"Right."

"I did. And we had a lot in common."

"Like what?"

"I don't know. Reading. She liked books. Liked animals." Tom hesitated — dangerous territory. "We got along well."

"I'm surprised you let her go." Fran stirred onions in a frying pan.

"Fran," Tom said.

"Really. Getting along so beautifully — and liking to read. That is rare."

"You're being ridiculous," Tom said.

Fran was quiet. Tom came into the narrow kitchen.

"Listen, I'm sorry she calls me. I can't do anything about it."

"You can't?" Fran turned astonished eyes on Tom.

"What?" Tom said. "You want me to tell her not to call?"

"I'm not going to tell you what to do." Fran went matter-of-factly back to the onions, pushing them this way and that.

"If you want that," Tom said, "you should say so."

"I just don't like it," Fran said. "Isn't it all right just to not like it?"

"I'll tell her not to call," Tom said, giving up. He looked over the rooftops. "But she won't understand."

"Of course she'll understand," Fran said. "Not that you should do it. She just doesn't want to let you go."

Tom regarded Fran with pity. "She's not like that. She's not as sensitive as you are."

"Men like to think women aren't sensitive, at convenient times."

"Maybe I know her better than you do," Tom said.

"Are you saying she doesn't have strong feelings?"

"Come on, honey." Tom stood behind Fran and pulled her to him. "Why are we talking about this? I love you."

"I just don't understand how you could have been with that person all that time," Fran said softly.

"It's pointless to think about," Tom said into her hair.

"It's not voluntary," Fran murmured. "It's a feeling."

Sunlight filled the windows of the chapel, and light-green leaves threw a leafy pattern over the empty pews in front.

"You know all these people?" Fran said.

"Mostly on Buster's side," Tom said. "Some of the bride's."

"A lot of blonds," Fran said.

"A lot of marriages," Tom said. "Buster's family alone could fill this chapel, if you included all the divorces."

"What's with that guy?"

"Mr. Harris," Tom said. "He hasn't had his daily ration of cocktails."

Fran watched people entering the church. She turned abruptly and faced front. "Guess who," she said. Tom glanced back. Fran toyed with her skirt hem. "Where's she sitting?" she said.

"Don't worry," Tom said. "Way back on the other side."

"I'm not worried. I'm just wondering."

After a few moments, Fran shot a look over her shoulder. "Oh, she looks good. Carefully avoiding our direction. Who's with her?"

"That's Heidi and Hilary. They're all friends of the bride."

"Old-home week," Fran said.

"They're nice, actually. I like Heidi and Hilary."

"I'm sure you do," Fran said.

"Honey."

"What?" Fran took Tom's hand into her lap. "I just feel a little out of it. Maybe I shouldn't have come."

"I wanted you to."

"I wanted to, too. But you know what I mean."

"Don't worry about it," Tom said.

The music changed as the groom appeared at the front of the chapel, biting his lower lip. The bridesmaids passed down the aisle, smiling stiffly, balancing garlands on their heads. The bride followed.

"What's that thing sticking out of her rear?" Fran whispered.

The sermon focused on the sacred qualities of marriage. The trembling of the bride's tulle veil could be seen from the back of the church.

The organ whined a jaunty tune when the couple flew out the door. Outside, the late afternoon was tranquil and bright. Tom and Fran strolled down the lawn to watch the members of the wedding party rearranging themselves in front of a photographer.

"Tommy Stanwyck!" A woman with a wide-brimmed hat engulfed Tom in polka dots. "Where are your parents? So naughty of them not to have come. Is this your girlfriend? Fran? How nice to meet you. Didn't I see your old flame up there, Tommy, coming out?" The woman winked at Fran. "I've got two exes here — two out of four! Don't let it worry . . ." the woman sputtered away.

Fran glanced up toward the church. "Maybe we should go say hi to her. Get it over with."

"Okay." Tom took her arm and they started up the hill.

. . .

On the way to the reception, they followed a car. In the backseat were Heidi and Hilary, with a familiar head in between.

"That was the shortest dress I've ever seen," Fran said.

"It looked ridiculous," Tom said, hands firmly on the steering wheel.

"If you've got the body, why not?" Fran said, weakly.

"To a wedding?"

"You know," Fran said, "I thought she looked sort of sad. My heart sort of went out to her." Fran watched the placid countryside go by.

Tom drove, eyes straight ahead.

"She seems different from how you talk about her," Fran said.

"You may not be the best judge," Tom said.

"I don't think she seems hard at all," Fran said.

'I didn't say she was hard. I said she wasn't that sensitive."

"She looked sensitive just now," Fran said. "I've never seen anyone go so white."

"When?" Tom said, but something was bothering him.

"Just now. At the church. She looked terrified."

"She was a little embarrassed," Tom said stiffly. "It's understandable. I don't think anyone would think it strange for it to be a little embarrassing."

"What did you think?" Fran said. "Here's a person I spent six years of my life with?"

"I didn't think anything." Tom bent to turn on the radio. "It was a little awkward is all."

"I think she has a certain dignity about her." Fran stared at the car in front of them. "With that long neck. Isn't there something sort of regal about her?"

"I don't know." Tom found a station playing music and left it on.

"Haven't you ever noticed that?" Fran turned down the volume.

"No."

"Makes me feel like a dwarf," Fran said.

"Stop it," Tom said sharply.

"I mean it. If I were you, I would rather be with her."

"You're insane," Tom said, angry. "I'm not in love with her."

Fran looked out the window. "I can't imagine why not."

"You don't need to," Tom said. "It's got nothing to do with you."

"She's been with you so much longer than I have," Fran said. "I hate that."

"Why do you want to make yourself unhappy?"

"I don't," Fran said. "What were you like with her?"

"That has nothing to do with us."

"What if I found out you were a member of the Ku Klux Klan before I met you—wouldn't that have something to do with us?"

"You're losing your mind," Tom said.

"Wouldn't it?"

"I don't know what you're talking about."

"Why won't you answer me?" Fran said.

"Because it's the question of an insane person."

They rode along in silence, past stone walls crumbling in the slanted light and ponds with green, glassy surfaces.

"You never had fights like this with her, did you?"

"No," Tom said matter-of-factly. "It wasn't like that."

"How could you not have fights?" Fran asked. "Was she too above it?"

"I don't know," Tom said wearily.

"You must think I'm so—so petty compared with her." Fran took some combs from her hair.

"Please," Tom said.

"I'm just letting out my feelings." Fran tried a few times to set the combs right. "I don't know what else to do with them."

"Keep them in," Tom said. After a moment he added, looking at Fran's stony profile, "That's a joke."

. . .

Night fell over the reception. Tom and Fran stepped down from the terrace onto the golf green. At the edge of the light, figures strolled into the darkness.

"So how do you know that lawyer guy?" Tom said.

"Who, Alex?" Fran said. "From around."

"Do you always kiss guys you know from around?"

"Well, I sort of . . ." Fran's voice trailed off.

Tom halted in his tracks. "Did you go out with him?"

"Sort of." Fran laughed. "Brief thing."

"You went out with that jerk?"

"Tom, you don't even know him."

"Yes, I do. Everybody knows him. He's a complete slimeball. How could you go out with him?"

Fran didn't answer.

"He's known for getting dealers out of jail and screwing models!"

"It didn't last long," Fran said. She looked through the windows of the clubhouse and saw Buster, the groom, at one end of the room and his bride at the other. "It was a short thing."

"But what were you doing with him at all?" Tom had become shrill.

"Let's drop it," Fran said.

"Oh, we can talk about my past but not about yours?"

"I thought you didn't ever want to hear anything about my past," Fran said.

"I don't."

"Good. Then drop it."

"Okay." Tom folded his arms. "As soon as you tell me what you saw in that greaseball."

"Jesus," Fran said. "Believe it or not, he did have some good qualities." Then she shook her head. "Listen, it never should have happened."

"You're so gullible," Tom said with disgust. "All a man has to do is say a few complimentary things, and you completely fall for it. Women are such fools."

"Excuse me, but I don't recall ever having told you what went on."

"I know what guys like that are like." Tom faced into the darkness.

"Okay. It was a mistake." Fran stood in front of him. "Haven't you ever made a mistake?"

"Not with a slimeball," Tom said.

"Come on," Fran said gently. "Let's stop. Let's go in and eat. See how Buster is."

"Who's hungry?" Tom said.

They left the reception after ten.

"Are you going to sulk all the way home?" Fran asked.

"If I don't talk, does that mean I'm sulking?"

"No."

After a while, Fran said, "So, did you have a good time?"

"Yup."

"You don't sound too enthusiastic."

"I had a fine time," Tom said. "Leave me alone."

They drove for a while.

"Can I ask you if you talked to her?" Fran asked.

"Yes."

"Did you?"

"Yes."

"Well, how was it?"

"She slapped me," Tom said.

"She what!?"

"She slapped me. Across the face." Tom began to look happier.

"Why?" Fran asked with astonishment.

"I don't know. She must have been angry with me."

"Obviously," Fran said. She gazed at Tom, waiting, but he didn't speak. "So?" she said finally.

"So what?" Tom said innocently.

"What did you say to her to make her hit you?" Fran enunci-
ated each word.

"Don't know." Tom shrugged. "I guess it was something about
her dress."

"What was it!?"

"I told her she looked like a hooker."

"You didn't."

Tom nodded. "Then she slapped me."

"That wasn't a very nice thing to say," Fran whispered.

"She didn't seem to think so either," Tom said. "Oh God, now
what? Are you crying?"

"It upsets me."

"Why?"

"It just does!"

"Okay, okay. Calm down."

Fran pressed herself against the door of the car. "She does care.
She obviously does. I knew she did!"

"It's the past," Tom said. "You can't do anything about the past.
Forget about it."

"I'm not thinking about the past," Fran sobbed. "I'm thinking
about the future."

"The future?" Tom tried to glimpse her expression as headlights flashed in the darkness.

"Ours."

"You're insane," Tom said.

"You always say that." Fran was suddenly hushed. She looked
at Tom. "Why do you always say that?"

"I don't."

"You do. A lot."

"Maybe because you act insane," Tom said. "Where do you get
these ideas?"

"They're not ideas, they're feelings." Fran attempted to com-
pose herself and sat up. "Why did you say that to her?"

"Because it was true." Tom shrugged.

Fran stared at him for a long time. "If you two had gotten married, a lot of those people would have been at the wedding, wouldn't they?"

"We were never going to get married," Tom said.

"Yes, but if you had."

"Not a lot of them." Tom thought for a moment. "Some."

"I bet she was thinking that, too." Fran looked out at the night.

"I doubt it. She does have another boyfriend, you know."

"Why wasn't he there?"

"Buster didn't invite him."

"Why not?"

"He doesn't approve. He thinks the guy's sleazy."

Fran laughed bitterly. "Buster probably liked her himself."

"Actually," Tom said, and the thought made him smile, "a long time ago, he did."

Honeymoon

By Mary-Beth Hughes

hon·ey·moon \'hə-nē-ˌmün\ *noun* [from the idea that the first month of marriage is the sweetest] (1546) 1: a period of harmony immediately following marriage or the establishment of a new relationship <As soon as a man burps in front of you, the *honeymoon* is over>. 2: a trip or vacation taken by a newly married couple, during which the tone of the entire marriage is set. <Fight on the *honeymoon*, it's Splitsville in a few years for sure.>

When Isabel stepped from her honeymoon bed and drew open the drapes, the view of Atlantic City was awful. Tilted houses, scattered parking lots, municipal buildings rusty from the sea air. The arrangement seemed badly planned or not planned at all, and the elevation of their bedroom was wasted, because the ocean was out of sight. *Just behind me,* Isabel thought, and turned as if to find it there. Tom was sleeping, and his lips sometimes vibrated on his exhalations. *I have wasted him with kisses,* she thought. Or at least she hoped she had. Marriage required a certain alignment of mind and body, and she was determined to make good on her end.

Isabel left the window and went in to draw her first bath in the heart-shaped tub. She chose the lavender bubble bath, half-remembering that lavender was for fidelity—wasn't it? Or was lavender for kindness? She couldn't recall, but earnestly allowed its stream to join the bathwater. She was twenty-two. The year was 1967.

At noon, a tiny bellboy, not more than a teenager, wheeled in breakfast. As the boy backed out of the door, Tom, who was barely sitting up, reached for various pockets, but couldn't find anything smaller than a twenty and said he would catch him later.

The bellboy nodded and smiled, but when Tom rose from the blankets and went into the bathroom, Isabel retrieved a five-dollar bill from her purse and settled the account on the spot. The moment the door whispered shut, Isabel felt uneasy, almost dizzy, and hoped that Tom would forget all about the bellboy. She imagined Tom's confusion when the boy would say he'd been tipped, even overtipped. Already she was making mistakes. She fiddled with the silvery tops on the dishes, piling them into an awkward stack before Tom came to the table. When he did, he mentioned that his eggs were cold.

Breakfast was brief. They were both anxious to get on with the day. Tom hurried into his clothes, barely glancing at Isabel as she sat with her legs crossed in her new stockings, wearing her new shoes and her pretty new dress. It was only in the lobby, as they were heading across the massive expanse of green carpet, that Tom pulled her to him. She was walking slightly ahead, looking in her purse for a booklet on sights that she had borrowed. He pulled her to him, as if overwhelmed by the sight of her, and kissed her just beneath the earlobe and whispered, My sweet wife. Isabel felt her heart would break open with relief. She was certain she heard the word *newlyweds* whispered by the admiring bystanders that she sensed all about them. The word danced very lightly on the air—*newlyweds*.

Beyond the gilded doors, she could see how thick and gray the day had become. The cold was nearly visible. She pulled the collar high on her pearl-colored, winter-white bridal coat and snuggled against Tom's arm. The boardwalk was immensely broad, its slats of wood arranged like a herringbone fabric. Far to the left, waves sputtered and coughed a gray spume. It seemed like a reel of film draped across the low horizon. Even so, Isabel was transfixed by the sight. She'd grown up inland and was unaccustomed to water sprawling just out of reach.

Tom released his arm from Isabel's and scratched his bare head. Sweetheart, you forgot your hat! Isabel almost said, then stopped. She satisfied the impulse with a brief loving stroke across his windblown hair, then devoted herself to the pages of her tour book and was pleased to find something that would interest them both. The World Famous Diving Horse! Certainly better than Skee-Ball or the merry-go-round. It wasn't far according to the map, and it was open year-round. So much was still closed in March.

Tom was willing to be led to the exhibition pier until a better idea presented itself. Did Isabel want to get a drink? Why not? They were on vacation. Honeymoon! Isabel cried. But she wanted to see the horse, didn't Tom? They could go watch, it wouldn't take long, and then they could go have a drink.

It was farther than Isabel's map had indicated. By the time they reached the special attraction, Isabel's cheeks were chafed by the cold. Tom's gloved hands were deep in his pockets, his collar pulled nearly over his ears. They paid the three-dollar admission, then went inside through a low, damp tunnel that led to the end of the pier. They were well out into the ocean when they emerged to find a rather rickety arrangement, something like a small arena. *Not very sturdy*, Isabel thought. The planks rigged for seating looked barely stable. One whole side of the tiny stadium was completely open, and a large chunk of gray ocean was revealed in the breach. In the white sky above, brackish clouds bumped against each other. A harsh wind scorched through the opening. Tom and Isabel waited perhaps ten minutes for other spectators to arrive, but no one else came.

Finally, a gate was released on a platform high above them. The platform had a long tongue, which extended through the gap and over a patch of ocean. Three men struggled above to bring a white horse — a beautiful, mammoth white horse — out onto the stand. Its eyes were covered with blinders, but even so, it seemed to sense that the waves below were sharp and unwelcoming. Isabel thought its eyes must be very gentle, very kind. Some animals have very knowing eyes. She could tell, even from a distance, that the white horse was one of them. The men struggled to get the horse to move forward, but it wouldn't. Each progression toward the sea was accomplished by the horse's being dragged as though its hooves were skates across the wood planking, and each forward pull was followed by a desperate skittering back.

Stupid horse, Tom said. What? said Isabel. But Tom didn't even look at her. He had his wallet out and was counting the bills inside. I'm not staying for this, he said, it's a waste of time and money. He stood up, indicating that they should leave. Well, said Isabel, stalling until she had a clear idea of what to say. She looked up at the horse. It was up on its hind legs, its front hooves drawn close to its heart. How could she leave? I think we should stay, she said to Tom, I think the horse will jump, don't you? Fine, he said, stay. Before Isabel knew it, he was ducking into the tunnel.

It had happened so suddenly. They had had a fight, or it seemed as if they had, and Isabel didn't know why. She sat, too confused to follow him and ask what was wrong. She huddled in her coat, which was far too thin for the gusts blowing off the water, and felt a sticky darkness opening up inside her. Sitting there, unable to budge, Isabel watched the horse being coaxed into a dive. Now the men had something tempting in their hands. They waved some treat over the edge of the platform so that the horse would be fooled into jumping, but still the horse stayed, impervious to threat or seduction. Isabel couldn't stop watching. When the horse went up on its hind legs again, she felt she understood the horse's actions better than anything she'd ever known.

She understood that drawing in, the way the horse's head lifted back and to the side, away from the foolish men. She understood all that.

Someone was gently touching her shoulder. She turned, relieved. Of course he'd come back. She knew he would, even if she'd been afraid to think it. But it was the attendant from the admission gate, offering Isabel her money back. Isabel shook her head. No, it was all right, she didn't want her money. The horse had done the right thing, she said. It made the right decision. It's too cold to jump into the ocean today.

When the horse was finally led off the platform and the gate was bolted, Isabel stood, wrapped her coat tighter around her body, and prepared to return to the hotel.

When she unlocked the door of their suite, Tom's back was to her. He sat slumped in the black leather armchair, facing the TV. Someone had sent flowers. Plump irises sheathed in pink cellophane had been placed uncentered on the coffee table, the card still sealed. Tom was having his drink. He set down an empty miniature bottle by way of greeting. Isabel approached him, unsure of what to say. He didn't ask her anything, didn't say hello. His face didn't have that hinged-shut look that he usually had when angry. Still, there was nothing to guide her, nothing to signal her.

She opened the drapes wider. He didn't stop her or comment. He watched the TV screen with indifference. Isabel shook back the gauzy sheers in the windows so that the whole of the sky and the topsy-turvy buildings laid out their unpredictable pattern before her. She pulled her coat close to her chest, though the steam heat was stifling, and turned to watch her husband. After a very long while, when he didn't say anything, she told him, deliberately, on the first full day of their marriage, that the horse had jumped.

The horse jumped, she said, it was incredible. Then she stepped up onto their double honeymoon bed without removing her coat or shoes. She let the black heels scar the silver spread. She didn't care. She pumped her legs up and down, shoes scraping against the bedspread, and held her arms tucked in close, her hands balled like hooves. She couldn't help it. She twisted her head back and let out a cry. The horse jumped, she said, and Tom got up from his chair, a little afraid. My God, Isabel, he said, thinking she was the prettiest thing he'd ever seen. She teetered on the edge of the bed, her arms starting to wilt, her face wrecked for a cry.

Come on, Isabel, he whispered, opening his arms. He gently pushed the black chair out of the way. Come on, Isabel, he said, and bit down on his lip when he stepped forward, needing to catch her.

ISLAND

By Jennifer Macaire

is·land \'ī-lənd\ *noun* [alteration (influenced by Old French *isle*) of earlier *iland,* from Middle English] (before 12th century) 1: a tract of land surrounded by water and smaller than a continent. 2: something resembling an island especially in its isolated or surrounded position. 3: an isolated group or area; *especially:* an isolated ethnological group; *specifically:* man.

There are geckos crawling up the sides of the tent. The moon is so bright that I can see their silhouettes as they trot across the canvas. The only problem is, I can't tell if they're inside or outside the tent.

Beside me in the dark, I can hear my sister's soft breathing and the harsher breathing of my mother and her boyfriend as they try not to make the cot squeak. It makes no difference to me. What bothers me is the thought that maybe a gecko will leap on a spider, and they will both fall onto my face during the night. The thought keeps me awake while the soft moans from across the tent fade and snores take their place. My eyes trace the geckos' paths across the tent, while the moon slides through the tropical night and the waves move slowly up and down the beach.

The next morning, we snorkel around the reef. I'm tired and let the waves carry my body where they will. Up and down I bob, my hands dangling beneath me, my hair floating all around, my eyes half closed, and the sound of my own breathing in the snorkel tube lulling me to sleep. I wake up when my sister touches my hand with her flipper.

"You're the only person I know who can sleep in the sea," my sister tells me. I crawl out of the water just far enough to reach my towel, and then I sleep again. Visions of parrot fish and angelfish swim through my dreams while my back burns to a crisp.

That evening, we eat at the cafeteria. We were going to have a barbecue, but we have no meat. Besides, the bright neon lights and white linoleum tables lure us into the cafeteria like moths to a flame. I take a tray and look at the food. Hamburgers wrapped in tinfoil, hotdogs, wilted salad with anemic tomatoes, half grape-fruits with faded maraschino cherries, and tuna sandwiches. I take a sandwich and a can of orange soda, then sit in a folding chair that rocks me as I eat.

We spend three nights camping on St. John. Each night I stay awake—listening, watching. There are rules to living in a tent. A blanket is suddenly a wall. In the morning, you take your tooth-brush to the showers and hold the toilet door open for your sister, so you don't have to pay an extra dime. When you fall asleep on the beach, make sure you're in the shade. No one tells me these rules; I learn them by myself.

When the sun sets, we take the ferry back to St. Thomas and drive through the deep, velvet night to our house. Easter vacation is finished.

Next Easter. Camping again. We take the wheelbarrow to get our supplies. There's no boyfriend to check the list. My sister pushes the wheelbarrow. My mother sighs when she looks in her wallet. We get sheets and blankets for the cots, a kerosene lantern, charcoal and lighter fluid, some hotdogs to grill, a bottle of soda, and a package of ice. Mom forgets dishes and cups, so we spear the hotdogs on sticks, drink from the same bottle, and tell ghost stories while the lantern flickers. Moths blunder into our hair and sizzle on the lantern. We wrap sheets around us and spray mosquito repellent on our bodies. Sleep eludes me, though. There is no moon, so I can't see the geckos, but I hear them walking on the canvas, stalking their prey, so I get up and sneak out of the tent. No one hears me.

I move through the campground in the dark. I can barely see the white gravel path, but barely is enough for me. Tents loom and subside as I wander down twisting paths. Some folk are sitting around barbecues; in other groupings, the tents are dark. I feel myself being lured toward the sound of a guitar. I round a corner and come across a group camp in a clearing, where five tents form a rough circle. There is another circle made up of children, who are sitting in front of a small fire. It seems to be a school field trip. Three men and a woman accompany the children. One is playing the guitar. I watch the children closely for a while. We're the same age, thirteen or fourteen. I'm the only one barefoot, though. I stay in the shadows. There is no one I know. They are from another island. I relax, take my hands out of my pockets, and smile at a boy standing alone just outside the light.

We talk, softly. A nearby tent flap is open, and the boy invites me inside. I slip in, no one notices, and we sit on the edge of his cot and kiss. I don't ask his name. When he runs his hands over my breasts, I don't pull away. My heart is beating like moth wings. I know this is against the rules.

Outside, one of the adults orders everyone to bed. There are giggles and groans, and the tent flap lifts again. Children hurry to bed, obedient. Without thought, I duck under the covers and press myself to the boy. I hear muffled goodnights, a flashlight flickers around the tent, and then all is darkness. I slip my hand beneath the boy's shorts. His breathing quickens and he jerks against me, uttering a surprised cry. My hand is suddenly wet, and I wipe it off on a sock. He trembles.

Soundlessly, I sit up and kiss him on the lips. He touches my face. We don't speak. Rules have been broken tonight, but so many that no one will ever believe him. Without a word, I slip out of the tent in the darkness. No one sees me. I make my way back to our tent in pitch darkness. Beneath my bare feet, the white gravel gleams faintly. There is still no moon, but it's hot and the bay-rum trees give off a subtle scent. I raise my hand to my lips and lick. It tastes like the sea.

The next morning, I sit on my beach towel and watch pelicans dive into the water. My mother goes to the pay phone and calls her boyfriend, and they talk until her coins run out. She hangs up, smiling, and decides to leave early. We rush to catch the last tour bus to the docks. I want to see the boy from last night, but I know that even if I do see him, we won't speak.

The next Easter. My sister and I tell our mother we're going camping on St. John. It's tradition, we say. She lets us go, too tired to argue. She stays behind with her new lover. He's glad to give us a lift to the ferry. We're glad to get away from him—he gives us the creeps.

At the docks on the island, we meet up with my boyfriend and three of his friends. At the campground, we don't rent a tent. We put our sleeping bags right on the beach and build a campfire near the rocks. My boyfriend has a guitar and plays music nearly all night long. People stroll up and down the beach, often coming to sit near us to listen to the guitar. Someone steals a cooler from outside a tent and we drink ice-cold beer and soda. A joint gets passed around.

My boyfriend sleeps with his head on my lap. I smooth his hair as I watch the sky turn pink. Then he wakes up and we make love. We move in slow motion, like the waves on the beach. He always digs his chin into my collarbone — often, I have small blue bruises there. I wrap my legs around him and close my eyes. I see the ocean behind my eyelids, though, rising and falling, white foam on the water. There are rules about making love. I haven't learned them all yet, but I have learned not to say that I love him. I understand that I frighten him in some way, and that he's more fragile than I am. Afterward, he sleeps again, and I wade into the ocean. I float on my back, watch the sun rise, and wonder about the rules of love and why I can't sleep at night.

There are rules about park beaches, too. The ranger comes to order us off the beach, and he takes our names and addresses. We all give fake names. The owner of the cooler complains loudly when he sees that it's empty. My sister and I slip away when no one is looking, and we hide for an hour in the showers. The light inside the showers flickers as if it's about to go out. My sister asks me if I made love to my boyfriend, and I say no. She believes me. Rules matter for her.

We hitchhike back to the docks. A man with a wooden leg picks us up. He drives a jeep, and my sister and I squeeze in the front seat while my boyfriend shares the back with his guitar, his friends, and the sleeping bags. The man's wooden leg sticks straight out in front of him as he drives; it rests on the rearview mirror. He hardly looks at the road. He shouts at us over the sound of his engine, screaming as he guns it up over the steep hills, telling us about his life as a German pilot during the war. His accent is so heavy that we barely understand him. He says he shot down thirteen English planes. The jeep swoops downhill and barely misses a tour bus. The man laughs and tells us he keeps a Mauser in his glove compartment. He drops us off at the docks and tells us to be careful of strangers.

On the ferry, I watch the white foam slipping by the hull, and I catch glimpses of flying fish skipping like silver disks across the water. I want to rest my head on my boyfriend's shoulder, but I don't. I wish he'd put his arms around me, but he won't. He's made up his own rules about love, and I follow.

When we arrive at St. Thomas, I manage to brush a kiss on my boyfriend's cheek. He tells me that he'll call me sometime, gets into his mother's car, and doesn't wave good-bye. I watch the car drive away. Sunlight flashes on the rearview window, and I realize he won't call me — that it's over, and I've failed again, somehow, to follow the rules. My sister and I hitchhike home. A rich lady in a BMW picks us up. She tells us we shouldn't hitchhike. In the car, leaning against my sleeping bag with my face in the sun, I wonder what other people do for Easter break and what rules govern their lives.

My sister sticks her hand out the window and talks about school. I think about stealing this car and flying to the moon.

JUSTICE

By Kathy Lette

jus·tice \'jəs-təs\ *noun* [Middle English, from Old English & Old French; Old English *justice*, from Old French *justice*, from Latin *justitia*, from *justus*] (12th century) 1: the maintenance or administration of what is just especially by the impartial adjustment of conflicting claims or the assignment of merited rewards or punishments. 2: vindication. 3: revenge, when achieved against a lover. Extreme acts are eminently permissible. *See also:* DISHES BEST SERVED COLD.

Looking back, I blame it on the man shortage. In Sydney, all the men are either married or gay. Or married *and* gay. And the rest have a three-grunt vocabulary of "nah," "dunno," and "errgh." Apart from the occasional Pommy poet passing through town, there is nobody. Nothing. Zilch.

That's how I ended up having a close encounter of the grope kind with an M.M.M. (middle-aged married man). As happens in most of these scenarios, I didn't know he was married until I found the teething ring in his pocket. But by then it was too late. He was tall, dark, and bankable with biteable buttocks and . . . I fell in love.

But did I fall—or was I pushed? I was too young to know that when a man says his wife "doesn't understand him" that what it means is that he wants you under, not standing.

There were drawbacks, of course. He was forever pulling away from my passionate love bites with a panic-stricken cry of "Don't mark me!" After a night of heartfelt declarations of adoration and devotion, the next morning I'd pass him in the sandwich line at the deli . . . and he'd stare straight ahead, as if he'd never laid eyes on me. Let alone laid me.

Even worse was never knowing when he was going to drop by. Invariably it would be the night I was in my pajamas, was covered in acne lotion, had one eyebrow plucked, had my hair plastered in henna, and was wearing an organic face mask. A knock at the door would send me torpedoing down to the bathroom. Not wanting to waste my precious R-rated moments with him, I'd hack and scrape away at my legs with a blunt razor in the shower, simultaneously inserting my diaphragm and spraying the old bod with aphrodisiacal unguents. Slashed, trailing blood, and covered in Band-Aids, I'd stagger breathlessly up the stairs and into his arms. (It was all right. He loved my "girlish charms.")

He promised he'd leave her. He promised we'd live together, forever, with a his-and-her harbor view. Marriage was in the air.

Well, I thought it was marriage. What it turned out to be was the car exhaust of his Alfa Romeo as he sped off into the sunset.

I truly believed my M.M.M. loved me, but it seemed I was merely a distraction—a little something to break the monogamy.

You can imagine how I felt when he *did* leave his wife a few weeks later. For a woman even younger than moi (a case of upward nubility). And ensconced her in a penthouse apartment with a his-and-her harbor view.

There was only one thing to do.

I enlisted the help of a girlfriend who lived on the less salubrious side of the street. One balmy evening, while she distracted the building superintendent, I snatched the keys to my ex's apartment. Once inside, I took down the bedroom curtain rod. Removing the stoppers at the ends of the rod, I stuffed the hollow cylinder full of raw shrimp, replaced the stoppers, and rehung the curtains. Now all I had to do was wait. . . .

It was a heat-wave summer. From my girlfriend's flat on the cockroach-riddled side of the street, we watched through binoculars as the lovebirds tore apart the flat, looking for the source of the odor. Within a week, my ex had called the Rent-a-Kill exterminator man. Fumigation was followed by a new carpet. Then, a complete rewallpapering. We watched them have their first fight. We watched as the new girlfriend started sleeping in another room. She then began to refuse to go back into his stinky apartment. Next, she moved out altogether. Shortly after, the apartment went up for sale.

Revenge is sweet. Sweeter than tiramisu. And, let's face it, with a broken heart and wounded ego like mine, it was cheaper than therapy.

We watched the moving men pack the van. And, the real beauty of it is this: They packed the bedroom curtain rod.

K I D

By Martha Southgate

kid \'kid\ *noun* [Middle English *kide,* of Scandinavian origin; akin to Old Norse *kith* kid] (13th century) 1: a young person; *especially:* CHILD—often used as a generalized reference to one especially younger or less experienced <the new *kid* on the block>. 2: the biggest reason for staying, going, or overall responsible decision-making.

I wanted him the minute I saw his hands. He had long fingers and wore three silver rings, two on his last two fingers and one alone on the other hand. The rings looked delicate against his skin, unexpected and graceful. He had long fingernails, wide and smooth, that looked like they'd been sanded down, maybe by holding wood or working with paint and steel. I wanted to touch those hands the way I always want to touch the sculptures in the museum but never do. I imagined them moving over my hips, shifting me this way and that as he kissed my stomach, feeling the rings brush against my flesh.

He was just a baby. That was the scariest thing. It was like walking into a wall, this desire, and who was it I wanted? A long-haired white kid, maybe twenty-two years old, whom my husband and I were hiring to paint the house. I could almost hear my mother's voice, "Suzanne, this is *not* the way we raised you. We are not that trash living down there in Cabrini-Green."

My mother had a horror of our acting like those other black people who lived over in the projects. To hear her tell it, all they did was throw bottles filled with half-drunk Orange-Crush into the piss-smelling corners of their building and sit around shooting up. She had grown up poor on the South Side of Chicago, but she'd married my father and escaped to a neat, politely segregated black suburb that was a lot like the one I live in now. She always told me and my brother how when she was coming up, even if you were poor, you could keep your place nice; but once the trash moved in, there was no hope. She spent most of her time guarding against trashy behavior in us. When I was little, "acting trashy" meant raising my voice or getting excited about anything; once I was older, it meant certain things about boys, too. When I was thirteen, my mother finally gave in to my begging, begging, begging to go to a Jackson 5 concert. I was convinced I was going to marry Michael at the time. I brought a friend, and we screamed like maniacs for the entire show. My mother didn't say one word all the way home. After we got into the house, with her voice like an ice shard, she said, "I hope you're happy with the performance you put on there tonight."

The house had needed painting for about six months. John had heard so many horror stories about contractors who put drop cloths everywhere for six months straight but who never finished the job that he felt we had to be extra careful. So he made me take a long time looking for someone. That was my job — anything to do with the house had always been my job — but John picked the color. The way we finally settled on C&M Contracting was that three of our friends had used them. I remember waiting a little nervously for the doorbell to ring that morning. Dealing with people who do things to the house always frightens me.

I jumped a little when the doorbell buzzed, but composed myself quickly and let him in. He said his name was Seth Jacobson. If I had seen him on the street, with his long, Indian-straight dark hair tied under a painter's hat, I would have said he looked kind of like a hippie. He had a nice face, though — hazel eyes and a sort of charming, avid look. His jeans had holes at both knees, and he was tall — more than six feet. He smelled of turpentine and Ivory soap.

As we sat down and he looked at me, I suddenly felt very conscious of my body, the even-brown tone of it, the long wavy hair that my mother always said was so good. I didn't usually think about my body much. It got me where I needed to go, I took it to the gym regularly, John liked it OK. The only time I had ever felt really connected to this muscle-and-bone package was when I had my kids, first Daniel, then Janie. A lot of women hate being pregnant, but I loved it. I loved watching my belly grow larger and smoother. I was fascinated by how my nipples spread and got darker and how I could smell everything around me. I didn't get sick, and I wanted to make love all the time. It wasn't that I wanted John specifically — I'd never desired him that way — but I just wanted to do it, to have the swelling and that release, to feel hands moving over my newfound, warm body. John liked it at first, but after a while he was downright alarmed. He couldn't figure out what had happened to the demure girl he'd married. But she came back after I had the kids. I transferred all that passion to them.

I hadn't felt that heat since Janie was born, six years ago now. But this kid was making me feel that way just by sitting in my kitchen, looking at me, drinking water, and flipping color swatches around with those beautiful hands.

Finally, he came up with a color that was close to what John and I had talked about, a soft blue-gray, a settled color. So I said, "Yeah, that's it. That's just what we were looking for."

He smiled. "I thought so. That'll look really nice. We'll have to mix it, but I can be back in a couple of days to get started. I mean, if the price is OK." Seth slid an estimate sheet over to me. It was a lot of money. But John, in his usual, methodical way, had already quizzed our friends, and the estimate wasn't much more than they'd had to pay. He would accept it. And I wanted Seth to come back. I liked the idea of those hands painting my house.

John and I were married eleven years ago, when I was twenty-four. He's an engineer—one of the few black ones in this area. We met when I was at Spelman and he was at Morehouse. He was bookish and orderly and wore neat, wire-rimmed glasses. He had dark skin and very clean, precisely cut fingernails. He was actually quite handsome, but most girls saw those glasses and the heavy book bag and passed him by. I looked behind the glasses and saw something I thought I could live with. When we were dating, he told me I was like a still mountain lake, quiet and cool. He didn't say romantic things like that often—less and less as time went by—but it impressed me.

My mother approved when we got engaged. "I'm so pleased you got yourself a man like John," she said. "He's really going to make something of himself. You should be proud." I was, I suppose, but my marriage was not some grand accomplishment; I was doing what was expected of me. I fell in love with whom my mother thought was appropriate, I married whom she thought was appropriate, I never felt much that she wouldn't have approved of.

I had a good job at a public relations firm in the Loop until the kids were born, then I stayed home with them, just like I was supposed to. I never knew passion until I had my children. When Daniel was born and they laid him on my stomach, he started looking around for my breast in that determined, desperate way, and I thought, I would do anything to hold onto this moment. It was the same way with Janie. They were always separate people to me, but separate people whom I adored so much that it hurt to look at them sometimes. I'm embarrassed to say how much time I spent kissing their unused, honey-colored feet when they were babies. Daniel was always sturdier—John used to call him the Tank. When Daniel first learned to walk, he would make his way around the house like a blind man. He seemed to feel that nothing was there until he touched it.

Janie is more like me, placid and light colored. She is impassioned about some things—her blankie, Trolls, *Ramona the Pest*—but her passions are few and carefully chosen. She has small hands and frizzy, half-straight/half-kinky hair. I think her curly hair is beautiful. My mother thinks I should straighten it.

It's funny, now that I think about it. I never observed John that closely, the way I looked at Seth or the kids. I knew John was handsome, that he had efficient hands and a warm laugh and a pretty mouth, but I never sat fascinated by each thing, as if each part of his body was revealing some elusive, crucial facet to me. We looked good together. And we had fun together sometimes. But it never hurt me to look at him. I never sat gazing at his hands, feeling my tongue behind my teeth.

The night after Seth's first visit, the kids were in bed, John and I were on the sofa, watching TV. I was also folding laundry, and we weren't talking until John pulled me toward him suddenly and began nuzzling my neck. "What do you say we go to bed ourselves?" he purred. Often, especially during the week, I put him off when he did that kind of stuff. I just couldn't be bothered. But this time, I put aside the laundry I'd been folding and stood up quickly. He looked a little surprised but walked behind me to the bedroom, kissing my neck and fooling with my hair. When I lay back on the bed and closed my eyes, I was thinking about Seth. I imagined feeling his hair spill forward across my face and breasts, hiding both of us, so different from the short, kinky hair I'd always touched before. I imagined what he'd smell like, the sharp, oily odor of turpentine and the baby smell of soap, and how I'd move under his hands.

Afterward, John rolled off me with a slightly bemused grin. "You haven't been like that in a while."

"I know. I guess it was just time."

"Well, it was nice."

"Thanks. It was for me, too." I kissed him and turned over to sleep, feeling like a liar.

When Seth came back on Thursday, he asked me to go with him to make sure he picked the right color. I thought it was a little weird, but I agreed to go. I liked the idea of riding around in his truck. John would freak: I could hear him now, "Don't they know what kind of paint they're supposed to get? What are we paying them for anyway?" I decided I just wouldn't tell him.

When Seth started the car, music leapt out of the stereo. It was so loud that I felt it in my chest. He turned it down but not off.

"What was that?"

"Six Finger Satellite. They're this band from Rhode Island. I really like them." He paused for a minute. "I'm in a band myself. We play over around Northwestern sometimes. It's called Trip-hammer."

"Yeah? That's nice."

"What do you think of them? I mean this music."

I listened for a minute. I could feel him looking at me. "It's kind of loud, isn't it?" I listened a little longer. "I don't hate it, though." I didn't either. It was nothing like the jazz that John loves so much — but maybe that's what I liked about it. "I think I'd just need to get used to it."

"I bet you could get to like it."

"I'm probably not your usual type. Of fan, I mean."

"There's no type. You just have to feel it."

I wanted to get away from this "feeling" stuff. I was feeling too much already. "Do you want to be in a band for good? What do you want to do?" I said in my briskest, most motherly tone.

We were at a stoplight, and he looked at me for a long moment. I imagined his hand resting on the back of my neck. "I don't know yet. I'm still thinking about it," he finally said. It didn't sound like he was talking about his career.

I looked out the window. This is a kid, I thought, a house-painter in one of those noisy, unwashed MTV-type of bands. My mother would be appalled. John would be appalled. "Where's the next place you're playing?" I asked softly, not turning back to look at him.

"I'll let you know." He reached over, his arm gently brushing me, and turned the CD up a little louder. "Here, listen to this. This song is amazing."

When we picked up the paint, I walked behind Seth back to the car. I studied the hair on the back of his neck that had caught in smooth tangles under his hat. I wanted to pull down just one of those dark curves and press it to my mouth, to taste the salty heat of his neck behind the smoothness of his hair, to take one of those narrow hands and hold it between my thighs. I'd make him leave his rings on so I could feel the silver pressing into my leg like a new part of my body, hard and shining.

By the time we got home, the other painters were there. There were three of them, all about the same age as Seth. They all set to work like old pros, carefully putting drop cloths over all the hedges and amiably discussing the best place to put the ladder. I watched them setting up. They seemed so young and sure of what they were doing. I couldn't remember ever feeling like that. I left them for a while, but I could hear their casual voices talking about this and that: some band that played downtown, this girl they knew, how long this job might take. As I lay on the sofa, reading in the late-morning light, I had the absurd thought that I would always remember this moment. The play of light on my legs, the young voices outside my window; it all seemed worth treasuring. I could feel Seth right through the walls.

I'd never even looked at a white guy before. That was another thing my mother wasn't having. From my first Jack-and-Jill meeting to my last class at Spelman, it was my people and my people only. But only those whom my mother thought were the right sort: light skinned (like us) with good hair (like us) and good jobs (like us). Her approval of John had surprised me a little because he's so dark. But I guess the '60s had some effect on her. I actually kind of liked Bruce Springsteen in college, but I didn't dare to admit it. I'd have been laughed out of my dorm. The music Seth listened to was so, well, so *loud*, so unpretty and unmelodic. It scared me some — but it drew me in, too, the way you sometimes feel when you're standing on the edge of a cliff. What would really happen if you jumped off?

They were still painting when I went to pick Daniel and Janie up at school, but they were gone by the time I got back. I felt oddly sad when I saw that I had missed them. Without the paint-spattered drop cloths, the hedges looked naked.

Daniel jumped out of the car and ran around the house, surveying it from all sides. The slightest change rattles him, but he covers it with a lot of bravado. I worry that when he gets older, people will mistake his bluster for true fearlessness, that he'll get hurt a lot as he grows up.

"I like this color, Mom. Can we leave the house half and half?"

"No, silly. It's all going to be one color."

"But if we left it half and half, it wouldn't be like anybody else's. It would be cool."

"Yeah, Mom. It would be cool," Janie chimed in. Her fondest wish is to be Daniel, or failing that, for him to respect her. She visibly puffs up when he deigns to pay attention to her.

"Well, someday, when you have your own house, you can paint it half and half," I said, resting my hands lightly on Daniel's shoulders. "Daddy and I are going to have this one all one color."

He looked put upon but agreed, shifting impatiently under my touch. Janie did her best to imitate his expression.

I've always found it hard to keep my hands off my kids. I want to feel the softness of their hair all the time, to check the round, gently hard surfaces of their skulls. When they were smaller, they didn't mind; but now that they're eight and six, they're growing more reluctant. Janie will still run to my arms for comfort, but she's beginning to see that she can do things on her own. And Daniel is starting to make friends and to resist my hugs, the way that boys will. I miss it, that body closeness we used to have. My skin feels empty a lot of the time.

The kids had their snacks and went upstairs to play. I started dinner, feeling like every woman since the beginning of time.

John came home, kissed me on the cheek, and headed for a beer in the fridge. He then went directly to the television—do not pass go, do not collect two hundred dollars. I followed him into the living room, something I didn't usually do. "Hon? What's up? How was your day?"

He started, surprised that I had followed him. "Huh? Oh, it was all right. They're sweating my department, as usual. But nothing special happened. How about you?"

"It was good. The painters came." The sports report started, and John's eyes drifted longingly to the set. I sighed. There was always something blocking us; there never seemed a way to talk. "Nothing special happened here, either. Dinner will be ready in a few minutes." I turned and left without another word.

I wondered what Seth's apartment was like. I imagined it would have CDs of bands that I'd never heard of scattered all over the floor. A Nerf football behind a thrift-store lamp, a heap of clothes on top of a tatty sofa. He'd probably come home and just shove the laundry out of the way and pick up his guitar, trying out a new song. Maybe he'd rehearse with the other guys in his band somewhere later, filling the walls with raw sound. After, he'd go out for dinner with a dark-haired, thin girl who'd be wearing a long, flowered dress. To someplace with candles in Chianti bottles. Maybe.

I called everybody down to dinner, but I was still thinking about Seth. I was distracted until Daniel started telling an elaborate story about Teenage Mutant Ninja Turtles: "See, then Michael-angelo was on top of this building, and he had to jump all the way across to the other one, and Donatello was over there waiting for him, and he almost didn't make it, but then he, see, he grabbed onto the side of the building, and Donatello pulled him up." He was in his best performance mode, assuming different voices for each turtle. I paid attention and asked lots of enthusiastic ques-tions; John listened with vague politeness, the way he might have to a maiden aunt who was given to lengthy stories.

Janie came into the kitchen after dinner and stood soberly watching me wash the dishes for a while. "What's up, sugarfoot?" I finally asked her.

"Is Daddy OK?"

"Yes, honey. He just feels tired because sometimes his job is very hard."

"Do you think it would help if I gave him one of my Trolls?"

"I think that would be very nice. Maybe tomorrow, though, huh? It's already past your bedtime."

"OK." She was quiet for another minute. "At dinner, he wasn't here. I like him to be *here* with us."

"Yes, honey. I know." My throat closed as she turned and walked upstairs.

When John and I were getting ready for bed, I took his hand in mine and said, "I know sometimes it's hard to come home from work and pay attention to the kids. It's hard to even pay attention to me, I suppose. But it means so much to them. They can tell when you're not listening. It hurts them." I paused. "And it hurts me, too."

He sighed and scowled. He looked rather like Daniel does when he can't find a favorite truck. "Suzanne, look. I'm here, aren't I? Every night, you know I'm going to walk through that door, that I'm not going to vanish. Isn't that enough?" He pulled his hand away and went to brush his teeth, leaving me sitting on the bed, sudden tears in my eyes.

A couple weeks later, the painters finished the house. Seth and I had spoken only a few more times — mostly about paint — in the time that they'd been there. I noticed that he took his rings off whenever he was working, to avoid getting paint on them, I suppose. Sometimes I could feel him looking at me with great keenness, or maybe I just wanted him to be. On their last day, as the other three moved quickly around, pulling up drop cloths and putting away paintbrushes, Seth walked up to me, a copy of the *Chicago Reader* in his hand. He smelled more like turpentine than usual. "Listen, I said I'd tell you the next time we were playing. It's this Wednesday, at the Rat. You should check it out."

I knew I should say, "Oh, thanks, Seth, but I really can't make it this time. I hope you kids do well." But I said, "I'll try to come."

I told John I was meeting my friend Sarah for dinner and a movie and wouldn't be home until late. As I said it, I thought, *This is the second time I've lied for this boy. I must be crazy*, but I did it. John didn't seem to care whether I might be lying or not. That made it easier. I felt like anything could happen as I drove into town, like I might just get on the freeway and keep going.

The Rathskeller was the whole name of the club, but the Rat was more appropriate. It was dark inside; some blue lightbulbs gave everything an unearthly glow. It smelled of old beer and new cigarette smoke and sweat. Graffiti and band posters covered every inch of the walls. I was the oldest person there, and one of just a very few black people. Everyone but me seemed to be wearing black leather and to have pierced body parts. I felt unshakably suburban as I ordered a beer.

It took a long time for anything to happen. Kids with hair hanging in their faces ran knowledgeably back and forth on the stage, turning knobs on complicated-looking machines and tapping on drums. A couple, a boy and a girl with shaved heads, kissed passionately against the wall.

Finally, Triphammer came on, and the crowd shifted its attention to the stage. Seth walked out, carrying a guitar and wearing a faded Flintstones T-shirt and ripped jeans. His hair was down. It looked beautiful.

When they started to play, I had that same feeling I'd had when I first looked at his hands. Ten times stronger maybe.

Nothing could have prepared me for that sound. It was so loud that it made the legs of my jeans vibrate, so raw I thought I might weep. Seth roared into the mike with his hair obscuring his face, flipping it back occasionally, his eyes closed. I was terrified. I couldn't take my eyes off of him. My ears were ringing.

When it was over, he pushed his hair back out of his face. He was lightly covered with sweat, but he had the same sweet, avid look on his face that he'd had when he first came to my house. But now he looked right at me without acknowledging me. I felt transparent, as if he knew every thought that I had, how I'd imagined his hands on me, his hair in my mouth. How I wanted him — not my children, not my husband, not my life. A girl stood at the foot of the stage, wearing an outfit almost like his, looking up at him with her eyes shining. I imagined them embracing, arms entangled, hair blending together, breathing. I couldn't stand it. I got up and left.

John was up watching a rerun of *All in the Family* when I got home. I watched him for a moment from the hall, thinking that he was not a bad man, not a bad husband. Maybe if I could just hang on to that. I wiped quickly at my eyes and went into the living room to sit next to him. "Did you have fun?" he said, without looking away from the screen. He didn't notice that I'd been crying, or that my clothes stank of smoke.

"Yeah, Sarah's good."

"That's good." I leaned over to him. Everything seemed to be narrowing to this one point between us. Turning his face to mine, I kissed him, hard. He smiled slightly and said, "Babe, I'm really too tired. I'll be up in a bit, all right?" Then he laughed as Archie Bunker gesticulated wildly at his son-in-law. I've always hated that show. I turned and went upstairs.

I looked in at Daniel, then Janie. I stood in Janie's room for a long time, stroking her hair, feeling the softness of her angel flesh under my hand. She stirred, moved her thumb toward her mouth, then stopped it; even in sleep, shied away. She was a big girl now. She was already learning to say no to what she wanted.

LDR

By Colleen Curran

LDR \el-'dē-är\ *noun* [origin unknown] 1: acronym for "long-distance relationship." 2: extraordinarily expensive, agonizing relationship. Usually leads to infidelity, gigantic phone bills, heartache, and breakups. Especially common when meeting partners over the Internet or at weddings. Often a consequence of relocating for graduate school or career moves. Often doomed.

My boyfriend told me he won't hold his breath for me. Like that's a surprise. He's in Chicago, I'm here in New York. It was not always this way. I said, "Oh, yeah, okay. That's fine. That makes sense." I hung up the phone and just stared at it. This doesn't have to be so serious. It doesn't have to be a big deal.

I actually told him I wanted to marry him. Don't ask me what I was thinking. I heard about girls doing that, on the third date spilling their guts about how their time's running out and how they want a family and how they want a house and that they think this is love and how they never felt this way before and how you, sir, *you* are the one, you are the love story they've been waiting for all these years.

I've never once blamed a guy for bolting. But not my boy, not two months into it, with my whispering in his ear during the middle of a movie, me saying this shit while his face is turned to the screen, watching him smile. Not Ben, who took my hand and held it, making me feel like it was more than okay, neither one of us really watching the movie.

He tells me things I've been waiting to hear since braces. He says all that stuff girls live for. At night, when the long-distance rates drop, I call Ben. He says, "Crazy, crazy girl. Took my heart and ran. What's wrong with you? Here I am, howling at the moon." And then he howls at the moon. It sounds retarded, but this kind of thing? I die for it. I kick back and put my hands behind my head, I hold the receiver between my chin and neck. I let Ben say this stuff for hours over long distance. I see dollar signs in my head every hour, but I've been in this one-room apartment in New York for two months already, and I haven't received a bill yet. I tell myself that I won't have to pay for this. I tell myself, "This will never hurt."

I've got this contest running with my best friend, June. The Best-Breakup-Ever Contest. She's got me beat with plain, dumb meanness. June, she's got this thing with bugs. Junebug, everybody calls her when they want to get her goat.

I learned this firsthand when we were roommates in college. We were catching some coffee in between classes at this dirty coffee bar on Michigan Avenue, when roaches started coming out of the cracks in the wall and running across the table. June scuttled right up and stood on her chair. Yips like hiccups came from her nose, and her hands did this wavy, palsied thing at her sides.

That was before June moved to Cleveland for a hotel management job. Now we talk long distance.

So in this story, June's only in high school. She's dating Leather Boy, who peddles dope at her school. She knows it's stupid, but she thinks he's dangerous because he wears a black leather jacket.

Two weeks into it, June feels like she's known Leather Boy for a millennium, and if she has to hear one more story that starts, "Dude, we were so wasted . . ." she'll start screaming and pulling him by the hair. It's just about this time that Leather Boy stops by her house, where she's sitting on the front porch.

"He starts ambling up to me, you know," June says, long distance. "So slow and sexy, my Mr. Cool. We're sitting there chatting, and Leather Boy picks a ladybug off my blouse. Now, a bug's a bug, babe. I don't care if it's got a pretty name, it still carries shit-all around on its legs. So naturally, I go, 'Get that thing away from me!' And he says, 'Okay,' and flicks his wrist.

"Then Leather Boy gets this stupid smile and puts a hand to his lower lip, like he's thinking. Like he can." June starts to giggle, and I know exactly what she looks like when she's telling this story. I can just see her shoulders start to shake, her magenta bob swaying at her chin. "So he gives me this really nice long kiss. He steps back to look at me, and I feel this dirt, this speck in my mouth. I put my tongue out, and sure enough, that asshole, that creepy bastard, put a fucking bug in my mouth." We laugh so hard that there's big spaces of dead air eating up the long distance. It's really our favorite game.

Bad boyfriends run in my blood, so I can beat June with sheer volume. Me, I get dumped every time. These boys I date, they dump me at the beach, in their cars, in my bed. Neal, who I saw for a week, told me after he kissed me, "I don't think this can work. You know, I prefer blonds. Or boys, sometimes." I was eighteen at the time, Neal was thirty with that almost-beard-thing happening. Adam told me he'd dated girls like me before, girls that do nothing for him. Normally, he'd give it a shot, but he just couldn't bring himself to do it, that we should nip it in the bud. That's all he said after we'd been dating for a year. Brett, who said he loved me, dumped me because I was twenty minutes late in picking him up for a party. He said, "Can't you do anything right?" Then he said, "Look, do you mind? Dropping me back off at the party?" I get points for this stuff. I score big.

. . .

For once in my life, I stopped racking up points. "Watch your step," June said when I called her up and told her about Ben. She said, "No matter what you think, it's always the same old story."

I put the Contest on hold for a few months. Instead of calling June and talking about our favorite kind of natural disasters, I called Ben and got him to pick me up in his old shockless Buick Riviera almost every night. I saved hundreds on my long-distance bill.

In the beginning, I thought he was just some guy. A friend of a friend. He had all this crazy, curly hair down to his collar. And this weird, galloping way of walking. When I'd get into his car, he'd say, laughing, "Hot stuff, coming through."

We went to bars in Bucktown and sat at tables that had long, skinny legs. We drank cocktails that our bartender had set on fire. We talked till they told us to leave. "Get a room," the bartender would say.

Ben. What can I say? His hands were always dirty, the gray of lead pencils from his drawings under his fingers. He wanted to be an artist, a painter, a famous, rich guy. I thought I never wanted something like that, ever. I didn't even think he was handsome until it was too late. He told me from the get go, "I've got this thing bad. You can take it or leave it. Anytime you want. I'll probably be here."

I said, "Not now. I don't think ever. I don't like boys like you. I like boys who break my heart." Still he kept calling. Still he picked me up in his big old terror of a car. These things, they can swell a girl's head. They can get her before she even knows what's happening.

I called June and told her I brought up the "M" word with Ben. That I started it. I told her I couldn't help it. I told her, "Off the record, I think I'm out of the game for good. Call it a sports-related injury."

. . .

In August, my first month in New York, June called and told me about her date with a short, heavyset stockbroker who had no neck. "Just head and shoulders, honey," she giggled. "Nothing in between." It was a blind date, a setup. She met him at a bar in downtown Cleveland. "He said he had to 'tinkle.' He actually used that word." June spit the words. "He was gone twenty minutes. I went to call a cab, and there's No-Neck in the corner with the waitress, his hands all over her fishnets."

Five points for June. Me, zero.

"So," she barked into the phone, "how's New York?"

"So far, it's just quiet. I go to work. I come home and sleep."

In August, I wasn't saying things June didn't want to hear. She had been thrilled when I had been promoted at work. I had listened closely when she said, "You have to take this. Move to New York. Think of your career. Don't stay in Chicago for any reason other than yourself."

So I let my boss ship me out to New York. Ben, he came with me. For one week only. Limited engagement. I told him that I couldn't lose him. I told him that it was only temporary. That we'd breeze in, get the job done in six months, be back for New Year's if not Christmas. I was lying, and he knew it.

Still, he said, "I can wait. I'll hate it, but I can wait. We've got days in our future," he said while he touched my hair. "I'm going to see you when you're seventy. I'll know you when you're a wrinkled mess, pruney even. We've got so much time, you don't have to worry."

To some people, maybe this doesn't sound like much. But I'm twenty-four, and listening to Ben talk, it's like learning a new language. It's like going to Paris and watching people eat brains. You can't help but say, "I've heard about people doing this, but I never thought I'd see it."

In New York, Ben carried my boxes into my new apartment. He put together my furniture. He stayed for one week, and we ate out every night as if we were celebrating. Like these were good times.

I drove him to JFK and cried as if somebody were dying. This old lady saw us boo-hooing for an hour and smiled at us. Like it was love, like she wished she had it. I wanted to knock her down and take her purse. I let Ben go at the terminal. Put my hand across my face all the way out of the airport. I don't remember anything but watching my feet walking. These big, black, ugly, expensive shoes.

The day after you've been kissed by a boy for the first time, you feel a little thin around the edges. Kind of like part of your skin's been rubbed off, like maybe there's less of you there. I always walk around my apartment with my hand to my face. Stepping very quietly. I wait a little while till I can call him up and ask him to come over and kiss me again.

The day after you've been kissed by a boy who's not your boyfriend, you try not to think really, really hard. By the time you sleep with the boy who's not your boyfriend, you've got this stone in your mouth, and you're not speaking. You let your pebble hold down your tongue, and you stop asking yourself questions that you can't answer. You find the trick is to keep very, very busy. Keep moving, keep walking, keep going in and out of doors all day long till the night comes out. Till you can go and get in the boy who's not your boyfriend's bed. Hold your stone and don't say a word.

June says I'm falling drastically behind on the Contest. She says, "I know you've got your Mr. Right and that everything is perfect. But doesn't he do one thing wrong? Don't you have one thing you can tell me to get you back up on the board?"

"Don't you get sick of talking to me long distance?" I ask her. "Don't you sometimes wish we could just meet each other at a bar and have a beer? How long have we been doing this? Five years?"

I twirl the cord with my fingers. "Five years since freshman year of sitting home in our dirty pajamas, racking up the phone bill like we're made of money, giggling cross-country instead of sitting down and having a good time?" I listen to June breathing.

"I'm twenty-five years old. You're twenty-four," she says real slow, like maybe I'm hard of hearing or just plain stupid. "I haven't made one girlfriend like you since I left school. I go to work and have lunch with the ladies. We get along real nice and ask each other about our days. But if I'm feeling lonely and like there's nobody on the planet who speaks my language, I don't call them up late nights. I call you. I call you, and we talk, and we make each other feel decent for a while. At this point, hon, I take all the good things I can get. I don't wish for things I can't have."

"My long-distance bill came today," I tell her. "Do you know how much it is?" I pick it up off the table and hold it out. Like I can give it to her, like I can show her something. "Four hundred dollars, June. Four hundred dollars could buy me a lot of nights out at a bar, laughing and talking and having a good time, instead of sitting here at home, yakking on the phone all the time."

"Please," June exhales. "Bring it down a notch, sister."

"I told Ben I want to see other people."

"What did he say?"

"'I won't hold my breath for you.' That's what he said."

"Smart boy."

"I just want one local call, June. Just one."

I dial long distance after eight P.M., after the rates drop low. Ben answers and asks me what I'm going to do. I tell him I don't know. I skirt around the issue as long as I can. I even ask him about the weather.

"Do you know anything about trains?" he asks me. "Do you know what happens when the engineer sees a suicide, just a crazy fucking guy, lying across the tracks? Do you know what that engineer has to do? He has to speed up. He speeds up the train. Because that's all he can do."

So I tell Ben that I don't love him. I tell him he's lousy in bed. I tell him he's a whiner and a loser and that there's no way in hell I'm putting that noose around my neck for the rest of my life. I tell him that I lied during that whole time in Chicago, that I was lonely and my bed was cold. That he was the easiest one to fill it. I tell him he does nothing for me, that he never did, that I just didn't want to hurt his feelings. I tell him I needed help moving all my boxes and that's why I didn't cut him loose sooner. I tell him I'm seeing somebody new, have been for weeks. That my new man is five times the man Ben will ever be. I pull out every single low-down, nasty, god-awful thing any guy has ever said to me before. I pull them all out plus add some of my own. I knock my love out at the knees.

When I'm done Ben says, "Well."

I call up June and tell her I can beat her bug story.

UAY THAI

By Rachel Resnick

mu·ay thai \\'myü-ā tī\ *noun* [origin unknown] 1: a style of kick-boxing; specifically, a martial art of Thailand. Incoprorates elbow and knee strikes as well as punches and kicks. 2: spectator sport that can provide an answer to the question, "Exactly *how* gay is my boyfriend?"

When we make our entrance—Walker with his shaved head, youthful bodybuilder stride, and illustrated arm, and me with my five-alarm red hair, pert tits, and skimpy tropical getup—Lumpini Stadium is already packed to capacity. Lights are low over the thronging crowd as we muscle our way toward the front, the circus roar swelling in our wake. When we pass, all eyes are on us. We've been tripping on each other for a crazy sleepless week, so the honeymoon heat comes off us in waves, blending with the humid, smoky air. I couldn't care less that Walker's got almost two decades on me with his half century. Everything's underworldly. The walls are dark and stained compared to the sanitized, super-clean supersports arenas of the States. Here, cigarettes glower their Cyclopean red eyes. The mood is carnivalesque. Drenched by the ring lights, some spectators at ringside wear shades, looking vaguely nefarious. Others sport garish gold-accented suits and jackets, sandals, and jewelry. Silver is considered second class. In the cheap bleachers, plainer-dressed Thais are standing, stamping, waving their arms, chanting, eyes egg-white shiny, even though the first preliminary is just beginning. There will be eight fights following. Eight fights, eight limbs fighting—hands and feet, elbows and knees. Weapons come in pairs.

My thighs are still humming from the motorcycle ride over from the cut-rate River City Guest House. As I wrapped my arms tentatively around the driver's waist, I saw Walker do the same, almost engulfing the slender Thai motorcycle driver. Arms around strangers, rice burners snarling between our legs, we were paramecia split and re-paired. Now we are seated at ringside, rejoined, our thighs thrumming, dizzy from smog and the titillation of the ride—everything is titillating in the state of heightened arousal that we are in, a week into round-the-clock sex and sightseeing.

Our VIP seats cost a whopping 880 baht. I pay my own way—a macho gesture, since Walker flew me over and has paid for pretty much everything. I figured what the fuck—free ticket, Southeast Asian adventure—even though I hardly know him. So here I am in Bangkok, a thirty-something in a strappy tank and sarong, my ass already sweat-suctioned to the creaky wooden seat. Everything is pleasantly sore from our elaborate couplings. My arms, forehead, even upper lip, are coated in a fine sheen of perspiration, as if I had just rolled out of bed.

"This is the shit, Blaise."

"It's wild."

"I ever tell you how puny I was as a kid? Sickly. Got picked on all the time. I was a foot shorter than the rest of the class up until high school, when I just got real tall and skinny with these big-ass eyes. Shaved my head before anyone even thought of it. Caused a minor scandal. But I played no sports. Barely went to school. Never finished. Junior year, I started working at the old porno theater on Sunset. The weights, the steroids, they came later. I was still trying to learn how to be a man. Here, they still teach that. There's a certain kind of toughness . . . the Thais, they have this . . . it's about the generations before. The masters, the fathers. How things get handed down. Ancestry. That's gone to shit in the States. The fathers? They're expendable. Dickless. Walking wallets, sperm donors, dogs. As a boy there, you might fight, you might even win, sure, but you are no warrior. You get me?"

I nod, run a finger down Walker's back, where sweat has already stained his white guayabera shirt, and the thrill of contact is like a seizure, but Walker is already tensed, studying the program, absorbed by the spectators and the ring only six seats away. We are close enough to see the talc rising from the canvas like miniature smoke signals.

"May I sit here?"

I hardly hear the man's voice over the pitched roar of the crowd as he gestures to the seat next to mine with his ticket, flashing some perfect bone-white teeth. Rather than try to speak, I incline my head toward the seat and smile back. If the seat is his, there was no need for the Thai to ask, so he's either being polite, as is the custom, or he's flirting.

I take Walker's arm, trace the deeply inked tattoo of the koi. Its green-gold fish body surges up through the frothing Japanese surf into Walker's elbow, covering old track marks. As usual, I avoid touching the sky demon, whose clawed foot steps rudely and permanently on the koi's majestic head. The demon's insanely muscular body torques over Walker's shoulder as if he owns it. I hate this guy, but it's his face that disturbs me the most—those bugged-out, malevolent eyes and the evil curled grin. The tat is such good quality that even after several decades, it's barely faded. Unlike Walker's fame as an avant-garde playwright and director, which reached its peak some years ago, then shrank a little more each year until he moved it with him to Bangkok.

"Excuse me . . ." The Thai is still standing. Waiting for my response.

"Help yourself," I say shortly. He's tall for a Thai, and dressed sharply in a knockoff Italian suit. Fine face, full mouth. Striking, and he knows it. Eyes completely obscured behind wraparound sunglasses. With no trace of sweat on his face, he sits, brushing my leg with his. No way am I going there; I have too much respect for Walker—besides which, the guy bugs me. I look at Walker, whose head gleams like a strangely formed egg about to hatch. Would Athena spring forth, brandishing arms, or some monstrous Caliban creature? I marvel again at how long his eyelashes are, like a girl's, when the rest of him is all square-jawed and buff in the manner of a thick-necked bull. He reeks of testosterone, that rarest and most desirable of perfumes. It is his formidable brain, however, that knits all the manly pieces together and makes him so magnetic. I am a sucker for self-made men, men who've shaped themselves out of the very mud.

"You are American?" the Thai hunk says in exquisite English, leaning close as if we have already been intimate. Horny bastard. Is he sniffing out après-sex? He himself smells of an expensive jungly cologne, and Singha beer. Instead of responding, I nod yes curtly, give a polite half-smile, then shut it down like a garage door. That should do it.

"Showtime," Walker whispers in my ear, but does not nibble it. So I drink in the way he inhabits the stadium, adopt his uncompromising focus, and rake my eyes over the scene as he does. Inhale. Incense chokes the air. Also beer, smoke, sweat, hair grease, peanuts, fried spicy beef. In the bleachers are energetic crowds, lots of shouts and gesticulations, fingers flying, bookies everywhere with books out in the open. There's a betting frenzy. Bits of colored baht exchange hands, waved in the air like small flags or secreted into hidden pockets. The music is haunting. Pervasive. A siren song to gamblers and fighters. Used to be they played live, Walker told me before we arrived, but now it is canned music, repeated over and over—a field of heartbeat percussion snared on top by a grinding, nasally flute and oboe blend. The top layer must be how fraying nerves sound, how adrenaline juices its high-pitched song into the bloodstream. Already I am tingling with anticipation. No man has ever taken me to the fights before, or fucked me so well.

While we watch the fighters do Muay Ram, the prefight ceremony, I feed Walker from a plastic bag full of beef satay. Stab the satay, dip it into another fat plastic bag full of peanut sauce, and then into another with cucumbers, onions, and tiny disks of red pepper, then spill the stuff into Walker's mouth, which looks so edibly red under the hyperlights. After a few mouthfuls, he holds his hands up to stop, and it hits me. In the past week, I have received his constant kisses. Now, the absence of his complete attention strikes at my core like a ball peen hammer, and I realize I have become accustomed. Or addicted.

"Toothpick?" The Thai hunk on my left holds out a flat, wooden stick with a sharp point in the center of his palm.

"What?" I say and shake my head no impatiently, but automatically check my teeth for food.

His gaze on my hair—which is flame-shiny under the lights and must stand out in the sea of dark heads—and then his gaze on my chest is somehow full of moisture and suggestion. I turn away abruptly, aware of his breath lingering on my bare arm. Thai women do not use toothpicks.

Up there on the stage, incense smoke sprouts from each of the four ring pillars, which are done up like mini-altars, hung heavy with flowers and garlands. There are garlands around the fighters' necks, and hanging from their heads are circlets that jut out in a sharp point behind so that the garlands dangle down their backs. Their tight, sculpted bodies are greased. Lascivious and lethal, lean. Each muscle articulated. The trunks are flashy and bright, silky and scrabbled with Thai words that look almost cabalistic under the heat lights. I think about the woman warrior—in Uganda, was it? Who mesmerized her hill-people army and told them to smear their bodies with some secret unguent so that arrows would not pierce them, nor bullets. They all believed. They all died.

Muay Thai was originally a war strategy, Walker tells me, for times when close combat made spears and clubs useless. The fighters' arms bobble as if they are dancing. Way back before they used Western-style gloves, they would simply wrap their wrists in soft bandages, then with rope, then soak the rope in tree resin, then, if both opponents agreed, coat the rope with bits of crushed glass. The winner would be the first to draw blood. I press my leg against Walker's, ignoring the Thai, who, I see out of the corner of my eye, is poking the toothpick at his front incisors. Walker uses envelopes to pick his teeth, a habit I find both uncouth and fascinating.

Already, the fighter in acid-green trunks has delivered enough bone-crushing low kicks that the other fighter's shins are purple with hemorrhaging and almost match his grape-colored trunks. The flower garlands are of marigolds and orchids, woven together with necklaces of peach and pink ribbon, with drugstore rose bows in matching colors—all these have been removed from the fighters and hang lushly from the corner altars, wilting in the heat of the fight. The bloom on the weaker fighter's shins is the color of those deepest colored orchids. What does it take to make the blood burst the skin? I wonder then if I am in the early stages of blood lust, and whether Walker is as moved by the violence.

"It's like they're floating," I say. They are so solid on their bare feet, and light at the same time. "Why does everything float in Thailand? You've got wing beans, floating ghost maidens, floating markets, floating sleeves in that Chinese opera."

"Floating sleaze? Is that what you said?"

Walker's wide-set eyes are on the ring. He doesn't even notice my bemused look at his mishearing. The two fighters and the whole stadium are rocketing with testosterone. The hypnotic, vaguely annoying music reminds me of snake charmer music—

the whining, insistent ducking and feinting of the flute, twining and untwining teasingly over the drums like a sonic bullwhip. The Thai hunk shifts in his seat, once again managing to get his leg near mine. Probably thinks all American women are whores. I wish Walker would notice.

"They look like snakes, right?" Walker turns to me excitedly, his eyes glassy. "Two killer cobras, dancing with each other. Hoods flared, fists up." I dig his mind, his stored-up knowledge, the way he sees the world. Everything is theater.

The Thai now bends forward to watch the fight more closely, simultaneously pressing his leg against mine with some urgency. That's it. Time for Walker to punch him out.

"Walker . . ." I whisper, lightly swatting his arm. The koi seems to jump in surprise. But just then, the weaker fighter makes a surprise flying knee move and catches the other in the eye, who goes down. Hard. Blood spurts from the brow as if squeezed from a lemon, arcs into the brightly lit air and seems to hang there, suspended like a necklace of blood in the lights, then finally splashes onto the dirty white canvas. I am sickened to find myself exhilarated. Without realizing it, I've risen to my feet, a floating ghost maiden filled with lust. Walker is already up. The Thai hunk, also standing, elbows me in the side.

"Hey! What is up with you?" I say. But the Thai hunk merely grins. Maybe this can all be chalked up to the cultural divide. Otherwise, he's a real asshole.

"A beautiful girl like you enjoys such violence, hmm?"

I scowl, but feel a pang of discomfort. Impulsively, I grasp Walker's hand, as if to steady myself, or to prevent a kind of falling into something deeper. I have to refrain from touching him more obscenely. I imagine wrapping my arms around his neck and wonder if, in this very moment, I'm gone for him. My blood pounds along with the speeded-up drums.

"Fuck me dead. That guy's hot," says Walker, staring off at a group of men who stand at ringside. "I'd let him fuck me."

The words are like a blow. An elbow to the temple. A knee to the psychic shin. Like something's just a little off now, tilting the landscape enough to make you seasick.

It would be one thing if it were some vampy ring girl. Some saucy, slant-eyed delicate dish with a curtain of black hair and schoolgirl tits, a delectable gap between her smooth legs, holding a round number card in her hands. *That* I've been preparing for, engaged in my own erotic Muay Ram, trained by the passionate, insatiable Master Walker. I was already wary about the downside of a man with a raging libido, especially one so skilled — once the focus slipped or the novelty wore off. But what is it really to be involved with a man who is turned on by other men? The whole world splits open, tsunamied with possibilities.

I follow Walker's gaze to a slender fighter in a pink silk robe that is patterned with red spots like silk measles and inscrutable Thai lettering, also in red. He is charismatic in a creepy way. His hair is cut wildly, probably a home job, short on top, with strange furrows here and there, like leftovers from bad ideas. When he stops talking, his mouth settles into a cruel expression. His lean body seems to vibrate with barely contained manic energy. Pumped up. Edgy. So this is the object of Walker's attention. My rival. I look at Walker and am surprised to see an innocent look there, a vulnerability, as if he's stricken with a schoolboy crush. I am in a man's world, a man's stadium, but I can see things. Beyond the crush, I recognize the look of a man who worshiped his father, who missed those arms and never got enough of them.

In the background, the first regular fight has begun, and the two men are dancing together, oiled and rock hard, measuring each other, unleashing kicks and elbows, knees and punches. They're using all eight limbs of the Muay Thai, as if they can't bear the masculine grace there before them, and the narcissistic desire it kindles. Walker's clearly obsessed with the hopped-up fighter in pink, who's taken the ring with a squat Thai who's just roundhouse-kicked Pink into the ropes with a resounding *thwak* on Pink's chest. One point. Two if it had been the head. Part of the crowd hisses, and part cheers.

"The Stanislavsky School of Muay Thai, huh?" I say, pointing out the sneer on Walker's crush as he arches his back insolently against the rope.

Pink refuses to give satisfaction, and Walker ignores my comment. At the end of the three-minute round, Pink's trainer lifts up the fighter momentarily to relieve his legs. There is so much touching of men and men here. The watering of faces and mouths, the tousling of hair, the shaking out of cramped limbs, the embraces. When I look around at ringside spectators, I am stunned by the rapture on the men's faces, their eyes pinned on the action. The only women I see at ringside are Westerners, *farangs*, and some have averted their carefully made-up eyes from the spectacle. Blood splattered on canvas, gaudy trunks, the dissonance of flower arrangements used for infernal purposes — I wonder if they appreciate the jazz fusion of blood and beauty. In the States, this is better hidden, in the country's communal dream sport — behind the crash of football helmets and the seemingly hostile tacklings, with the nubile cheerleaders reassuring everyone of the heterosexual aggression taking place on the field.

"Sonchai's got heart. The panache of the underdog. I bet he grew up poor, in the provinces. I'm sure of it."

"How do you know his name?" I am as disoriented as if I had been slugged.

Walker taps the rolled-up program against his thigh by way of an answer. The bell sounds, the round ends, but Walker keeps his eyes on Sonchai as he walks with attitude to his corner. The loss of Walker's full-on attention acts like an ice pack on my heart, numbing it out. Even his voice sounds distant, and the delivery is stiff.

"In the old days . . . they've been doing Muay Thai for three centuries . . . the way they'd measure rounds? They'd mark the competition ring in the dirt, then float a coconut in a pool of water nearby. The coconut shell, it'd have a small hole in the bottom. When the water filled that hole, when the shell sank, that's when the round would be over. Too bad they don't sell coconut."

Walker slings his heavy arm over my shoulders like a flesh boa and draws me in for a squeeze. I remember how we got stuck one day last week in the middle of the insane Thai traffic, stranded on a thick island of sidewalk at Silom Road, for almost an hour. And how Walker had wrapped his arms around me while I tried to breathe through my shirt, and he'd said, "Every minute that we stand here, breathing, I swear I can feel pieces of me dying." And held me tighter, as if the dying would be okay, would be bearable, if it were in each other's arms. We'd sucked down some young coconut juice on our return to the River City Guest House and had revived completely, and instantly. It had felt like a miracle. Like we'd both been saved for something. I made the mistake of thinking it was about us.

The next round begins. Sonchai immediately doles out a slamming low kick, gives the other guy his own orchid bloom on the shin.

"To condition their legs, they break Coke bottles against their shins. Used to be they'd hammer them with banana trees. Weird thing is, there's a high rate of shin cancer in Thailand."

"That the kind of fighting you favor?"

"Street fighting's what I like. Practical. Take from here, from there. The Thais are some of the toughest fighters in the world. At the Bangrajan Muay Thai Camp, where these fighters train, I learned a lot of moves. I use their elbow techniques. Other stuff's not so practical, someone fucks with you in close. Then you use wrestling moves. They throw you to the ground? Jujitsu's the ticket. A man's got to be able to defend himself. I do not welcome shit. I am not beyond using a pair of brass knuckles if I need to. Or a brick. Whatever. I tell you the time the cops stopped me on my way to a Hollywood meeting? I happened to have a cricket bat in the truck. These cops, they wanted to know, what was I doing with a cricket bat in my truck? I don't even think they thought it was a weapon. They were laughing. 'We know what you use this for,' they said. I don't know what the fuck they thought."

I look at Walker but can't read him. Maybe that's another appeal — this sense that there's a glowing ball of mystery floating in his head, a ball that explodes at random, like a radioactive piñata. With him, I am constantly alert, alive. One of the fighter's kicks lands and makes a resounding, sickening *thud*. I can't imagine how much force must've been behind that kick. What kind of snap. I can't imagine what I'm supposed to be learning here.

The bell sounds and the rival comes out dancing, but Sonchai is on; Sonchai is a blur of movement. With a flurry of jabs, Sonchai gets in close and executes a deadly low kick to the shin, followed by a smashing uppercut to the jaw. The crack is thunderous. For a split second, the rival looks surprised as he hovers there, uncertain. Then a shower of sweat — or is it sparks? — flies off the falling body as he crashes to the canvas, out. Down for the count. A rush of dark blood leaks from his mouth and the trainers and medics leap into the ring, surround him so he can't be seen. The crowd explodes. Walker rises to his feet, punches his fist in the air, and yells out, "Sonchai! Sonchai! Sonchai!" along with all the sports-crazed, beer-high, money-mad, adrenalized Sonchai bettors and fans. The fight is over.

That night I tell him. We are both sprawled on the scratchy bedspread, each reading — him, some Orton; me, a book on Thai divination, this part about how pimples are portentous — and he has just said, "I love you." Those words that change the world, or not. I take a breath. "I want to date other people," I say. Walker sits bolt upright, fury gathering in his eyes like a fuel injection. He's wearing a black Ren & Stimpy T-shirt with the sleeves cut off and the neck cut out *Flashdance* style, so his beefy arms and chest are on display. He moves so suddenly that the T-shirt slips and hangs unevenly off his collarbone. A vein throbs in his neck, in between a few thick folds, like a trapped worm.

"That's not acceptable." And I, immediately panicked, and flattered, and panicked, and freaked, I hold onto my skinny raft of honesty, even though the world has become white-water rapids.

"I just told you I loved you. I'm in too deep," he says, choke-voiced, throaty, pleading. "I am in love with you."

"Walker, we've only known each other a month or so . . ." *You want to fuck men.*

"I'm in love, goddammit. I'm willing to move back to L.A. for you. I have to be with you." He sees my face is unchanging, slams a fist into the headboard, hard enough so it rattles, and pushes all one hundred and ninety pounds off the bed with breathtaking speed for such a large man, so solidly built, well over six feet. "What the fuck did you come to Bangkok for then? Huh? What do you think I am, a mark? You think I'm some kind of fucking mark?" I can see flashes coming from his eyes, his face is so close. His voice is harsh now, shredding words. The demon tat won't stop grinning, flexing. The koi tries to break through the surf, knock the demon off his aching fish head once and for all, but it's no go. Not in this lifetime.

"Walker. Calm down. I can't make that kind of commitment so soon—you don't even live in L.A., I don't know you . . . I came to check things out with you . . . we're seeing . . ."

Without warning, Walker launches a killer punch right into the wall and, presto, knocks a raggedy hole in it. I watch the plaster drift down, in clumps, and in a fine kind of sifting of smaller bits.

"Fuck that shit. You think I'm not good enough. Not good enough for your middle-class, college-educated ass. I'm going out. You should go back to L.A. Tomorrow. Tonight. Right the fuck now. I can't stay here." He glares at me, and I, I shrink, that's how fierce the glare is that he trains on me. A *withering gaze*, now I understand that phrase. He is burning the skin from my bones, frying the fat truth away from my brain's hard kernel.

"Fuck you," he says. He says this with incredible precision and relish, and vicious conviction, like an actor who's finally cracked his character, who's made his pivotal choice, and it fits him like a glove.

The words crucify me, nailing my limbs to the blanket. I can't move. All I know is that I am curled on the bed, looking at the wall, where there are strange discolorations and stains.

Walker gets up, slams around his belongings — it's funny how books sound one way, with their shudder-flutter of pages, the crisp smack of hardcover binding against tile; and clothes another, like soft, draping exhalations, sighing onto the floor; bottles yet another way, plasticky and sloshing, staccato and plinky. Walker crashes into the bathroom, throws articles into a bag, drops the bag on the floor, kicks it against the door. God, he's strong. He has that muscle burst of energy — is that what bodybuilders have? Where they concentrate the bunches of muscles to do low reps, with massive weight.

Walker comes back, I feel the air churning; he comes back to the bed. Me, I don't move. There's no noise, but it's deafening. What if I were in a trench right now, enemy peering overhead? I would play dead. I would not move. No breath would escape from me. I would not be there. And if they saw me, somehow, and if they shot me, or ran me through with a bayonet, or cut my throat with a gaping slit smile, I wouldn't even feel it, I wouldn't even give them the satisfaction of a cry or gasp, because I wouldn't be there, and it would all be their stupid G.I. Joe war fantasy anyway.

Is he standing at the foot of the bed? Yes. The bed creaks. Why? The saggy bed tilts toward him. I strain my muscles to maintain my chosen spot, my area. He is lying down again. Close, very close, but not touching me. Around my body, I have fashioned a magical flexible net of finest threads and wires, all of remarkable tensile strength, impenetrable.

A hand grips my thigh. It is a meaty hand, a hand shared by his Polack ancestors — did they have pogroms? — a hand that does things, can hoe and build and plant and please. Once upon a time, there was a comic book called *The Flailed Hand*. In it, the hand, unattached to its body but still suffering after death, went on digital rampages around I think it was a rural British country town, inspiring horror. I remember being amazed at what one hand could do and how it could be more frightening than two hands of a whole person. Those comic books would be worth a lot today, but unfortunately my grandmother stuck them in the incinerator, thinking they were tasteless, creepy, and inappropriate for teenagers. She was the type who only read Dickens and Jane Austen, and equestrian magazines.

A hand manifests between my legs, trapping my cunt. I am amazed at how heavy it is, as if the skin is packed full of earth. He's got me pinned, my legs close to falling off the edge of the bed and my upper body wedged near the headboard. I can't think.

"You're burning up," he says. In wonder, his voice throaty and soft. Maybe I breathe. My cunt is a cute little furnace. The little cunt that could. He takes me in his arms. "What're we going to do?" he whispers.

"I love you," I say, for the first time. Red Rover, Red Rover, send Blaise right over. And just like that, I am on the other side.

NIGHTMARE

By Pam Houston

night·mare \'nīt-"mar, -"mer\ *noun* [Middle English, from ¹night + ¹mare] (14th century) 1: an evil spirit formerly thought to oppress people during sleep. 2: a frightening dream that usually awakens the sleeper. 3: something (especially a dating experience, situation, or object) having the monstrous character of a nightmare or producing a feeling of anxiety or terror.

What I was *supposed* to do that night was to give a reading from my latest book at a tiny but wonderful bookstore in Laramie, Wyoming. Where I found myself instead was in coach class on United Flight 956, from Denver to Chicago, nothing but fog outside the window and the glow of a runway whitened with snow.

"Just tell them your fiancé was in an automobile accident," my publicist said.

"We broke up last month," I said, "he couldn't handle the book tour."

"That makes it all the more believable," she said, "the unexpected twist."

The audiences at the little bookstore in Laramie are always generous, intelligent, forgiving, and the very best part is that there is an apartment off the back where the visiting writer gets to sleep for the night. After the owners lock up and go home, you can walk through the aisles with just your socks on and squint through the darkness at all the books.

So it was against my better judgment that I lied to the nice people in Wyoming, people who understood me, people who would have been delighted to share an evening with me. And all for what? To go on a blind date with Cupid.

The magazine thought it would be perfect. A double publicity stunt. Pam Houston, the author of a new book filled with tales of failed romance, goes out on a date with Cupid, just as he gets ready to launch his TV show by the same name.

"They'll do a photo shoot with him all day," my publicist says, "I mean, since he has, you know, visual recognition, and then you'll fly in and meet him for your date. You'll start out at Michael Jordan's restaurant, Blue, I think it's called, and where you go from there," she added, her voice turning mildly suggestive, "is entirely up to you."

"And then I'll write about it," I said.

"Two thousand words," she said, "by Monday."

"And what if nothing interesting happens?" I said.

"Come on," she said, "he's a star."

The plane landed a half hour late into sheets of Midwestern December rain.

I'll admit right now that, considering I would be in Chicago a total of thirteen hours, I had brought way too many things to wear, too many choices. Black jeans and a new Eskandar blouse, a black velvet skirt with a slit up the back, and a high-collared wool jacket. Three pairs of shoes. And even though I was the only one who had to know about the consideration, the indecision I had gone through, it suggested a shred of expectation that I was embarrassed to admit.

At the hotel, a woman in a tight blue suit informed me that she was terribly sorry, but the room that my publicist had booked was not, after all, available. Unforeseen circumstances, a couple on their honeymoon who decided that they weren't quite ready to go home, but they had put me up at another hotel only a few miles away, and their shuttle driver would be happy to . . .

I looked at my watch. I would certainly be late to meet Cupid.

"Do you have somewhere I can change at least?" I said. "I have a date."

She raised an eyebrow at me but did not smile, "The lobby bathroom is around the corner."

I crammed myself and my rolling carry-on into a faux-marble stall after having considered and rejected using the larger, handi-capped area. I tried the jeans, then came out to look in the floor-to-ceiling mirrors. I tried the skirt.

"Which do you think?" I asked a Korean attendant, who was making perfect little pyramids out of seashell-shaped soaps.

She waved her hand at what I had on. "The skirt."

I said, "Yeah, that's what I thought, too." I left my roll-a-bag behind the counter in the lobby and went out to catch a cab.

The driver had deep-black skin and was wearing an Oakland Raiders cap pulled down over his eyebrows. "You're a long way from Raider country," I said.

He grinned. "We're everywhere," he said. "Where to?"

"Blue," I answered, "the restaurant."

He whistled through his teeth. "Fannnnnncy," he said, "I heard they stack the food there real high, like edible skyscrapers."

"It's an assignment," I said.

"I can dig that," he said and grinned again. It was the second time in ten minutes that someone had taken me for a whore, not counting the Korean woman. Being in Chicago was starting to seem like a very bad idea.

"No," I said, "I'm a writer."

The explanation that never worked. It came out as more of a sigh than language. I remember the very first time, ten years ago, the publication of my first book imminent, when on another plane, between two other cities, I'd been brave enough to say those words for the very first time. The woman next to me, with her cotton candy hair, had looked at me, blinked twice, and said to her husband, "Howard, this young lady over here says she's an underwriter. Imagine, at her age!"

"A writer," the driver said, "Really, and what do you write?"

"Fiction," I said. Mostly. I remember another time when I had told a long-limbed, fantastically beautiful and equally androgynous checkout guy at Whole Foods market that I was working on a screenplay for Danny DeVito. The checkout guy had taken one look at my sweatpanted, unshowered self and said, "Right, and my daddy is Richard Nixon."

"Fiction," the driver said, "No shit. What kind?"

"Just fiction," I said. It was another difficult question. "Not mysteries or westerns or true crime or fantasy, just fiction. Some people call it *mainstream*," I said, conscious of the tone in my voice, hating myself a little for it.

"*Mainstream*," he said, like he was trying out the word, "and by using that word, you might be referring to, oh . . ." he scratched his head through the Raiders cap, "maybe John Updike, or Tim O'Brien, or Jayne Anne Phillips, or Annie Proulx?"

His eyes were suddenly wicked in the rearview mirror. I wanted to stay in that cab for the rest of the night. For the rest of my life.

"Yes, that's it exactly." I paused, then confessed, "I have a date with Cupid."

"Come on, girl," he said. "Let's hear it."

When I told him, he said, "Well, I thought I knew a lot about writers, but I never guessed they'd make y'all do shit like this. You think Annie Proulx would do shit like this?"

Back in Denver, I had recently had dinner with Annie. I said, "Never in a hundred million years."

"We're here," he said.

I looked at the dark street, empty of people or signage. "It's subtle," I said.

"Of course," he said. "Good luck." When I had paid him, he asked "You sure you don't want me to wait?"

I walked into Blue twenty minutes late. I went to the desk and asked for Cupid by his real name. The hostess looked at me pityingly and bent her head sideways to indicate a man standing behind her and to her left.

I walked over to him and stuck out my hand. "I'm sorry I'm late," I said.

"I am, too," he said, then turned his back to me and strode over to the bar.

He was short, balding, and smoking a cigar.

Like a stubborn dog, I followed him. "I did come all the way from Denver," I said.

He ignored me. He appeared to be internally combusting.

I looked around the room, which was golden and glassy, some kind of warehouse out near the ballpark, entirely remade to resemble some designer's idea of utopia; it was both elegant and warm. The bartender put a napkin down in front of me. There were cosmopolitans on all sides of me. Cupid was drinking something brown. "Club soda," I said, getting my bearings. "And cranberry, with a lime." Cupid still had his face turned away.

"The plane got in late . . ." I said.

He looked at me with more fury than perhaps I have ever deserved.

He said, "I saw your face when you came in here . . ."

"Yes?" I said.

"You . . ." he stretched out each word, "have . . . no . . . idea . . . who . . . I . . . am!"

I tried to think quickly. "Well," I said, "that's . . . true. I mean, I know you have this new TV show, and I know you've been in movies, but I'm not a TV watcher really, at all, except sports sometimes, and I tend not to go to the more violent movies, which if I understand correctly are the ones . . ."

He let out a breath that was slow and hot.

"I know your publicist said she was going to FedEx me a copy of the movie and the pilot of the show, but I waited at home as long as I possibly could before I had to go to the airport, and it just didn't come. This whole thing happened so quickly at the last minute. I'm actually supposed to be in Laramie right now."

"Where?" He squinted at me through a cloud of cigar smoke.

"Laramie."

He looked at me blankly.

"Wyoming. At a bookstore."

He waved for silence. "Just tell me one thing," he said, his face screwing up around the cigar like the face of a much older man, "how on earth are you supposed to do an interview with me if you don't know my work?"

Again, each word seemed to have its own internal punctuation.

"Well . . . it's not an interview," I said, a little like a conductor who knows the train is nearly at the place where the bridge has washed out and still can't find a way to reach for the brakes.

"Then what is it?" he said.

I took a deep breath and felt iron give in to gravity. "It's a date," I said. Though I had wanted it to be strong, it came out as a whisper.

"A date?" he shouted, loudly enough to interfere with everyone at the bar as well as several tables' utopian experience. "Why would I want to go on a date with you?"

I made myself not look away.

It had been nearly a month since David, my fiancé of a year, had waited until I returned *home* from therapy to tell me that he didn't want to see me ever again. He had made up his mind without me, he said, while I was out on tour. When I begged him to reconsider, to see a therapist with me, to give us a chance to repair things when I got back from the rest of my tour, he yanked on his much-too-long hair and talked with so much vehemence that little flecks of spittle showered my face.

I spent the next and final month of the tour on autopilot, doing my job, making people laugh, and feeling increasingly worse about myself, about my looks, about my life. I can say, with some objectivity, that I am a reasonably attractive woman, though clearly not the kind of woman a star of television and movies would ordinarily find himself out on a date with. I don't wear makeup, for one thing, and I rarely do much of anything to my hair. And although it's likely that I was at my thinnest for that tour, I'll bet I weighed a full twenty pounds more than anyone Cupid has dated since he got his first leading role in junior high. Though at this point too much time has passed for me to say this with any certainty, I may have been a shade taller than Cupid, had we both gotten down to our socks.

Had I to do it all over again, I would have thrown my club soda in his face and stormed out of the restaurant, teaching him no lesson at all, but preserving some shred of dignity. What I tried instead was reason.

"It's not a *real* date," I said, reminding myself of the tone I had misused on the literary cabdriver. "It's a publicity date. I write books about failed relationships; you are going to be Cupid. Somebody at a magazine thought it would be funny. Didn't you have a photo shoot for this today? What did you think you were doing, out there on the sidewalk with flowers in your hand?"

"The photo shoot was fine," he said, "I knocked on doors, I held the flowers behind my back, they took my picture."

"A-ha," I said, "you see, not an interview. A date."

He thought about this for a minute, and some vestige of the person he might have once been nearly came to the surface — the part of him that understood that I wasn't out to get him, the part of him that wanted to laugh . . . but just as quickly as the understanding crossed his face, it was gone, and the movie star returned.

"Are you suggesting . . . ?" he asked, his face twisted again, "that you and I would be *in-ti-mate*, and then you would write about it?"

"No," I said, "I don't believe intimacy ever crossed anybody's mind."

"I swear to God," he said, "on all sides of me . . . everywhere I turn . . . I'm surrounded by idiots."

"I hope you don't mean me," I said.

He eyed me for another moment before he went on.

"If that's true," he said, "then why would you agree to do this?"

From where I sat at that moment, he had a point. "Well," I began, "first of all, I try to do whatever my publicist tells me to do. I feel like she knows better than I do about that end of the business. And secondly, I just got dumped, about a month ago. This date felt serendipitous . . . a date with Cupid . . . like I might get some information I needed, like you might have something to tell me that I could use."

He gathered up his patience from unimaginable depths. I felt it coming, the karmic payback. "Do you not understand," he said, "that I'm an actor?"

"That is one thing," I said, "I definitely do understand."

For a minute there seemed like there was nothing more to say.

"Well, then," he said, at last, "do you want to at least get some dinner?"

"Okay," I said, just like a trained seal, just like a trained woman.

The food did come, as the cabdriver said it would (I held on to his memory like a life preserver), in multicolor erections. Cupid had a hard time staying at the table, getting up to relight his cigar every couple of minutes and also to talk on his cell phone.

He took a big bite of ahi tuna and looked me in the eye for the first time.

"So, you promise you won't do the assignment?" he stated more than asked.

"I don't think this is what the magazine had in mind," I said.

"That doesn't sound like a promise."

"I'm not a secret agent. I owe the magazine nothing. If you don't want the story to appear, I'm sure you can stop it. You are, after all, the famous one here."

"So, you're saying you are going to write it, and make me responsible for killing it?"

"That would be a ridiculous waste of my time."

"All right, then," he said, "so should we just try to have a normal conversation?"

"What would you like to talk about?" I asked.

He put his head in his hands and shook the resulting sculpture back and forth.

"Nothing," he said, "I can't talk about anything, because how am I supposed to trust you not to write down what I say?"

Had I to do it all over again I would have hurled a dinner roll at his considerable forehead and walked out of the restaurant at that point. What I did instead was ask, "How about if I talk?" I put the roll back down onto my bread plate. "I'm planning a trip to Laos and Cambodia. Would you like to hear about that?"

He would have just as soon not, as it turned out, but I told him anyway. He got up and stood in the corner of the golden-lit Utopia, which was not, come to think of it, Blue at all, and he made another call, this one with a bit more urgency. I wondered if he was asking some of the other idiots who surrounded him to come and deal with the one who was currently taking up his time. I checked out the other diners. I took great pleasure in knocking over my little skyscrapers of food.

When he returned, I said, "What about you, is there anyplace where you would like to travel?"

He drew a long, cleansing breath. "Look," he said, "I don't want to hurt your feelings, but I really think if we make it through dinner, we shouldn't even think about extending this date any longer than we already have."

Had I to do it all over again, I would have upended my little towers of rare ahi into his lap and walked out of the restaurant.

"I meant in the *world*," I clarified. "I meant by *yourself*."

Seven years later, dinner ended. We both declined coffee and dessert. We shared a cab back in the direction of Michigan Avenue. I prayed for the Raiders fan, but he did not appear. Cupid and I rode silently through the wet streets until at his stop, which came first, he leaned over and kissed me very briefly on the cheek.

I went back to the originally booked hotel, where I had changed in the bathroom. I rode the shuttle to the other hotel, where my room was right next to a conference center and in which an insurance company was holding their annual blowout. The band was scheduled to play until one. It was just after ten.

Had I been in Laramie, it would have been just after nine, I would have just finished my reading, everyone would be applauding, and a few loyal fans would be lining up to have me sign their books.

I walked back out to Michigan Avenue. It was 1998, and for reasons I couldn't imagine at the time, someone had lined the streets with individually decorated life-size papier-mâché cows. The one in front of Neiman Marcus was wearing pink toenail polish and pearls; the one in front of the Rand McNally store had the world painted all over him; the one in front of the *Tribune* building was jumping over the moon.

I've never liked Chicago much, but that night, its cows saved me. I went back to my room and watched an *I Love Lucy* marathon on Nickelodeon until it was time to get ready for the airport.

ORGASM

By Darcey Steinke

or·gasm \'òr-,ga-zəm\ *noun* [New Latin *orgasmus,* from Greek *orgasmos,* from *organ* to grow ripe, be lustful; probably akin to Sanskrit *ūrjā* sap, strength] (circa 1763): intense or paroxysmal excitement; *especially:* an explosive discharge of neuromuscular tensions at the height of sexual arousal that is usually accompanied by the ejaculation of semen in the male and by vaginal contractions in the female. <If *orgasm* is not achieved within a relationship (after a reasonable amount of getting-to-know-each-other time), get out. Quickly.> *See also:* BED BUDDY, GRAFENBURG SPOT, BRAIN CHEMICALS RELEASED BY CHOCOLATE.

Mary heard her husband's key in the lock. The dead bolt gave and she jumped up from the tub, wrapped a towel around her body, and tucked the corner in between her breasts. She'd been planning what to say to him, how to tell him that she was hurt that he had stayed out so late on Christmas Eve. But now, as usual, she was just glad he'd come home. Cold drops of water fell onto her bare shoulders as she stretched up on her tiptoes to kiss him.

He grinned like a teen idol. "Missed me, huh?" he said, pulling her into the front room, plugging in the Christmas tree lights, and yanking a Macy's bag from his backpack.

"Go try them on," he said.

Mary went into the bathroom and opened the bag. She was hoping for a flannel nightgown in a pattern of rosebuds, maybe fluffy pink slippers, but instead she pulled out a white bustier, panties, and thigh highs. Was he trying to mock her? Her stomach muscles were like Jell-O, and she had ten more pounds to lose. But she wanted to be a good sport. Life was short—what was wrong with a little sexy underwear? She let the towel drop and secured the bodice backward, then twisted it around so that the harsh material pressed into her nipples. Wouldn't he be disgusted? But he liked the look of white lingerie against pink skin.

Mary walked out and threw herself down beside him on the couch. She was chilly in the outfit. In the raw, overhead light, her skin looked as powdery and loose as a latex hospital glove. She looked, even to her own eyes, like a washed-up hooker. But he didn't seem to notice her body's imperfections—the loose stomach, the heavy upper thighs—and this fact comforted her. His oversight, a connubial manifestation of her place in his heart. But then his eyes dilated out of focus, and she knew the lace was mesmerizing him, encouraging the curtain to rise on the private slideshow in his head. Who knew what items were on the playbill? A sullen fourteen-year-old with puffy nipples and fuzzy blond hair, in platform shoes. A few Barbies. A couple hundred gin and tonics.

Her husband unzipped his black jeans, let his cock flap out, and moved, looking flushed and boyish in his white T-shirt, till his head was in position between her spread thighs. He flattened his tongue against her, causing the stiff nylon to push against her pubic bone, and she felt the imprint of the synthetic rose outlined there. Sensations like sound waves moved into her pelvis and bloomed like one tiny wet flower after another. Her husband came back up and kissed her mouth as he pushed his cock inside her. Really, he was a sweet guy, a little misguided but nice, she thought, as she watched over his shoulder as the light illuminated the weave of the linen-covered lampshade.

Mary turned into a baby-sitter with a thin teenage body, entwined with her boyfriend's thin teenage body, as they fucked crazily on the couch. And for a while, that was OK, the scent of Coca-Cola and sweat emanating as their flat stomachs and sharp hips collided. But then it wasn't enough, and it was time for the father of the house to walk over to the couch, lower his pants, and offer the baby-sitter his cock. This worked immediately. A sweet sting infused her flesh. But just as quickly, the water began to leak out of the drain. Mary tried frantically to inhabit each of them: father, baby-sitter, boyfriend. Each had characteristics as specific and mysterious as the Holy Trinity. She decided to kick the baby-sitter out, but it was too late. She was the baby-sitter, the unbaby-sitter, the ur-baby-sitter, the ghost in the baby-sitter, and so she paused a minute and concentrated on the cock within her, rotating around in a motion that made her think of the name Roto-Rooter. That in turn brought the picture of a toilet brush getting at the film in the hole of the toilet bowl, and that did give her a little charge. It was weird, the things that were sexy. Of the two sticks that sparked fire, each had their own philosophy, excruciatingly particular. Wanting to help her husband along, she reached down into the crack of his rear and ran her fingers over the webbed skin between his testicles and his anus. Jesus Christ. Even the words. *Testicle. Anus.* It was enough to make you put a gun to your head. He sped up the motion of his pelvis, and that was it, that was the point in the universe, the shiny one, the one one, the place where restlessness was transformed into ice cream, gravel into flowers, and dirt into love.

Pain

By Leslie Pietrzyk

pain \'pān\ *noun* [Middle English, from Old French *peine,* from Latin *poena,* from Greek *poinē* payment, penalty; akin to Sanskrit *cayate* he revenges] (14th century) 1: punishment. 2a: localized physical suffering associated with a bodily disorder such as disease, injury, or termination of romantic relationship; *also:* a basic bodily sensation induced by a noxious stimulus, received by naked nerve endings, characterized by physical discomfort (as pricking, throbbing, or aching), and typically leading to evasive action. b: acute mental or emotional distress or suffering: GRIEF. 3: one that irks or annoys or is otherwise troublesome—often used in such phrases as *pain in the neck.*

Want to feel suddenly single? First: Hurt yourself. By accident, of course. Do something stupid — say, use a sharp knife to pry wax from a candleholder and direct the sharp point of the knife toward your hand. Let a bagel slip sideways on a cutting board while you're slicing it and slice your thumb instead. Try to wrestle gristle from a slick piece of beef with a dull knife. Drop a wineglass

on the hardwood floor and step barefoot on a shard as you're trying to clean up the mess; curse yourself for breaking expensive
crystal, for not wearing shoes, for being stupid. There are many
possibilities.

But what's important is that you don't hurt yourself badly
enough to warrant an automatic trip to the emergency room. You
want to think about your injury, to study the flow of blood. Is it a
flow? An ooze? A drip? Examine the size of the cut—wider than a
nail head? Longer than an eyebrow? Deeper than a thumbtack?
Wonder.

You want to avoid doing something that makes blood gush.
Gushing blood may well mean the need to visit the emergency
room. Instead, aim for this thought: hospital, followed by a big
question mark. Like this: *Hospital?* Immediately followed by
another question: Or will Band-Aids and hydrogen peroxide be
good enough? (Make sure you do not have gauze pads anywhere
in the medicine cabinet or in your overnight travel toiletry bag.
It's okay to have a roll of the sticky white tape for taping gauze
pads, as long as there is no gauze to be taped. Cotton balls are
okay, because you aren't sure if they're sterile.)

It helps if you hurt yourself on a Saturday, when your doctor is
at home with her husband. Perhaps she and her husband are
spreading mulch on their front yard flower beds. Perhaps the two
of them are getting ready to go to the mall to buy him a new suit
at a store that is having a one-day sale. Perhaps they are upstairs in
the guest room making love on the bed up there because it's
someplace different, something meant to be exciting (the suggestion of a friend—you know exactly this type of well-meaning
friend—who said something like, "What have you got to lose?").
Actually, it doesn't matter where they are or what they're doing,
because the point is that your doctor is *not* in her office. That's the
point.

What you want, what you're looking for here, is to achieve the
perfect type of injury that should be shown to someone else,

someone trusted, that one person who can say with certainty and in a soothing voice, "Yes, you need stitches," or "No, you don't need stitches."

Of course, the goal here is not the stitches.

Second: Get sick. Better yet, start to get sick. Have a scratchy throat, glands that are tender when you squeeze them obsessively with your thumb and index finger. A slight fever, ninety-nine degrees perhaps. Struggle into work, anyway, because you think you should. Cough whenever someone intercoms you. Build up a pyramid of used Kleenex in your garbage can. Sneeze into the phone when you have to take a call in someone else's office. Maybe—if you're lucky—by lunchtime, the receptionist will ask if you're okay. By two, your boss will suggest that you go home.

Go home. Discover that you have no soup in the house. Begin to crave ice cream. Want Jell-O. Need tea with a squeeze of honey from a plastic container that is shaped like a bear. But have none of these things—not in your cupboards or your refrigerator or your freezer. Instead, call the *other* Chinese restaurant—not the one you like, not the one you used to call all the time, not the one where they know your name and could write out your order at the sound of your voice—no, the other one—and ask them to deliver wonton soup. If you're especially lucky, they will inform you that there is a minimum order of ten dollars for delivery. How many containers of wonton soup are in a ten-dollar order? Find out when your order arrives. Late. This Chinese restaurant does not take checks the way the other one does. Cough so hard that your eyes water while you dig your fingers deep into the couch cushions, looking for change so that you can tip. Later, run out of Kleenex and carry a roll of toilet paper up to bed with you.

Third: Work on projects. Decide that the house needs a new roof. Or that the crumbling driveway needs a new layer of asphalt. Or discover a colony of carpenter ants, nesting at the base of the oak tree out front. Let two companies give you estimates with two very different treatment plans with two very different prices;

both companies are highly recommended, both have excellent reputations.

Even better—refinish a bathroom floor. Best—refinish a bathroom. Talk to plumbers and contractors and guys who do tile. Let them ask you what color of tile you want. When you say *white*, let them spread out six different shades of white tile.

Bring home a hundred paint-chip samples and set them out on the living room carpet in neat rows. (Maybe you also need new carpet—but don't be sure if you do or don't. Wonder if getting new carpet and painting will lead to wanting new slipcovers. Plaid? Flowered? Checked? Is white upholstery chic, or is it a huge, huge mistake that you will regret for years? What about window treatments? Possibly look into putting in a bay window. Wonder if that room is really too small for a bay window.)

Another option: Buy a new car. And insurance. (Don't rely on getting a flat tire. Getting a flat tire is for amateurs. Anyone can get a flat tire. You just call the auto club for a flat tire.)

Somewhat related: Get involved in a car accident. Preferably, this accident is not your fault. In fact, your best bet is if the other driver takes off after ramming into you. Maybe you've parked your car in an end-of-the-aisle spot (even though there are those who warned you repeatedly—though kindly—about the hazards of parking in the end-of-the-aisle spots) and you are returning to your car, lugging several bags of groceries that contain a number of expensive, perishable items (shrimp and three cartons of your favorite premium ice cream), and you discover that someone has bashed in the side of your car but did not leave a note.

The goal is: not your fault. But there is no one who will listen to your explanations or watch your reenactment with salt and pepper shakers on a restaurant table, no one to appreciate the magnitude of the other driver's stupidity. The insurance agent is mildly interested, listening politely to your rant, but he is quick to note that you did not pay the extra $2.57 monthly premium that would have given you rental car coverage in the event that your car sustained damage.

Take the f—ing bus to work. Be late every day for five days in a row. There is no one to drive you, no one's car to borrow. On one of the days, it rains.

Fourth: Begin to crave—deeply—a particular item of food that is prepared exclusively in an enormous quantity. (Bonus points if this product is made from a very, very special recipe and this recipe is so special and so right and so perfect that similar products sold in the deli near your office do not at all duplicate this particular product, do not come remotely close to satisfying this immense craving, and the thought of eating the deli version is ludicrous. Extra bonus points if you happen to no longer have access to this recipe.) Examples: bread pudding, mashed potatoes, chocolate soufflé, stuffing, crepes, collard greens flavored with ham hocks and Tabasco, any kind of pie (but a pie such as apple or peach that requires a great deal of peeling and slicing is preferred). Note: These are not foods that produce leftovers that can be popped into the freezer. These are not low-fat, low-cal foods, not foods such as baked potatoes. Obviously. Baked potatoes come in all different serving sizes. You can make one baked potato exactly as easily as you can make two.

Fifth: Plan this little adventure of suddenly feeling single around your birthday. Certainly, someone will take you out to dinner or buy you a drink or tie a Mylar balloon to the arm of the chair in your office. Maybe people in the office will all sign a card that insults you—humorously, ha, ha—for turning another year older. (Laugh at this card even if it's not funny—and it won't be—and prop it on the corner of your desk for one day. Then you can secretly tuck it underneath other papers in your garbage can.) There even may be a present from somebody, the kind that is dropped into a gift bag instead of the kind that is wrapped with paper and Scotch tape. Perhaps a surprise party will be given, if you have those kinds of friends. Maybe when you are taken out to dinner, waiters in a restaurant will sing "Happy Birthday" and everyone will clap, including the tables of people you do not know.

But there will not be *the* present, the thing you'd been dropping hints about for two or three months. That present—opal ring, KitchenAid mixer, Fendi bag—you will have to buy for yourself. Be sure to use your credit card. Be sure not to pay the full balance on that bill so that you can have the pleasure of (*a*) paying more money than the cost of the item through excessive— but legal!—18 percent interest charges and (*b*) sensing that particular item lingering, lingering, endlessly lingering on your monthly statement.

Sixth: Look for ways to fill out lots of official forms, forms that want to know the name of your spouse. Your spouse's employer. Your spouse's employer's address. Your spouse's work phone number. Some even ask for your spouse's social security number!

Bonus points: Have to go somewhere where you have previously filled out those forms (in ink) and tell those people to remove those pieces of information. Smile while you say that. They will smile back, but it will be a different kind of smile.

Extra bonus points: Fill out a new form that asks who to contact in case of an emergency. Is it so terrible to write down your mother's name and phone number, even though she lives two time zones away? Do not make eye contact when you hand that form to the person sitting behind the counter.

Seventh: Go to a wedding. It should be a very romantic, very loving sort of wedding, not the other kind, not the kind where people are snickering behind their hands and reminding each other that according to Emily Post it's okay to wait a year to give a wedding gift.

No.

This should be the kind of wedding where the bride and groom feel like incomplete people unless they're standing next to each other. And when they stand together, they are always touching—a hand on a shoulder, two elbows rubbing, one foot brushing up against the other's. That kind of bride and groom. Perhaps they finish each other's sentences on occasion? Maybe they tilt their heads to the same side when they smile? Both families are very happy; each family likes the other. Sense no brewing arguments about where to spend holidays. Hear someone comment that the honeymoon is a trip to fill-in-the-blank, somewhere you've dreamed of going.

This wedding must have a towering cake (perhaps decorated with real flowers), a band, lots of people taking flash pictures, champagne that is better than average, at least one grandmother on both sides, and a noisy, noticeable, prolonged bouquet toss. There should be one other single person seated at your table. Loathe this person on looks alone. When this person talks, think of fingernails scratching spiral after spiral on a blackboard. Dance with this person anyway. You are the better dancer.

Send a present from the registry to this couple. Do this with one phone call and a credit card. The person on the other end of the phone will ask, "What would you like to say on the gift card?" This is what you should say: "May you have many happy years together." But this is what you actually manage to say: "Congratulations."

Of course, these are just suggestions to get you thinking. There are more. But the important thing is this: It all starts with injury. Start with pain.

QUEER

By Pagan Kennedy

¹queer \'kwir\ *adjective* [origin unknown] (1508) 1a : differing in some odd way from what is usual or normal. b (1): ECCENTRIC, UNCONVENTIONAL (2): mildly insane: TOUCHED c: absorbed or interested to an extreme or unreasonable degree: OBSESSED. *syn.* see STRANGE.
²queer *transitive verb* (circa 1812) 1: to spoil the effect or success of <*queer* one's plans>. 2: to put or get into an embarrassing or disadvantageous situation.
³queer *noun* (circa 1812): one that is queer; *politically re-appropriated so as not to be disparaging:* HOMOSEXUAL. Related issues, especially concerning sexuality or gender identity, can seriously interfere with a relationship.

The Anatomically Correct Irishmen was the name of his band, Janet told me, as we scooted into a booth at the back of the club. We ordered home-brewed root beer that had silt floating in the bottom of the glass, and we watched four guys and one woman huddle together on the minuscule stage. They played songs by Public Enemy on pennywhistles and Autoharps with so little skill

that it was obvious they'd obviously started practicing that afternoon, probably in somebody's kitchen.

Seamus lurked in the back, drumming on a collection of ten-
gallon buckets that, according to the labels still clinging to their
sides, had once held bulk tahini. He managed to be handsome
yet also goofy—at first I might have classified him as an Asian-
American surfer dude, because he'd bleached his thick hair and
let the jet-black roots grow out, and he wore about fifty Mardi
Gras bead necklaces around his neck.

"He's getting his Ph.D. in Celtic Studies," Janet whispered
to me.

"He *is?*" I whispered back.

"Yeah, I know. He's Japanese-American, but he says he *feels*
Irish. That's why he changed his last name. Now he spells it like
this." She pulled a pen out of her backpack and printed some
block letters on a napkin, then twisted the napkin around so I
could see: O'SHIMA.

"Wow," I said. "I guess he has identity issues. Like me." I had
decided to become a lesbian. My friends scoffed. They told me I
was deluded. They tried to set me up with men.

Onstage, Seamus thwacked his buckets so hard that the Mardi
Gras necklaces windshield-wipered across his chest. He struck
me as already broken in, like a pair of jeans that you buy used at
the Salvation Army, soft in all the right places. If I squinted, I
could almost imagine that he'd been my boyfriend for years.

I felt this way until the lead singer—a black guy who also did
not appear to be genetically Irish—announced, "Well, that's all
the songs we know," and the band threw their instruments into
some milk crates, and Seamus O'Shima stepped off the stage and
headed, bearlike, toward our booth.

That's when I decided I hated him. I'd just started to get the
hang of being single, and now *this*. Seamus O'Shima marching
toward me, determined to rob me of my calm and my newfound
lesbian identity.

He would ask me to go out, the jerk. Bowling—that's the kind of date he'd suggest, and he'd crack jokes about the rental shoes and I'd laugh too loudly. Afterward, he'd walk me to my front porch and hug me tightly enough that my breasts would mash against his chest, but his demeanor would be buddy-buddy. "You're a good sport. Let's do it again," he'd say.

For days, I would have to obsess on those moments at the door. Had he wanted to kiss me? Did he find me attractive at all? Why hadn't he called already? I would force my friends to listen to a detailed account of the date and demand them to tell me what I should do. Each one would offer completely different advice: call him, don't call him, sleep with someone else to make him jealous, meditate, eat kelp, get drunk, masturbate, breathe.

When my friends would fail to comfort me, I would consult some of the great minds of Western civilization: Heidegger, Foucault, Simone De Beauvoir, W. E. B. DuBois, Hannah Arendt. The simple question—why hadn't he called?—would lead me to reexamine the most fundamental questions of self and other. I would consider DuBois's and De Beauvoir's ideas about the political construction of identity and the ultimate unknowability of an Irish-identified Japanese-American drummer to a Jewish eco-feminist. But my theories would trail off into dead ends. Finally, I would shake my Magic 8-Ball and wait until the little plastic hexagon swam up from the inky depths to announce, "Ask again later."

Then he'd call. Then we'd kiss. But none of this would provide any relief. I'd have to lure him into bed, coax his clothes off, instruct him about the best methods for touching me, figure out which positions he preferred. Then, the clothes would have to be picked up, washed, dried, folded, placed in bureaus. Condoms would have to bought and thrown out. Keys to apartments would have to be copied and exchanged.

By the time he walked across the club and slid into the booth next to Janet, I was heartily sick of Seamus O'Shima and all his demands. He seemed to sense this. Wisely, he chose to ignore me.

"Hey, Master Po," he said, lightly punching Janet on the shoulder. "You been practicing those kicks?" They'd met in karate class, so a lengthy discussion of martial arts ensued, during which I pointedly remained silent.

And then somehow, while I was spacing out, Janet and her girl-friend jumped to their feet, stabbing their arms into the sleeves of their coats. "Can you give Erica a ride home?" Janet said to him. "OK. Great. Thanks. Bye."

They bustled away and abandoned me to Seamus. I hunched down in my seat, staring into my root beer. Seamus did not seem perturbed. He swung an arm over the back of his booth, took possession of the space where Janet had been, slapped on the wood bench in time to the song blasting from the speaker behind us—I hadn't even noticed any music until just then.

"So," he said, "Janet tells me you're an emotional wreck, too. How long have you been broken up?"

"About a month," I stammered. This was not at all what I'd imagined would happen—the two of us bitching about our failed relationships. And yet, now that we'd started, I realized that I would much rather commiserate with Seamus than date him. "We split up so suddenly," I heard myself say. "Just a few weeks ago, we were in Sears, shopping for a DVD player. And then another week later, he's emptied all his stuff out of my apartment. It makes you see how flimsy everything is, not just relationships, but everything."

Seamus made a low purr in his throat—an oddly sympathetic sound. "You're not just losing a person, you're losing all your old habits. Suddenly, you don't know who you are." His voice went husky. "The nights are the worst."

"Yeah," I said, swirling around my root beer, refusing to meet his eyes. My cheeks burned. "The nights" evoked a vivid picture in my head: both of us in our respective beds in Northampton, simultaneously squirming under sheets that we refused to wash, curling up like pill bugs around our useless genitals. "Why did you guys break up?" I asked, in an effort to insert his ex into the conversation, like our chaperone.

"Hell if I know." He threw his legs along the length of the bench seat, settling in, as if he meant to stay there until he had figured it out. "We kept getting annoyed at each other, then we'd have to process why we were annoyed, until we couldn't even cook spaghetti together without analyzing why she thought the sauce needed more oregano, and why I didn't, and what that had to do with our childhoods. But now that we're not sleeping together, we're friends again."

"That's admirable," I said.

"Actually, I sort of have to get along with her." He took a slug of beer and shot a glance at me. "I've been apartment-hunting for two months—can't afford anything. I'm still living with her."

I couldn't believe that Janet had failed to warn me about this. "Why don't you crash at a friend's house?" I asked, a bit scandalized.

He shrugged. "All my papers are in that apartment, my computer. I'm in the middle of my dissertation—it was the worst possible time to break up."

I nodded as if his reasoning made sense. "So, isn't that kind of awkward, though? How do you guys date?"

"We don't. At least I don't," he said.

Then he drove me home. His two-door Toyota spewed heat from its dusty vents as we glided through the dark. Except for downtown Northampton, most of western Massachusetts is the country. At night, it's darker than city folk ever imagine the night could be. Your headlights seem to invent the road out of nothing; tree branches and junked cars and fences jump in front of you as you drive along. I hadn't ridden in cars much since my ex-boyfriend took his away, and I realized how much I'd missed the countryside outside of town, where the streetlights fell away and the stars freckled every inch of the sky.

"So, if you don't mind my asking, why the Irish? Why not the Japanese?" I asked.

Seamus sighed. "I wish I had a better answer. All I can say is, too much baggage. When I see the word *Japanese*, I picture my dad on the back patio in a brown bathrobe, eating Egg Beaters, reading the stock page. But the Irish—no baggage. I can write about the potato famine, and in some underground, coded way, I'm really writing about the internment of the Japanese-Americans and all the rest of the stuff my family refuses to talk about."

I nodded. "That makes sense."

"Really?" he seemed pleased. "Not many people think so."

"It makes a lot more sense than still living with your ex-girl-friend," I said, and got a laugh out of him.

When he pulled in front of my apartment building, he jumped out and ran around to the passenger side to open the door for me—not out of chivalry but out of necessity. The inside handle of his Toyota was broken.

"It was great talking to you," he said, and hugged me, but not the kind of hug that's a borderline kiss. Instead, we clung together like two people on an icy sidewalk, holding on for balance.

The first "why can't we be friends" message came the next night. I was leaning into my refrigerator, sniffing a container of tofu for freshness, when my answering machine clicked on. Suddenly, my ex-boyfriend's amplified voice boomed through the apart-ment. I ran into the living room and bent over the answering machine, watching the wheels of the cassette turn as they recorded that familiar voice. "Erica," he said, "why haven't you returned any of my calls? You're making this a lot more awkward than it has to be." He stopped for a moment, and the *cree-cree-cree* of the tape cassette filled up the silence. "We've known each other too long to end this way. We're going to be friends." It sounded like a threat. Then the machine clicked, the tape rewound, and a red light began blinking.

I slid down to the floor. Five blocks away, my ex-boyfriend had just placed a receiver into its cradle and gone off to do something else—if I knew him, he probably was now sitting in front of his editing system, playing and replaying segments of film, so that the actors on the monitor stuttered as he moved them back and forth through time.

Occasionally, as he worked, his thoughts would flicker toward me. I was the woman who had once pedaled around town on her bike, tears glittering on her cheeks, searching for him in every bookstore and drugstore, desperate to beg his forgiveness after a fight. I had worn a push-up bra, canceled my subscription to the *Whole Earth Review*, eaten a Junior Whopper—all to please him.

If he decided to barge back into my life, I had no power to stop him. For the next hour or so, I stared at the scratches on the floor, contemplating my inevitable future of abasing myself to him. Soon, I would invite him over. He'd show up at my door, eyes cast downward, and give me a stiff hug, as if he were comforting someone at a funeral. I'd lead him into the kitchen, and he'd pull out a chair, which would groan as it slid across the floor. I'd offer tea.

"I keep the tea on this little shelf now," I'd tell him, to point out that, on my own, I had adopted new wall furnishings, new ways of organizing my life.

But as I would lean over to hand him his mug, I'd catch a whiff of the air that wafted out from the neck of his shirt, that smell of a zillion Sunday mornings when we'd nestled under the fleece comforter, gossiping about the other couples we knew, and congratulating ourselves for being more loving than all of them. Then, right there in the kitchen, when I was supposed to be proving that I didn't need him, I would turn back into his Erica-ferica, his pink cat.

Now I ran my finger over one of the scratches in the pine floor, breathing in a presobbing way. I could sense him only a few blocks from me, deciding that it was unacceptable that I ignore him.

And then a random image flitted into my brain: those goofy beads that Seamus had worn around his neck, the color of lollipops, dangling next to the frayed rim of his T-shirt. Suddenly, I knew exactly what to do. I fished a scrap of paper out of my jeans pocket and called it.

A woman answered. "Hi," she said brightly.

When I asked for Seamus, her voice changed. "He's right here," she snapped.

As soon as I had him on the line, I got right down to business. "Listen, you want to be my roommate? I need one by next week."

"I probably can't afford it."

"It's a disgusting basement apartment. Two hundred a month."

"I'll take it," he said.

"Don't you want to see it first?"

"No, that's OK. Can I start bringing stuff over tomorrow?"

Sunday night, I was walking home when I caught sight of a giant turtlelike creature, trudging along the sidewalk ahead of me. It turned out to be Seamus, bent underneath his futon.

I ran to catch up. "Here, let me help." I took the end that hung behind him and carried it like his bridal train.

We huffed down the stairs, getting caught in the corners, and finally managed to wedge ourselves and the futon through the door and down the hall. He collapsed on top of it.

"OK, now I live here," he said. Boxes teetered all around us. A snare drum sat on top of the refrigerator. A file cabinet leaned against the sofa, one drawer spilling papers. "I'll put it all into my room tonight. Just let me catch my breath," he added.

"I can't believe you moved everything so fast," I said, squatting down so I could talk to him eye-to-eye.

"It would have been faster except that my ex and I had to process our feelings for hours. As soon as I took the bed, the breakup became real to her. I explained a million times that you and I are just roommates, but she cried, anyway."

"That's terrible. Listen, if you want, you can tell her I'm gay."

He shook his head. "She's not stupid."

"No, really," I said, and then I explained about how I'd made up my mind to be a lesbian. "I don't want to date men right now. Because what if I got married and lived my whole life and died without ever figuring out whether I'm gay?" I said. "I'm going to settle this for once and for all."

He leaned toward me over his crossed legs, engrossed in my argument. "You're right," he said. "More people should have that attitude."

"All my other friends think I'm crazy." I slumped against one of the boxes of books and felt the cardboard settle against my shoulder blade.

"You're just taking some time to find out who you are." He uncrossed his legs and then flung himself on his side, propping his head up on his hand. Seamus liked to throw his body around, stretching his legs out, claiming the space around him. Tonight, he wore a ragged T-shirt with a line drawing of a ukulele on it; the shirt appeared to have shrunk. It stretched over his pot belly. "Look at it this way," he added. "What has monogamous heterosexuality done for either of us? Maybe it's time to shift your paradigm."

He would have elaborated, but I was bouncing up and down on my haunches, signaling that I needed to speak *right away*. "I just had a great idea, Seamus," I blurted. "You should be gay, too! It would be so convenient." I pictured him in the bleachers as I hit home runs for my dyke softball team; he'd wave a sign that read YOU GO GIRL. Best of all would be the look on Janet's face when I told her, "You know that guy you tried to set me up with? He's *gay* now. Ha!"

Seamus flopped backward against the wall and squinted at me dubiously. "Oh, man. Do I have to be gay? I'd rather be nothing for a while. I'm so sick of relationships."

"OK, you're nothing," I said, though I was only humoring him. I knew I'd wear him down eventually. One day we'd both be gay, and Irish, too.

Regret

By Jennifer Weiner

re·gret \ri-'gret\ *verb* [Middle English *regretten,* from Middle French *regreter,* from Old French, from *re-* + *-greter*] (14th century) 1: to feel sorry, disappointed, or distressed about. 2: to remember with a feeling of loss or sorrow; mourn. <I *regret* telling him that I had lunch with my ex>. *See also:* CHAGRIN, PINING AWAY, 20/20 HINDSIGHT.

1986: At the Vince Lombardi service area on the New Jersey State Turnpike, my mother tells me that she and my father are getting a divorce This sounds like it should be made up, like it's the first part of a joke, but unfortunately, it happens to be true.

"I've got something I need to tell you," she begins. I'm sixteen years old, and my mother and I are on our way back from visiting colleges in Philadelphia and New Jersey, on our way home to the two-story, four-bedroom colonial in Connecticut, to my sister, who is fifteen, and my brothers, who are thirteen and nine. We sit down under the flickering fluorescent lights, alongside stainless-steel steam trays full of tired-looking fried chicken and biscuits, and my mother tells me that my father's leaving, that he's probably packing, even as we're sitting there, that he'll be gone by the time we get home.

"You know things haven't been right for a while," she says, and I nod, because I've sensed this, in the vague, nonchalant way that teenagers keep track of their parents' emotional lives. My mother talks about how sorry she is, and how sad, and how hard it will be. I pull apart a piece of fried chicken with my fingers and think about my boyfriend. He is my best friend's older brother. He's twenty-three, done with college, living at home until he figures out what he wants to do besides me. My parents have decided that they don't want me to see him — have, in fact, forbidden me to see him, which means that I spend a lot of my time sneaking around and a lot more of my time thinking up new and elaborate lies to cover the fact that I'm rarely where I say I am. But if my father leaves, and my mother's going to be preoccupied with guilt and grief — which, judging from our conversation here at the Vince Lombardi service area, is clearly the case — it's going to be a lot easier for me to see him. I nod in all the right places, I ask the correct anguished questions ("Why? *Why!?!?*"), but in truth, I decide, this will not matter much. I am sixteen years old, and next fall, by this time, I'll be in college, I'll be free, I'll be gone.

That spring, with my bags packed, I find out that the circumstances of my parents' divorce are not as they were initially presented. My mother had given me the standard party line: grown apart, difficulty communicating, relationship broken down. The rest I'd figured out on my own. It boiled down to this — my father had decided he didn't want to be a father anymore. I felt proud of myself for arriving at this conclusion. I say it a lot, imagining how sophisticated it sounds, like a strand of pearls slipping from my fingers.

"He doesn't want to be a father anymore," I repeat to my friends, whose own fathers had decamped for other cities, other beds. I say this in the cynical, hard-bitten, world-weary manner that we decided to adopt.

In fact, that's only part of the story. In fact, there is somebody else. I learn this from my mother's friend Julia, who is tiny and chic, who drinks vodka and tonic and smokes cigarettes, and who has herself been divorced for years. "He's having an affair, Jenny!" she says from her perch on a wooden bench on our porch. It's getting dark, and the only lights come from inside the house and from her lit cigarette, but I can still see the look on her face, a look that strongly suggests that I've been naive and foolish to ever think otherwise. "Everyone knows!" The reason everyone knows is because my father leaves his red sports car parked in the other woman's driveway, for all the world to see. The other woman's name is Vicky. She is my mother's boss.

"Excuse me," I murmur, getting up from the table, all of the cynicism and sophistication gone *whooshing* out of me as surely as if I'd been kicked in the throat. I'm ashamed, and furious at him for being such a dumb cliché. And I feel mad at myself, because I don't care . . . or, rather, I shouldn't care. I've already decided not to.

The night before my high school graduation, my father picks me up to take me out to dinner. He's drunk and drives too fast, and he quickly confesses to the girlfriend, like he's been waiting for me to ask, like he wants to talk about it. Vic, he calls her. I imagine a foreman at a construction site, a hard hat, tattooed, beefy arms. At the fancy restaurant, I try to charm him in the manner that I've seen other teenage girls successfully employ on different sitcoms. "Do you like my new shirt?" I ask. He glares at me, gulps his drink. "No," he says. I bow my head over my plate, blinking back tears, because if this is a scene from a sitcom, and if he's just a cliché, why should it matter what he thinks of me? Why should it hurt?

The meal progresses at an agonizing crawl—oysters, duck, vodka, and wine. My father wobbles disconcertingly down the

g lot. I ask for the keys. He snarls something in
ids like it contains both the words *fuck* and *you*.
talk to their daughters that way . . . not even
ided not to be fathers anymore. Do they?
me alive. He roars into the driveway, swaggers
out of the sports car, and decides that he wants the keys to my
mother's car, too. "It's *mine!*" he bellows at the door I've locked
behind me, in an unprecedented display of foresight. "Mine!" he
yells again. My mother doesn't answer. My grandmother, who's
come up from Florida for my graduation, looks scared. "Frances,
should I call the police?" she asks. My mother's face is stony. On
the other side of the door, my father starts to cry. "Please, Fran,"
he begs, from the other side of the back door. "I don't want this
divorce. Please," he says, weeping. I sit in the living room, thinking of the jokes I will tell about this to my divorced-father friends.
I think about my boyfriend, how I'll tell him the story of this
night, how I'll spin it for maximum sympathy, how perhaps I'll
even cry.

At some point in the years after the divorce, in his sporadic com-
munications with the four of us, my father has stopped referring
to himself as our father. He's not "Dad" anymore. In private, my
sister and brothers dismissively call him Pap. He calls himself the
Old Man, in what I think is a reference to Hemingway. "Jenny!"
his voice booms on my answering machine. "It's the Old Man!"
He has news, he says. "Tying the knot," he announces, and tells
me where and when. I decide to go. I decide this the same way I
decide to slow down and look at wrecks on the side of the highway, the same way young men decide to cough up five dollars
for a peek at the bearded lady and the two-headed man. I'm not
choosing to be there—I'm impelled, by invisible forces much,
much larger than I am. Plus, I figure, I could maybe use the material some day.

In the years since his departure, my father has always had a girlfriend. He's run through Vic (for Victoria) and Jack (for Jacqueline), and some woman whose name I can't recall but who kept her Brazilian parrot, Rio, at his apartment. "Rio, Rio," my father crooned at the brilliantly colored, green and gold bird. Sometimes Rio would say hello, and I'd amuse myself by making up internal monologues for the parrot, most of them consisting of lines like, "I left the jungle for this?!?"

But at the time of his phone call, I'm living in Philadelphia, I haven't seen him in years, and I have no idea who he's seeing. My first sight of his intended will be on their wedding day.

My father's second wedding takes place by a lake in Connecticut on a sunny summer day. My brothers and I huddle by a picnic table, carefully examining every female who walks by. Is that her? (No, it's the photographer.) Is that her? (No, just the justice of the peace.) Our father emerges, natty in a dark suit, his hair and beard carefully clipped. His bride—or, as my brothers and I quickly start calling her, the Second Future Ex–Mrs. Dr. Weiner—is tall, short haired, and round faced, like our mom, only twenty years younger. She's in her thirties, closer to my age than my father's. Also, she's wearing a loose-fitting pink dress with an Empire waist. I look at this and wonder.

The lunch after the wedding—her parents, her sister, her sister's husband, their little kids, and the three of us, in an upstairs room at the lakeside lodge—is exquisitely awkward. There's lots of silence, lots of strained small talk, and, in my youngest brother's case, lots of drinks from the open bar. From the conversation—the things that are said, the things that aren't—it's clear that this wedding was hastily planned and something of a surprise to the bride's family. It's her second wedding, which is maybe why she's happy with such a tiny handful of guests, such a sad excuse of a celebration. Nobody says anything about what may or may not be under the loose-fitting midriff of her wedding gown, or about the fact that the bride is twenty years younger than the groom.

The bride passes pictures of a tropical vacation she and my father have been on — here they are swimming, and here, on the beach. There's palm trees, white sand, turquoise sea, schools of brilliantly colored tropical fish. I think how my mother's told me that my father hasn't paid the child support that he owes her in months because, he said, he's out of work, and even though I'm trying to be a detached observer, a fly on the wall, even though I am, by this time, a professional reporter, even though observation is my job, I feel sad. I'm sad that my father's life has become this bad collection of clichés, this pastiche of the predictable: the younger woman, the fights about the checks, the shotgun wedding, the second family sure to follow, the family where he would get it right. Because whatever else I'd thought of my father, I'd always believed that he was special, that he was different (and, as a result, of course, that I was also special and different). And here he was, just like Mindy's father and Pam's father and Elaine's father: younger woman, late checks, a second family in a doubtlessly futile attempt to wipe the slate clean and start over. How disappointing.

I see my father and his second wife for the second and last time three months later. My siblings and I are invited over to their brand-new house for Christmas dinner. My father is Jewish. The Second Future Ex–Mrs. Dr. Weiner, evidently, is not. I travel through the cold with my brother Joe, my then boyfriend, X, and my little dog. My father's new wife opens the wreath-bedecked door, her belly bulging beneath a fluffy, red and green sweater, and I want to scream because it's so fucking predictable. My father takes Joe and me on a tour. X is left in the kitchen, eating nachos and trying to make conversation with his girlfriend's father's new wife.

"Beautiful house," he says politely.

"Well," she replies, "I won't be living here much longer. Larry's leaving me, and the baby's coming in the spring!" ("The only thing I could think of saying was, 'Could I have some more salsa?'" X tells me later.)

Somewhere between the basement steps and the start of dinner, X whispers to me what's happened. Dinner is bizarre. I know that she's pregnant and that my father's leaving. He doesn't know that I know he's leaving. Poor Joe doesn't know any of it. My dog, Wendell, refusing to be intimidated by my dad's new wife's much-larger dog, Harley, helps himself to various fluffy toys that squeak when he bites them. After dinner, the Second Future Ex–Mrs. Dr. Weiner drags me downstairs to pour out her tale of woe. "He's mean," she whispers, and I nod, having experienced his meanness firsthand. The specifics don't matter, but she's happy to share them. He's yelled at her, belittled her, called her a lesbian, locked her out of the house. I nod and make appropriate noises, but meanwhile, I'm thinking, *Well, lady, what did you expect? You married a man with four grown-up children whom he doesn't really speak to, doesn't care for, doesn't know, and you thought you were going to be different? What did you think was going to happen? What did you expect?*

Outside, the air's so cold it hurts to breathe, and our boots crunch through the ice-crusted snow. My father and the Second Future Ex–Mrs. Dr. Weiner stand side by side in the doorway, waving, silhouetted in the doorway with the Christmas tree twinkling in the background. From a distance, they could be a greeting card, or a commercial for this season's piece of jewelry or hot holiday toy. From a distance, you can't tell that he's twenty years older, that the marriage is falling apart, that two weeks earlier she had to call the fire department to let her into the garage. "Weird," says X. Joe says nothing. Wendell hops into the backseat with one of Harley's choicest fluffy toys clenched between his jaws. It's as if he knows we're never going to see her again. It's as if he knows we're never coming back.

You don't get fairy-tale endings outside of fairy tales. You can get happy endings, but not perfect ones. And there is, sadly, a part of me that will always crave perfection, search for it, mourn its absence.

If I were writing the story of my life instead of living it, the phone would ring. My father would be on the line. He'd thought about things, he would say. He'd seen what he had done to me, to the four of us, and he was sorry. Was it too late? he'd ask soberly. Was there still a chance to fix things? I'd say that I wasn't sure, and he'd sigh (a sane sigh, a nonmelodramatic sigh, uninflected with tears or curse words) and say that he understood, and that he would always regret not appreciating me and loving me while he had the chance. Can we try? he'd ask, and the urgency in his voice would let me know that trying was the most important thing in the world. "I'm sorry," he'd tell me. "I wish you happiness," he'd say.

I know this won't ever happen. I regret that most of all.

SAVAGE

By Maggie Estep

sav·age \\'sa-vij\\ *transitive verb* [Middle English *sauvage,* from
Middle French, from Medieval Latin *salvaticus,* alteration of Latin *sil-
vaticus* of the woods, wild, from *silva* wood, forest] (1880) 1: to attack
or treat brutally. 2: to rip out the heart of another, jump up and down
on top of it, whir it around in a Cuisinart for a while, then restore it to
its rightful owner (with a pinch of salt sprinkled into the open wound).
Sometimes accompanied by bad behavior such as infidelity with the
heart-owner's close friends or relative. <the divorce wasn't just bad, it
was *savage*>. *See also:* LOVES LOST.

She walked into my shop one day in early spring. I was hunched
over my worktable, carefully shaving the hammers of a tinny
sounding Kawai baby grand. The radio was on, blaring the salsa
station at an invigorating volume. My shop is wedged between a
bodega and a bicycle repair shop in a predominantly Spanish part
of Brooklyn. Full-volume Bach doesn't go over well with the kids
from the bike shop. Arturo, the youngest of them, likes to come
over and yell things ("That shit sounds like math, man"). So I
mostly play salsa when I've got the shop windows open.

That day, I had the door open, too. It was beautiful out. The sky was a violent blue, exploding with life. I had my back to the door, and she must have walked in and watched me work for a spell. Eventually, she spoke.

"Hello?"

I turned around and looked up, startled.

"Oh, hello," I said, setting down the razor blade I'd been using on the hammers. "Can I help you?"

"I need a piano," she declared, jutting her chin out.

She was verging on tall and on the odd side of beautiful. There wasn't much meat on her, but that was fine. I'd just been dumped by a voluptuous Cuban prodigy. I'd had enough curves to last a lifetime. Not, mind you, that this girl was indicating she wanted me to contemplate her lack of curves. Her eyes were hungry, but they were focused on a Steinway with troubled dampers. Not on me.

"I'm Lucinda," she said, extending a surprisingly weathered, small hand.

I told her my name was Albert. She smiled, as if this pleased her.

"That's a handsome Model B," she said, indicating Steinway #238659, the 1926 Hamburg B with damper problems.

"Play," I said. I stood up and pulled a bench from the chaos near my worktable. The shop was particularly crammed that week. I'd just bought two broken-down Yamaha uprights off a music school that was going out of business, and I now had fourteen pianos stuffed into my small, low-ceiling storefront.

I dusted off the cracked leather bench and put it before the Model B.

I had a sense that Lucinda could play. In spite of those strangely damaged little hands.

She hesitated. Looked from me to the bench to the big black piano.

She could have been anywhere from fifteen to forty, but I figured probably in the middle there. Her eyes seemed to be gray.

"Go ahead," I said, waving her toward the instrument.

She frowned, turning her forehead into an appealing little accordion of flesh.

"What's wrong?" I asked softly.

"I can't afford it."

"Oh, don't be sorry about that. No one can. No one ever buys my pianos. Even the cheap ones. Just play."

"Oh," she said.

She sat down. She removed her watch and a silver charm bracelet. She kicked off her dirty brown shoes, then lightly rested her hands over the keys.

She started playing, very softly. Schumann's Romance in F-sharp major. I'd never heard it quite like that. She seemed to be doing the same things any other pianist would do, but there was something that made it odd. *Good* odd. Before I could pinpoint the source of the oddness, though, she abruptly shifted to a strident Prokofiev piece. Whipped through it. Violently.

When she finished, she looked up at me from between the two wings of her hair.

I'd never liked Prokofiev's piano sonatas, but right now they were working for me just fine. In fact, she could have played a putrid rendition of the Moonlight Sonata, and it wouldn't have mattered. I was sold on her.

Before I had time to compliment her playing, she stood up and started inspecting the walls. I had all sorts of things affixed to the blistered green paint. Photographs of musicians and pianos and a cat calendar that the Cuban prodigy had given me. Off to one side was John Black's holy card, which I'd gotten at his memorial service at St Patrick's. This was the thing Lucinda focused on, staring intently at the laminated photo of Captain John Black. It was a nice picture. He was wearing his FDNY uniform. He was grinning, and his close-set blue eyes seemed to be laughing.

"How do you know him?" Lucinda asked, still staring at the card.

"Bought a piano off me," I said. "Turned forty, decided it was time to take up piano."

"And he's dead," she said.

"World Trade Center," I said.

"Oh."

"That's his piano," I said, indicating a humble mahogany Model M. "His family gave it back to me to sell. I'll give the proceeds to Ladder 3 in Manhattan."

"Oh?" she said.

"He was captain there."

She went back to staring at the picture.

Amazing that, even from the grave, John Black still had a way with women. She would have been his type, I guessed. He'd gravitated to pretty, smart, half-crazy girls. Not that I'd been his best friend. He bought a piano from me, I helped him to find a teacher, and we'd stayed in touch. We had dinner now and then. Sometimes I'd stop by Ladder 3 to say hello.

The morning it happened, I'd been on my way to Manhattan to, ironically, tune a piano in the World Trade Center Marriott. I was on my bike, approaching the Brooklyn Bridge bike path, when all hell broke loose. Crashes, smoke, and chaos. Thousands of people started pouring across the bridge, fleeing lower Manhattan. For a while, I kept going, toward it, walking my bike. About halfway across the bridge, I stopped. Stood off to one side, holding my bike against my body as thousands of strangely quiet pedestrians hurried across the bridge. There were women in bare feet, carrying their office pumps, evidently having evacuated without retrieving their walking shoes. There was a group of large black women, praying aloud. Dozens of pale men with cell phones glued to their ears. And just ahead, the towers burned. A few seconds before the first tower fell, I realized I was watching thousands of people die. I had a sick feeling at the time that John was one of them.

Lucinda stared at John's holy card for a very long time. I didn't understand quite what was going on, but I left her to it.

Eventually, she dragged the piano bench away from the imposing Model B and put it in front of John Black's piano. She sat down and ran her right hand over the instrument's lid.

I turned back to the Kawai hammers I'd been working on.

She played a Bach prelude. A beautiful thing in E-flat major. Simple and heartbreaking. I wanted to say something about it, but felt like this would be invasive.

When she'd stopped playing, I asked if she was hungry.

She frowned and seemed to consult herself. Then, "I think so, yes."

I took her to the Caribbean place on Myrtle Avenue. JouJou, the big sexy waitress, pulled a long face, seeing me with another woman. Not, mind you, that we were dating or anything close. I'd certainly noticed the way her glorious ass looked under the lively print skirts she favored, but she wasn't the kind of woman to date a white man, anyway. You knew that just to look at her. Still, she liked to pretend she had dibs on me.

We ordered and the food came quickly. Steaming piles of collard greens, yams, and cabbage. Lucinda didn't say much. Was far too busy shoveling food down herself. I'd never seen anyone eat like that. Particularly not someone so thin.

As if reading my mind, she looked up from her immense plate of food: "I burn it off."

"Oh?" I said.

"Horses," she said.

"What?" I asked.

"I ride. At the track."

"You're a jockey?"

"Exercise rider."

"What's that?"

"I ride 'em in the morning. The jocks just ride 'em in races. But it's fools like me that go out on the track every morning at five and work those suckers."

"Wow."

She shrugged. Then: "How much you want for John Black's piano?"

I was taken aback. She'd remembered John's name.

"I dunno. About twelve."

"Thousand?" Lucinda frowned.

"That's cheap for an M. You must know that."

"Uh," she said—then shoved more food down her throat.

"Do you want to go to the movies tonight?" I ventured.

"I get up at three A.M.," she said, completely matter-of-fact, not seeming to feel strongly in any direction about my having asked her out. She was just stating the obvious, that a nighttime movie would conflict with her schedule.

"Oh," I said.

"So what do you do?" Lucinda asked then. She had finally put her fork down, and she was now actually looking at me.

"What do you mean what do I do?"

"With all those pianos."

"I sell 'em."

"You told me earlier you almost never sell them. How do you earn your keep?"

I started feeling defensive. And, simultaneously, wanting to take her clothes off.

"I'm a tuner, too. I have a good amount of tuning clients. I get by that way."

"Oh. So what's with all the fucked-up pianos, then?"

"They're not all fucked up," I said, wanting to reach across the table, grab her small pretty face, and kiss her violently.

"You play?" she asked then.

"Not really. I was a violinist. But I have a tremor. I had to stop."

"A tremor?" She squinted.

I noticed tiny, pale orange freckles smattered across her nose. Her hair seemed too dark for freckles.

I held my hand out in front of her. It trembled like it does. Early onset of Parkinson's. Mild at this point. Just enough to have ruined any violin dreams I'd had.

"Oh," she said. Her gray eyes went black with sadness.

A few minutes later, JouJou brought the bill. I paid. Lucinda thanked me and for the first time really smiled. She had handsome, even teeth.

As we walked back toward my shop, she looked all around, taking in the bodegas, the manicure shops, and the gas stations. They seemed to please her.

We reached my block. I unlocked the padlock, pushed the gate up, and ushered her inside, advising her to steer clear of the Chickering's keyboard that was laid out on a blanket near the door.

Lucinda took two steps into the shop, then turned around, draped her arms around my neck, and pulled my mouth to hers.

I'd been thinking about this very thing, but I definitely hadn't expected her to pounce like this. Though I can't say I minded.

Her tongue found its way into my mouth and traced my teeth. I touched her lower back. It was barely wider than the expanse of my hand. I leaned my body into hers. She sank down to her knees. I did the same. I touched her ribs and her jutting hipbones. I cradled her neck. I kissed her ears. She grew more savage, forceful, kissing me violently, grabbing at my lower back, grinding her hips into me.

I had thought that, with luck, I'd get her to take in an afternoon movie with me later in the week. Maybe two or three weeks down the line, we'd get intimate. But now this.

And then, as abruptly as it had started, it ended. She stood up. I was in a heap on the floor, probably looking like a dumb, stunned mess.

She smiled slightly and said, "I'm confused."

"Ah," I said.

She smoothed her shirt, ran one of her strange hands through her hair, then went over to the door.

"I'll be back," she said, then walked out of my shop.

I sincerely doubted I'd ever see her again. I frowned at John Black's holy card. Then shrugged. Then laughed to myself and went back to shaving down the Kawai's hammers.

The next day, Lucinda was back. She was wearing strange little boots that had mud all over them. I guess I was staring at these.

"Paddock boots," she explained. "I came right from the track. Somebody ripped off my locker, too; my change of clothes was gone. And twenty-seven bucks I won on this long shot that Bridgemohan rode last week," she said.

"Oh?" I said.

"Bridgemohan tried to pick me up once," she said, frowning at the memory of it. "But I don't like bulimic men." She said it emphatically. I didn't know what the hell she was talking about.

"You know they've all got to vomit, right?"

"What?"

"The jocks. To keep the weight off. Gotta puke and sweat and take Ex-Lax."

"Oh."

"Females got it easier. We're smaller, but the reason you don't see many female jocks is usually a small woman doesn't have as much upper-body strength as a small man. You know how much strength it takes to hold a thousand-odd pounds of Thoroughbred back when he wants to go?"

I shook my head.

"Yeah. Well. Me, I'm five five, and I've got big shoulders. I have upper-body strength, but I can't get my weight under one-twenty without getting sick and weak." She shrugged. She looked at me then, finally seeming to actually see me. She leered a little. Then stopped.

" Can I play? You mind?" she asked, and before I could tell her she could do anything she damn well pleased, she marched over to John's piano.

There were thousands of things I wanted to ask her, but I was slightly afraid of her. I had the impression that she was the kind of woman to come and go as she pleased. No fanfare, no pronouncements or commitments.

She sat down at John Black's piano. She played.

At some point, she stopped playing and I looked up. She was standing, staring at John Black's holy card again. I felt like ripping it off the wall.

She came over to me. I put down the damper I'd been fussing with. I rested my hands on my knees and stared at her. She was very beautiful at that moment.

She put her hands on my shoulders, kissed me lightly. Pulled back. I thought she was going to turn around and walk out the door again. Instead, she took her shirt off. She had well-made, tiny breasts. She was thin, but her arms were muscular. I put my hand at the small of her back. I felt a strange swelling in her skin.

"Scar," she said, turning around to show me a long pink scar that started between her shoulder blades and ran all the way down her spine, disappearing into her pants.

"What's that from?" I asked her back.

"Fell off," she said.

"Fell off?"

"A horse. Ballistic. Grandson of Native Dancer."

I was getting attached to the way she'd spout out horse talk, even though it must have been obvious that I had no idea who or what she was talking about.

"Oh," I said.

"Ballistic spooked at some geese on the track during a workout. I got thrown off, then stepped on by the horse running behind us. Broke my back. I was laid up a long time. That's why I have to have a piano."

"What?"

"I couldn't do much. I listened to music again. I hadn't in a long time. Now I'm obsessed again."

"Oh," I said, increasingly confused. I didn't know what the hell to do. About anything. Least of all this crazy creature, half-naked in my shop.

"You studied music as a child," I said.

"Yes. But I stopped when my brother got locked up."

"Oh?" By now, I knew she would tell me the whole story. I also knew it would be quite a story. Nothing to do with Lucinda was boring.

"The prison he was in, they had this program where the convicts took care of broken-down racehorses. You know they get auctioned off for meat, right? Horse could win a shitload of stakes races, make someone half a million dollars, but then, minute it breaks down, off to the meat wagon. Literally. So they started this thing. In Kentucky. Inmates taking care of fucked-up racehorses. My brother was incarcerated there. He had two horses he took care of. I went to visit him often. One day, I was probably fifteen, he put me up on one his charges. A little chestnut mare that was sound enough to ride. I never wanted to get off. I'm like that. I get obsessed with things.

"Two days later, I went over to Churchill Downs and just walked around the backstretch until I found this trainer that gave me a job walking hots. That's where you walk the horse around to cool it down after a workout. The trainer I walked hots for, he put me up on a horse within a couple of months. I knew I'd fuck up my hands. Working with horses, you're bound to. I didn't care, though. It was like all those stories you hear, how some overzealous parent makes the kid play piano six hours a day. I'd been doing that so long that all the joy was gone. When I got on a horse, the joy was back. So I didn't care about my hands."

She studied these hands now. She seemed totally oblivious to the fact that she was still half-naked.

"I never broke 'em," she continued, "just my back. Nine months I couldn't get on a horse. I thought I would die. I listened to Bach."

She fell silent now. I folded her into my arms. I put her down on the floor on top of the blanket that the Chickering's keyboard had been on. She was wearing red cotton panties that were a little too big for her.

"My lucky panties," she whispered into my ear.

"Oh," I said.

"For riding I mean. Everyone's incredibly superstitious on the backstretch. I try not to be. But I have to wear these."

I covered her mouth with my hand. Ran my other hand under the elastic of the lucky panties. I pushed the crotch of them to the side as I entered her. She seemed to like this.

. . .

Within a few days, she had moved in with me. For the last five years, I've lived in the back room of my shop. There's a toilet, a shower stall, and a sink. I have a hot plate and a very comfortable futon that I keep under a Knabe concert grand. Lucinda loves this.

Most mornings, Lucinda gets up before three to head off to the track. Sometimes, I feel her kiss me good-bye.

She's always full of stories. About the track. About her brother,who's still incarcerated but now looking after Kentucky Derby–winner Monarchos's full brother.

She never makes any pronouncements about love or a lack of it. She plays the pianos. Mostly John's piano.

One afternoon, she fails to appear.

Two days go by without any word from her. I don't have a phone number for her. All I know is that she shares a small house in Queens with two other racetrack people. I consider calling over to Aqueduct, but, as ridiculous as it sounds, I don't know her last name.

She's left some belongings here in a pile to the right of the Knabe concert grand we slept under. There's a pair of crusty pad-dock boots. Some books. A lipstick she never wore. And I realized that she had stolen something. John Black's holy card. Took it right off my wall.

Three weeks after she's disappeared, I get a phone call: "I'd like to speak to Albert Rauch," a nasal voice says.

"That's me."

"You know a Lucinda Shoemaker?" the voice wants to know.

"Yes, I do, yes, what is it?" I say.

"I'm afraid there's been an accident."

My heart weighs too much.

"Is she dead?"

"Oh, no. No. She lost consciousness, though, so we have to keep her overnight. And she has some fractures."

"Hands?"

"I'm sorry?"

"Did she break her hands?"

"No. Both legs."

"Oh." I sighed. "That's good."

The nurse, no doubt, thought me sick.

I wrote down the hospital's address. Closed the shop. Drove out to the nether regions of Queens.

I didn't know why she'd had them call me. She must have had friends at the track. I hadn't even been aware of giving her my phone number.

Her legs were in traction. Her head had been shaved and was partially bandaged.

"It didn't work," she said by way of greeting.

"What?"

"I thought John would give me my nerve back."

"What?"

"This," she said, reaching for her bedside table, where, I now saw, she had John Black's holy card. "I thought if I rode with this in my helmet, it would give me my nerve back."

"Oh?" is all I said.

"I hope it's okay I had them call you," she said then. She was so tiny and pale-looking, the bandage on her head almost bigger than the head itself.

"Sure. I can't say I understand it, but I'm glad to find you alive." There was more I could have said. Like that over the last couple of weeks I had cut myself, gotten felt glue stuck in my hair, tripped, banged my head into the ceiling, and been bitten by a previously friendly dog. All because I'd been distracted by the absence of Lucinda.

"Maybe I should go now," I said.

I found myself rising from the plastic hospital chair I'd pulled up to her bedside.

"Go?" She looked aghast.

"I'm not sure what purpose I serve."

"Albert, please," she said.

This was all she had to say.

She was released from the hospital two days later, and I brought her back to the shop. We never talked about what made her leave in the first place. But now, there was no getting rid of her. For one thing, she couldn't walk. For another, I would have been hard-pressed to drag her away from John Black's piano. Though his holy card had apparently failed to keep her safe from harm, his piano was certainly doing something for her. She would carefully arrange her plaster-encased legs and play for hours. And her playing improved monstrously. She'd been a good—albeit out of shape—pianist to begin with, but now she was pulling savagely beautiful things from the clunky old Model M.

One night, about a week after the accident, as we lay half-asleep on our futon beneath the Knabe, I felt her hand on my chest.

"Albert?" she said tentatively.

"Yeah?" I opened one eye. I didn't really like the sound of that *Albert*.

"I will never get my nerve back, and that probably doesn't bode well for our future."

I sighed. I could live without the incomprehensible statements that she was partial to.

"What are you talking about?"

"I told you I thought having John Black's holy card in my crash helmet might help. With my nerve. Which I lost after the injury on Ballistic. I knew I lost it, but I tried to pretend I hadn't. I had a bad feeling it would catch up to me, and it did. Now this," she said, motioning to her casts.

"And how is it this doesn't bode well for us?" I asked.

I hadn't really realized there was an "us" to begin with. "Us" implied keeping each other informed of whereabouts and feelings. Lucinda had not mastered anything resembling this.

"I can't ride anymore. Maybe for pleasure eventually. But not as a living."

"I understand that and I'm sorry," I said, cupping her chin in my hands, "it doesn't mean anything has to go wrong between you and I."

"You and I was the sire of You. Great filly," Lucinda said.

"What?"

"You. Gangly bay filly. Went off as the favorite in the Breeders' Cup juvenile fillies but didn't get the job done. Had a great career, anyway. She was by a stallion named You and I."

"Lucinda," I said, taking my hands away from her face, "I'm sick of this."

"Of what?"

"Of cryptic fucking horse talk whenever you have something serious on your mind."

"Oh," she said. Then: "I'm probably going to leave New York."

"No," I said.

"No?" she asked, letting one of her small battered hands travel down the front of my pajama pants.

"No," I said. Then, I let her savage me. Because that was what it felt like. Savaging. Which was another damned horse-racing term. Unruly stud colts were sometimes known to savage their handlers by grabbing them with their teeth, throwing them down, and sometimes stomping on them.

I let Lucinda savage me. And there wasn't any more discussion about her leaving New York.

Our bodies did the talking for several weeks.

I started falling behind on work. We would make love, and then she would immediately hobble over to John Black's piano, arrange her plaster-encased legs, and play.

I would lie under the piano and listen.

Weeks passed.

Her casts came off in early May.

Her already slender legs were now lumpy and malnourished-looking. Her hair was growing back in frantic spikes. I found this deeply sexy.

On the first Saturday in May, we watched the Kentucky Derby on my tiny, black-and-white TV. Lucinda was certain that a horse named Jack Valentine — a long shot — would win. As we watched him romp across the finish line more than sixth lengths ahead of the pack, Lucinda told me that she'd had money on him. I was surprised, since she had previously told me she'd only bet on horses she'd ridden — and she'd never been given a horse of the caliber of Jack Valentine. I didn't think much about it, though. After we'd watched the race, we made love for the third time that day. Eventually, she drifted off to sleep. I kissed her sleeping face, then went back into the front of my shop to investigate some separation in a Mason & Hamlin's pinblock. A few minutes later, Lucinda emerged from the back room, fully dressed. She came and draped her arms around me.

"I'm going out for a little bit. Do you need anything?"

"Where you going?"

"Just out. Get some air."

"Oh," I said. "I don't need anything. Thanks."

I watched her walk out, pulling the door closed behind her.

I had a bad feeling.

I worked.

When Lucinda came back two hours later, I felt like crawling inside one of my pianos and going to sleep.

Instead, I put down my tools and looked at her, sensing that something big was coming. No doubt she would first launch into a horse story. Maybe her disappointment over Point Given's not running as a four-year-old. Perhaps a discourse on the history of racing. A mention of Seabiscuit or Ruffian or Cigar. Maybe she'd even root through her pile of stuff and produce her tattered photo of Secretariat, winning the Belmont Stakes by twenty-one lengths. She'd pulled that one out several times already, when something was particularly troubling to her.

She came over and kissed me on the cheek. She was very pale. She reached into her Churchill Downs tote bag and produced a big envelope.

"I have this," she said, opening the envelope, "twelve thousand dollars," she added, fanning endless bills out on the lid of a Yamaha baby grand.

"For John Black's piano," she explained.

"But it's already yours," I protested.

"Now it is, yes," she said, pushing some of the bills toward me. I was furious. I contained it.

"Are you going somewhere?" I asked.

"I am, Albert. I am."

"May I ask where?"

"Back to Kentucky."

"Where on earth did you get twelve thousand dollars?"

"Jack Valentine. He went off at 13-1. I bet him to win, and I used him in an exacta with Hellcat Helen, the filly that ran second. She went off at 55-1."

"Lucinda, this isn't right."

"What isn't?"

"You just walked in one day, and now you're going to walk out?"

"I'm sorry."

"I would have liked to have had some input into all this."

"Of course. I don't know how to conduct myself in love."

"You love me?"

"Possibly."

"But you're going to give me twelve thousand dollars and leave."

"Yes. I warned you, didn't I?"

"Warned me?"

"That I'd lost my nerve. I can't ride anymore."

"So? You don't have to ride. Live here. Play the piano."

"No. I can't stay here."

"Why?"

"I can't explain it. I have to go back where I came from. With John Black's piano."

She went to sit at the piano. Lovingly dusted her fingers over the keys, not making any sound, just saying hello to it, and to John.

Over the next few days, we didn't say much to each other. We were painfully polite and solicitous. We made love innumerable times. Horrible, final love. I felt like my chest cavity was on fire.

Sometimes, when Lucinda was playing or sleeping, I would stare at her, trying to memorize every millimeter of her. It's possible that I could have coerced her into staying, but, had I done this, it would have hung between us forever. I preferred heartbreak to guilt.

The day came. She'd hired a truck and three men to hoist John's Steinway out of my shop and to drive it to Kentucky. I sat at my work table, pretending to fiddle with the innards of a lovely Chickering upright that I'd just gotten. Lucinda was nervously overseeing the moving of her piano.

When the movers left, she gathered the last of her things into her Churchill Downs tote bag. She wouldn't let me drive her to the airport, which was fine. I liked the idea of saying good-bye to her in the very spot where I'd first seen her.

We stood holding each other.

I had my hand at the small of her back, just where the scar was.

She pulled away from me. She was very pale. She smiled slightly, put the tote bag on her shoulder, and walked out.

I sat in my shop for several hours, trying to work, blasting Bach without any regard for the Spanish kids from the bike shop next door.

By early afternoon, when it was clear I wasn't getting any work done, I closed the shop, got in the car, and drove to Manhattan, to Ladder 3.

A big guy whose name I couldn't remember, but who I recognized as one of John's close friends, was hanging in front of the station. Wearing those firefighter boots and that dark slicker with the yellow stripe across the back.

He was staring off into space, even though he didn't seem the type who'd be prone to daydreaming.

"Hey," I said, walking up to him, "I'm Albert, the guy John Black bought his piano from."

"Oh, yeah? How ya doin'?" the big guy said. I was embarrassed to have forgotten his name. At John's memorial at St. Patrick's, after the priests and government officials had said their bit, several of John's fellow firefighters had gotten up and told stories. This particular fellow had lurked up to the podium, stared out at the crowd, and said, "Those suicide bombers were promised a flying carpet to Allah and forty virgins. Imagine their surprise when they got to the other side and all they found was one very pissed-off John Black."

"I sold John's piano," I told the big guy now.

"Oh, yeah?" He didn't seem that interested.

"His family wanted the proceeds to go to you guys. Here," I said, handing him Lucinda's envelope.

He took the envelope, held it for a moment, then looked inside.

"Holy shit." His eyes grew huge. "What, was that thing made outta gold?"

"Steinways are valuable," I shrugged.

The big guy stood there, looking baffled.

"I gotta hand this over to the captain," he said.

"You do that," I told him.

I went home to my shop.

Lucinda was still gone.

But I now noticed that she'd put John's holy card back on the blistered green wall.

I stared at it. John's close-set blue eyes laughed at me.

THREESOME

By Dana Johnson

---

three·some \'thrē-səm\ *noun* [origin unknown] (14th century) 1: a group of three persons or things: TRIO. 2: a bad idea.

For their anniversaries, other women get, what? Like a box of chocolate and roses if they got a boring boyfriend, or dinner at the Olive Garden or someplace like that if the guy's half-trying. A stuffed animal? Or even jewelry if he's for real. Not no cheap bastard. *Something.* Me, I get something else not even close. I get Bobby coming home from work a few weeks before, telling me somebody there at the gym has a crush on me. He was all excited, grinning like he had new teeth and wanted to show them off.

I didn't get what he was up to. Not because I wasn't hella smart. I was. Bobby admitted that one time after we did it for an hour in the desert, in Palmdale somewhere, in the middle of nowhere. I'd taken this astronomy class at L.A. City College because I had a lot of time on my hands, and I was learning a lot about stars and stuff. I told Bobby about how all the stars were just distant suns and that the sun we saw in the daytime is just the largest of all the suns, of all 100 billion suns—at least. The largest object in our whole big crazy solar system. He squeezed me really hard. "Damn, you're smart," he said. Bobby waited till I gave him a big sunshine smile, and then he said, "But everybody ain't perfect."

Ha, I'd said.

But, lately I was hardly smart enough to know what he was up to anymore, because since his brother had died, Bobby treated everything like a big hurry. He didn't take time for anything—or when he did, it was like he forgot why he was taking the time in the first place. He was treating his life like something he wanted to get over with, to do, but not to see.

He was still grinning at me about this crush, so I asked him, "What? You glad some man at your work's wanting me? That don't sound like you, Bobby." What sounded like Bobby was jealousy. He made me quit stripping because of it. I put my hand on his forehead, and he slapped it back down.

"Quit playing with the smart-ass comments." He ran his hand through his wavy black hair and stared at me. He was dyeing it because he was only thirty-six and going gray.

I stared back. "So? Who's this guy?" All this time, Bobby was standing in front of me in his favorite gray sweat suit. He unzipped his jacket, tossed it on the futon, and started making his way to the kitchen to cook.

"You thaw that chicken like I told you?"

"It's in the sink. Is it that Furio guy? That actor guy?" He worked out at the gym, and he was always giving me the eye. "Please," Bobby said. "Where the fuck's the olives? I was going to make cacciatore."

"Ate 'em."

"OK, Big Ass," Bobby said. "That's the last thing you should be eating. A whole goddamn *can*?" He shook his head. "I'm just going to broil this, then. What else you eat up in here?"

Bobby Cantadopolous was militant about cooking, his kitchen, food, and me involved with any of these things. I'd moved in with him in his apartment, and it always felt that way—like his.

"Who's got the crush on me, Bobby? I'm tired of waiting for you to tell me." I just knew it was some nasty dude. Otherwise, Bobby wouldn't think it was so damn funny. "What's his name?"

Bobby was washing the chicken and was seasoning it. He looked up at me, mouth serious, eyes cracking up. "Amber."

"Amber? Amber," I repeated. Bobby got me to thinking. "Is it that transsexual dude? The one who just came back with all the changes?"

"Uh-uh," Bobby said.

"Amber," I said again. I watched Bobby chop onion and crush garlic. "Is this dude, like, Irish or something? Got one of them names that sounds like a lady? Like Carol or Adrian? Like that?"

"Nope," Bobby said. "And whoever heard of a guy named Amber?"

I couldn't figure it out. Bobby poured olive oil in the pan and stirred in the onion and garlic. I was hungry. "We eating rice with that?"

"No, *we* ain't," Bobby said. He was policing my weight more since I quit stripping. I wasn't doing a lot of exercising no more. "Broccoli for you, rice for me."

"Fuck," I said.

"Watch it, tough guy. Keep that filth out your mouth."

I rolled my eyes. "So *who*, Bobby? I practically don't give a shit anymore."

He gave me the eyebrows and then swatted me on the ass. "What I tell you?"

I leaned against the counter with my arms crossed, pouting. Bobby tap-danced on my nerves sometimes. He concentrated on browning the chicken, stirring it around and staring at it like it was his life's work. Finally, he said, "Remember that thing I did down in Mexico last year? With the four girls?"

"Yeah," I said slow. That was before me and Bobby were together, when he was just starting to do porn. It don't matter to me, the porn on the side of training folks at the gym. I'm just saying, Mexico was a long time ago, at least a year. Telling me about it when we first met, Bobby bragged that he made eight hundred dollars just to go down to Mexico and be with a bunch of women. I thought eight hundred dollars was a bit cheap to have your life out there, floating around forever and ever, but he said he would've been with all those women for free.

"I guess," I'd said, and Bobby'd said that was the trouble with me. I never opened my eyes to see the bigger picture.

But now I was trying. "What's Mexico got to do with all that?" Before Bobby could answer, I got a picture in my head of this blond woman he was always talking about like something he missed, like his mother's goddamn home-baked cookies, waiting for him after school on a rainy day. "Amber," I said. I sucked my teeth and rolled my eyes at Bobby. She had blown him in this other video he did.

"Yeah, right? The blond? With the tiny waist and the lips?" He tore his eyes away from the chicken long enough to bite down hard on his fist. "Fuckin'- A," he said.

"If you want to call those lips," I said. "They look like life rafts. A little collagen goes a long way. You should tell her that."

"You're one to talk," Bobby said. He motioned a finger and then tapped his lips, so I could come to him and kiss him.

I stood where I was. "On me, it looks normal. You ever see a black girl with thin lips? No. You ain't," I said.

"Eh, what're ya gonna do," he said and shrugged, like some things you just can't help. He finally stopped babying his chicken, mixed everything together, and put it in the broiler. When he straightened up, he stretched out his arms and wiggled his fingers. "What I tell you? Get over here and give me a kiss."

I was getting worked up. "No, and what's so great about her ass?"

"Nice and big."

"But you keep telling me that mine's getting too big. What's up with that?"

"Since when did big mean gigantic? Huh? Answer me that, Whole-Can-a-Olives."

Because I was hugging myself and wouldn't come to him, Bobby came to me and put his arms around my waist. "I'm just breaking your balls, you know that, right?" He kissed me and held me so close and tight that I felt wrapped up, completely. His hands traveled down my waist and under my ass. "I'm just giving you a hard time. I might even let you eat some rice—if you go to the gym tomorrow. Get on that treadmill."

I laughed, waiting for Bobby to say, "Just kidding." But he didn't.

Late in the night, when I was trying to fall asleep, Bobby wouldn't shut up about Amber. What if she hit on me, would I do her? Didn't I think she was sorta cute? Would I do it, just for him even? Just for fun? What was the big deal? It wasn't like he was asking me to be with another man. What'd I think?

I told him that I thought he was a sex fiend, but if he was nice to me, I just might. And he finally shut up, which was all I wanted. In bed with Bobby, when it was quiet, was the only time I could talk to him about serious things. So I asked him how his mother was doing with Louie being gone. It had only been three months.

"How you think she's doing?" he said, and then I didn't hear anything else from him. We just lay there in the dark.

Before long he was snoring, holding on to me tight, his left arm lying across my body like a weight. This threesome thing seemed to come out of nowhere, but Bobby did seem restless, a little more wild since his brother died. Bobby says I'm full of shit when I say he changed after his brother got killed. But how could he not? Louie was his heart, a younger version of Bobby, a nice kid with a big mouth. Louie took to calling me Sunshine, just like Bobby. Some asshole shot him at the ATM and only got forty bucks off him. I was there when Bobby got the phone call from his father. Bobby'd just gotten off me. We were happy, wiped out. When the phone rang, he got up, went to the phone, and stood there naked. We had two candles burning, and the moon was so bright that we didn't even need the candles. And Bobby, Bobby was so beautiful to me, the curves of his muscles, hard and rocky with smooth, shiny skin from the sweat on his body. I don't remember what Bobby said, if he said anything into the phone. He just fell to his knees and dropped the phone. His daddy was hollering, "Bobby! Bobby!" in a tiny cartoon voice, coming from the phone, but Bobby was curled up in a ball with his eyes squeezed shut and his mouth wide open. Nothing coming out. When I went to him, Bobby grabbed me and held on to me so hard that I thought he was going to crush something inside me. I knew his kid brother was dead. Nobody had to tell me nothing.

When I tried to get out of going to the funeral with Bobby — because his family was always asking if he was still dating me, the black *kargiola*, and did he think he was the fucking Greek Robert De Niro, with the black chicks every time they turned around — Bobby told me, "La Donna, fuck them. I need you there." I asked him what *kargiola* meant, and he told me, "Never mind. It ain't nice." At the funeral, Bobby held my hand tight and leaned forward in his chair while they dropped dirt onto the casket. Then they lowered the casket into the grave. Bobby didn't really cry until then, and later he told me it was because his brother was deep in the dirt, covered with dirt, and was going to turn into dirt. I told Bobby that Louie wasn't in the casket. Louie's *body* was there, covered in dirt, but the Louie that Bobby loved — his spirit — was with us and the whole world. Bobby told me to shut up and kissed me on the forehead, so I knew I made him feel better, some kind of way.

"That's why I love you, Donna," he said. He took my hand. "You know how to take care of me, Sunshine."

Now, Bobby was snoring even louder, his mouth open just a little bit. I turned my head to kiss him on the lips. They felt soft, and I wanted him to wake up and make love to me. I kissed him again and played with the black waves of his hair. But he didn't feel a thing. He just kept right on sleeping.

. . .

Bobby worked out and trained at Gold's Gym off Santa Monica Boulevard. All the stars and a lot of famous people worked out there. Like I care. One time, though? Bobby almost broke his neck in three places trying to get a look at some skinny model bitch, and that pissed me off. Kind of wished he'd broken *something*.

Getting to the gym was the same routine every time. It took us a thousand stoplights to get down Santa Monica, park the car, give the homeless guy in the parking lot a couple of bucks for wiping down Bobby's Mustang, Bobby "how ya doin'" everybody, me wishing I was at Zankou Chicken eating a drumstick. When we walked in, Bobby gave me the regimen.

"Cardio . . . You gotta hit the ab machine, no doubt. And after that, some lunges." He raised his voice over the techno crap they were playing, and he looked around the gym, scanning the joint like he was looking for someone.

"This really, really sucks," I said.

"What?" Bobby wasn't paying attention. He was looking around the gym.

"If you hadn't made me quit dancing, I would still be lean." I made sure I said it right in his ear so he could hear me over the bass and noise from all the clinking weights and machines.

"Lean," Bobby said. "You a lot of things, baby, but better cross lean off the list." He laughed. He was cracking himself up. "I gotta appointment," he said. "See you about an hour."

When Bobby walked away, I couldn't help but notice that he *did* look good in his wife-beater T-shirt against his tan skin. From the tanning salon, but still. That's why I put up with him, I thought. That, and he always looked out for me, was always on my side. I told myself that he had me at the gym for my health, for my own good. Plus, once — and only once — he told me that I was so fine, he didn't need to do nothing to make himself look good. I did it for him.

I found a StairMaster and stepped on it, bored off my ass after two steps. I pushed the button that made the machine go faster — but not too fast. I daydreamed I was at the club I used to dance at, the Eight Ball, where I met Bobby. Those were good days. I missed the girls, and I missed the money. I worked where I wanted to work, doing what I wanted to do. I didn't have to do any of that gym shit.

Somebody was talking to me. Amber.

"It's better to lower the resistance. If you're just wanting defini-tion. You don't want to cover your body with a lot of muscle," she said in a soft, clear voice. She sounded like a therapist.

"Yeah," I said. I gave her a half-smile. A polite, now-you-can-go smile. She didn't seem to catch what I was doing, though. She stretched some, and then she got on the StairMaster next to mine. She was wearing one of those I'm-at-the-Gym-to-Be-Looked-At outfits. Cute and strappy. Whenever I tried to wear something like that, Bobby told me to put some clothes on. She worked out on the machine next to me, taking cute little baby steps and swinging her white-blond ponytail around. Everything about her was light and golden tanned. If somebody was looking for the opposite of me, they would have pointed out Amber in a heart-beat. What was the matter with Bobby?

The whole time I was working out, she kept looking at me out of the corner of her eye, making me nervous. I never knew no woman who had a crush on me before. I didn't know how I felt about it. I ignored Amber until Bobby came up behind me and told me to stop leaning. That was cheating, he said. It wasn't good to cheat. Made the whole workout easier.

"Just pretend you're on the stairway to heaven, baby," he said. "And I'm up there waiting for you." I swear, Bobby thought he was a regular actor, a porn actor, a trainer, *and* a comedian.

"La Donna can cheat," Amber said. My name sounded funny coming out of her mouth. She stopped stepping and looked me up and down. "She doesn't even need to work out."

"Rii . . . ight," Bobby said slowly. "Uh-huh."

"La Donna has the most beautiful body in the world. And face, too," Amber said. She winked at me.

"Tiny fuckin' world, eh?" Bobby said. "Yeah? Right?" He looked at Amber for a laugh, but she didn't give it to him. "I'm just kiddin', baby," he said. He popped me on the ass.

"Then why'd you say it?" Amber asked him.

"C'mon," Bobby said. "Donna knows I'm joking, right, baby?"

I gave Bobby my fuck-you eyes. I was kind of pissed at both of them for talking like I wasn't there.

"Anyway, it's not a tiny world. It's a big, big world, Bobby," Amber said. She stared at me. "A whole universe."

Bobby looked at Amber and then at me. "You want we should get some lunch? Maybe I could make us something at the house. I got a bottle of wine, too." He put on the sweet and innocent face. I got loose with wine, Bobby knew. He looked back and forth at me and Amber.

"I've got a previous engagement," Amber said. "Engagement" sounded like she'd added "loser" to the end of it. Bobby just hadn't paid attention. "But, La Donna?" She pulled the band from her ponytail and shook her hair out. "Maybe if we're around here together sometime, we could have a coffee or something."

"That sounds good," Bobby said. But Amber ignored him and touched my hand. "Nice talking to you," she said.

"Be good," Bobby said, and then she gave him the smile I'd given to her earlier. Now go away.

There was going to be what they called an annular eclipse, my astronomy teacher said. On me and Bobby's anniversary, this was going to happen. Professor Salazar spent a whole class period talking about how annular eclipses come once every couple of years or so and only happen when the moon passes right in front of the sun. But it's not able to cover the sun the whole way, because the moon looks smaller than the sun. I thought that was all pretty cool. Stuff I hadn't really thought about. I was trying to tell Bobby all this when we were sitting in front of the TV, watching some dating show where one person goes on a date with a bunch of people and has to get rid of them one by one until they end up with the person they really want.

"And you know what else, Bobby? I learned something else. The moon?" I looked over at him to make sure he was still listening. He didn't seem to be, but I kept talking anyway. "The moon? It's this, like, cold rocky ball of stuff. Doesn't have its own light coming from it. You know why the moon looks so bright at night, Bobby?"

"Why?" He pulled me to him and started twirling one of my braids in his fingers. "Can you believe this? This moron's gonna pick the short girl, the one with the mouth on her, always talking all the time. They oughtta let me on the show." He blew out some air, disgusted.

I snuggled up against Bobby and rubbed his belly under his T-shirt.

"That's nice," he said. "Keep doing that."

"I was telling you about the moon," I whispered, and kissed him on the soft part underneath his armpit. Bobby got still when I did that.

"What about it?" His voice was soft and low, way down his throat.

"I learned that the reason the moon looks so bright is because of the sun. We wouldn't even see the moon if it wasn't for the sun."

"Fascinatin'," Bobby said. He undid the top button of his jeans and waited for me to do the rest.

Amber always seemed to find me at the gym. This time, I was just finishing my workout when she came up to me. I was sweating so much, I looked like I'd just gotten hosed down. I walked real slow on the treadmill and slowed down the speed until I was barely walking. When Amber walked up to me, she said, "I hate the treadmill. I'm so bored when I do it, it's like I'm not even there."

"Mm-hmm," I said. And then, because I sounded like a bitch to my own ears, I said, "Uh, you look like you hardly ever need to do anything in the first place." It seemed like a nice thing to say. I thought she was too skinny, to tell you the truth.

She smiled and stared at me. She had these huge, blue, Barbie doll–looking eyes. A lot of her was Barbie doll–looking. I'm not saying that's bad. I'm just saying.

"I like your body better," she said. "I'd kill for your ass."

That was nice, what she said. I finally smiled at her for real. "Yeah, well. Tell Bobby that."

"I did."

I pretended I didn't hear her.

"*Bobby,*" she said, after a second. Like *please*. "He shouldn't have to be told something so obvious."

I didn't like her talking about Bobby with that tone. But still, what she said had a ring of truth to it.

"Listen," Amber said. She had a nice voice, soft but sure of herself. She came closer to me, and I stopped the treadmill altogether. "Do you—would you like . . . I would love it if we could maybe grab a bite to eat."

I looked around the gym. "With Bobby?"

"No. Not with Bobby."

"Oh," I said.

I felt funny. The thing was, Amber was OK and all that. Even if she looked fake, she wasn't. There was something down home about her. Never thought I'd say that. I talked trash about her for the longest. But a couple of days before, I saw her do something. She got in this big dude's face about leaving the StairMaster all sweaty and disgusting. *Did he think his mother was going to come clean up his filth?* she asked. *Or did he expect one of us other women to clean his shit, before we got to do our own workouts?* He called her a bitch, but wiped it off like she asked. Amber wasn't playing with that fool. I liked that. Lunch with her was something different, though.

"I don't know," I said. "Maybe next time? I kind of want to get home." I did want to get home, even though I didn't really have anything to do once I got there. I just kept seeing Bobby's face, cheesing it up, ecstatic that Amber and I were going to lunch, like he was one number away from winning the lottery.

"Oh," she said. "OK." She stared at me some more, but looked down at her shoes after a second. When she looked up again, she had a little halfhearted smile.

"Real soon, though," I said. Don't ask me why I did this, but I touched her shoulder.

"Next time, then," Amber said, and then walked away. "Next time" sounded like a contract.

Later, at home taking a shower, I turned on the radio real loud, since Bobby wasn't home to have a fit about it. I played music to make me want to dance. Evelyn "Champagne" King. *Champagne.* I liked her attitude. *Got to be real, got to be real.* It was music that I used to dance to when I worked at the Eight Ball. Thinking about being real, Amber came to mind. Every time I saw her, I kept expecting her to get all giggly and white-girl silly over Bobby. Or just be slutty. Everybody else did. But she looked like she could take or leave Bobby. Mostly leave, and keep on stepping. That just made Bobby get even more stupid over her. Amber this and Amber that. I half-wished she'd hit on Bobby so he'd shut up.

Taking a shower was the best part of working out. I stood there and let the water massage my body, little warm needles with dull points. I started laughing out of nowhere, because I remembered this time when me and Bobby decided to smoke some weed and drink about two bottles of red wine.

Bobby had eaten like food was going out of style, but I hadn't eaten a bite because I was trying to be all skinny and dainty and cute and shit. Bobby was on top of me, covering my whole body, practically. He was being extra sweet, extra slow, saying my name in a voice I heard less and less lately. I was hypnotized. High, too. "La Donna," Bobby had whispered, and put his tongue in my ear. Right then, I got sick to my stomach. I jumped up, had to balance myself on the edge of Bobby's futon couch.

"Where's your bathroom?" I moaned.

"What?" Bobby was confused — and hard. "What's wrong with you?"

"I don't feel too good," I said. Bobby only had a studio, so the bathroom was just three steps away. I thought I could make it. Bobby's apartment was practically all white or cream colored. That was a shame. I did make it into the bathroom, but it didn't matter, because I threw up red all over Bobby's clean white bathroom, all over his pomade and creams and ten bottles of cologne. I stayed in there for what seemed like days and months and a lifetime before Bobby knocked and came in without an answer from me. I was on my knees, holding on to the toilet like it was my long-lost friend.

To his credit, Bobby didn't say a word — at first. He just looked at all the red covering every single thing in his bathroom. I hadn't known him long, but I already knew he was the kind of guy who turned a book back to the *exact* position it was in before you picked it up from his table. Bobby only had two books in his house. *His Way*, Frank Sinatra's biography, and *How to Train Your Dog*. But still.

"Are you fuckin' kiddin' me?" he said finally. "You OK? What the hell?"

"Yeah," I said. "No."

"Lemme look at you." Bobby pulled my braids from my face and grabbed a towel from a rack. He wiped all the vomit from my face. "Can you stand up?"

"Yeah." I lifted my head. "There," I said.

"Fuck," Bobby said. He stood me up, leaned me on the sink, and started undressing me. "You gotta get cleaned up. Lemme clean you up."

Somehow, he got me in the shower, bathed me, dried me off, put a T-shirt and socks on me, lay me down on the bed, and pulled the covers over me. Before I passed out, I saw Bobby working in the bathroom with a mop and pail. The same bathroom I was standing in now. I had to remember that thought whenever I wanted to smack Bobby with him getting on me about everything and nothing at all.

I turned off the shower, dried off, and looked at myself in the mirror. I thought I looked OK, everything did except the tits. I'd gotten them done a couple of years ago, when I thought I was supposed to look like all the other strippers with big tits — except I was big all over. I should of known that I'd never look like the skinny white girls, unless I stopped eating — and fuck that. They never ended up feeling like a part of my body, these tits. They were from some other place. But maybe Bobby was right, and Amber was wrong. Bobby could fit a whole inch of my fat in between his fingers when he pinched me, and I didn't want to hear it. I could at least tighten up here and there. Cut down.

I ran out of creative ways to blow off Amber. Every time I saw her, she came at me, asking to have a coffee or lunch, like it was the first time she'd asked me, like I hadn't said, "No, I can't," five times before. So we grabbed a coffee, because lunch seemed like getting in too deep. Once you start eating with somebody, it's hard to get away from them. If I couldn't stand her, I wanted to be able to get up out of there right quick.

Having coffee with Amber made me nervous, like going out on a date. Small stuff was always on my mind, like who would get to the door of the coffee shop first, and who would open it? Was she going to offer to pay for my latte, but why would she, though, since it wasn't a date? Would I trip over my own feet? And was she checking out my body when I walked in front of her? Bobby said she'd mentioned the shape of it more than once. I'd never been nervous around no white girl before, and it felt weird to be jumpy and jittery.

We walked around the corner to some small place, and she *wouldn't* let me pay for my own coffee. When I put my money down, she said, "Please, let me. For the pleasure of your company," and smiled at me. She had two deep dimples in both cheeks that I never noticed before. She said, "Why don't you find a place for us to sit? I'll wait for the coffee and come to you." So that's what I did. My eyes skimmed over everybody reading their papers and typing on their laptops. In a minute, I saw that the coffees were ready, and she came over to me, already talking.

"Did you know that La Donna means 'the woman' in Italian?" She slid into her chair and pushed my coffee toward me. "*The* woman, not even *a*. Like, there are no other women." She grinned at me, showing teeth just as white and perfect as Bobby's. Then her lips closed over them real slow while she stared at me.

"No, I didn't know it meant that in Italian. I think my mama just liked the way it sounded." I was having trouble looking her in the eye, so I looked around the café and stared at some other tiny white girl, who was talking too loud on her cell phone about her doctor's appointment.

"Don't you hate how everyone's always on the phone everywhere you go now?" Amber said, following my eyes. "Like we really want to hear about her shrink's advice or whatever she's talking about."

"I know," I said, because it was all I could think to say. The other tiny woman flipped her blond ponytail and propped her feet up on the table. I thought about how she was making herself at home, taking up space and filling up everybody's ears, as small as she was. I thought about how my mama would smack me for putting my feet up on somebody's table, especially in public. She kept me in check, my mama. *I don't care if you are grown*, she was always saying. Looked like nobody had ever checked this girl before in her life.

"What does Amber mean?" I finally asked, hoping that would get her to stop staring out me so hard.

"Well," she started, running her thin fingers over the top of her coffee glass, "I don't know what it *means*, but I know that amber is this stuff that comes from trees from millions of years ago—"

"I know," I said. "It was this liquid that, like, oozed out of the trees and trapped all kinds of stuff in it, like twigs and bugs . . . all kinds of stuff it picked up along the way. It got hard and turned into stone." Amber's mouth was open and she was squinting her eyes like she was having trouble seeing me. "I just thought maybe Amber meant something else. I don't know why I was thinking that." I kind of laughed at myself and took a sip of my coffee. Amber reached across the table and touched my wrist, real light, with just the tip of her finger.

"Hey, I forgot, you probably know all about this kind of stuff. You're always reading those astrology books and stuff at the gym."

"Astronomy. Astronomy's different. From astrology. And from rocks and stuff."

"I know. I meant astronomy. I'm just saying. I shouldn't have talked like you didn't know what amber was."

"That's OK," I said. I was thinking about her touching me on my wrist. She'd touched me once before, and this time I could still feel her finger there, like a warm spot. I remembered something else I knew about amber. "You know how you can tell fake amber from real amber?

Amber shrugged.

"I learned this once: If you rub real amber with something, it'll turn electric, but plastic fake stuff that's supposed to be real doesn't feel as warm, and it doesn't feel electric."

Amber leaned into the table, put her elbows on it, and then

put her face on her knuckles. "Bobby's real lucky you're his girl-friend," she said. She sat up straight and then pulled at her feet so she was sitting cross-legged in her chair. "And I know you proba-bly think it's weird that I would want to have coffee or lunch with you, but I think you're just beautiful, and I would love it if we could get to know each other better, because I love beautiful, smart women." She took the little paper thing from around the glass that keeps you from burning your hands when your drink is hot and started ripping it into little pieces, just staring at me. She was the worst about that staring, like you were a damn meal and she was starving.

Something about her made me like her, even though she made me feel weird, too. Before, I used to think she was just a silly, blond little white girl, like the one who was *still* talking on her cell phone a few tables over. But there was something real about Amber, even if her lips were fake, her hair color was fake, and all kinds of parts of her body fake. Maybe it was just that she told me I was beautiful in a tone I hadn't heard from Bobby in a month of Sundays. Or maybe it was because she said I was smart matter-of-fact, wasn't being funny about it, believed it. Whatever it was, I felt so weird that I wanted to leave. I looked at my watch and then back at Amber, who looked sad.

"I shouldn't have said what I said."

"No," I said. "What you said was nice, really." And then before I really thought about it, I said, "Maybe we could go out some-time, get to know each other better." We laughed about some of the people at the gym for a little while, and then she told me about how she was a composer, wrote music — and who would have thought that? I took one last sip of my coffee before I stood up. "I should go, though. Bobby's waiting for me back at the gym to give him a ride home."

"OK." She gave me a weak smile and stood up. She came closer to me. "Mind if I give you a hug before we go?" I wanted to make her feel better, like things weren't weird. So I hugged her first. And

I gave her a real hug, I held on for a long second. When we pulled away from each other, she gave me one of those big toothy grins.

"You're a good hugger," she said.

"That's what Bobby says," I said.

"Hmm," she said, like *Bobby, who? Like I give a shit.* Then she turned to leave the café.

Driving Bobby home, I was tired. It was hot, the air conditioning was busted, and traffic was working my nerves almost as much as Bobby.

"So, OK. Wait. She buys you the coffee, and then you guys sit down, and then what?"

"*Nothing.* We just talked." In the car ahead of us, some kid, a boy it looked like, was waving at us from the backseat. I waved back. When I did, though, he gave me the middle finger.

"Motherfucker," I said, my voice high. I flipped the kid off.

"Whoa! Hey!" Bobby said. "A kid and everything. *Nice.*"

I rolled my eyes. "They ought to do something with this street. This is ridiculous."

"She ask you out again? What?"

"*Bobby.*"

"C'mon. *Bobby.* Did she or didn't she?" Bobby bit down on his knuckles.

"You should have drove," I said. Everything about everything bothered me. The kid in front of us was waving something in front of us now, a goddamn doll. He kept flipping me off and waving it, and Bobby kept running his mouth about the three of us fucking, and I couldn't breathe in that hot-ass Mustang anymore.

"Fuck!" I yelled, and banged my hand on the steering wheel. "Fuck!"

"What I tell you?" Bobby said. He thumped me hard on the thigh. "What is your *problem*?"

. . .

He was wanting to know what I wanted for our anniversary. "A whole year with me, sweetheart. Paradise or what, huh?"

"Or what."

"All right, smart-ass. See? Try and be nice to somebody—"

"I'm just playin'!" I stood behind him and hugged him tight.

"Seriously, though," Bobby said. "I want to do something nice for you." He turned and faced me. He kissed me on the forehead.

"I don't know. Maybe just a romantic dinner? Here even. Make me something special, just for me."

"I don't know how to make no chitlins or collard greens or whatever the fuck."

"Well, I don't want none of that weird Greek health shit you're always trying to give me." I pinched him on the side.

"Ow! Bitch." He laughed. "OK, how 'bout I take you out, spend a couple of bucks on you. Someplace nice."

"And I can eat any kind of fattening thing I want without hearing it from you."

"Fine," Bobby said. "I'll hook you up nice, baby."

"Better hook me up nice."

He squeezed me hard, tighter and tighter until I screamed at him, laughing. "Stop, Bobby! Stop! I mean it!"

We went to a place kind of far from where we lived. It was Sandy's in the Marina. I ordered fried chicken, collard greens, macaroni and cheese, and corn bread. Bobby tried to come between me and my macaroni and cheese, but I wouldn't let him. I was feeling good, had a buzz on from the wine we were drinking. All the planets were lined up right, even though Professor Salazar said talk like that was astrology. A world of difference from what he was trying to teach us.

"Happy anniversary, baby," I said. I fed him a bite.

"Hmm, this is good," he said. "How come you never make this for me?"

"What? And hear fat this and fat that? Gimme a break."

"Well, you're right about that. You like my choice, though? A couple of people at the gym said this would be a good place."

I nodded and smiled at him bright. "It's good, Bobby." Really, it was just OK. "You know Hattie's in Leimert Park? That would have been good, too." It would have been a *lot* better. It was in a black neighborhood where they didn't have no marinas.

"Never heard of it." Bobby shook his leg under the table. He was being jittery and distracted all during dinner. Biting his nails, jiggling his leg, and playing with his hair.

"What's wrong with you?" I worked on my peach cobbler.

"Nothing," Bobby said. He lifted our wine bottle off the table to show the waiter we needed another bottle of wine. He smiled and winked at me.

"'Member the time," I took a drink from my glass, "that time I threw up in your bathroom?"

"Christ, La Donna, you gotta bring that up now?" He nodded at my wineglass. "Better slow down with that."

"That was funny, though, Bobby. Almost a year ago. Can you believe it?"

"Yeah, funny to you."

I put my fork down and pushed my plate away some. Bobby took my fork and finished off my pie. "That was sweet, though, Bobby. How you cleaned me up, cleaned up everything." I leaned into the table, trying to get as close to him as I could. I thought I was the luckiest woman sitting with the finest man in the whole place. I felt so close to Bobby, so happy, I was thinking he must have been feeling it, way across the table, me shining everything on Bobby.

"What," he said. "Like I had a choice."

I was smiling at Bobby before, but I stopped. "What do you mean? Course you had a choice."

"If you think I was gonna let my bathroom stay vomity, you're crazy, and if you think I'm gonna let a vomity woman sleep passed out next to me, you're even more crazy."

I hadn't ever thought of it like that. A cloud passed over my face.

Bobby looked at me. "Don't start."

I looked around the restaurant and sank down in my chair.

"Come on. Don't get mad. Come here."

I sat still.

"Come here," Bobby said. When I ignored him, he said, "All right. I thought it was kind of cute, you puking all over my god-damn bathroom. The cutest, sexiest shit I ever saw."

I tried not to smile at that, but Bobby could be funny some-times. He saw me trying not to smile.

"Lemme kiss you, then I'll tell you your surprise."

I sat up straight. Hard to do after my fourth glass of wine. "What surprise?"

"I ain't gonna tell you till you kiss me."

I did. "Well?"

"OK," Bobby cracked his knuckles and then took both my hands. "I got something waiting for you back home."

"What? What Bobby? What is it?" I got happy, got rid of that cloud real fast. I knew it was that telescope I'd pointed out to Bobby one day when we were shopping. It cost a fortune — a fortune to me and Bobby, but if he'd been thinking about me at all this year, even a little bit, he would have been saving up for it. I'd dragged him into the shop and pointed it out to him, plain and obvious. He said I must have wanted to blow my teacher; that was the only reason I'd be so into the "most boring shit on the planet. The fuckin' stripping astrologist. That's funny," Bobby had said.

"Astronomy," I had said.

He turned down the corners of his mouth and shrugged. "Whatever."

But maybe he was just trying to throw me off the trail. "You got me that telescope, didn't you?" I said it like I was accusing him of something and happy to bust him.

Bobby stopped grinning. "Wha? Nah. I didn't get you any fuckin' telescope. This is better. Way better."

My heart started beating real fast and my hands started shaking. Bobby had gotten me a ring. "It's a ring!" I screamed. Some folks in the restaurant turned to look at us.

"What? A *ring*," Bobby said, blowing out of his nose. "That's funny. Wow," he said, shaking his head.

I blinked and frowned at him. I was confused. "Then what? What'd you get me?"

Bobby looked into my eyes. Serious. He glanced over his shoulder before he leaned into me as close as he could. He smiled. "OK, don't freak out."

"Yeah?" I smiled back at him.

"At home? Right now? I got Amber waiting for you."

"Amber?" I was still confused. "What for?"

"What *for*," Bobby said. "Don't be cute."

My hands were in Bobby's. I squeezed his hands as hard as I could, letting everything he was telling me find a place to settle in my head. "You're telling me" — I took a deep breath — "that Amber. Amber from the gym. She's in our apartment. Waiting for us. For all of us to have sex."

"That's right," Bobby said, hopeful, kind of holding his breath.

"That's your present. To me. My anniversary present."

I didn't know whether to cry or punch Bobby in his perfect actor face. I couldn't look him in the eye, because I was afraid I'd cry, which would have made me real pissed at myself.

"It's *part* of your present." He reached into his jacket pocket in the chair next to us.

Bastard. He was just playing. He handed me a long velvet box. When I snapped it open, there was a shiny gold chain in it, with a little white stone attached to it.

"You like it? I got you this, too. It's a moonstone. I told the guy at the place what you liked, and he said this, you'd like." Bobby looked like he was really wanting me to like his present, but I couldn't fake it.

I turned the stone over in my hand. It was beautiful and felt cool in my palm. "*Too?*" I said finally. "So you're not kidding about the Amber stuff."

"Uh-uh," Bobby said.

I held the chain in my hands. Amber was in my apartment. Bobby asked her to be there. Or did she ask?

"Ah, fuck. I shouldn't of told you," Bobby said. "I should of just got you home. See what happened when you got there."

"You should have seen." My voice had no life in it. "You're really fucking crazy, Bobby. You know that?"

"What? You said you were down, might try this someday."

"I was just *playing*. I wasn't for *real*."

"Then why'd you say all that stuff then?"

"I was just half-kidding!"

"What half, Donna?" Bobby was yelling. "And we got Amber waiting there and everything. . . . She's going to feel really shitty about this. I told her it would work out."

I poured myself more wine, shook my head slow and careful.

Bobby threw up his hands. They dropped down loud on his thighs. "She's supposed to be waiting in the closet. I'm supposed to call, and she's supposed to get in the closet when we get there, and I'm supposed to put a blindfold on you, get all sexy and loose with you, and then that's when we were going to surprise you."

I put my head in both my hands and coughed out a laugh.

"Then what am I supposed to tell Amber?"

"What do I care, Bobby. Tell her whatever you want. You did that already. She can stay in the closet all night."

Bobby's eyes followed people leaving the restaurant. "We gotta tell her something, Donna. It ain't nice."

"It ain't nice, Donna," I said in a deep, fake Bobby voice.

"You're fuckin' drunk," he said. He saw the waiter and then motioned for the check. "And you better not get sick in the car."

I fell asleep on the way home. I was full of wine and food. I felt heavy. I didn't dream about stuff, nothing at all. I stayed asleep until we got off the freeway. You always do that, stay asleep when you're riding, until you get off the freeway. Something about going so fast, the sound of the air *swooshing* by, like floating, being in a trance. But then, when you feel the car slowing down, going down the off ramp, you can feel some kind of change, something about the ride feels different, even if you're in a deep sleep, dreaming. You wake up.

We were in the garage of the apartment building. The building was shitty, the stucco all stained and peeling, but all the cars in the garage were nice.

"Hey," Bobby said. He touched my face. "You all right? You not sick or nothing? You can get out, right?"

I nodded. Bobby came around and helped me out. He was trying to be nice.

"Didn't you say there was going to be one of those eclipses today?" He put his arms around me and walked to the elevator.

"It wasn't that great," I said. Bobby pushed the UP button, and we got in and went up. Earlier that day, I'd spent a half hour standing outside. I put a hole in a piece of paper, turned my back to the sun, and looked down on the sidewalk while all the cars sped by me on the street. I saw a little bitty old shadowy thing that looked like a moon with a bright light all around the edges. It wasn't as cool as Professor Salazar said. But he said we had to see it that way, with the filter and everything, or else we'd burn the shit out of our eyes. He didn't say "shit," but he said we really,

really didn't want to look straight at the eclipse or else we could really hurt ourselves.

I wasn't drunk — *as* drunk — as I was at the restaurant. I thought of Amber waiting for me in the apartment, and I thought it would be nice to see her.

The elevator bell rang when we got to our floor. When we got to our apartment, Bobby put his key in the door and looked at me before he turned it.

"I don't care," I said, which was the truth. Being with Amber sounded better than being alone with Bobby just then. She would look at me like she really wanted me, like she knew what I was, and I wanted that.

Bobby opened the door and I went to the couch. I started taking off all my clothes. Bobby, too. He stood in front of me and put a scarf around my eyes. There was a little slash I could still see through, so I squeezed my eyes shut. I still wasn't sure how far I was going to go, even if I was already in the middle of it, anyway. I lay down on the carpet. Bobby didn't want the lights off. He wanted to be able to see everything; but me, I wasn't supposed to be able to tell when Bobby stopped touching me and when Amber started.

I knew right away, though. Amber's hands were light and smooth. They moved all over my hips and breasts, between my legs. Warm, soft hands, gentle hands that felt like liquid. Her hands were so warm I felt tingly, like I was on fire. I still had the blindfold on, but when I looked through the little slash, I saw Amber on her hands and knees between me and Bobby. Amber felt good, but she didn't come close enough to what I wanted. I wanted how Bobby used to make me feel. I wanted something bigger than me. I could sort of make out Bobby moving slow behind Amber, like a shadow. "You like that, Sunshine? You like that?" he was whispering to me. But I didn't feel like sunshine, not like I usually did when he called me that. Bobby thought the three of us together in that room was big, a big thing that would take his mind off Louie. But he was still trapped, doing without seeing. And now, there was something, *somebody* between us. I was in it, seeing it. Me and him and Amber wasn't half as good as he talked about it being. I was disappointed in everybody and everything. But at least I could finally see clear.

U NDERDOG

By Judy Budnitz

un·der·dog \'ən-dər-,dóg\ *noun* [origin unknown] (1887) 1: a loser or predicted loser in a struggle or contest. 2: a victim of injustice or persecution. 3: a neglected, underappreciated guy. *See also:* JESUS COMPLEX, TEACHING NEW TRICKS TO OLD DOGS.

My wife makes a patchwork man and hangs him in the garden.

"Is that really necessary?" I say.

"The rabbits," she says, "have been getting into the tomatoes." She shows me one with a huge gouge in it. No rabbit could have made that. Unless it was a monster bunny. It looks like the work of a rabid beaver.

"Rabbits don't even like tomatoes," I say.

"It's an acquired taste," she says.

"They can't even reach the tomatoes."

"They have cute little stepladders," she says.

I don't care if they take all the tomatoes, since I don't even like them. They're heirloom tomatoes, which to her means they're precious and gourmet, and to me means they're big and mutatious and ugly. And my wife used to love *all* animals, great and small. Why would she want to scare them away?

The patchwork man, out there on his stick, is undeniably waving at us.

"It's a windy day," she says brightly.

I look at him harder. "Hey, isn't that my tie?"

"But you never wear it."

"You gave it to me. For my birthday."

"Exactly."

I go out to the garden to study him closer. He's smaller than I thought. Pretty flimsy. The wind keeps tugging him around. He seems flexible, fluid in the joints, and moves in sudden, unpredictable spasms. The way he moves reminds me of those horrible mimes. You never know when they're going to come up to you and do their creepy invisible wall thing. Or even worse, do that mirror thing where they imitate you in front of a big crowd of people.

The patchwork man is all pieces, like a jigsaw puzzle stitched together. My wife is a decent sewer. Bits of her clothes, and mine, and other stuff all mixed up. The guy's got a huge stupid smile on his face. I'm not a smiley guy. I'm a nice guy, I'm a good person, I just don't smile much. He's got a little curly mustache. I don't. What's that supposed to mean?

He's thinner than me, I admit it. He doesn't have a gut like I do. She could have given him a gut, easily, if she'd wanted to, with a little extra stuffing.

I give him a good punch. He whips around on the stick but doesn't really go anywhere.

I can't stop thinking about *The Wizard of Oz*, and how Dorothy liked the Scarecrow best. They never really explained why. Just because he met her first? Is it all about longevity? In that case, I should get points. I punch him a few more times. "Ha. Beat you to it, straw man."

Where does jealousy come from? I can't remember when it

started, when suddenly it seemed that everything with eyes started ogling my wife. We used to be so happy.

I punch him until he sags and stuffing is leaking out of his seams. He's almost falling off his post, his head drooping. There's something familiar about it, his knees together and turned to one side, head down, arms stretched out. Oh, no. He looks like Jesus. This is not good. Those door-to-door people with their pamphlets will never leave us alone now. I try to fluff him back up, separate his legs. Eventually, he lifts his head and smiles at me.

I go inside. I hear her rustling around in the bedroom. I go up there and find her naked in bed under the patchwork quilt. We've had that quilt for years, but now it makes me feel queasy to see her body covered in patches. I look out the window and, sure enough, there's the scarecrow looking right in, checking her out and smiling.

I met my wife at a low point in my life. It was after I wrecked the van, after the grease fire, after the sexual harassment accusations, after the memos placed in everybody's office mailbox and posted in the bathrooms (both male and female), showing my picture above the words DO NOT DATE THIS MAN. It was the year I became a walker.

"A walker?" I'd said to the woman at the employment agency. "You mean, like, dogs?"

"No," she said. "I mean, like, people." I did not like her tone; I wanted to tell her that she had no right to judge me. I could see all the places where she'd tried to cover up pimples with pink makeup, I could see the line along her jaw where the foundation ended. She had fat fingers. But she had every right to judge me. That was her job. She'd looked at my credentials and seen I was not really qualified to do much of anything. The one thing I was good at was focus groups, getting paid fifty bucks a day to sit around a table in front of a one-way mirror, talking about potato chips or shampoo.

I found out that being a walker meant occasionally offering an arm or carrying a bag of groceries but mostly just walking beside a person, an elderly person, just being there. In case something happened. Spontaneously broken hips; rollerbladers knocking them down; tripping over dog leashes; forgetting their keys or where they were going or where they lived; arguments with impatient bank tellers; untied shoelaces (most of them could not bend); sudden bouts of incapacitating sadness that made them freeze, weeping on the sidewalk. This happens more than you might expect. And not just to old people.

I got a walker job with a Mr. Murray. On the first day, he informed me that I was a temporary replacement; his usual walker was on maternity leave. "She's had three kids in the time she's been with me. As soon as this little niglet gets big enough, she'll be back."

I didn't know what to do. "Um," I said. "That's an ugly thing to say. You shouldn't say things like that."

"Oh, so you're going to call me a racialist now? Jim?"

"Joey."

"Is that some kind of fag name?"

"No," I said. Maybe it is; I don't know. Looking back, I wonder if maybe saying no makes me a homophobe. Maybe I should have taken a stand. These things get so confusing sometimes. I wanted to tell him that I was quitting, but then I thought of the flyers, the picture of me grinning maniacally in front of horizontally striped wallpaper that made it look like I was in a lineup.

"Are you some kind of mental patient? Why would a healthy, young man like you need a job like this?"

"Carpal tunnel syndrome," I said. "Bad back. Lots of chemical allergies. A.D.D."

"You have a kind of nutty look. I'll keep my eye on you."

I spent a few hours a day with him. I wondered if he had

Tourette's. It was the most hazardous job I've ever had. He had a loud, stentorian, professorial voice and would comment on every person he saw on the street. He used ugly words, he used words I had to look up later. He used words like *coolie* and *coon*. He called a pretty teenage girl a sodomite, and then he told her friend she looked like a woman of ill repute. I had to be constantly explaining, making excuses, blocking blows. The sharp corner of one woman's purse left a triangular dent in my forehead for weeks. I dredged up words like *Alzheimer's, senility, Parkinson's, dementia* — anything that sounded vaguely medical and mitigating.

On the weekends, I went around tearing down the flyers. They were everywhere; they seemed to be multiplying. That woman really had it in for me. I couldn't get away from them. Strangers on the street would look twice at me; a few times people would say, "Haven't I seen you somewhere before?" I couldn't escape the thing. I hadn't done anything wrong. Or maybe I'd done one little thing wrong. But I wasn't a bad person. I was a good person — *I was.* Wasn't I a better person than someone like Mr. Murray, who'd spent his entire lifetime calling people niggers and fags? I knew better than that.

There were fresh flyers on the lampposts every weekend. A bike messenger ran over my foot. A toddler shot a bird at me as his mother wheeled him past in a stroller. When I shot one back, his mother stopped and lectured me for half an hour. That night, I got thrown out of a bar for barging into the women's bathroom. I'd only been trying to get to the flyers in there, but no one gave me a chance to explain.

I overslept the next day, missed my usual appointment with Mr. Murray. Later, I got a call and learned that he'd gone out without me, had an accident, and was now in the hospital. He'd been hit by a car, the nurse said. "Just tapped, probably," she said, "but he's very delicate." I suspected he'd probably been pushed out in the street by someone he'd said something unpleasant to. Someone Asian or bald or fat or Irish or wearing the wrong pants — the possibilities were numerous.

I went to see him in the hospital. His face was a mess of purples and greens, it looked all crumpled and caved in, like a wet paper bag; his arms and legs looked frail and spindly. There was still dried blood in his white hair. I felt terrible. "You're the worst walker I've ever had, bar none," he said. "You're a pathetic human being." He picked up his cane from the bedside and heaved it at me like a javelin. It hit me smack in the nose.

It didn't hurt all that much — the cane had a rubber tip for traction — but it must have hit at a lucky angle, or something, because I felt a pop deep inside my head, then blood started gushing out of my nose and wouldn't stop. It was warm and wet, on my face and neck and all over my shirt; it felt like tears. Not that I cry much. I tried to be quiet and just watch the television, but after a while, Mr. Murray told me to leave because I was making him nauseous. "Give me back my cane before you go. Where's the clicker?"

I walked out of the hospital and around the parking lot to a different entrance, the one with ambulances, and I waited a long time in the emergency room. The blood pulsed out steadily. Big drops kept splatting on the floor. I'd been fired from my walker job. I was lower than low. I was bleeding out through my nose, and I imagined my heart all parched and dried out, wringing out the last few drops. "Clear!" the doctors would say, the way they do on medical TV shows, as they pressed electrical paddles to my nose, which was now an enormous throbbing thing barely attached to my face.

Finally, a nurse noticed me. She kneeled before me, right in the blood, and looked up into my face. She was a vision of lightness and purity. "How long has it been bleeding?" she asked, looking up my nose. She had large green eyes with skinny eyebrows puckered up in a concerned frown. Her nostrils were tiny and perfect. Her hands were cool and smooth on my face. And then she smiled, and she had, honest to God, the biggest teeth you've ever seen. She could gnaw down a forest with those teeth. They were just gorgeous, dazzling. I tried to tell her this but couldn't with all the blood in my mouth. I tried to tell her again, much later, and somehow didn't phrase it correctly — I'm no poet — and it made her cry for days. Forever after, she'd smile in a self-conscious closed-lipped way, except when she forgot; and then, the smile would burst out again, and it would be like one of those blinding summer days that burn into your retinas, making you feel like you'd be able to see even with your eyes closed. Magical, like that.

That was the beginning of it, and I had high hopes about her; but I wasn't certain until a few weeks later, when she brought me to her sister's wedding. It was a Jewish wedding, and when the groom stepped on the wineglass at the close of the ceremony, a big shard of glass went right through his shoe and into his heel. My future wife didn't blink an eye as she whipped out her little medical kit from her jeweled purse and stitched up his foot then and there, to the sounds of the band playing "Hava Nagila." That just blew me away; that was when I knew she had to be my future wife. She completed me. She was everything I was not — resourceful, responsible, intelligent, capable, compassionate, employed.

You'd think I'd never have half a chance with a woman like that. But fortunately, she had a weakness for sad and pathetic creatures. The three-legged dogs of the world.

"Now what are you doing?"

She's all set up at the window with her bird-watching book prominently propped up and the binoculars pointing nowhere near any birds. "Watching beautiful Billy next door," she says.

I give her two chances, because I'm a nice guy. But when I catch her at it again, all camped out at the window with the birding book not even open — well, that's the straw that breaks the camel's hump. Or something.

I go over there in my steel-toe boots, with my hedge clippers, thinking I'll crunch the lock off his door if I have to. But I don't have to, the door's wide open, so I breeze right in. God, it's a mess in here. We're not neighborly, I've never met him, I don't even know how long he's been here. Many stenches are emanating from many different locales. I walk through, kicking stuff. "Billy? Billy?" Maybe he's dead. Maybe someone killed him already. Then I won't have to.

"Billy?" I hear dripping. I find him in the bathroom. He's propped up in the tub, one arm trailing on the floor, head tipped back, blissful face. He looks like Marat in his bath in that famous painting that my wife likes. Minus the turban and stab wounds. "Hey," I say. The eyes open and blink.

"Might you be Billy?" I say. I've got those hedge trimmers, understand.

"I might," he says, and stands up. The water streams off him. My God, he is beautiful. He's svelte and languorous, with long, greasy black curls. He's dark and high cheekboned in some Mediterranean or Hispanic or Native American way.

He says, "Who are you?"

I say, "I'm the jealous husband." When he doesn't say anything, I say, "Next door. Binoculars. Get it?"

"I don't even know your wife," he says.

"When I get through with you, you're gonna wish you did," I say.

"What?" he says. "What's that supposed to mean?" He leans on my shoulder to climb out of the tub. I don't get it. He's not only unarmed, he's naked. And little. And yet I'm the one getting pushed around? I'm a big person. I don't push easy. I'd like to really, really hurt him.

I get all close to him and all up in his face. He'll squash like a bug. But I can't do it. I just can't. He's too beautiful. It would be like smashing a Ming vase, or a Grecian urn, or even a really nice pitcher from Crate & Barrel. It would be such a waste.

He offers me a beer. We go sit in the living room. Or should I say the many-piles-of-crap room. He looks like a guy who smokes a lot of pot. I wonder why he doesn't offer me any. Do I not look like a fun guy? Am I too old?

"Man," he says, "you need to get your priorities straight."

"You're right," I say. He is.

We watch public television for a long time. "Man, those antelopes are really something," he says. "Look at 'em go. *Boing, boing, boing.*" He makes an antelope of his fingers and hops it around the furniture. His hand lands on my knee for a second, and I wonder if he's making a pass at me. But he doesn't seem to notice and keeps bouncing his hand around. If that's flirting, he's flirting with his couch a lot more than he's flirting with me.

"Those are gazelles, anyway," I say.

"But antelopes, man," he says. "Wow. Crossbreed 'em? Antelopazelles?"

He must be high. Somehow, he smoked a joint when I wasn't looking. Or just stuffed a big handful of weed in his mouth. Either that or he's just really, really stupid.

"Are you leaving?" he asks.

"I might be," I say.

"Here's your clippers," he says. He's been playing with them.

"You should maybe put on some clothes," I say.

"Come back when you're in a better mood."

I go back across the yard. My wife is waiting for me, tapping her foot. I wonder how long she's been tapping. It's probably just for effect, but it would be cool if she's been doing it for two hours. We could make a video and send it to the Guinness people.

"What were you doing?" she says.

"Just straightening things out," I say. "Beautiful Billy. Ha."

"Was that really necessary?"

"Beautiful my foot."

"You're getting worse and worse. Do I need to take you back to the hospital?"

"Why? So we can volunteer for experiments again for a lousy

thirty bucks? So they can do that thing where they stick me full of needles and darts, and you act like you can feel my pain?"

"No. So they can do that thing where they stuff you full of pills, and you act like a normal human being."

"I don't like that experiment."

"Now what are you doing?"

She says, "Jesus, Billy, what does it look like I'm doing? I'm feeding the birds."

"What did you call me?"

"What? I said Joey."

"You are treading on thin ice, woman."

The birds are swarming all around her. You can't even see the driveway. I don't know what kind they are, I should grab her bird-watching book. There are big black ones and brown ones and small black ones with yellow beaks and sparkly bits. They're coming so close to her, not to the point of perching on her shoulders or eating from her hands, not that Disney-ish, but close. They're huddled all around her, warbling, and cooing. Her face, before I came out, was lost, blissful. You could say they're just there for the food, but I know the truth. They're leaving their splotchy white love letters all over the driveway.

What I don't like is the way they keep flapping around. Up, down, spiraling around her in a whirlwind. Between her face and mine.

"You can't do this."

"Why not?"

"They're mine."

"What?"

"These are my birds. You can't feed them. Find your own."

She doesn't even argue, just flounces into the house, kicking birds out of the way.

I stand looking at my flock for a minute. They're just dumb, dirty birds.

I go back inside. She's waiting, tapping her foot. She's still wearing her raincoat, it has little, white bird-splatters on it. She doesn't look at all sexy, but I'm sure there's some pervert out there somewhere who would find a shit-splattered raincoat with my wife in it a huge turn-on.

"Just tell me, Joey. What is it? What do you want me to do?"

"I want you to stop looking at other men. Is that so wrong?"

She rolls her eyes.

I spell it out: "Other men. Other males. Males of any species. Mammal, reptile, fish, fowl. Inanimate objects in the shape of a man."

"What do you suggest I look at then, Joey? There's not much left."

"Look at the walls. Look at the TV. Look at the sunset. Look at yourself. Look at our kids, for God's sake." Our kids! I forgot all about our kids! Where have they been all this time? What if there's been an accident? Are they okay? I race up the stairs to their room, yank open the door, my heart pounding, expecting to find a couple of curled-up, starved-to-death corpses.

There's a mop. The vacuum cleaner. A dusty, old card-board Rubik's Cube Halloween costume. "Where the hell are the kids?"

She's standing right behind me. "We haven't had the kids yet, remember?"

"Of course," I say. Strange how I forget. When we moved here, we labeled this room the kids' room. Sometimes, we'd pretend there really were kids in it; I'd go in there and yell at them to clean it up, and then my wife and I would laugh like mad and then make love, the whole time whispering to each other, "Shhhhh, shhhh. The kids might hear." At some point, I'm not sure when, we stopped playing the game. But I keep on thinking they're in there, the kids. When my wife's eyes veer away when I'm talking, when she disappears for hours and comes home smelling of perfume samples, when she pushes my hand away— I think of the kids. I tell myself that she won't ever leave me, if for nothing else than for the sake of the kids. She cares about family; she wouldn't want to raise kids in a broken home.

There's a disease I read about— histoplasmosis. You can catch it from bird droppings, even bat guano. You breathe in the spores, and then it infects you; it causes a swelling of the membranes around the heart. I'm not making this up. Bob Dylan had it. I think I have it, too. I have an ache here, under the sternum. It gets worse when I look at her. Can you get histoplasmosis from your wife?

She's decided that if she's not allowed to look at anything else, she'll look at me all day. It's nice for a while, I like the attention. But after a whole night of feeling her eyes creep over me like beetles, I start to feel like my skin is blistering and peeling away. I wish I had a job; I'd go to it. I'd work overtime. I'd make tons of money, buy her piles of gifts, buy her anything she wants, buy a bottle of champagne for her, buy a huge steak for dinner and come home and tape it over her face to stop her staring at me like that.

"Stop it!"

"Stop what?"

"I can't stand it anymore! You with your wanton eyes!"

"I'm just sitting here."

"I feel like a piece of meat."

"You used to like it."

"You're lascivious and unsubtle. It's disgusting."

"These are my bedroom eyes. My come-hither eyes."

"Yeah, come hither and I'll bite your head off and gnaw on your bones' eyes."

"What are you watching there?"

"I don't know! A television program! It's funny! You'll love it! Watch it! Please!"

"I can't," she says. "There are men in it."

"How much longer are you going to keep this up?"

"I thought men loved being the focus of attention."

She puts on sunglasses, but that's even worse; I can't see her eyes, but I can feel them sliding all over me. I go in another room, and her eyes are boring through the wall.

I leave, slamming the door behind me. I move in with beautiful Billy. I don't really move in, but I hide there quite often. He doesn't notice for a while. It's nice to be invisible for a change. Then he notices, but thinks I just happen to be visiting a lot. At night, I sit in his living room and impersonate a pile of random crap, and he doesn't even see me. Then finally, he really notices and says, "Are you ever going to leave?"

Not for a while. I feel safe here. I brought my wife's binoculars so I can keep an eye on her and be sure she's not spying on us.

Why does love turn bad? How do these things happen? I didn't do anything wrong. I'm a good person. I was honest with her. I was never unfaithful or unkempt. Why did she pull away from me?

I stay at Billy's until I see her packing up her car. I'm afraid she might pack up the patchwork man to take with her (put him in the front passenger seat — then she could use the car-pool lane) or invite beautiful Billy to come along. But she leaves them both behind. She waves toward Billy's house as she gets behind the wheel. I see the flash of her splendid teeth. It's like the flash of a shipwrecked sailor signaling for help with a mirror. She knows I'm in here watching. She can probably see my eyes between the window shade and the sill. I want to run out to her, but I know I have to make her come to me. She knows I'm here. She has to prove herself. So I wait. And wait.

I stay here until she's long gone.

And then I stay a little longer, because the house over there is empty and sad, because our kids' room is full of cobwebs and will never have kids in it (barring some freak of nature), and because the driveway is full of bird shit. Nothing is waiting for me over there but histoplasmosis and heartache. I stay because Billy really is beautiful to look at, even when he's picking spilled shreds of marijuana out of his navel. I am far from homosexual, but I can appreciate beauty in art, and in cars, and in living things. I stay until Billy says my child-molester eyes are creeping him out and messing with his high, and he pushes me out the door.

V ITRIOL

By Shelley Jackson

vit·ri·ol \\'vi-trē-əl\\ *noun* [Middle English, from Middle French, from Medieval Latin *vitriolum,* alteration of Late Latin *vitreolum,* neuter of *vitreolus* glassy, from Latin *vitreus* vitreous] (14th century) 1: a sulfate of any of various metals (as copper, iron, or zinc); *especially:* a glassy hydrate of such a sulfate. 2: something felt to resemble vitriol, usually in caustic quality; *especially:* virulence of feeling or of speech as exhibited by a lover.

One morning, I found a puddle under my bed. It was small and the dull yellow-green color of the foliage in old paintings and had a halo of tiny, shiny blisters that burst incessantly and were replaced by others that showed not the puddle's own volatility but the devastation of the varnish on the floor. I dipped my finger in it and brought my finger to my nose. It smelled bitter and familiar.

"My mother has cut me out of her will," you said, "and will not allow my name to be mentioned in her house." You showed me a punitive gift from her. It was a family portrait in which you did not appear. In your place was a hole in the shape of you. Only your fingers were left, clenched in your sister's hand. The edges of the hole were not scissored but rough, brittle, and discolored.

"What happened?" I asked.

"Vitriol," you said. "Bile."

It smelled familiar and remorseful, and it seethed slightly upon my fingertip and stung under my nail, and when I wiped my finger on my jeans I noticed that my fingertip had gone white and powdery and that my cuticles still burned. I washed my finger and found that some of the white wiped off, but not all, and my finger felt unpleasantly smooth. Later, my same finger wandering found a hole seared through my jeans where I had wiped the finger.

Your mother's difficult love had made all love difficult for you. When you began to love me, you asked me to let you read my journal. "Now that I love you, you have power over me. I need you to give me something personal so I have power over you, too," you said. "How can you expect me to trust you if you won't trust me?"

"Let her," Nolan said. "Love invents its own rules."

"Let her," Madeline said. "But then leave her."

You took my journal into the bathroom and locked the door. When you came out, I saw your face, severe.

You wouldn't give my journal back. So much for trust.

Where I had wiped the finger, my leg hurt. I could see through the hole that my skin had gone intricately bumpy, as if nettle-stung. The pain gave me a peculiar satisfaction. It was my pain, only mine. I went to the puddle and I dipped my finger in it and I painted my mouth with it. It hurt, fizzing softly.

I might have left you, but I couldn't let you keep my journal. I went to get it back. In your anger, you had thrown my shoes out the window into the neighbors' yard. You pointed them out from your window. One was caught in the top of a bush, the other lay next to the rotting sofa, where the stray cats fought or fucked — you could never tell the difference. My shoes looked worried and foolish there. We laughed at them. Then we had sex.

Fizzing softly in the darkness, my obnoxious secret grew. I checked it every morning. I cultivated it like a grievance.

When you gave my journal back, you said, "Someday I will ask to see this again." Although you had already read it (but surely not every word), I went through the whole thing and scribbled out everything I thought might offend you. I tore out whole pages, adding lines to the tops of the following pages to close the gaps. These offending pages I destroyed. I mailed my other notebooks to my parents for safekeeping. I congratulated myself for my cunning.

I cultivated it like a grievance I would one day charge to you, and every day I took a little from the growing puddle with a turkey baster and made ablutions with it. I washed my hands with it. I douched with it. I squirted a little stream from the baster into my eyes. When I could see again, it was with eyes that had learned not to trust too easily.

I showed you photographs, but when you saw a naked picture of me, you railed against me, not believing I had taken it myself with a tripod and self-timer. I went through my photographs and got rid of all the other ones I thought might bother you, like an old picture of my ex with no clothes on; I even destroyed the negatives, knowing you were subtle.

I made ablutions with it, and I learned to love its rigors. It stripped my fingers of their prints. My hands grew as anonymous and smooth as marble. My period stopped. My eyelashes fell out. I gargled, and grew mute.

There was nothing I did not examine with your eye for the unfor-givable, because I knew you noticed everything. You paid atten-tion to syntax, to sentences interrupted in midstream, to wrong numbers and non sequiturs. I lied about these things even when the truth was blameless, because it was easier than explaining, and more and more I kept my mouth shut.

I grew mute, but I could write. One day, I dipped a pen in the bile. At first my writing was invisible, but pretty soon the ink ate into the paper, leaving a hundred holes in the shape of letters. It was not impossible to read these missing words. The silhouette of a girl cut out of a photograph can still be recognized and may be a better likeness than her image was.

When I wrote in my journal, I typed it up on the computer that I used at school, gave the files deceptive names like English 101 Syllabus, crumpled the handwritten originals and hid them inside take-out boxes and paper cups, which I discarded in other people's wastebaskets. I learned that I was a deceiver after all, just as you had feared. I took a vengeful pleasure in this.

A hundred holes were not enough to speak my mind. I injected the bile into the ink cartridge in the printer that I use at school. I am printing out my journal. I would like you to have a copy. Every page is blank, but the acid is at work in the paper fibers. By the time you get it, my life will be written down in absentia. You can read every single thing I thought about you. Read that I loved you, and that I'm gone.

If you can't say something nice, don't say anything at all, your mother always said. I've taken that advice. But take a good look at what I haven't said. I've learned to write that way. Now you'll learn to read.

WORSHIP

By Michele Serros

wor·ship \\'wər-shəp\\ *noun* [Middle English *worshipe* worthiness, respect, reverence paid to a divine being, from Old English *weorth-scipe* worthiness, respect, from *weorth* worthy, worth + *-scipe* -ship] (before 12th century) 1: (*chiefly British*) a person of importance—used as a title for various officials (as magistrates, mayors, or members of the Rolling Stones). 2: reverence offered a divine being, supernatural power, or celebrity. 3: a form of religious or dating practice with its creed and ritual. 4: extravagant respect or admiration for or devotion to an object of esteem <*worship* of a rock star>.

I didn't dig drummers anymore. They sweat too much, never make the front of any band photos, and always whine 'cause nobody ever wants to hear the songs they write. Singers—well, singers are just pretty boys with ugly egos. And lead guitarists? *Please.*

Leonard played bass. I'd never been with a bassist before. "A Fender Precision," he bragged. "With an extra-long neck." The minute he said that, I knew it would only be a matter of time before I moved out on No-Talent Gary, leaving that drum-banging loser to cry with that stinky ol' cat of his.

Angela introduced me to Leonard backstage at one of his shows. Unlike Gary, Leonard was already on his way up. He was from the East Coast. Not New York City, but a town pretty close, he said. Minutes into our first conversation, I was already play-fully tugging at his arm, sharing his drink, and calling him Lenny. By our third date, he became Wenny, a name I pouted in a full-blown baby voice.

Maybe it was the pouty voice that did it, 'cause in less than a month, Lenny had helped me to load all my stuff from the studio apartment that I shared with Angela and had moved me into the band's house with him. *The band's house.* Does it get any better than that?

Our first weeks together as lovers, we were too selfish to share time with anyone else. Afraid we'd miss out on each other's new-ness, we'd stay awake for hours into the night, sometimes just looking into each other's eyes, not saying anything. Sometimes we'd get more playful and fling rubber bands at some water beetle racing across the bedroom wall.

I remember one morning when Lenny had his head on my belly, half-asleep and gazing at all his amps, basses, and equip-ment and stuff. He confided in me a dream he had just had.

"Man, Lenny," I responded, after hearing the whole thing, "that was something. You know, I read somewhere that crazy dreams like that are the sign of a creative person."

"Really? You think I'm creative?"

"Absolutely, yeah."

"I wish the guys would think so." It was then that he realized just how important I was in nurturing him as an artist, supporting him and his music. And it was the following month that Lenny demanded to his unsupportive band mates that I go on their European tour with him. He warned me that it was to be a short tour, only six weeks, he said. It would be winter and it would be hard, but please, would I go?

I had seen enough VH1 specials to know what touring with a rock band was all about. Yes!

. . .

But that conversation now seems so long ago. It was already March. We were leaving Holland and heading out to Spain to play La Musica Mania, the big outdoor music festival. The grand tour bus I had envisioned turned out to be a small, cruddy van, overcrowded with bodies and personalities I never bargained for. Only two weeks into the tour, and I was already sick of the road. Sick of the same CDs skipping at the same spot; sick of the same banter that bounced off the van's interior; sick of the same scenic snowcapped mountaintop after scenic snowcapped mountaintop. But most of all, I was sick of Lenny.

We were sitting in our usual seats in the middle of the bus. His head was on my belly, and he was passed out, again. Lenny was always passing out. Not from overindulgence in partying, recreational drugs, or even booze. Oh, how I wish! Lenny was just plain tired. He was *always* tired. After every show, he'd just wanna go back to the bus and crash. He was never writing songs or coming up with new bass lines. He was never rushing back to the hotel room to explore craziness with me. He never wanted to do anything. After he was done with a show, all he wanted to do was sleep.

"So, I'm guessing you had fun last night."

I didn't have to look up to know it was Z-Man. He was sitting at the front of the bus. I pretended not to hear him, but he kept at it.

"Yeah, while your man and I were at the Weg, breaking down the stage, you just took off for the party. Man, must be nice to be a groupie who made good."

"What? Who are you calling groupie, *roadie?*"

I adjusted Lenny's head higher up on my lap and leaned my seat as far back as it could go. I closed my eyes. Groupie? *Me?* Z-Man was the one kissing ass! I mean, he's the one who looks to the band for approval after every little joke or remark he makes! How could he even *think* that I was a groupie?

I glanced down at Lenny. He was breathing with his mouth

open, and I could see his dark tooth. When I first met him, I thought the tooth made him look tough, macho, like he had been in loads of barroom fights or something. Like he didn't take shit from anyone. But when he told me he killed the nerve playing kick-the-can when he was a little kid in Clinton, New York, I tried to not let it bother me. But I gotta admit, it did. A lot.

Three days later, when we finally pulled into Valencia, I was so happy. I couldn't wait to check into the hotel, take a hot bath, and have some fun time with Lenny. But as if Gunter was reading my mind, he announced to the whole band that we were behind schedule and that we would have to go straight to the venue and do a sound check.

"Sound check?" I called out. "Are you serious? We sounded fine in Amsterdam. Why do we always have to do a sound check? "

Z-man looked back at me. "We?" he smirked. Gunter ignored both of us and helped Jorge navigate through the narrow Spanish streets.

I shook Lenny to wake him up. "Come on, Wenny, make Gunter take us to the hotel. Come on . . . let's go rest before your show, let's order some room service and kick it like real rock stars."

Lenny stretched and slowly took my arms off his shoulders. "Man," he yawned and looked out the bus window. "Why do you always have to make it harder than it already is? Come on."

I sat back in my seat. I was beginning to learn that no matter how cool bass players seem, they really don't have much clout in any band. They're pretty much just second up from the drummers.

I looked up and saw Z-Man was still looking right at me.

"What?" I asked.

"Nothing." He smirked again.

At La Musica Mania, I saw the buses for Les Les and even Grand Plastic Rap. There were already loads of kids hanging around, trying to get into the sold-out show. I started to get excited.

"Come on, Wenny." I squeezed his arm as the bus pulled up. "Let's go check out backstage. See if there's something else other than a wheel of dry Brie."

"Can't." He stood up in his seat and rubbed his eyes. "I gotta set up for the sound check."

"Help? Are you serious? Isn't that a roadie's job? Come on, you gotta eat."

"I will, later. I'll meet you there."

As soon as I got off the bus, I took off for the backstage area. Just as I thought, the catering table was stacked with mini bread slices and mounds of Brie. I found a bottle of orange juice inside a tub of ice and poured some into a paper cup.

"Hey, wouldn't this make it better?"

I turned around. It was Marco from La Maquina. He was waving a bottle of vodka.

"Oh, hey." I knew who Marco was, but I didn't really *know* him. I suddenly felt embarrassed, self-conscious after three days on the road. I patted my bangs down quickly.

Marco flopped down on the torn couch behind the table and motioned me over.

"You come here. Let me fix you up right."

"Huh?"

"Your drink. I can't let you drink naked. Come here."

I looked at my cup. Oh. I went over to the couch and flopped down next to him. "Um, shouldn't you be helping with the sound check?"

"Sound check? That's for the peons. Or the roadies. There's partying to be done, no?"

Marco leaned into me and smiled. I smiled back. Man, he was something. Yeah, he was a lead singer, but, well, I dunno.

"Take a drink." He motioned at my orange juice. I took a small sip. He took a large swig of vodka, then leaned into me and pursed his lips against mine, shooting the vodka into my mouth. I swallowed and pulled back to laugh. Just as I was gonna take another drink, Z-man barged in.

"Hey, am I interrupting something?" he asked from the doorway.

I pulled away from Marco.

"Nuh-uh. What's up, Z-Man?"

"I just came to get you. We're getting out of here."

"What?" I sat up on the couch. "Whaddya mean?"

"He means we got booted from the bill." Gunter came up behind Z-Man. "Fucking bastards didn't even wire us. We drove three days for nothing."

I got up from the couch. "Are you serious? Wait, why?"

They didn't even bother to answer. They were already heading toward the bus.

"Shame you have to leave." Marco clicked his tongue. "My band still has a show to do. Plus, we are going on to Greece next week."

I sat back down next to him. "You're going to Greece?"

"Yeah, the big . . ."

"Yeah, I know. The big AMI festival, right?"

"Right."

"Wow, that's like the best show."

"Yeah, maybe you can come."

"Wow, really?"

From the couch, I could see Lenny and Z-Man through the doorway. They were heaving equipment into the back of the van. I watched Lenny wiping his forehead and scratching the back of his head. If you didn't know him, you would think that Lenny was a roadie, just like Z-Man. His black T-shirt was faded and ripped, and the soles of his Converse were cracked. I looked back at Marco. There was no way I was gonna get back on that bus with Lenny. No way.

"Oh, so this is how it is? Like this?" Lenny said when I told him. "How are you gonna get home? How are you gonna get around?"

"I'm gonna hitch a ride with Marco, from La Maquina."

"Marco? From La Maquina? Are you . . . serious?"

"Yeah." My voice suddenly felt soft. "Yeah. I'm just gonna kick it with them for a while. Come on, Wenny. Don't make it harder than it already is."

I returned backstage to be with Marco. From the couch, we both watched Lenny board the van and take a seat in the back.

Marco laughed. "He's got a long way to go." He took another sip from his drink and walked over to me. I put my arms around him. He looked over my shoulder. "Well, I'm gonna check out who else is here. I'll be right back, but if I'm not, I'll catch you in Greece, yes?"

"In Greece?"

"Yes. Look for me."

Marco took my arms off his shoulders and went toward the crowd at the food table. I looked out after the van. Jorge was pulling out, and Gunter threw my backpack out the side door. I saw Lenny pull the drapes away from the back window. And then I saw Z-Man. He was watching me from my old seat. I couldn't tell from his expression what he was thinking. Was he finally happy that I was off the bus, off the tour? Would he stretch out his legs on my old seat?

I suddenly felt more than anything that I really, really needed a hot bath. I turned and saw the last bits of Marco as he faded away into the crowd.

X

by Suzanne Finnamore

[1]X \'eks\ *often capitalized, often attributive* (before 12th century) 1a: the 24th letter of the English alphabet. b: a graphic representation of this letter. 2: an unknown quantity. 3: a former lover, also EX. [2]X *transitive verb* (circa 1849) 1: to mark with an x. 2: to cancel or obliterate with a series of x's—usually used with *out*.

> *"One should never know too precisely whom one has married."*
> Friedrich Nietzsche

I am soon to be divorced, for the second time. I should be ashamed, but I'm not. I'm inconvenienced mostly. Sometimes sad, sometimes grateful, as though I have been untied from the train tracks of life. You can be sad and grateful at the same time; that's one thing I've learned. Also, property is everything. Buy the bastards out if necessary.

This is, as they say, a long story, but one with undeniably entertaining moments—some of which informed my work as a functioning adult, one who has recently turned two hundred. Actually, thirty-six. I just feel two hundred.

As always with a major breakup, and particularly divorce, I feel devastated yet freed, much like one of Lincoln's slaves: I don't know quite what to do with myself, but I am aware that a pressure has been lifted, constraints broken. For example, I am writing this while eating an individually wrapped Ding Dong, a small detail that I can't help but include. Could I do that while married? Interesting. Like a photographer at the scene of a crime, I am intent on documenting everything, so that it may lessen the blow of actual firsthand reality which assaults me daily.

I suppose I should start with Ex#2—also known as Soon-to-Be-Ex #2, or S2BX2—my currently estranged husband, forty-two years old, of five years. (*Estranged* is a perfect word; it efficiently includes the word *strange*.) I have recently been forced to acknowledge that ever since my second trimester last year, when I began to look like a gourd with legs, S2BX2 has been having affairs, even though he is, on the surface, remarkably trustworthy and likable. Perhaps that has been the problem. He has been too well liked, mostly by people with large breasts and an *ie* at the end of their first name. He sells luxury cars for a living and is strikingly good looking, in that eventually you want to strike him. He cannot pass a mirror without doing the Sears-model half-turn, with hand-in-pants-pocket-and-one-eyebrow-cocked move.

Historically, there is X1—my first husband, who is convinced that we should have stayed together, even though he tried to poison me with Snail Death after an argument concerning joint checking. He sprinkled some on my English muffin. "Just a little," he said. "I didn't mean it. If I had meant it, you'd be dead now. I always follow through on the things that are important to me." So it was just a gesture. A shot across the bow. I ate half and was fine, if you don't count the vomiting and headaches that persisted for a month, too long for X1 to suppress the brilliance of his plan. I did not press charges. Instead, I filed for crucifixion (his), otherwise known as divorce.

X1 has never remarried. He is far too busy making my life a living hell and poring over mental scrapbooks of our sordid years together in the eighties (Reagan was president; a lot of bad shit went down). He will call and say, "Do you remember the time we made spinach lasagna in the middle of the night?" "We were stoned," I say. I don't remember. "Well, it was raining," he said. "We were watching *Bewitched* on Nick at Nite, the episode where Dr. Bombay cures Darren from telling the truth." X1 is like a damn elephant. He never forgets anything, except the small detail of the Snail Death incident. "Why can't you forgive me?" he asks. He says I need to work on my doubts, jealousies, and insecurities before I can rediscover our love.

X1 says we will always love each other, and that it's because of my Karma that my marriage to S2BX2 is breaking up. He generally feels that the fact that I got married to and had a child with X2 was just a minor passage. He will not validate any portion of my life that took place after October 11, 1990, which is the day we divorced. Every wedding anniversary, he still sends flowers, and on the anniversary of our divorce, too, with a card that says *We Are Mean to Be Together.* I don't know whether he means to leave out the *T* in *Meant* or not. It's the kind of joke he would enjoy, especially the not explaining part. He is about an inch away from being one of R. Crumb's brothers—the one that's a street person, who swallows string and then pulls it back out his ass and starts over.

Then there's the Crazy-Ass Bitch (CAB). CAB is the woman my temporarily still husband (S2BX2) sold an Audi TT to and with whom he had his most recent affair; but then she turned out to be a bit of a psychotic—sewing his boxers shut and Krazy-gluing the pockets of his suits shut when he had the temerity to suggest that perhaps this was a "transitional relationship." So, whereas once he was proffering yellowfin tuna down her paper-white throat and knocking back sake as if it were oxygen, now he wishes she would fall down a cement stairwell. She turned out to have quite the stamina and imagination. I will give her that. She has taken the job of torturing S2BX2 right out of my hands. It's really too delightful. The irony is that now that he wants to get rid of her, he attempts to hide out at my place. I never allow it, except for when he comes to see our daughter. There's a grease spot where his car used to be, and I like seeing it. I don't like his car covering it up again.

"I told her we reconciled," he says. "Can I just park my car here in the driveway?" "Absolutely not," I say. "I don't even want your toothpicks here," I say. The toothpicks that I packed up along with his martini shaker in the final box of his belongings, which he was loading into his car as he asked for sanctuary. Imbecile.

The night he brought the silver martini shaker home from Restoration Hardware should have been my first clue that there was serious trouble. Its "James Bond time in the suburbs" vibe should have been my clue. James Bond never married and was an international spy. He never gets old, either; he is just recast. S2BX2 was trying to be James Bond. I was in the way, like someone standing in front of the television. It is possible that CAB was originally cast as Pussy Galore.

CAB calls me on the phone, making heavily nuanced statements (for example, "You need to let him go, you bitch!"). CAB sends me chihuahua turds wrapped in heart-embossed tissue, a dozen clam pizzas, and nasty notes in her childish scrawl. Like Glenn Close, CAB will not be ignored. She is the artist formerly known as Small-Foot Bitch, because while we were still together, I found a charge on S2BX2's credit card from Neiman's, and he swore it was a gift for me and that it was in his office. So he brought it home that night, and it was a pair of Manolo Blahniks—size four. He said he was going to just give me the sample size, and then I could exchange it for my own size, which is nine. And I believed him. That was during the time when I wanted to believe, was desperate to believe. If he had said that the earth is flat, I would have said, "As a fucking pancake."

But that's all over now. We're in the vortex of uncoupling. Working on the legal settlement, alternately hating each other's guts and waxing nostalgic, still having occasional sex. It's incredibly complex, and you can't explain it to people. They either make you feel pitiful or guilty; neither are emotions that I covet. No one got this excited when we got married. They just showed up and drank too much, ate the roast beef and the poached salmon. Plus, it was over in a day. Divorce is much slower, more protracted. It's like LSD time. Not that I would know. I mean, I don't even take Tylenol, not after it killed those people. (It's not like I'm lucky, either. I mean, look. Take a good look. Maybe you can avoid my life. Maybe you can steer around it.)

Divorce, unlike marriage, has a crazy schema of its own. It's like the soapbox derby that they have at the top of Twin Peaks every third Sunday in San Francisco: *There are no rules.* You can put a 1950s stove on wheels and wear a chef's hat, and that can be your soapbox derby racer. Or, you can make a ratmobile with a long, hairless tail made of licorice. Mine would be a Pottery Barn couch on wheels with me and the baby and no husband, careening down the hill, screaming. CAB would be right behind on a Ninja bike. X1 would be on a huge, Styrofoam English muffin that's embroidered with live snails that spell out COME BACK, BABY.

S2BX2 is always saying he loves me, too. The way he expresses it is through filing for divorce and screwing the Crazy-Ass Bitch. "And that's just the one we know about," my best friend, Sarina, says. "Yeah. Right," I say. She would like his penis to fall off, the way a baby's umbilical cord does, in the middle of the night. "Noooo, I'm still using it," I say thoughtfully.

"What would Gloria Steinem say?" Sarina asks, mildly reproachful. "I don't know," I reply. "What would Camille Paglia say?" she asks. "I don't know," I say, annoyed. Let the lesbians duke it out among themselves. This is my divorce. I can do it however I want. I can have a party if I want to. I can frame the divorce petition. I can do that. In fact, I have done that. It's in my office. It makes a fantastic conversation piece.

S2BX2, though admittedly great in bed, is a lifetime-achievement cheater. He was the kid who always insisted on being the banker in Monopoly games and then won, pulling five-hundreds out of thin air. But it's all he knows how to do. He's never been faithful to anyone. He's like an epileptic pilot that way and should not be working for Air Monogamy. Here's something interesting. Since we separated, we are having more sex than ever. I have become the Other Woman. Plus, I get checks now. I never got checks before. So there's that. It's called Spousal Support monies. It should be called Keep Quiet, Bitch monies. Stay Away from My Lexus with That Icepick monies. Why don't they call things what they are?

I've decided I am through with clever, charming men. I want someone simple, maybe even slightly retarded. I'm thinking one ear. A simpleton. Anyway, I call my girlfriends for talk. Men don't want to talk after the first year; they just want you to do their laundry and screw doggy style. Men are nice, but they are not strictly necessary, the way ketchup is to French fries. You can do without. I will do without. For at least the next few hours. God, this celibacy is grueling. I mean, divorce. Divorce is grueling. But I will keep doing it until I get it right. Either marriage or divorce. One of them I must perfect. Clearly, this is my life plan.

Tomorrow, I see S2BX2. He's coming over to visit our daughter. What should I wear? I must look fantastic. I must harm him in at least one aspect. Even though he filed for divorce, winning still seems possible. I will meditate on it. I will go to the closet and exclude mercy from my selection of attire. This is war.

I decide on the outfit from Bebe, a store I formerly eschewed because its clothes would perfectly attire a prostitute on Nob Hill. And yet, last week I could not resist the blatant allure of the flimsy and the stringy and the clothes that say, "Come get me, you great big hunk of a man."

Bebe. The saleswomen all appear to be from an alternate planet, where there are no pores or breasts. Not a menstrual period among them. They twirl about like skeletal tops and pay no attention whatsoever to me, and for this I commend them. I need none of their attention, I am more than capable of humiliating myself on my own and prefer it thus. One of the girls is on the store telephone to her boyfriend, telling him that she hates him and then laughing maniacally, putting the phone down for a minute to her bony chest, and then bringing it back up to trill, "I do. I do hate you!" She has a diamond in her nose, a precious rock fastened onto her very nose. I have nothing fastened anywhere and resolve to keep it that way, for aerodynamic speed and efficiency. Also, I feel no urge to have tiny metal spikes rammed through my body tissue so that I may look like a Zulu warrior gone gay.

I choose a pair of capri pants that are a Gucci knockoff, bright sixties paisley against black background, side zipper. My blouse is silk chiffon and terrifyingly expensive; it matches the pants perfectly in that let's-kill-all-the-homeless kind of aplomb. These clothes are the opposite of actual clothing. For this, I am thankful, because actual clothing has gotten me to the exact place that I'm at. I need costuming—the more inappropriate and scanty, the better.

S2BX2 calls from his cellular telephone to say he will be late because he thinks—no, he is certain—that CAB is following him in a red Ford Escort GT. I ask him how he knows it is her, and he says she has a pink garter belt hanging from her rearview mirror. I wonder aloud how far one has to search to find her exact blend of intelligence, wit, and style. S2BX2 screeches around a corner, announcing that he has lost her, breathing heavily. It is entirely possible that he is masturbating. I put nothing past him.

When he finally arrives, he is red faced and somehow icy at the same time. He forever seems to feel a sense of effrontery that I have kept the connubial home. He wanders around, picking up cigar ashtrays and candlesticks and coasters, his lips curled tightly. He is taking a mental inventory of everything I have bought since he left. It all seems to insult his memory, his legacy.

I am certain he felt that after he left, I would transform our home into a museum, along with my vagina. He is so often mistaken about the most basic truths of life.

"When did you get this?" he asks, holding up the edge of a pumpkin silk chenille throw.

"Oh, that," I say brightly, walking past him just close enough so he can smell me. I have taken the liberty of daubing Jil Sander No. 4 behind each ear. I have spent perfume on him, and it is not in vain. I can see by the way he shoves his hands into his pants pockets that he is nervous and excited. He wants to discuss CAB, but I wave my hand in the air, as if to dry my fingernails. My work is done here. I escort him to the door, kissing our daughter and saying, "Have a wonderful time with Daddy!" I am channeling Rosalind Russell in *Auntie Mame*, only younger. I shut the door behind him and twirl the deadbolt shut, so that he can hear its sound. So that it is the last sound. Not only have I had the last word, I have had the last sound.

After he has gone, and upon checking my e-mail, I am horrified to discover that yes, the whole world has gone mad and is calling it spiritualism. I am in receipt of an electronic *Tantra Nepalese Totem*. I am instructed to send copies to whomever I think is in need of good fortune. In my mind, of course, I choose both my husbands, past and present, and their respective mistresses. The Tantra Nepalese Totem includes vital advice, such as "Eat plenty of whole rice" and "Don't believe anything you hear" and "Do not sleep as much as you would like to." It's just this kind of thing that keeps me believing that computers are instruments of Satan and should be avoided as much as possible.

In continuation of intestinal self-destructive mode, I drive through Burger King for lunch. Waxing maternal, I decide I am a growing girl just as my daughter is, and that I need protein. I order a five-piece chicken nugget pack. After nearly maiming a pedestrian who has stepped out into traffic—as if it is his right as a United States citizen—I grab the paper bag, take one bite, and am startled. It turns out that the food handlers had temporarily lapsed in their blinding efficiency. It is a jalapeño cheese nugget pack. Outraged, I take another bite: terrifyingly delicious. I save the rest for cocktail hour, reheating them in the microwave — even better than I had originally estimated.

Meanwhile, S2BX2 is coming on Saturday with Irish movers to get his furniture and boxes. Arguments loom over who gets the pewter pepper grinder, electric pencil sharpener, weather vane, et cetera. I think this will be the last horrible thing we have to go through, until he moves in with a size-zero receptionist and the whole travesty begins again. I myself have an invisible sign that reads DON'T DATE ME, I CHAIN-SMOKE, I'M BITTER, AND I INCLUDE A GRABBY TODDLER; this has dramatically decreased my social life. Have now resigned myself to a lifetime of jalapeño cheese bites, midrange wine, and *Seinfeld* reruns. Why has no one proposed yet? I feel bad about that. I should have been asked by now; divorce will be final Tuesday. Lowering standards by the minute, but still nothing. Recently decided that the contractor working on the construction site down the street looked like Harrison Ford. Slowed car down and tried to look available, despite toddler seat in the back and Elmo sunshade. Then, today, he looked like Ray Liotta. I know my vision is impaired and cannot be trusted with even the simplest tasks, much less dating. Not that I have come within talon distance of a man.

I would have to run over the Ford/Liotta contractor to meet him: jump the curb, ruin German car, chance arrest. Even running him over may not ensure an introduction. Maybe I could just clip him as he crosses the street? This would require keener eyesight than I apparently have. I would probably clip him into a coma.

I'm not sending out the right alpha wave lately. Perhaps the fact that I frequently wear antique sweatpants and free, editing-house, XL T-shirts is holding me back. Save for the recent escapade with the Bebe attire, I just can't seem to get back into the daily donning of intelligent-slut-for-hire outfits that lure men. Even shoes with laces evade me. Plus, my hair is Fran Lebowitz–esque. I think my eyes are getting closer together. I don't know. Judgment clouded.

To make matters exceptionally worse, my brother is getting married next month. It's all I can do to keep from chopping his foot off to deter this obvious mistake. Still, I feign happiness for him. His wedding should be interesting. They're doing it in a Catholic church, and I plan to wear something smart, like army fatigues. I may accessorize with an assault rifle. I don't want anyone to get married right now. Why can't people consider my feelings? The selfishness of the world continues to astound me.

Mail-order shopping is shaping up as an issue. Bought a floor lamp last night, plaid cashmere pajamas, and twelve pairs of cotton ragg socks. This should fill out my divorce wardrobe nicely. New lines on my face are popping up with hideous regularity. The beginnings of a mustache intrigue me — surely, this is not the right response. One leg seems longer than the other. Where will it end? Yet, just now, I am unexpectedly cheered by a news item appearing on my computer screen:

> Chronic work stress and divorce can be a deadly combination for men, a new study has found.
>
> Researchers from the University of Pittsburgh School of Medicine and the State University of New York–Oswego studied data from 12,366 patients who participated in the seven-year Multiple Risk Factor Intervention Trial.
>
> Of 10,904 men who were married at the beginning of the trial, the researchers found that those who stayed married were less likely to die from a number of causes than those who divorced. Of those who divorced during the trial, 1,332 died from various causes, including some 663 from cardiovascular causes. (Reuters)

Information is so invigorating, yet enigmatic. So much of it on how to get a man, so little of it on how to get rid of one. To this end,

I proffer a handy list, which I have been compiling for my divorcing girlfriends, some of whom have clearly been born yesterday and need my advice as well as physical intervention. One of them actually had moved out from her home after she caught her rabbi husband with his hand up the nanny. I immediately alerted said girlfriend to the folly of her actions, installed her back in her home, and changed the locks myself. As for the mezuzah on the doorframe, I bashed it off with a sledgehammer and mailed it to his temple, along with the Polaroids (one needn't ask what was within the photos; Polaroids are never lucky, I am afraid, unless properly dealt with). She looked on as I sealed the envelope, tears frozen on her once-blossoming cheeks, which had turned the color of ash.

Yes. It is sad what ignorance does to women without resources who have been struck with an infidelity. It can and will render them childlike, like palsied Shirley Temples, throwing themselves on the floor and crying about the general unfairness of life, et cetera. I try to be kind but firm, and in the end they all thank me. It is a veritable hothouse here come Christmas, so numerous are my bouquets of thanks from women who have lost neither their minds nor their shirts.

I hope that no one reading this will ever be faced with the travesty of divorce. It should not happen to any good woman. But if it does? If you fall in with the wrong kind, the way I did? Be glad for divorce. It is God's way of telling you, "Girl? You have fucked up again! Now, here I'm going to give you a chance to start over. Go out there and please, please, *please* show some sense. Don't make me come down there again and bail your ass out."

Ten Simple Yet Elegant Tips on Divorce

1. Change the locks.
2. Make him pay for the divorce—and anything else you can.
3. Keep everything beginning with consonants (children,

money, house, cars, furniture, real estate, medical benefits, retirement funds, linens).

4. Allow him to keep everything beginning with vowels (armoires, umbrellas).

5. Sequester precious items at a friend's house. Men never remember what they have—if they did, they would not have ruined their lives by running around with whores.

6. Don't fight in front of the children . . .

7. . . . This includes your X/STBX—it only adds gasoline to the fire, and they don't care how angry you are, because they exist wholly in their own tiny birdcage of a brain.

8. Take frequent hot baths; get manicures and pedicures; have your hair expensively cut.

9. Everything, no matter how ludicrous and squalid it seems at the time of the split, will get better and better, until you will wonder why you cared so much in the first place.

10. When confronted with a question regarding fairness to your ex, err on the side of Lifetime Vendetta. That way, you will never feel a fool, and you will also have kept everything of worth in your rightful possession. In short: You may have once been in love, or you may still be in love—but you are not crazy.

Y
UPPIE

By Lucinda Rosenfeld

yup·pie \\'yə-pē\ *noun, often capitalized* [probably from *young urban professional* + *-ie*] (1982) 1: a young, usually college-educated adult who is employed in a well-paying profession and who lives and works in or near a large city. 2: anyone employed in the Internet industry during the late 1990s' economic boom.

All the women in my family—minus me, since I don't cook—take turns putting on Thanksgiving. This year, it was Aunt Judith's turn. I figured that whatever she served up couldn't be any worse than the cremated turkey my mother laid out last year. My boyfriend Rob and I had set off from the city that morning. We arrived in the Berkshires around noon. "Hey, Judy," I said, walking into the kitchen, where my aunt, a curator of Renaissance painting at the Met, stood in a black cowl-neck dress and fresco apron, chopping a bulbous-looking head of celery root. She looked even more anorexic than usual.

"Well, fancy seeing you here, Rachel Epstein!" she announced with those popping eyeballs of hers. She laid down her knife, wiped her hands on a pair of rosy-cheeked putti, and came over to kiss me hello, smelling faintly of after-bath splash.

"This is Rob," I said, motioning to my left.

"It's a pleasure to meet you, ma'am," said Rob, extending a hand.

"Well, it's a pleasure to meet you, too, *sir*," said Aunt Judith, returning the compliment, but you could tell she was mocking him with that whole "sir" business. And then she leaned toward him, chicken neck extended, as if she were gearing up to take a bite out of his nipple, her thumb and forefinger affixed to the right hinge of her oversized red frames. "In and Out Burger," she said, squinting at his T-shirt like she was reading hieroglyphics. "What in the world is that?"

"It's a fast-food chain in southern California," he told her.

"A fast-food chain—how extraordinary," she muttered incredulously, as if ours were a family for whom the taste of frozen hamburger patties was an alien one—as opposed to a bunch of *New York Times Magazine* recipe victims brainwashed to believe that the greater the number of ingredients, the tastier the meal.

"We're going to go put our stuff upstairs," I said, already ready to get out of there.

"Okay, you two," she said, waving us away with a flick of her microscopic wrist. And then, "Oh, Rachel—I think Joan wants you in the red room . . ."

"No problem," I called back, even though the red room was the only one in the house with twin beds in it (thanks, Mom). No doubt my dork-face of a federal prosecutor/brother Ben and his ugly, human rights lawyer/fiancée with the short bangs, Nathalie, had gotten the yellow room, which had a nice queen-size bed in it. It was all so typical. I didn't even know why I'd bothered coming.

Except, of course, for the opportunity to flaunt my white trash boyfriend in everyone's face.

. . .

The ride up had taken forever. It was sleeting, or hailing, or freezing-raining, or whatever it's called when little turds of ice fall from the sky and make a racket on the windshield. All these cars had gone off the road. There were dead animals everywhere. Rob and I passed the time looking for good songs on the radio and talking about which Hollywood actresses we thought were hot. Of course, I ended up getting insulted because everyone that Rob named was blond with big breasts. (I'm a small-chested brunette.) But I could only blame myself, since I was the one who started the conversation.

At another point, I tried to prep Rob on members of my family to avoid having prolonged conversations with, beginning with Aunt Judith, but continuing with my cousin Delmore, who was probably just another depressed Ph.D. candidate when he was back at U.C. Santa Cruz studying the history of consciousness, but who, in the company of the extended Epstein clan, felt somehow compelled to inject the word *queer* into every sentence he uttered (it was like — *yes, Delmore, we know you prefer cock to pussy*) in a barely disguised attempt to make everyone else feel guilty about still being heterosexual.

But Rob was like, "Don't worry about me — I get along with everyone."

It was scarily true. Half the time, he didn't even notice when people were busting him. The other half, he didn't seem to care. He had this talent for disarming people. At least, he'd disarmed me. He was like, "Hey, I'm Rob" — we were both at this bar in midtown after work — and the next thing I knew, we were sitting across from each other over dinner, and he was telling me all these stupid high school driving stories that were actually pretty funny, especially the one about rear-ending a bus containing an entire Little League team.

That was nine months ago. But it was already pretty serious. I saw us moving to Westchester or Connecticut in a couple years' time, to a three-bedroom colonial at the end of a cul-de-sac, where we'd watch obscene amounts of TV on some convertible sofa bed, when we weren't busy going at it on the wall-to-wall carpeting. That was my fantasy. I dreamed of culture-free days spent pushing strollers through the mall. I saw Rob and me floating on our backs in some kidney-shaped pool, eating Pringles and reading thrillers by Dean Koontz.

All I'd ever wanted was to be normal—to have had an adolescence shaped and honed by Pat Benatar and Big Macs and fast cars and cute guys and Ron Duguay and Def Leppard and softball and Sabbath and Sylvester Stallone.

Instead, I spent my formative years being force-fed a steady diet of Modified Marxist Cultural Criticism written by midcentury German-Jewish émigrés (Dad) and two-thousand-page works of Victorian literature (Mom). Indeed, the concept of leisure was an unknown one to the Epstein family of West Sixty-seventh Street (and, on holidays, Great Barrington, Massachusetts). When I tried to watch TV, my father turned it off. I still haven't forgiven my mother for canceling my subscription to *Seventeen*. For my parents' efforts, I awarded them with a learning disability and developmental issues. I had an imaginary friend named Zemulus the Pontificator. I had to go down one step for every two steps I went up. I was obsessed with palindromes. *Able was I ere I saw Elba*, and *A man, a plan, a canal—Panama*. It was the seeming impossibility of those phrases reading backward as they read forward that gave me hope. They seemed like proof that life was this magical thing that could turn course at any moment, as opposed to boring and lonely and predictable, which turned out to be closer to the truth. I went to Friends, and had none. Later, at Sarah Lawrence, I developed a recreational heroin habit and launched my own line of baby-doll dresses under the label "Blow Up Doll." I was angry at my family for putting so much pressure on me to succeed, but also at myself for being such a failure. I had some body-image issues left over from all the years of mandatory ballet. I had issues with my sexuality, too. (My parents could only talk about screwing in the context of French people.)

After two years of college, I'd had enough. I moved to Seattle with my boyfriend, Dewey. Everyone called him Dewey Nothing behind his back, and, eventually, so did I. At which point I moved back to New York and got a job in the promotions department of a luxury leather goods conglomerate—mostly to spite my parents. True to form, they took the news badly and tried to lure me back to school with promises of unconditional love and interest-free loans. That was six years ago. Since then, I'd been promoted to Director of Special Events for the United States and Canada. I was currently pulling in twice as much money as my mother ever made teaching her students about George Eliot at the CUNY graduate center—as if it made an impression on anyone in my family. They still treated me like a charity case. Not that I cared what they thought of me. I was through with trying to please the Epsteins.

Still, I admit that a critical, petty side of myself would have been happier if Rob had been wearing another shirt—really, any-thing but that "In and Out Burger" one. (With any luck, he'd change for dinner.)

Just as Rob and I were climbing the stairs, the whole "gang" came in—a whole Subaru station wagon's worth of them outfitted in corduroy and Polartec, their arms loaded up with white paper bags filled with McIntosh apples, their faces gleaming from the cold. Rob and I stopped on the landing. "Rachel!" someone said, but everyone was looking at Rob.

"Hey, you guys," I said, trying to pretend I was happy to see them. "This is Rob."

"Hi, Rob," said everyone, practically in unison.

"Hey," he answered, palm raised like a mellow traffic cop. "Nice to meet you all."

"Did you just get here?" asked Sara, my beyond-boring, East Asian studies professor cousin, trying to be conversational, I guess. (It was like—*no, we're just toting our weekend bags around the house for fun.*)

"Just a few minutes ago," volunteered Rob, as usual picking up my slack. "It was pretty slow going with the weather."

"We're going to put our stuff away," I said, offering a glacial smile and climbing another step, so the point wouldn't be lost.

"Well, just let me know if you two need anything," said my Aunt Lila, moving to the front of the pack. Lila was my mother's incredibly earnest younger sister. She worked with disadvantaged students in Cambridge and lived for National Public Radio. "Joan and Susan are antique shopping in Stockbridge."

"Okay, thanks," I said, climbing another step.

"Seem like nice people," was all Rob said when we finally got upstairs.

Unable to offer up any compelling evidence to the contrary, I made a face and said nothing.

Dinner was still an hour off, so Rob and I took off our clothes and got under one of the garish Marimekko quilts that had won our bedroom the red room designation. Rob started pressing into me, but I wasn't in the mood. "Let's just cuddle," I said. He didn't seem to mind. It hadn't always been that way. One night, when we were first together and I'd had my period, he'd gone and slept on the sofa because he didn't think he could make it through the night just lying next to me. More recently, his Chia Pet-like tendencies aside, he'd learned to turn his sex drive on and off like a light switch. In fact, within minutes, he was snoring his weird ventilation system of a snore. At some point, I must have dozed off, too.

I woke to find him on the other bed, feet up, leafing through *Sports Illustrated*. "Mornin', sweetheart!" he said in his fake country-bumpkin accent. (He had grown up near Atlanta, but was born in Tennessee.)

"I wish it were morning," I grumbled into my pillow.

"Yeah, well, Miss Bitter, it's time to rise and shine," Rob went on. "I think we're the only ones not down there. They're probably getting paranoid that we don't like them or something."

"Where would they get that idea?"

"Hey, you just sit there glaring at everyone, and I'll make the small talk. Okay?"

I had been staring at a framed copy of that *New Yorker* poster in which the rest of humanity is reduced to a suburb of New York City, and thinking how annoying and insider-y it was. Now I looked over at Rob—at his pink cheeks and giant sock feet—and a wave of tenderness washed over me as I contemplated the possibility that life had its whimsical aspects, after all. "Will you give me a wake-up kiss?" I moaned at him.

"One wake-up kiss—coming right up," he declared, hoisting himself off his bed and delivering the promised smack.

"You're cute," I said, stroking his flushed cheek.

"Not as cute as you," he said, squeezing one of my nipples.

"I wuv you."

"The feeling's mutual."

We got dressed—Rob, to my relief, in an unobtrusive, pale blue button-down shirt and khakis—and went downstairs.

I kissed my short, fat, sweet, bald, totally irritating father, who was currently the publisher of a (snooze) middle-of-the-road Jewish newspaper hello ("Hi, Honey"), then my short, not-quite-as-fat-but-equally-if-not-more-annoying mother, Joan ("Hello, Rachel"). Then I introduced them to Rob. As far as I was concerned, my brother didn't exist. His main crime? Living.

"So, Rob, I understand you sell coffee," my father began. "Tell me—what's the most popular flavor these days?"

It was so like my father to ask a retarded question like that. The guy was a genius, except when it came to real life. "Dad," I hissed. "Rob trades coffee on the commodity exchange—he's not a frigging street vendor!"

"Well, I didn't—" my father started to say, all defensive, as usual. But Rob interjected with, "Actually, I wish I knew the answer to that question, Mr. Epstein, but I don't sell coffee so much as I speculate in coffee futures." (I don't know how he did it.)

"Coffee *futures*—I see," said my father, lips pursed, head waggling like an Orthodox Jew reciting his morning prayers, even though you knew he had no clue what Rob was talking about, and no interest in finding out, either. (Thanks to the classic six apartment we'd inherited from Mom's parents, he could afford to be a moron when it came to money.)

We all sat down. My uncle Ralph, who taught Literature Between the Wars at Columbia and fashioned himself a kind of one-man anti-political-correctness militia, was seated at one end of the table. (The guy was convinced that Toni Morrison had only won the Nobel because she wrote about slaves. Whatever.) My father was at the other. I was between Rob and Aunt Lila. "So, what glamorous things are you two city slickers planning for New Year's?" she asked me. (Why did everyone in my family have to be reduced to a type?)

"We haven't really planned anything yet," I told her, then turned my back to nuzzle Rob. Which seemed to shut her up for the while.

My mistake was to compliment Uncle Ralph on his choice of wines. "There's actually an interesting story behind the Château Cos d'Estournel label," he began to sermonize while undoing the first cork. "A love story of sorts . . ."

I felt my lids begin to droop.

There were toasts, a family tradition. My father raised a glass to Edward Said, "For enlightening those of us in the intellectual community who were under the apparently mistaken belief that the pen is mightier than the sword—or, perhaps I should say, mightier than a certain kind of naturally occurring, hard, round object." A sprinkling of clinks. A few tight smiles. I rolled my eyes. Ever since chucking that rock on the West Bank, the great Palestinian orator had become my father's Public Enemy Number One. (It was getting a little tired.)

One of the younger generation, a habitually ironic policy-wonk cousin named Jake, followed with a raised glass to "Paul Stanley né Stanley Eisen and Gene Simmons né Chaim Witz on the twenty-fifth anniversary of the release of their breakthrough album, *Alive!*, for ushering in the Golden Age of the Kabuki Jew." Real laughter. More clinks, especially among the younger generation. "Who is this?" said my father. More laughter. Rob looked equally baffled by Jacob's toast. In lieu of trying to explain to him why it was that secular Jews were so obsessed with identifying their "own" in the fields of sports and entertainment—not that I knew the answer—I gave him an under-the-table hand squeeze and whispered, "Don't worry—they're all insane."

Next up was my mother, who raised a glass to Judith, "For lending her infallible culinary skills to this evening's festivities." (A classic Mom articulation.) We all here-here'd.

"Oh, it's nothing," said Judith, simpering from behind her wineglass. But you could tell she was pleased. In fact, you got the feeling that she was a little *too* pleased—that she lived for the tiniest showings of appreciation. There were rumors in my family that my Aunt Judith was the long-suffering mistress of some octogenarian Old Masters dealer. I was still pissed about that whole "sir" business—never mind the "In and Out Burger" recitation—but I was capable of feeling sorry for her, too.

Which is probably why, a few minutes later, I told her, "Judith—this is, like, the best matzo ball soup I've ever had." (We'd accidentally skipped the stuff at Passover, so we were having it now, six months after the fact. That's how seriously we took Judaism—*not very.*)

"Believe it or not, it's Wolfgang Puck's recipe," she warbled back at me, but loud enough for everyone to hear—and cease their own conversations in the interest of this far more scandalous one. There were huhs, mms. Someone—my mother?—repeated the guy's name as if it ended with a question mark: "Wolfgang Puck?"

My nonexistent brother, Ben, piped in with some idiotic "Nothing wrong with Nazi matzo balls" line.

I guess Judith could dish it out a lot better than she could take it. Her mouth frozen, she looked like she was about to spit her soup clear out of her mouth. Instead, she reached for her water glass and held it to her lips like some kind of protective shield. It was of no use. The Epsteins were off and running, wondering aloud whether (beyond snooze) the *next generation of Germans were in denial about the deeds of their jack-booted elders.*

"To be honest," started up my cousin Delmore, dressed for the occasion in a calico housedress over a pair of tattered blue jeans, "I don't see how eating 'Nazi matzo'—to borrow Ben's expression—is any more or less of a hypocritical gesture than swooning over the peasant bread at some pretentious little Frog restaurant on Bank Street, as my mother and father here are so terribly fond of doing."

I let loose a semivoluntary yawn: the Vichy France theme was a perennial with Delmore—as was Uncle Ralph's display of condescension toward his only son (and chief ideological rival). "I always appreciate hearing your perspective on things, Del," Ralph bantered. "In fact, I suspect it keeps me young! But I'm afraid I find your position an extremely shortsighted one, not to mention ignorant of major historical develop—"

"Sorry, Dad," Delmore shot back, "but I think your ongoing fellatio of the French race is not merely ignorant, but, frankly, a little on the *creepola* side."

"Delly, sweetheart." It was my aunt Susan's turn. "Maybe you and Daddy want to take this up after dinner?!" After miraculously surviving Stage-Ten-Million Breast Cancer, she'd given up a going-nowhere fiction-writing career to write inspirational books about surviving cancer. One had even hit the best-seller list. Admiration aside, you had to hate her a little for having such a positive attitude about everything, in particular her son. (One Passover, Delmore had made us all read from some "post-gender" Haggadah; all the *mankinds* had been changed to *humankind.*)

Now he roared back at them, "Actually, Mom, I'd prefer to take it up now! And I'd like to add that the Jews weren't the only victims of European supremacist ideology. The Gypsies were decimated. Queer populations were virtually eradicated. More recently, the Palestinians . . ."

"This is exactly what I was talking about," I whispered in Rob's ear, while Delmore droned on about the valuable educational services provided by the terrorist organization Hamas — and about how Anwar el-Sadat had been a total sellout to ever recognize the *fascist, colonial, police state of Israel.* (The rest of the family took a more nuanced view.) In short, nothing new to report at the Epstein family Thanksgiving.

Except, of course, for Rob being there. "Huh," he grunted in acknowledgment of my comment, but his thoughts seemed elsewhere — on his turkey leg, I guessed. I had never seen anyone go at a piece of meat with that kind of enthusiasm.

His turkey leg stripped bare, however, he laid the thing on the side of the plate, reached for his wineglass, took a long, Adam's apple-y sip from it, and cleared his throat. Then, drowning Delmore out with his best commodity-trader voice, he declared, "Speaking of the Camp David Accords, I've always thought Nixon was underrated as a president."

Silence. Even Delmore looked stunned. Nixon? Surely, Rob had to be kidding! But no, his face was straight. I wanted to die. Disappointed to find myself still breathing, I opted to choke. Aunt Lila hit me on the back. (Maybe she'd learned how on NPR.) "Do you mean Carter?" asked my father, the Expert on All Things Jewish, displaying, in this case I have to say, admirable restraint. "Carter was the one who brokered peace between Sadat and Begin."

My boyfriend seemed unsettled by the news. For a moment or two, he even looked pissed. Finally, he came back with, "Are you sure it wasn't Nixon?"

"I'm sure," said my father.

More silence.

"Well, then, what accord was it that Nixon brokered?"

"I can't really think of one. Unless you mean his restoration of relations with Communist China."

"Maybe that was it," said Rob, sheepish now. He went back to his dinner.

I could no longer stand to look at mine. From where I sat, it was one thing to be spouting far-left, anti-Zionist rhetoric like my cousin Delmore, and another to be confusing a benign Southern Baptist liberal such as Jimmy Carter with a disgraced reactionary and notorious anti-Semite. (I couldn't believe that anyone I knew—let alone regularly slept with—was capable of that kind of gaffe.)

"Rachel, would you pass the turkey around?" asked my mother in a clipped voice I knew only too well. As if her disappointment in her only daughter was already so extensive as to barely register the addition of a future son-in-law with the mental capacity of a chimpanzee.

"I'd love to, Mom," I said, not knowing who I hated more in that moment: my mother for being so critical, or Rob for forcing me to identify with her superior ways (Rob, probably. I was used to my mother).

Indeed, as much as I had brought Rob home to horrify my parents with his unlearned ways, it had never occurred to me that his ignorance would be of such a magnitude as to succeed in horrifying me, as well.

The conversation moved on—to the latest Philip Roth novel. Why was the guy so obsessed with sex? And what exactly happened with him and that pretty actress, Claire What-Was-Her-Name, the one who was in *The Spy Who Came in from the Cold*? But the damage had already been done. Out of the corner of my eye, I could see my nonexistent brother smirking—the prick.

After dinner, I tried to talk to Rob about his gaffe in the manner in which my therapist, Carla, had encouraged me to resolve conflict—that is, without accusing anyone of anything, but rather stating my needs and suggesting how they were and were not being met. We went back up to the red room, where we sat on facing beds. "Look, Rob," I began, "you're totally entitled to being a moron. But the next time you visit my family, could you do me a favor and do a better job of disguising it?!"

His mouth flew open; his face turned red. In retrospect, I can't say I blame him for being offended. "Look, Rachel, I may have gotten my facts wrong at dinner, but I have a fucking M.B.A., unlike you, who never even made it through college. So don't you be telling me who the dumb one is around here!"

"Well, at least I know the difference between Nixon and Carter!"

"Well, at least I treat my guests with respect when they come to dinner at my house!"

"You don't have a house, Rob. You live in an ugly little studio in a depressing neighborhood." (In Battery Park City, actually, and I was exaggerating—it wasn't so bad.) "And no one ever comes over to dinner at your house, including me, because you don't even know how to boil water!"

I could see the spittle collecting between his incisors. He finally got it out: "Fuck you, Rachel."

"No, fuck you, Rob!" I shot back, the words spewing from my mouth as if I'd been waiting my whole life to say them. Maybe I had. Maybe I had never loved Rob Muhlenberg, and he was just the latest in a long line of escape fantasies that had begun with palindromes and continued into poppy seeds. They always worked for a while. The magic inevitably wore off. Maybe there was no escaping who or what I was, and I would never fit in anywhere as well as I did here, among the Epsteins, with their Ph.D.'s and their Provençal hand-towels and everyone peppering their sentences with references to Ruth Bader Ginsburg, Stanley Fish, and Michel Foucault. Maybe the truth was that I was just as much of a snooty bitch as my mother.

And maybe the best I could hope for in a mate was someone who would pass scathing judgment on others along with me. "And no one cares about your M.B.A.," I went on, unable to stop myself. "My father's right—you're just a glorified street vendor." (It happened in all my relationships; one day, my heart just shut off.)

That's when he tried to gag me. I couldn't even breath, let alone repent. Have you ever had your oxygen supply cut off? It's really scary. OK, I'm exaggerating slightly. I could still breathe through my nose, but Rob wouldn't get his hand off my mouth, thereby compelling me to pick up the first book I saw, which happened to be *An Early View of the Shakers* (God only knows who had picked that one up at the local book sale), and swatting him over the head with it as hard as I could. His hands fell away from me, and then he, too, fell—backward onto one of the twin beds, clutching his skull and groaning, "Jesus Christ." (As if *he* had anything to do with it.)

I closed the door behind me and went downstairs.

I found the bulk of the Epstein clan playing (too many snoozes to count) Botticelli in the family room. ("I'm thinking of a famous artist whose last name starts with D—No, I'm not Degas.") Mozart's "Eine Kleine Nachtmusik" was playing in the background. I guess not all Wolfgangs were unwelcome in the Epstein household.

I had never been so happy to volunteer my services in the kitchen.

My Greenpeace cousin, Matt, and I loaded up the dishwasher. Then we went out on the screened porch and smoked a bowl. The skies had cleared for the moment, but it was so cold out there that our breath was indistinguishable from our smoke. We were both hunched over, hands buried in the sleeves of our jackets and—after the second hit—laughing uproariously. Matt reminisced about the time he was out in Tahoe, when he'd been so fucked up that he'd tried to ski uphill. (He was definitely my favorite cousin.)

I spent the rest of the evening zoning out in front of the fire with the last of the Château Cos d'Estournel, while my bachelor cousin, Bill—actually my stepcousin, since he was the product of my aunt Lila's husband Milton's failed first marriage to a Serb— performed Schubert Lieder ("Mein Fader! Mein Fader!") in a high-pitched mewl that gave me more insight than I ever needed into what Bill sounded like when he got it on. Meanwhile, at the same hour of the evening, to the best of my knowledge, Rob Muhlenberg and my cousin Delmore could be found playing Mastermind in the coatroom (our version of a TV den, minus the TV), over a couple of beers they'd found in the bottom of the fridge. I know, because I saw them in there on my way back to the kitchen, where I'd gone in search of extant pumpkin pie. (Pot always gave me the munchies.) I guess they were the closest thing to an ally either could find that night. Still, it was hard to imagine what they found to talk about—maybe other than what a bitch I was.

I had my mother to thank—for possibly the first time in my life—for assigning Rob and me separate beds. Not that I even heard him come in. I was out cold by midnight, drooling on the pillow and dreaming about who knows what.

By morning, the bump on Rob's forehead had expanded to the size of a jawbreaker. I could tell it was going to be a fun breakfast. "So, Rob—is there is a domestic explanation for that large tumescence on your forehead?" trilled Aunt Judith, the Nosiest Woman Alive. "Or are we to believe that you snuck off to the local pub last night, after we'd all gone to sleep, and found yourself a country brawl?"

I held my breath for fear of hearing the words "Actually, your charming niece here," exiting Rob's lips.

To Rob's credit, however, he wasn't the type to go around telling everyone everything. "Nah—just a little accident with the wall," he told her.

My gratitude for his discretion aside, I would have been just as happy (again, for possibly the first time in my life) to spend an extra day with my family as I was to get back in the car with him. "Bye, Mom. Bye, Dad. Bye, everyone," I said, feeling inexplicably kindly toward the lot of them, give or take a few exceptions (my brother, Judith, Delmore, my mother, my father, Aunt Lila), as I kissed and waved my way outdoors. We were the first ones to leave. Rob had to get back for work. The commodities exchange apparently stayed open even on holidays.

It had begun to snow, and for real this time. There wasn't much accumulation yet, but it was coming down pretty hard. The visibility was about two inches. Rob was leaning over the steering wheel like a student driver. "Shit, this is really bad," he said, or the equivalent thereof, about five hundred times.

"Yeah," I kept saying, thankful for the distraction from our own problems.

We hit the cat on a two-lane blacktop road outside Pittsfield. It came running out of someone's driveway—a little gray thing with psychedelic eyes. That's all I remember. Rob stepped on the brakes, but it was as if the car had a will of its own, and it wanted to go sideways. And we followed—into the other lane, mowing down the thing in the process. We were lucky not to have been killed ourselves. That was my immediate reaction. I felt bad for the cat, of course, but I figured it wasn't our fault any more than it was the cat's for running out in front of our car.

Rob seemed to feel otherwise. "Oh, man," he kept saying. By this point, he had pulled over to the side of the road. Then he got out, and I followed, though, at that point, I didn't precisely know what for. (What could we do about it now?)

It was a winter wonderland out there—everything white, white, and whiter, and the sky indistinguishable from the ground. Plus, windy and freezing. "I'm going to get him," he said.

"You're going to do *what*?!" I cried. I admit that I just wanted to get back in the car and go back to New York.

"Get him out of the road, so his owner can give him a proper burial," he explained in a pedantic tone, as if it were obvious.

"You could get rabies or something!"

"Jesus, Rachel, it's a cat — not a bat!"

"I'll watch for traffic," I mumbled, feeling chastened — even as I suspected, suddenly, that Rob's prime motivation for stopping was to prove himself the morally superior one of us.

I watched him walk into the road, grab the lifeless cat by its hind legs, and drag it back to a nearby driveway. From where I stood, it wasn't even a cat anymore. Or, at least, it didn't look like a cat. It looked like a bloody rag, and it was dyeing the snow around it a shocking shade of pink. Disgusted, I turned away and started back to the car. But Rob wasn't finished. "I'm going to ring the doorbell of the house," he called after me. "You can wait in the car if you want."

All I wanted to do was say, "Okay," and keep walking. But the desire to deprive my boyfriend of his little victory was even stronger than my desire to keep warm. I called back to him, "Wait, I'll come." And I did. I followed him up the front path of a small white house with a sloping front porch.

An elderly lady in a shawl-collar sweater greeted us at the door. Rob did the talking, his eyes downcast. "It must be Belle," the old woman whispered at the end of his soliloquy, her nearly lashless blue eyes blinking and glistening with fresh tears.

It had somehow never occurred to me that there might be a human dimension to the story of our roadkill. And now — now — I couldn't believe how fucked up it was, or my own blindness in imagining that it was no big deal. Moreover, the thought struck me that Rob's sense of "doing the right thing" maybe had less to do with showing me up, or even with some self-conscious notion of correctness, than it did with some genuine sense of cama-raderie with all the world's creatures.

It wasn't entirely my fault. My family had taught me to be suspicious of tenderness, what with its close links to sentimentality and nostalgia, never mind its diametrical opposition to logic and reason. But what if the Epsteins were the ones missing out? Growing up, I was literally the only person I knew who didn't have a cat or a dog. We didn't even have fish! My family didn't believe in pets. Pets were too cute. Pets weren't ideological enough. Pets were for the kind of people who got their art on calendars. We had an original Hans Hofmann hanging in the living room.

It was an hour before we were back on the road. First, we had to wheelbarrow what was left of Belle to an outlying barn. Then, we had to drink tea and look at photographs of Belle in her better days. Rob left his number in case there was "anything more we could do." The woman assured us that there wasn't. Eventually, we got back in the car.

The snow had let up some, so the driving wasn't quite as treacherous as before. But relations between Rob and me remained strained. We hardly spoke a word until lunch, which we stopped for at a diner off the Taconic. I ordered a turkey club on toasted rye — Rob, a grilled cheese and fries. After the waitress disappeared, Rob turned to me with an accusatory expression, as if the whole thing were my fault (maybe it was), and said, "So, are we going to make up, or what?"

I shrugged, as if I didn't care one way. In truth, I didn't know how I felt anymore. Rob was a good guy. A compassionate guy. I saw that now. It was the fact that he wanted to be taken seriously as a thinking, breathing, feeling *man* — I realized that now, too — that presented the greatest obstacle for me. In my mind, he had always been the rock to my paper and scissors, desirable by virtue of his density; the soundproof wall that muffled the voices in my head, voices that had haunted me since childhood with their tireless directives to keep up, because I would never keep up, because time was running out, because it was already too late, because there was no escaping history, it was only ever a second ago. Such was the mantra, and the curse, of families like mine, families who could never just live, never just be, but who were forever looking over their shoulders, measuring their own lots against the travesties and triumphs that had come before. In that sense, I didn't know whose legacy had proven more pernicious: the Nazis', or Marx's, Freud's, and Einstein's.

But how could I begin to explain that to Rob? How could I begin to admit that I had picked him among all men for his dead weight when he crushed me? "I don't know," I finally answered, purposefully avoiding the point. "You almost suffocated me to death last night."

"Gimme a break!" he protested. "I didn't almost suffocate you."

"Then what do you call cutting off someone's oxygen supply?"

He shifted his gaze away from me, into the parking lot, looking wistful. "Look, I'm sorry I gagged you. I was just pissed because you kept calling me a street vendor."

"Only after you said 'fuck you' to me."

He turned back to me with a heavy sigh. "Look, Rachel. I'm sorry I said that. I shouldn't have said it. And I didn't mean it. But none of what happened matters. I just want to make up with you. I love you." His eyes honed in on mine. I didn't know what to do. I couldn't think under pressure. We sat in silence for a few minutes—him waiting, hopeful, me looking anywhere but at Rob. Finally, our lunch arrived. That bought me a few minutes. But Rob started up again halfway through his sandwich. "Rachel—do you love me?" he wanted to know.

A feeling of weightiness suffused my chest and my lungs. I felt like sliding under the table. At some point it occurred to me that I ought to get it over with right then and there—admit that I didn't love or respect him; that I would never value his M.B.A. half as much as I did my father's Ph.D. That was just how I'd been raised.

But I couldn't convince myself that I wanted to lose him,

either. Staring into my half-eaten lunch plate, I pictured myself drifting away from him, coming home to a dark apartment, a cold bed. It had only been nine months. In the larger scope of things, that wasn't so much time. I was still young. Barely thirty. I had another ten years to meet someone, to find a sperm donor for my strollers through the mall. I was outgoing. Other than a few lines in my forehead, I still had my looks, my figure. Some people would say I had a glamorous job. At the very least, I was self-supporting. I would probably meet someone new within the year. Someone more intellectual, more Jewish, more like an Epstein. But would he treat dead cats half as nicely as Rob did?

I glanced up at my boyfriend, at his vibrant yet indistinct face, which sported a quarter-shaped protuberance. That's when I noticed the ketchup on his stubble. It drove me crazy the way he always got food on his face when he ate! But there was also something endearing about it. He was like an overgrown baby. *My* overgrown baby.

"Look, I love you. Okay?!" I lit into him suddenly, furiously, as if I were the victim. In a way, maybe I was — the victim of my own skittishness. Maybe I couldn't even accept the fact that Rob Muhlenberg made me happy.

Just then, a tickling sensation seized my thigh. I went to scratch it. Then I realized it was my boyfriend — dragging his unused fork against the inside of my thigh. His drooping mouth had firmed up into a goofy grin. "What are you doing?" I whined.

But he didn't answer, just kept smiling — and dragging.

"Stop that," I said, but just phlegmatically enough to imply that I didn't actually mean it. I felt suddenly powerless. I was just an animal looking for a set of warm limbs to wrap around. I figured I could always run away later, if I had to. In the meantime, I closed my eyes and allowed myself the pleasures that kitchen utensils occasionally afford the lower regions of the body.

I wanted Rob again. I wanted him on top of me and inside me, sucking the wind from my tunnels and the thoughts from my head. Until I was just gray matter. *A woman with no plan — just a canal.* To be living in the present!

And to be freed from the past — the future, too. (Maybe that was enough.) We paid the check and went back to the car.

A half-mile up the road, behind a hubcap store closed for the holiday weekend, we found an empty parking lot and climbed into the backseat.

Zero
ERO

By Erika Krouse

ze·ro \'zē-(ˌ)rō, 'zir-(ˌ)ō\ *noun* [French or Italian; French *zéro,* from Italian *zero,* from Medieval Latin *zephirum,* from Arabic *sifr*] (1604) 1: the arithmetical symbol 0 or Ø denoting the absence of all magnitude or quantity. 2: the point of departure in reckoning; *specifically:* the point from which the graduation of a scale (as of a thermometer) begins. 3: an insignificant person or thing: NONENTITY. 4a: a state of total absence or neutrality. b: the lowest point: NADIR. 5: something arbitrarily or conveniently designated zero.

It's hard to stop looking for something without simultaneously giving up hope. I don't know how. Buddhists learn the art of non-attachment, or they say they do. But have you ever seen a Buddhist lose his car keys? I have, and they're just like the rest of us.

Now that I reached my thirties, being single was entirely different. It meant candid discussions with a date, both of us saying, "Naaaaah . . ." but friendlylike. It meant peeling singles out of my wallet, splitting the tab exactly down the middle. I was starting from zero. I'd forgotten all my exit lines. I'd lost that "Good morning, Vietnam" feeling. I just wanted a little peace.

Two things told me I was getting older: Last Christmas, three people gave me tree ornaments. And second, when my friends described the men they wanted me to meet, they listed their qualities. "He's an individualist, losing his hair but in a good way, Harvard grad school, wants children . . ." It felt like shopping—shopping blind. It used to be that we all went out, drank a jug of wine, and woke up the next morning to see what had happened during the night. These days, you go on a date with a pen and notepad. They're more like job interviews.

"That's why I believe dates should be conducted in a formal office setting," said my friend Jack.

Shouldn't it feel natural, spontaneous, like falling out of a tree?

Other people think I've made a mess out of my life, but I disagree. I think that I've just been efficient. I've managed to cram a lifetime of mistakes into a span of ten years. I'm still young, thirty-two, and I'm watching other people take their time with it, sticking with husbands or wives who won't have sex with them, who won't clean up after themselves, whatever. I've done all that. Somewhere along the way, I'd gotten selective. My condoms had dust on them. I wanted a mail-order prince. Either that, or nothing.

"Here I am, baby," Jack said, thumping himself on the chest. "Prince Charming."

"Prince Alarming," I said.

I took a test out of a magazine. "What Kind of Girlfriend Are You?" There were questions that went like this: "He wants to eat burgers. You want Chinese. What do you do?" I scored a zero. I made Jack take the same test. He scored a one. He was delighted.

"Together, we're a ten!" he said.

The morning after every first date I went on, I would buy a fifteen-cent feeder goldfish from the pet store and put it in a giant jar that used to hold pickles. I would name the fish after my date. And I wouldn't give him any advantages. Instead of distilled water, I would use tap water—overchlorinated, radioactive. I would not change this water. I would not feed the fish. If my date called and the goldfish was still alive, I would go out with him again. If the goldfish had died before he called, I would give up on him.

"It's Darwinian," I explained to Jack.

Jack said, "That's totally crazy."

I said, "When it comes to dating, you have to be a little crazy to be sane, because a sane person would go crazy."

"Jesus. Feed it, at least."

My instincts are always wrong, but I follow them anyway. I read somewhere that you can find your way out of any maze by touching the wall with your right hand and following that hand wherever it leads. Eventually it will lead out into the open air, even if it takes a million billion years.

Jack said I was just looking for someone whose metaphors matched mine. He said I should give up, that I'll never find that because my metaphors are stupid.

I suspect that my problem is this: I have never been able to tell the difference between longing and love. This, Jack says, is my dysfunction.

"There *is* no difference," he says.

Jack and I went to the gym and got on stationary bikes. Jack said, "This is ridiculous. A stationary *bike*?"

"It's cold out, though," I said, beginning to sweat.

"I'd rather freeze," he panted. But he kept pedaling next to me.

I met Jack five years ago at a party. He got down on one knee and said, "If I don't take you home tonight, I'll never recover." But the way he said it, looking over my shoulder and nodding at someone he knew, told me that he had said this before, maybe as recently as last night, and he had recovered quite well, considering.

Jack is thirty-five. Jack is attractive. But I say that grudgingly, because with Jack, you do. He has dark brown eyes, and they change expression so rapidly that talking with him is like watching television.

When he was sixteen, Jack lost his twin sister in a party-related drug incident—he won't discuss the details. She had an extreme allergic reaction and died. Jack spent the next three years at home in Tucson, comforting his mother and father; then he left and didn't go back again, not even for Christmas, which he spends with my family each year. My family adores him. They think it's cute when he says grace at the table, and we all humor him, shouting "Amen!" or "Halleluiah!" afterward.

Unlike me, Jack had a religious upbringing. He and his twin sister had been forced to take two hours of religion classes every day in school, K through twelve. One day, Jack's third-grade teacher spotted him daydreaming and asked, "Jack, why do we worship Jesus? Why don't we worship, say, you?" Startled, Jack said, "Not enough people know me yet."

Enough people know him now, but I'm his only follower. Jack and I had settled into a friendship over the past five years that had flowed seamlessly out of his come-ons. Every now and then, he would throw out another one, but I handled them like dents in my windshield, swerving my head for the clearer view. We were each other's oral historian, always calling to record every little event in our lives: that our ficus plant wasn't doing well, or that the guy at the gas station had shortchanged us by five dollars. Sometimes I was confused and would forget what I had told Jack versus what I had planned to tell Jack, and it would take us some time to iron out those details.

At the very least, it was nice to have a compatriot. There at the gym, I slid over a retro seventies postcard I had just bought next door. It vibrated on Jack's machine. It was a picture of a smiling blond woman curled up on a couch, watching her date croon a love song to her, his open mouth wide. In a cartoon bubble over her head, the woman is thinking: "The good times are killing me." Jack laughed, pedaling faster.

I told him about the date that had inspired the purchase. I had gone out the night before with a man who told me, "I'm not religious, but I'm very spiritual."

So I said, "I'm not at all spiritual, but I'm deeply religious."
He asked, "What religion?"
"Oh, you know," I said, waving my hand. "Any of 'em."
"I see we have some differences," he said.
Jack now explained. "He was just trying too hard, that's all."
"Oh."
Jack told me about his last date, a woman who described in tortuous detail every other man she was currently seeing. She knew how much money each man made. She proceeded to ask Jack about his income, and then repeated the number back to him to make sure she had gotten it right.

Jack had met her at a dance club, where she had written her phone number on his stomach in red lipstick. He sweated too much at the club, and by the time he got home, he was missing a number, so he tried number combinations until he reached her. She didn't remember who he was, and it took him an hour of all his funniest jokes to convince her to go out with him. He said that the date had gone so poorly because he had used up his best material on the phone.

My legs hurt. I looked at the exercise machine, unable to decipher it. "Help me with this thing."

Jack leaned over and punched some buttons. A drop of sweat fell from his forehead onto the panel. The pedals got looser. I stared at the sweat shimmying on the plastic as I said, "I don't know why you're even bothering with her."

"Because she doesn't want me. Once she changes her mind, I can leave her alone." He wiped his forehead with his arm and glanced at me.

"You always go after unavailable people."

"If the available people were all that great, they'd be unavailable," Jack said.

"Not true."

"Yes it is."

"I refuse to live in your Tom Cruise world," I said.

But was he was right? Don't you live in the world you're stuck with? I mean, I never wanted to live through two Bush presidencies, but here I am, saying it again: President Bush. And here we were, Jack and I in T-shirts, pushing some pedals around. That night, we'd each go on a different date. We'd call each other the next day and complain about it. He'd tell me something, like how during sex (and there would be sex) his date said, "*Hup* two-three-four . . ." and I'd tell Jack something, like how my date said he was only interested in women who could ski.

When do the stories end? Is that why people get married, and why married people are so boring? Because you marry the guy who will give you no stories to tell? Is that what I wanted? No more stories?

Jack created a "Chicks I've Nailed" database. When he disclosed this information over lunch one day, I said, "Never tell this to another woman."

He said, "Eleanor, it's a wonderful introspective tool. For example: Although I *say* I like hippie chicks, the plurality of girls I've slept with have been artsy types."

"Oh, my God."

"I'm just trying to figure out what I'm doing wrong. I printed out a pie chart . . ." He started groping in his bag.

"No. Put it away."

"But—"

"No."

Jack was working a new job doing sales and marketing in the building next to mine downtown. He said that he had taken a two-thousand-dollar pay cut for the convenience of seeing me. Of course, I didn't believe this, but we did have lunch almost every day, like now. I picked up my sandwich. Jack did the same, but just held it in front of his mouth while he talked.

"This is what I'm so sick of hearing: 'I really like you, Jack. You're a great guy, *Jack*, but I just don't feel that spark with you.'"

"Oh. Nice-guy syndrome." But he wasn't a nice guy, so I didn't get it.

Jack put down his sandwich without biting into it. "I want to figure out this 'spark' thing. And control it."

"Don't you think you're missing the point?"

"I want to gently open my hand and see a little flame in the center of my palm, dancing." He stared at his hand.

"On the prowl again," I said.

"That sounds a little more . . . real than I'd like it to," Jack said, finally eating, mouth full. "I'm on a mission. I have a list." Jack flashed me his list, maybe twelve women long, with phone numbers next to them. Some had question marks instead of last names. One woman he simply called Satellite Girl. He kept the piece of paper on the table while he talked, explaining that he had finally, seriously considered what he wants, and who fits the image. He wants the big, big love, composed out of an aggregate of characteristics. I peeked. Halfway down the list, I saw my own name.

I had a big love, once—Richard. The way it started was this: I had met Richard at a bar and was instantly smitten, but he didn't notice me. One day, Richard called for my roommate Pete, who wasn't home. When I answered the phone, I was lying on my bed, playing with a stone that a geologist friend had given to me. She had explained, "See the shiny parts? See how it's kind of oily looking, chipped in weird places? Long ago, a dinosaur ate this stone and kept it in its gizzard with other stones to help digest its food." I sometimes tried to put it in my own mouth, but it was too big.

When I knew Richard was about to hang up, I said, "You'll never in a billion years guess what I have in my hand."

Richard paused then bit, asking questions. Is it old, new, pretty, ugly, what color, what shape? When I finally told him, he asked me out. We were in love for three years, and then he abruptly fell out of love and left me for a woman who makes bagels.

Despite all that, maybe that's what love is, after all—holding out your hand and saying, *Here. I'm holding this small, simple thing, as old as time itself. Do you want it? Is this what you want?*

Now, Jack asked me what I wanted, pen poised over an old receipt.

"It depends," I stalled.

"Come on," he said. "Any nonnegotiable requirements? Any personal habits you can't stand?"

All I could think to say was that I didn't want a man who picked up his plate in restaurants and licked it. Not like last time. Jack wrote, "No plate-lickers." He stared at the paper for a minute and then said, "Well. I think we can find you something."

We both looked up suddenly. The woman at the table next to us had just started crying. "Michael . . . that's . . . so . . ." she said, her cheeks turning red and wet. "I tell you I have feelings for you and you just laugh at me like that. I can't believe you made me say that stuff out loud when you don't care about me. I feel sick; I'm going home."

Her chair screeched back and she rushed away, shoving her arms into her jacket sleeves. The man, Michael, stood up, threw money on the table, and said, "Ellen, wait! Ellen!"

Ellen did not wait. She pushed her way toward the door.

Then, in a voice probably meant to be just loud enough, but overcompensating at the last minute when he realized that he was losing her forever, Michael boomed, "STOP! ELLEN! I LOVE YOU! TOO!"

Ellen stopped and turned around. They stared at each other across the room. Nobody moved. The place fell silent. Even the music stopped, stuck between songs.

Someone called out, "Kiss her!"

Michael walked over to Ellen. She looked up at him. The music began again, an accordion winding through the melody. A voice sang in another language.

They kissed.

People cheered.

Michael and Ellen kept on kissing, as if they were alone, as if the world were whirling around them in a hurricane, and they were caught right in the middle of its beautiful blue eye. Then they walked toward the doors, holding hands. This, what we were witnessing, was the extraordinary beginning of something ordinary. Or maybe the other way around, I don't know. Strangers smiled at each other. A little boy started laughing. A woman reached across the table to hold her husband's hand.

Jack and I stared at each other, then at the lists fluttering on the table as the double doors opened and closed.

I had to drive down to Colorado Springs for a meeting. On the drive back, I was hit with a freak spring blizzard, almost a white-out. Peering through the shooting snow, I saw a solid black billboard on the highway with giant words in white: WHO'S THE FATHER? It was sponsored by an adoption agency. I wondered how many pregnant women drove down this highway, suddenly snapped their fingers, and said, "Come to think of it, who *is* the father, anyway?"

Waiting for Jack that night, I threw part of a leftover bagel into my new goldfish's jar. It sank slowly and rested on the bottom. The fish stared at it.

It was still snowing when Jack drove me to a party at his friend's house. In the parking lot, he combed his hair with the brush end of the ice scraper before we went inside.

We took off our coats in the hallway. Jack looked at my outfit and made a cat noise, deep in his throat. I didn't know men could make cat noises.

"Nice skirt."

It was tight, made out of old neckties sewn together. I said, "Thank you."

Jack ushered me inside, saying, "I need a girl exactly like you. Except maybe with lower standards."

"How about her?" I asked, pointing with my head at a girl in a silver tank top and a gold miniskirt. I could remember times when I felt that desperate. The girl was smiling at Jack. He said, "She's sparkly."

"She's pretty." She had a big, red nose. She looked like she was terrified that nobody would talk to her all evening. She held a glass of wine by the stem with one hand and caressed the rim with the other. She meant to be suggestive, I'm sure, but instead it was just vulgar. I wanted to wrap her in a big fireman's raincoat. "She seems nice, Jack," I said.

Jack moved so close to me, I could smell his soap. I looked at his left shoulder as he whispered above my ear, "I don't like her, um, breasts."

"What?"

"They look bitchy."

I looked immediately at the girl's breasts. Maybe it was the power of suggestion. They did seem somewhat bitchy in her silver tank top, like they were gossiping together. Even though I was staring directly at her breasts, the girl's eyes passed right over me and on to Jack. She slowly walked toward us.

Shouldering me aside, she asked Jack to dance, without even glancing at me. He took her in his arms and maneuvered between laughing and drinking people, guiding her in a pretty two-step. I settled back to watch, next to a random couple by the seltzer water and pretzels. The couple was arguing loudly. It's hard not to listen, especially when you can.

Boy: Hey. I'm sorry things didn't work out between us. I just don't want the closeness.

Girl: The closeness? I mean . . . Jesus. People need people.

Boy: Not me. I am alone. Without warmth. Without need.

[I spilled my drink.]

Girl, voice wobbly: Well, you have some of my things. My book.

Boy: Should I mail it to you?

Girl: Mail it to me.

Boy: I don't want to mail it to you. That's so impersonal.

Girl: Mail it to me.

Boy: Maybe instead you could come over —

Girl, voice of steel: Mail it to me, you cocksucker.

I laughed. Then immediately I felt lonely. I looked for Jack. The sparkly woman was leading him away by the hand. In passing, he grabbed me with his other hand and rumbled in my ear, "She's taking me home to show me her —" then was yanked away. He waved on the way out. He was my ride.

In a few seconds, he was back again, thrusting a twenty in my hand. "Can you get a cab?" he asked, holding my shoulders and bending down to catch my eyes. "Is that okay?"

"Of course," I said, suddenly furious.

Jack landed a giant kiss on my forehead and left again. His absence seemed as absolute as his presence. I stewed, looking around. Men played air hockey in the corner, while women watched. Someone spilled a bottle of vodka and just left it there, leaking onto the carpet. A little terrier scrambled under the couch, then lit out of the room.

A blond guy now sidled up to me and slurred, "So, what's your story?" He was wearing a Hawaiian shirt with hula girls all over it.

"My story?"

"Have a boyfriend? You married?"

"No."

"Wanna be?"

"I don't know."

"Want kids?"

"Yes."

His eyes finally managed to focus on my left eyebrow. "Can you speak a foreign language?" he asked.

I excused myself and crossed the room. I leaned against the wall and nodded at the girl next to me, who was rolling a joint. She lit up and we silently smoked it together. Then she wandered away. In a few minutes, I realized that it's not rude to ditch a party if nobody notices you're there, so I called a cab and went home.

That same night, still stoned, I took off my clothes and stood in front of my full-length mirror. Did I have bitchy tits? How about the rest of me? It was a cold early spring, and my limbs huddled together. Desperate legs? Was my crotch . . .

No. No. I covered my face with my hands.

Images of my breakup with Richard flared up. Mardi Gras beads swaying from the rearview mirror as he said, *Don't love you*, the rim of dust on the speedometer, *Not anymore*, a dog crossing in front of the car and looking back at me for a long moment, *Maybe I never did*, then turning its head, following its leash, its sweeping tail the only happy thing in the world.

Nothing was worth that. I pulled the covers over my head and stayed that way until I fell asleep.

Since I've thrown away all my lone socks, their mates have returned from the sea. I hold them in my hand, thinking, *Where have you been all this time? Why can only one of you exist in a single space?*

Back in the saddle, I told myself, and went on a date with a beautiful consultant at my office named Andrew. He picked me up and took me around town, holding my hand. It was a warm spring night, and he stopped me in the street to touch my face and pull me closer. As he was kissing me, I was already wondering if he would call, his lips on my lips, our eyes closed.

Later, Jack said, "What a loser."

"What do you mean? I haven't said anything bad about him."

"I can just tell." He picked a leaf off my shoulder and rolled onto his back on the grass. His shirt poked up an inch, his pierced belly button showing. The park was empty except for the two of us. "This is a new one, right?"

"Jack!" I pulled up some dead grass and threw it in his face. He blocked it with his arm and squinted at me.

"Frankly, I can't keep track of all the men you're not sleeping with," he said.

"What about sparkly girl?"

"I drove her home but didn't go inside. I kissed her on the cheek. Went back to the party, but you were gone." I stared at him. He waved a fly away and said, "She'd never pass my test, anyway. I had a feeling." I was still staring. "I didn't fucking feel like it, Eleanor, okay?"

I had the goldfish test; Jack had the buyer's remorse test. It's very complicated — I don't understand it. It's a Pavlovian-response-voodoo kind of thing, involving the girl's phone number, whether or not you feel like buying new underwear, what you do when you drive past her house, and a hair sample. I don't know what you do with the hair.

I didn't see Jack all the rest of that week. Then, early Sunday morning, he showed up unannounced. He banged on my door until I let him in. I was in pajamas, my hair bunched up. He didn't say a word, just walked over to my goldfish jar and picked it up.

"What's his name," he demanded. The goldfish lurched around inside, bug-eyed. Stringy fish shit whirled up from the bottom.

I rubbed my eye.

"His *name*," Jack barked.

"Andrew," I said. I felt like a caught sadist.

Jack looked at the fish. "Andrew," he said firmly. He walked out with my jar, my fish, my date. The door stuck open behind him.

The next day, Jack called me at work. He was mumbling. I leaned back out of my cubicle and looked at the window, open a slit. I caught my own dark eyes in the pale reflection on the glass. It was beginning to rain, quietly.

"Andrew died, didn't he," I said.

No sound but the start of rain on dead grass. Then, "Yes."

"He didn't call," I said.

. . .

The weather was doing its crazy spring thing. Snow, then sun and seventy-degree weather, then many days of incredible wind. Then power outages and the sudden peace that they bring. I tried to fly a kite, but it was too gusty and the kite lodged itself in a tree. Downtown, the wind kicked up and people's white shirts simultaneously billowed out, making them look like pirates stranded far from their ships. People did strange things. As a homeless man passed by, he pointed his finger at me and said, "You just try speaking your mind in *Tehran*, missy." A woman in a pink suit stood at an intersection and sang loudly into the traffic, "Don't Go Breaking My Heart."

Jack was also beginning to act different. He stopped telling me about his women, and he grew quiet when I told him about my latest nonadventures. He now sometimes became angry at me very suddenly, for nothing. For dropping a chopstick. For pointing at a painting in a museum. Once he grabbed my arm and hissed, "Eleanor. You are making me lose my mind." All I had done was show him a bruise on my elbow. Then he released my arm and wandered over to the pay phones and back.

One time, he put his head in his arms and shook it, as if my mere presence were torturing him. I burst into tears, right there in the delicatessen.

Jack was immediately contrite, stroking my face, pulling tissues out of his pockets. Only Jack would come prepared with tissues.

"I'm sorry," he said again and again.

"I don't understand. You suddenly hate me. You pick on me."

"I don't hate you. I'm just going through something."

"What?" I asked, blowing my nose.

Jack didn't say anything.

"Why?" I pushed, sniffling.

"Eleanor. Cool it," Jack said.

"What? What? Whywhywhywhywhy?"

That night, I went to dinner with my Turkish friend Deste, who had "erased" her last boyfriend and now had another. Things were going well with them, she said, because she treats him badly. "He has all these extra weights on his belly. I call him Fatty."

"Deste! He'll be traumatized."

"It's better this way," she said. "Walking in the street or out with friends, he's going to say bad things and I shut up. But at home I say, 'I don't like the lunch you packed for me. Make it again. I don't like ham today.'" Her eyes wandered to the window. "Tonight, you will make a list of what you want . . ."

"Another list," I said. Apparently this was cross-cultural.

". . . and think about it, all those little things. Like, I want a man who will shave his armpits. American men won't, so I want a Turkish man. So you make a list, and you look at the list every day, and *fuck us* on it. Fuck us hard. If you don't fuck us, you will never find that guy."

I stared at her. Then, "Oh," I said quickly. *Focus.* "But I want someone who makes me forget about that stuff," I said.

"That's dangerous," Deste said. "Never forget anything. Only forgive."

I looked out the window, and there was Jack outside in the street, waving a cell phone at someone or something. This often happened—he was everywhere, all the time. I was beginning to think that he was actually a yogi, inhabiting more than one body at once. The lights from the buildings tinted his skin orange. I pounded on the window to catch his attention. He turned our way, but didn't see me and walked away again.

"How about that man?" Deste asked.

I was kind of daydreaming. I said, "Jack. That's Jack." Jack passed by once more, and I banged again on the glass, louder and louder, until people started twisting around in their seats to look at me. Jack turned his head in all directions. Deste pulled at my fist, but I used the other one until Jack finally walked away, stopping and looking back once as if he suddenly remembered something.

. . .

I had to go to a Saturday wedding. A coworker was getting married, and my pseudo-friend Marcy was going to be there. Marcy had married a lawyer, and I could no longer stand to talk to her on the phone. All she talked about was what her husband had fixed that week — the toilet, the patio door. She said she had a friend whom she wanted me to meet, named Paul. She had never been nice to me. I asked Jack to be my date.

Throughout the ceremony, Jack kept pretending to weep. The priest forgot the vows and instead made some up on the spot, insisting that Kathleen "obey" and telling Fred to say, "with this wing, I thee wed." Fred said it verbatim, teeth clenched. Jack kept trying to hold my hand, and I slapped it away discreetly, biting the inside of my cheek.

While Jack scouted hors d'oeuvres at the reception, Marcy grabbed me and pushed me over to a short, chubby man who had a kind face. He breathed hard as he gripped my hand.

Marcy said, "Paul's a doctor."

Paul said, "I do medical research."

"Oh, yeah?" I asked. "That's wonderful. Because everyone needs . . . medicine."

"I enjoy my specialty," Paul said, hands in his pockets so that his stomach pooched out and his hips looked a yard wide.

"What do you specialize in?"

"Mucus."

"Oh, mucus," I said.

Paul nodded quickly. A cracker crumb fell out of the corner of his mouth and onto the floor.

Marcy said, "Paul's the leader in his field."

"There aren't too many of us," Paul said, waving his hand.

"Still," Marcy said.

I said, "Where's the bathroom? Do they have a bathroom here?"

I didn't get more than a few steps away before Marcy pulled me aside, her fingers pinching my upper arm. She hissed, "I was kind of thinking you and Paul would get along. But you brought that guy." She was holding me in place.

"Jack," I said, glancing at him. He waved a cracker at me and mouthed, *The good times are killing me.* I turned to Marcy. "I wanted to bring a date. Everyone else has a date."

"But I thought I had made it clear on the phone."

"What?"

"That I wanted you to meet Paul."

"Yeah. I met him."

Jack sat down next to Paul and said loudly, "Soooo . . . you're a mucus man."

"Ha-ha," Paul said sourly.

Marcy whispered, "I don't know, I'm disappointed. Paul's been so lonely."

"So get him a goldfish," I said. "I have a goldfish."

Jack boomed (for my benefit), "How do you get your samples? Do they use special tissues?"

Marcy said, "Give him a chance."

"I don't want to," I said.

Paul said, "I don't work with the actual mucus. I have assistants for that. I do the more theoretical stuff."

Marcy said, "You think you can be so picky, Eleanor?"

Jack said, "*Theoretical* mucus?"

Marcy and I finally sat down, me next to Jack, Paul on my other side. Marcy and her nondescript husband sat facing us across the round table. We dug into our scratchy, filmy salmon and waterlogged yellow squash. Jack and I drank a boatload of wine, toasting everything. The waiter spilled a glass of water. We toasted him, too. Halfway through the wedding torte (Kathleen and Fred's attempt at noncontroversial originality), Marcy smiled and said, "I'm so proud of you, Eleanor. I mean, you don't have it easy. Your life's not what I'd call great."

Oh, no, I thought.

"Look at you," she said. "You're unmarried, alone, struggling financially, you're unmarried . . ."

"I'm twice unmarried," I explained to everyone at the table. "Some people just do it once, but I'm an over-underachiever."

Smiles shot from everyone's faces at different intervals, like bullets at a firing range. Jack glared at Marcy.

She said, "You don't have a house, you don't have any of the things we talked about wanting when we were in college. Remember? And here you are, still so . . . hopeful."

"Yeah," I said.

"I can't believe this shit," Jack said.

"She's a trooper," Marcy told Paul.

"I'd like to make a toast," I said, glass raised. The others raised theirs, too—it's a reflex, the way applause breeds applause. I paused. "Here's to suicide," I said. I drained my glass and turned to Jack. "Wanna dance?"

Jack stood up and faced Marcy. "You suck," he told her.

I said, "Yikes," jumped up and pulled at Jack's arm. He hung back, staring, lower lip slack. He looked as if he were going to challenge Marcy to a fight. Marcy's husband stirred, realizing that he should do something. Marcy shrank in her chair. Paul's mouth opened, food still in it. Jack took a loud, deep breath, as if he were going underwater.

"You . . ."—we all waited, motionless—"*really* suck," Jack finished. He swayed a little.

I said, "I love you."

Jack jerked his head to stare at me. His mouth was open. Mine was, too. So I said it again, experimentally: "I love you?"

And I did. Why? Because I did.

"What kind of love?" Jack asked. His fists were loosening.

"You know," I said. "Love."

Paul snickered.

Jack just stood still for about nine seconds. Then he quickly pulled me to his chest and dipped me all the way backward until I could see the ceiling above his head. "Really?" he asked. "Really?" I nodded, upside down.

Jack pulled me up and kissed me deeply, in a way that showed practice, forethought, and intoxication. I kissed him back, with all the ardor of my own experience. *This is Jack*, I thought. *This is crazy.* I heard some vague heckling from the table beside us. But Jack kept stubbornly kissing me until everything else faded and we were left alone with this newborn thing that we had somehow created from nothing—strange, imperfect, so much better than the best of what's around.

CONTRIBUTORS

Elizabeth Benedict is the author of four novels, *Almost, Safe Conduct, The Beginner's Book of Dreams,* and *Slow Dancing,* which was a finalist for the National Book Award; she is also the author of *The Joy of Writing Sex: A Guide for Fiction Writers.* Benedict writes for many publications, including *Salmagundi, The New York Times,* and *Tin House,* and has taught writing for almost twenty years. She lives in New York City and Somerville, Massachusetts. (www. elizabethbenedict.com)

Judy Budnitz is the author of the novel *If I Told You Once,* which was selected as an Orange Futures book by the Orange Prize for Fiction judges, and of *Flying Leap,* a collection of dark, witty, and weird short stories. Her work has appeared in *The Paris Review, Story, Glimmer Train, Harper's,* and *25 and Under.*

Colleen Curran lives in Richmond, Virginia, where she is the associate editor of *www.richmond.com,* a commercial Web-zine. Her fiction has appeared in *Jane* and *Meridian.* She is finishing up a collection of short stories and working on a novel.

Maggie Estep has authored two published books, *Diary of an Emotional Idiot* and *Soft Maniacs*. Her third book, *Hex*, the first in a series of crime novels about horse racing, misanthropes, and Coney Island, will be out in March 2003 from Three Rivers Press; *Love Dance of the Mechanical Animals*, a collection of short stories and essays, will be published in fall 2003. Maggie's work has appeared in *The Village Voice*, *New York Press*, *Black Book*, and on *www.nerve.com*, and she has performed her work on MTV, HBO, and PBS TV. She lives in Brooklyn, New York, and likes to hang out at racetracks, cheering on long shots. (www.maggieestep.com)

Suzanne Finnamore is the author of *The Zygote Chronicles* and *Otherwise Engaged*. She lives in Larkspur, California.

Pam Houston is the author of a short story collection, *Cowboys Are My Weakness*, and a novel, *Waltzing the Cat*. She lives in Denver, Colorado.

Mary-Beth Hughes is the author of the novel *Wavemaker II*. Her short stories have appeared in a number of literary journals, including *The Georgia Review*, *Ploughshares*, and *The Saint Ann's Review*.

Shelley Jackson is most widely recognized for *Patchwork Girl*, a hypertext reworking of Mary Shelley's *Frankenstein* that has been compared to Katherine Dunn's *Geek Love* and Angela Carter's *The Passion of New Eve*. She has written and illustrated two children's books: *The Old Woman and the Wave* and the forthcoming *Sophia, the Alchemist's Dog*. Her new collection of stories is called *The Melancholy of Anatomy*.

Dana Johnson won the Flannery O'Connor Award for Short Fiction in 2000 for *Break Any Woman Down*. She is on the faculty of Indiana University, where she teaches creative writing.

Johnson holds an M.F.A. in Creative Writing from Indiana University and a B.A. from the University of Southern California. She was born and raised in Los Angeles. At present, she is working on a novel.

Heidi Julavits lives in Brooklyn, New York, and Brooklin, Maine. Her short stories have appeared in *Zoetrope, Esquire, McSweeney's,* and *The Best American Short Stories 1999.* She is also the author of a novel, *The Mineral Palace.* Her new novel, *The Effect of Living Backwards,* will be published in June 2003.

Pagan Kennedy is the author of a novel, *The Exes,* and a biography about explorer and human-rights activist William Sheppard. She lives in Somerville, Massachusetts.

Erika Krouse's stories have appeared in *The New Yorker, Atlantic Monthly,* and *Ploughshares.* Her debut collection of stories, *Come Up and See Me Sometime* (Scribner, 2001), won the Paterson Fiction Prize and was a *New York Times* Notable Book of the Year. She is currently living in Boulder, Colorado, and working on a novel.

Kathy Lette achieved *succès de scandale* as a teenager with *Puberty Blues;* afterward, she spent several years as a newspaper columnist in Sydney and New York (collected in the book *Hit and Ms*) and as a television sitcom writer for Columbia Pictures in Los Angeles. Her novels, *Girls' Night Out* (1988), *The Llama Parlour* (1991), *Foetal Attraction* (1993), *Mad Cows* (1996), *Altar Ego* (1998), and *Nip 'n' Tuck* (2001), became international best-sellers. *Mad Cows* was recently made into a film starring Joanna Lumley. Kathy Lette's plays include *Grommits, Wet Dreams, Perfect Mismatch,* and *I'm So Happy for You Really I Am.* Her novels have been translated into fourteen foreign languages and are published in more than 100 countries. She lives in London with her husband and their two children.

Jennifer Macaire is an American freelance writer and illustrator living in France. A former model for Elite in Paris, she is married to a professional polo player and has three children. Jennifer has published short stories in magazines such as *The Advocate, Bear Deluxe,* and the *Vestal Review.* One of her short stories was nominated for a Pushcart Prize. She has also written a series of novels based on the life of Alexander the Great.

Anna Maxted lives in London with her husband, Phil, their son, Oscar, and their two cats, Disco and Tasha. Her first novel, *Getting Over It,* was published in June 2000, and her latest, *Running in Heels,* was published in May 2001.

Eliza Minot was born in Beverly, Massachusetts, in 1970. Her first novel, *The Tiny One,* was published by Knopf in 1999. She lives in New Jersey with her husband and their two children—succeeding relationships all around—and is at work on her second novel.

Susan Minot is the author of *Rapture, Evening, Lust and Other Stories, Folly,* and *Monkeys,* and she wrote the screenplay for the film *Stealing Beauty.* She lives in Maine.

Thisbe Nissen is the author of a story collection, *Out of the Girls' Room and Into the Night;* a novel, *The Good People of New York;* and a "thing" called *The Ex-Boyfriend Cookbook* (with co-author Erin Ergenbright), which is a work of fiction, recipes, and collages. Her new novel, which will have the word *osprey* somewhere in its title, is due out in 2003 (Knopf). Nissen lives in Iowa with her cats, Maisie and Fernanda.

Leslie Pietrzyk is the author of *Pears on a Willow Tree* (Avon Books), a novel about four generations of Polish-American women. Her short fiction has appeared in many journals, including *TriQuarterly, Shenandoah, The Iowa Review, The Gettysburg Review,* and *The Sun*, and her work has been nominated several times for a Pushcart Prize. She lives in Alexandria, Virginia.

Rachel Resnick was born in Jerusalem, Israel. The daughter of a secular Talmudic scholar and a peripatetic Boston debutante, Resnick moved frequently as a child and into adulthood. Her concern with place and setting, paramount in her debut novel, *Go West Young F*cked-Up Chick*, is an outgrowth of the constant moving she experienced as a child; so is a taste for travel. A graduate of Yale with an M.F.A. from Vermont College, Resnick worked various jobs for years in film and television. She currently lives in Topanga Canyon, California, with her severe macaw, Ajax. Her work has appeared in publications such as *Tin House*, *Alaska Quarterly Review, Bakunin, The Minnesota Review, The Crescent Review, Chelsea, The Ohio Review*, and *The Los Angeles Times*, and has been honored with a 1998 Pushcart Prize Special Mention. Following a stint as a private investigator, she is presently at work on a detective novel.

Lucinda Rosenfeld is the author of *What She Saw in. . . .* Her next novel, a sequel, will be published at the end of 2003. She has published essays in *The New York Times Magazine*, the *Sunday Telegraph* (of London), and *Creative Nonfiction*, among other publications. Her fiction has appeared in *The New Yorker*. She lives in Brooklyn, New York.

Michele Serros was still a student at Santa Monica College when her first book of poetry and short stories, *Chicana Falsa, and Other Stories of Death, Identity, and Oxnard*, was published. An award-winning poet and commentator for National Public Radio (*Morning Edition, Weekend All Things Considered*), Serros has released a spoken-word CD on Mercury Records and toured with Lollapalooza. Serros, who was called "one of the top young women to watch for in the new century" by *Newsweek*, made *The Los Angeles Times* best-sellers list with her collection of fiction,

How to Be a Chicana Role Model. Currently living in New York City, Michele is working on a young adult novel tentatively entitled *Notes for a Medium Brown Girl.*

Amy Sohn is the author of the novel *Run Catch Kiss* and *Sex and the City: Kiss and Tell,* the official companion guide to the hit television show. Her second novel, *My Old Man,* will be published in 2004. She lives in Brooklyn, where she was born and bred.

Martha Southgate is the author of the novels *The Fall of Rome* and *Another Way to Dance.* Her short fiction has been published in *Redbook* magazine and in various anthologies. She has held fellowships at the MacDowell Colony and at the Virginia Center for the Creative Arts and is at work on her next novel.

Darcey Steinke is the author of *Up Through the Water, Suicide Blonde,* and *Jesus Saves.* She also coedited a book of essays on the New Testament with Rick Moody called *Joyful Noise.* Her work has appeared in *Spin, George, Artforum,* and *The New York Times Magazine,* as well as other places. She teaches at the New School for Social Research in New York City and resides in Brooklyn with her daughter, Abbie. Her new novel is called *Milk.*

Jennifer Weiner is the author of *Good in Bed* and *In Her Shoes.* She lives in Philadelphia.

ACKNOWLEDGMENTS

Part of the joy of publishing one's first book is the opportunity to thank everyone who has passed through one's life. Sociologist David Grazian calls it an "exercise in performing authenticity." I prefer to think of it as a public way of expressing my thanks to the vast number of people who helped to make my life delightful while this magnum opus gestated.

The first and most fervent shout-out goes to my family: Delma, Ray, Lauren, B.C., and Scott. You guys rule. Thanks to my agent, the incomparable Rosalie Siegel; Carrie Thornton, a friend, a generous critic, and a magnificent editor; Jonathan Ames, Dave Daley, Colson Whitehead, and Jerry Stahl, for the invaluable assistance with mapping the literary landscape. Thanks to my extended family: the Cranes, Hunts, Seatons, Alteveers, Kinseys, Johnstons, and Zikmunds, as well as my grandparents Ann and Tom Hedges. Love you all, and I wish Mary and Burnee could catch this episode. Many friends deserve special mention for their forbearance, kindness, and acceptance of a wide range of eccentricities: Kelly Gartner, Caitlin McLaughlin, Tanya Bezreh, Jordan Ellenberg, Sarah Manguso, Bill Hansford, Jerome Hodos,

Dave Grazian, Sam Adams, Debra Auspitz, David Warner, Frank Lewis, Paul Curci, Juliet Fletcher, Deirdre Affel, and the entire Ill Hindu Posse.

The contributors to the book are the most talented, utterly fabulous group of writers I've ever had the pleasure of knowing. Thanks, gals, a billion times over.

And to the real Tony Columbo: Tony, thank you. If you hadn't been such a prick, this book would've never come into being.

ABOUT THE EDITOR

Meredith Broussard is a freelance writer based in Philadelphia. A literature and arts critic at the *Philadelphia Inquirer* and the *Philadelphia City Paper*, she has also written for *Philadelphia Magazine*, the *Hartford Courant*, the *Chicago Reader*, and the *New York Press*.